PRAISE FOR

THE YEAR OF OUR LOVE

"A layered, riveting story of love and complicated friendship set against a tumultuous period in Italy's history. Fresh and stylistic, with characters that will remain with you, this modern saga has a clear ring of authenticity. Caterina Bonvicini delivers a thoughtful, enthralling story full of twists and turns . . . not to be missed."

—Jan Moran, *USA Today* bestselling
author of *The Chocolatier*

"Caterina Bonvicini has created a vivid, engaging, and utterly convincing world in these pages . . . Few writers are able to capture so perceptively the human tragicomic yearning after happiness. *The Year of Our Love* is a book for these times: compassionate, funny, and dead-on accurate."

—Eleanor Morse, author of *White Dog Fell
from the Sky* and *Margreete's Harbor*

"A deeply moving and memorable novel that captures love's intensity and the losses that come with adulthood. In prose that is restrained but pulses with emotion, Bonvicini reminds us that the compromises we make in our youth can haunt us all our lives, and the people we love are often, in equal measure, the source of our distress and our only comfort."

—L. Annette Binder, author of *The Vanishing Sky*

THE

YEAR

OF OUR

LOVE

Caterina Bonvicini

Translated from the Italian
by Antony Shugaar

OTHER PRESS

NEW YORK

Originally published in Italian as
Correva l'anno del nostro amore in 2014 by Garzanti, Milan
Copyright © 2014 Caterina Bonvicini
Published in agreement with Piergiorgio Nicolazzini Literary Agency (PNLA)
Translation copyright © 2021 Antony Shugaar

Production editor: Yvonne E. Cárdenas
Text designer: Jennifer Daddio / Bookmark Design & Media Inc.
This book was set in Goudy Old Style and Helvetica Neue
by Alpha Design & Composition of Pittsfield, NH

1 3 5 7 9 10 8 6 4 2

Library of Congress Cataloging-in-Publication Data
Names: Bonvicini, Caterina, 1974- author. | Shugaar, Antony, translator.
Title: The year of our love / Caterina Bonvicini ; translated by Antony Shugaar.
Other titles: Correva l'anno del nostro amore. English
Description: New York : Other Press, [2021] | Originally published in Italian as
Correva l'anno del nostro amore in 2014 by Garzanti, Milan.
Identifiers: LCCN 2020052812 (print) | LCCN 2020052813 (ebook) |
ISBN 9781635420623 (trade paperback) | ISBN 9781635420630 (ebook)
Classification: LCC PQ4902.O68 C6713 2021 (print) | LCC PQ4902.O68 (ebook) |
DDC 853/.92—dc23
LC record available at https://lccn.loc.gov/2020052812
LC ebook record available at https://lccn.loc.gov/2020052813

Publisher's Note
This is a work of fiction. Names, characters, places, and incidents either
are the product of the author's imagination or are used fictitiously, and
any resemblance to actual persons, living or dead, events,
or locales is entirely coincidental.

TO

RIC

TRANSLATOR'S NOTE

An effective cinematic device is the flitting, sinister streak of a shadow, moving somewhere just outside of the central frame, purposeful and elusive. What such an image does—and what many forms of visual and verbal shorthand do—is to communicate telegraphically a hint at something that is stored in the reader's or viewer's brain. It's economical and effective, because of all the things that don't need to be said. All it requires is a pointed finger, widened eyes, and a full-body startle response.

There is a dark, flitting shape, sinister and murderous, in Caterina Bonvicini's *The Year of Our Love*. But for any reader wishing to gain an understanding of how the book reads in its original Italian, to an ordinary Italian reader, it is necessary to bear casually in mind what that shape was a reference to.

The Year of Our Love begins in the Years of Lead. The Years of Lead and the Years of Berlusconi that followed, temporal and spiritual bookends of a sort, are shorthand for an Italian half-century that runs basically from 1967 to 2015, but that sinks its roots in the previous century and, in a sense, the previous millennium. But then the snarling creature flitting through the shadows in our suspense films and our fever dreams sinks *its* claws back tens of thousands of years, if not longer, in our limbic system and fight-or-flight synapses.

A good starting point is the formation of the Italian nation, around the time of the American Civil War. Poets as early as Dante and Petrarch had been singing the anthem of Italian unity, but until the 1860s the peninsula was carved up into warring principalities, looming large among them the vast and militaristic Papal States. South of the Papal States lay the Kingdom of the Two Sicilies (namely the island of Sicily and the mainland kingdom centered on Naples). When the industrialized North finally invaded the agrarian South under the putative leadership of Garibaldi, it was seen by many as very much an act of war, not liberation. A chaotic but serious resistance movement sprang up and lasted for years, characterized by the northern Italian press as "anti-unification brigands." The repression of that uprising was savage. One French journalist at the time described "the extermination campaign, here in Europe, not unlike that being practiced against the Red Indian in America." Summary execution by firing squad could be the penalty for disrespect of the new Italian king, queen, or flag. That was the queen we still memorialize when we order a Margherita pizza, with the green basil, white mozzarella, and red tomato sauce of the Italian flag, just to be clear.

Carlo Levi, writing after the Second World War but referring to his time in political house arrest in southern Italy in the years prior to the war (thus neatly bracketing the period), wrote about the persistence of the legend of that uprising:

> The myth of the brigands is close to their hearts and a part of their lives, the only poetry in their existence, their dark, desperate epic. Even the appearance of the peasants to-day recalls that of the brigands: they are silent, lonely, gloomy, and frowning in their black suits and hats and, in winter, black overcoats, armed whenever they set out for the fields with gun and axe. They have gentle hearts and patient souls; centuries of resignation weigh on their shoulders, together with a feeling of the vanity of all things and of the overbearing power of fate. But when, after infinite endurance, they are shaken to the depths of their beings and are driven by an instinct of self-defence or justice, their revolt knows no bounds and no measure. It is an unhuman revolt whose point of departure and final end alike are death, in which ferocity is born of despair. The brigands unreasonably and

hopelessly stood up for the life and liberty of the peas-
ants against the encroachments of the State. By ill luck
they were unwitting instruments of History; they were
on the wrong side and they came to destruction (from
Christ Stopped at Eboli, translated by Frances Frenaye,
pp. 139–40. NY: Farrar, Straus and Giroux, 1947).

One brigand told his judge, "Your Honor, if the world
had one enormous heart, I'd rip it out of its chest." Another
brigand leader rode down into a southern town leading an
army of three thousand men. They proceeded to loot, plun-
der, and feast, executing all the liberals and the lawyers, and
melting down all the confiscated watches, as much for the
gold as to simply *stop time.*

Eventually, the uprising was put down, but a massive
flow of southern Italian emigration to both North and South
America ensued. Before long, this profound national trauma
had largely been erased from the historical record—but
never entirely forgotten.

Then came Mussolini and the Fascist revolution, in part
prompted by the trauma of the First World War. What people forget is that, while Hitler was in power for a dozen years,
Mussolini held Italy in his iron group for a quarter-century.
They also forget that Italy fought alongside the Germans for
part of the Second World War, then overthrew Mussolini,
imprisoned him, and made a separate peace with the Allies in 1943. The Germans promptly invaded Italy, restored
Mussolini to power, and occupied the country with savage

ferocity for the rest of the war. That's a somewhat simplistic description, but it definitely led to an insurrection of partisan forces battling the Germans with tactics and names that hark back to the southern Italian brigands fighting another northern invader seventy-five years earlier. Among the most noted Italian resistance forces were the Brigate Garibaldi—the Garibaldi Brigades—and if there is no connection between "brigand" and "brigades" then I am leaping to a facile conclusion. Let's wait and see.

After the war, in the ambiguity of Italy's status as an occupied nation that had *wanted* to free itself from German occupation (after twenty years as an inspiration to a rising Hitler and a staunch ally and fellow collaborationist in the Holocaust), the occupying forces did their best to quickly forget the crimes of the Fascist party. US General Mark Clark, who led the Allied fight in Italy, once joked that the greatest disappearing act in history was the overnight evaporation of fifty million Italian Fascists.

But not all Italians were willing to forgive and forget. La Volante Rossa—The Red Flying Squad—was an organization that systematically murdered, or executed, people considered guilty of collaboration with or leadership in the Fascist war and prewar crimes. Let's remember those names, La Volante *Rossa* and the *Brigate* Garibaldi, because they appear again just twenty short years later, in the name of the *Brigate Rosse*—the Red Brigades.

Which takes us to the Years of Lead and the grim slinking beast that lurks behind the story of *The Year of Our Love*.

It was in the middle of the summer of 1964, when Pietro Nenni, the leader of the Italian Socialist Party, was trying to form a center-left coalition with Aldo Moro's Christian Democrats, that the first ingot of those Years of Lead was cast. In the negotiations to form that ruling coalition, there had been discussions of the government takeover of Italy's privately owned phone system. Powerful economic and political forces were opposed to such a move, the same kind of shadowy coalition that later resulted in military coups in Greece and Chile, among other places. July in Italy is an intensely vacation-oriented month, the run-up to the sacred monthlong holiday of August. July Sundays are when pretty much every family in the country is in a car heading for the mountains, the seaside, or a farm somewhere outside of town. That Sunday, at the command of a notoriously political military police general named Giovanni De Lorenzo, convoys of slow-moving military troop trucks, crowded with men, filled Italy's highways, jamming traffic, ruining the holiday cheer, and sending a clear and cacophonous threat of further, if vague, disorders. Nenni withdrew his party's proposals for a government takeover of the telecommunications infrastructure, doing so, the Monday after that fraught Sunday, with an explicit reference to "saber-rattling" on the part of the military. Clearly, there were fears of a right-wing coup.

From that summer Monday in 1964 through the seismic social changes of the sixties and seventies and on into the eighties, when Silvio Berlusconi stepped onto the national political stage, Italy struggled through a nightmarish gauntlet of darting, obscure, shadowy plots and maneuvers. Much was unclear, tension was high, and life was vaguely—and occasionally, suddenly and violently—turbulent.

There is a classic Italian novel by Elio Vittorini, published in 1942 but written in the years just prior to the Second World War and first published in installments in 1938 and 1939, called *Conversazione in Sicilia*. It has been published in English with the strangely pluralized title *Conversations in Sicily*. It opens with these coy, censor-proof lines: "I was, in that winter, in the grip of abstract furies. I won't say which, that's not the story I'm here to tell you."

Caterina Bonvicini also did not set out to recount the story of the Years of Lead. But that story keeps butting in, in various permutations, in various shadowy lunges and prowls. Much like the frenzied times of Italian unification and the fraught years of Mussolini's quarter-century dictatorship, the two-decade span of the Years of Lead was a time of violence and obscure plots, of lives lived in the lowering shadow of "abstract furies."

A shorthand for those years refers to the Red Brigades and the kidnapping and murder of Aldo Moro. But in fact it was much more a titanic struggle between two worldviews, a progressive left-wing revolutionary movement and a repressive right-wing reactionary force. It is sometimes calculated that five hundred or so people were murdered in the Years of Lead, and that the headcount falls about equally to the "red-flag" radical Communists and the "black-flag" Neofascists.

Things became so tense and deranged that there was actually a splinter movement called the Nazi-Maoists.

There are references in this book to the Italicus train bombing, to the Bologna train station bombing, the Banco Ambrosiano and the Vatican, Sardinian kidnappers and the Sicilian Mafia, the Red Brigades and Silvio Berlusconi. A famous cover design of a German newsweekly in this period showed an appetizing bowl of spaghetti with a black revolver instead of sauce and meatballs. (The largest flow of tourist visitors to Italy has always been Germans, who in the Years of Lead looked at their neighbor to the south much as we now view Mexico: sunny, cheerful, exciting, with good food and cheap vacations, but also worrisome, dangerous, chaotic, and possibly fatal).

There is not enough room here to tell the tale of the Years of Lead. It is a sprawling saga, vast and chaotic, and perhaps in a sense Italy's third great schism, after the two earlier times of chaos marking Italy's birth in the 1870s, then its rise as a colonial empire and thunderous downfall under Mussolini. It was a hallucinatory revolt of starry-eyed revolutionaries who had grown up listening to stories of anti-Fascist and anti-Nazi Resistance fighters battling against foreign—German—occupying armies. From there to the belief that Italy in the 1970s had been occupied by American multinationals like Esso and IBM seemed like a small and logical step. The Red Brigades were not the only revolutionary group of that era, but they are the name that has survived, largely because of their kidnapping and murder of the head of the leading political party, the Christian Democrats, and a former prime minister and international statesman. Aldo Moro was killed in the spring of 1978, roughly midway between the 1974 Italicus train bombing referenced on page 7 and the 1980 Bologna train station bombing described on pages 15–17.

These are minor, passing references to "abstract furies," and they are not the story Caterina Bonvicini is here to tell you. But I feel confident that any story of Italian lives stretching from the 1970s to the present day is a story told with this sleek panther prowling somewhere in the *anti-camera del cervello*, the waiting room of the mind.

The events of those years were horrifying and relentless: a bombing in an agricultural bank in Milan in 1969 killed nearly twenty and wounded almost a hundred, seemingly planned for the Friday afternoon when the bank lobby would be thronged with farmers come to town for the weekly fair. Three days later, an Italian anarchist being questioned in connection with the bombing, and who almost certainly had had nothing to do with it, fell or was pushed out of a fifth-floor window in Milan's police headquarters. Many assumed the man, Giuseppe Pinelli, had been killed by his questioners. Nearly three years later, the police detective in charge of questioning the anarchist, Luigi Calabresi, was shot and killed in retaliation for his suspected role in Pinelli's death. Thirty years later, Italian playwright Dario Fo was awarded the Nobel Prize for a career that included a 1970 play, *Accidental Death of an*

Anarchist, based tacitly (not explicitly) on Pinelli's death, one of the many "abstract furies" of the time.

Bombings followed bombings, shootings proliferated, judges and politicians were kidnapped and murdered, civilian airliners were shot mysteriously out of the sky, bank administrators were murdered by Mafia hitmen, gray eminences of finance were, variously, poisoned by arsenic-laced espressos in their prison cell (Michele Sindona) or else found hanging by the neck under a bridge in London, with heavy rocks in the pockets of their pinstripe suits (Roberto Calvi). The bridge, by the way, bore the sinister name of Blackfriars, literally the "Dark Brothers," irresistibly evocative to the Italian newspaper-reading public.

The Red Brigades and other radical-left revolutionary groups murdered or simply "kneecapped" middle-level managers of major corporations on an almost daily basis, usually outside their homes as they left for work. It became a grim joke in Turin, epicenter with Milan and Rome of much of the violence, that a typical morning for a Fiat middle manager was to wake up, turn on the radio, shower, shave, don his suit and tie, drink his espresso or cappuccino, and once *another* middle manager, not him, had been shot, kiss his wife and leave for work. That joke became intolerably grimmer, and no longer useful, the morning that the Red Brigades shot *two* middle-level Fiat managers.

"The Years of Lead" was clearly a description of a time when lead bullets seemed to be flying in all directions. Given the intense study of philosophy and ancient civilizations in the Italian educational system, it was also a widely understood reference to Hesiod's description of the ages of history, a Golden Age, followed by a Silver and then a Bronze Age. The present age, in ancient times, was the Iron Age, but "the Years of Lead" seemed a fitting epithet for a time of dispiriting violence and rage.

The great anti-Fascist thinker and activist Carlo Rosselli, murdered in France at Mussolini's orders, wrote about the life of the mind in such leaden times. Fascism, he said, paraphrasing the philosopher and politician Benedetto Croce, was "a murky state of mind, a mix of a lust for pleasure, a spirit of adventure and conquest, a frenzy for power, a restlessness and at the same time a disaffection and an indifference, *all typical of those who live in an uncentered way, those who have lost that center for a person that is an ethical and religious conscience*" (Rosselli's emphasis). Rosselli considered the cause of Fascism to be an absence of inner liberty.

Roughly a hundred years later, Doug Glanville, a sports commentator and former major-league baseball player, wrote this in a *New York Times* op-ed piece (May 18, 2019) about a briefly notorious on-air incident: "Ambiguity has always been a friend to racism." A fan behind him wearing a Cubs sweatshirt had flashed the arguably white supremacist "O.K." sign behind him. Afterward, Glanville wrote, "my [Twitter] feed was overrun by strange avatars, unrecognizable handles, aggressive trolls and a heated debate about racist imagery [. . .] We often project our biases in ways that shape how we see a vague situation, initially leading to opposing viewpoints where each one dogmatically sees itself as truth. The middle ground evaporates into thin air." It's a brilliantly argued, subtly reasoned essay about belief and conviction. It might have been written about the Years of Lead, a time of either great confusion or a titanic battle between two dominant world systems, depending on who's telling it. Glanville posits a person who, unlike him, rarely if ever experiences racism. "How do I talk with this person and convince him of the pattern I see? [. . .] If you innocently decorate your office with a rope shaped into a noose because you like rodeo cowboys, I can still be offended."

The assassinations of John F. Kennedy, Robert F. Kennedy, and Martin Luther King Jr. have roiled the consciousness of American democracy for more than half a century. Italy has struggled with the murders of national leaders and hundreds of others for just as long. But everyone on earth knows about the Kennedys and King. Italy's struggles have largely been Italy's alone.

Silvio Berlusconi, who is emblematic of much of the money-making and discontented wealth in the second part of Caterina Bonvicini's book, emerged from the dark years of civil unrest as a self-proclaimed pragmatic businessman, looking optimistically to a bright, industrious Italian future of modernity and opportunity. In fact, however, he emerged from a dubious past involving membership in a sinister Masonic lodge called the Propaganda 2. His rise was protected by a political leader referenced in this book, Bettino Craxi. Craxi notoriously kept a lion cub given him as a gift by a

Mafia kingpin; he died in exile in Tunisia, evading a twenty-seven-year sentence for corruption and judicial inquiries into suspected involvement in arms trafficking. He was the best man at Berlusconi's wedding to his second wife. The two men reportedly vacationed together.

These stories can turn you into a conspiracy theorist. Or they can seem like the ravings of a conspiracy theorist. But one thing I can tell you, from personal experience. If you lived for any length of time in the Italy of those years, these stories flitted, a sinister shadow, in the vague reaches of your peripheral vision.

The main characters of this novel live in a time of confusions. Kidnappings, bombings, the cynical amassing of cash, the relentless corruption of politics: all of these violations of the human spirit seemed to flood Italy in the years this story spans. But one of the great thinkers of twentieth-century Italy raised his voice on this subject early and clearly.

Pier Paolo Pasolini wrote an op-ed for the Milan daily, *Corriere della Sera*, one of the largest and most influential newspapers in the country. It was electrifying, and is still remembered as a clarion call of sanity in what seemed to be an induced state of national madness. It's remembered for a shortened version of the headline: "What Is This Coup d'État? I Know."

Pasolini proceeds to lay out what he knows. He knows the names of everyone responsible, he knows the names of those who protected them, those who directed them, those who absolved them ("between one Mass and the next," he adds). But then he comes to the crucial point. "I know. But I have no proof. I don't even have evidence." He goes to explain that, though he can't prove anything, he is a thinker, and facts have weight. Thinking clearly, you can't miss the pattern.

Over time, proof and evidence have, in fact, emerged, but that's another story, one much longer and more interesting than all of this. But what Caterina Bonvicini knows, and what her characters would have known, is that almost exactly one year later, Pasolini was murdered. He was murdered on the beach at Ostia, and it may have been the result of a sexual tryst with a seventeen-year-old boy, it may have been related to the theft of reels of one of his films, or it may have been a gang murder designed to punish Pasolini for being a gay Communist. Almost as soon as Pasolini was dead the deeply Italian tendrils of confusion, scandal, and endless bickering set about obscuring the meaning and causes of his death.

James Joyce, who conceived his masterwork *Ulysses* in Rome and composed much of it in Trieste, wrote a line that might have resonated with Pasolini, with the characters in this novel, and with all of Italy as it lived through the Years of Lead. "History [...] is a nightmare from which I am trying to awake."

Antony Shugaar

PART ONE

1975–1984

1

THE BERETTA

EVERY DAY we went off to nursery school together, and Olivia's grandfather would swing by to pick us up in his armored, bulletproof car. We both carried identical straw lunch baskets. My mother filled mine with mortadella sandwiches and bottles of pear juice. Mama would tell us not to drink right from the bottle, that it was bad manners. So drink right from the bottle we invariably did, once we were sure no one was watching.

"Swear that you'll never tell a soul."

"I swear."

The drive to nursery school was an adventure. First of all because her grandfather drove us in person, and he was one fast driver. Then because there was a bullet hole in the windshield of his armor-plated Fiat Ritmo, with a spidery array of cracks radiating out across the glass.

"Gianni, who shot you?"

We weren't allowed to call him Nonno. He said that the word made him feel old. In 1979 he was sixty-one years old, still an attractive man who delighted in casting his smoldering spell in all directions. The family was untouchable, as were his weaknesses. He'd take his granddaughter to nursery school with the same devotion he spent waylaying and seducing women.

"You always ask the same question, what a pain. I've told you before, these aren't stories for little kids." And his eyes would crinkle into a smile. Of course, he couldn't explain to us who the Red Brigades were.

There was a pistol in the car's glove compartment. There it lay, tucked in amidst the registration and insurance, next to a ballpoint pen and a glasses case. We'd see it anytime he reached to get something out.

"You are not to touch it, ever," he'd say. "It's a real gun. It's a Beretta."

There we'd sit, breathless, never taking our eyes off the dashboard for so much as a second. And we'd reel off a string of stupid questions, always the same ones. For instance, we'd ask what would happen if the glove compartment popped open by accident and the pistol fell out—who knows, because he would have to slam on the brakes.

4

"Not a thing," Gianni would reply, "the safety is on."

I was dying to get my hands on that Beretta. At least once. But Olivia would pinch my arm. "Watch out, Valerio, it fires real bullets."

When we pulled up in front of the nursery school gates, the excitement subsided. All the other children would leap toward the driver's seat, wedging themselves between the front seats, to hug their mother or father goodbye, practically sprawled atop the stick shift. Not us. Because there was that Beretta in the glove compartment. We'd open the door, get out carefully, and walk around, cautiously.

"Ciao, Gianni." And then we'd plant a kiss on his face.

He'd muss up my hair and give his granddaughter a bite. Olivia would rub her cheek dry with one hand.

"No, not the saliva," she would whine.

Her grandfather would just laugh back. "You little monkey, it's a seal bite. It's good luck." Then he'd turn serious again: "I'll be back to pick you up at one o'clock. Remember, this is important: wait for me *inside the gate*."

AT FIRST we attended a public nursery school; only then there was an incident, and our parents decided to send us to a nursery school run by nuns. Or, to be exact, it was Olivia's parents who made the decision. My mother, who'd always been a social climber, was happy to go along. She was happy to have me mingling with high society, even if I was only four. My father, an atheist and a Communist, not quite so much. But he had no real backbone, he wasn't capable of standing up for himself, especially when it came to his wife.

The incident occurred one evening in May 1979. Giulio and Elena, Olivia's parents, had invited a dozen friends over, and my mother was serving caviar canapés. They were all in the living room, drinking champagne as they waited for dinner. I was at home with Papa, probably watching the children's show *Carosello*. We lived downstairs, because my father was not only the Morganti family's gardener but also the villa's caretaker.

Given her preferences, Olivia would have been watching *Carosello* with me, but when her parents had friends over, she wasn't allowed to venture downstairs and come over to our place. She had to greet the guests and be shown off. She let herself be dressed up like a doll, patiently shaking hands with everyone, and even curtseying to the elderly matrons. Then she was free to play, but in the living room. Because she was onstage and was expected to stay there.

So there she sat, on the carpet, by the fireplace. She was playing alone, with a plastic toy train, bothering no one.

"Boom," she said.

The grown-ups watched her, beguiled, and kept repeating the same litany of customary comments. Why, what a lovely little girl. Why, what stunning dark eyes. Why, what cute little pigtails.

Olivia, impassive, indifferent to everyone in the room, kept saying, "Boom! Boom!"

After a bit, a young lady with long hair hanging down to her bottom got up off the sofa, crossed the living room with a glass of champagne in one hand, and sat down beside her, crossing her legs.

"What game are you playing, sweetheart?"

Olivia looked up, stared at her for a moment, then answered with a friendly smile: "I'm planting bombs under trains."

Silence.

That was hardly an appropriate game to play, especially in that particular period. The mayhem attendant on the Italicus train bombing was seared into recent memory, still rife with telling details: the tunnel brightly lit, the mountain shaking, the sudden roar, and passenger car number five enveloped in flames. Everyone could picture the twisted metal of the Rome–Brenner Pass express. My mother stood there, frozen, no longer handing around canapés, no longer collecting dirty glasses. Olivia's nanny was immediately summoned, but she had no answers to give.

"Cecilia, who could have taught her to play such a game?"

"I don't know, Signora, I really don't know."

Olivia was sent straight to bed. But in the living room, a grim cloud of disquiet was less easily dispelled. Everyone got to their feet, as if to convey a need to move elsewhere, preferably to the dining room.

My mother rushed straight into the kitchen: "Dinner!" she shouted to the other household help, "the Signora says that we're to serve dinner immediately. Get the pasta started now."

In the dining room, the discussion was blazing. Some were of the opinion that the little girl must have overheard some mention of the train, possibly on the evening news. Olivia's parents kept shaking their heads: "Impossible, in August 1974 she hadn't even been born yet."

Others, tired by now of the obligation to take that conversation seriously, ventured to crack sarcastic jokes: "Maybe there are terrorists who send their children to the same nursery school. Ha ha ha."

But the joke landed with a thud, and nobody laughed.

Luckily, the roast was brought to the table at that point and with the roast came another topic of discussion. One that unfortunately cut close to the bone. Namely, whether it was better to send your children to public or private schools. Nearly everyone came down on the side of the latter.

"The way things are these days," they tutted.

"I'd rather have an ignorant son than a dead one." It wasn't clear how ignorance was supposed to stave off death, as someone pointed out. But that question was soon forgotten.

"Such a tender roast."

"Delicious meat, no doubt about it."

And so the following day my parents were summoned upstairs. Signor Morganti, the engineer, and his lady, Signora Elena, invited them into the drawing room, just like the guests from the previous evening. They sat down and smoked a cigarette together, sociably.

"Would you care for one of mine, Sonia?"

For the first time, my mother was allowed to sample one of the thin, white cigarettes that Elena always seemed to have clamped between her lips, smearing the filter with her lipstick. My mother kept gazing at her forefinger and middle finger, like a little girl wearing new shoes who can't take her eyes off her feet. In reality, though, each drag brought little or no satisfaction because those cigarettes were so much lighter than hers. Still, they were much better looking, no doubt about it, far prettier.

"We'll pay Valerio's tuition, too. The children are so fond of each other, it would be a shame to separate them."

My father listened without looking up. After all, my mother had promptly accepted on both their behalves: "The nuns, why of course. Right, Guido?"

ON SATURDAY AFTERNOONS, we'd go to the Giardini Margherita with the nanny and two members of the police protection detail. We learned to ride bikes with the police. The police were there to help us up, when we fell over onto the asphalt. They were there to run after us children when we pedaled awkwardly, there to get out a screwdriver and tighten our training wheels as needed. They could load the bicycles into the trunk of the car when it was time to go home.

Olivia squirmed uncomfortably in the presence of those young men in uniform. Not because of the incongruity of their care, which meant little or nothing to her. Simply because the youngest of the two was always flirting with her nanny, and it made her jealous.

Any time she fell down, she'd scream for Cecilia, afraid anyone else might approach, unasked for.

"Naaanny."

Olivia might as well have been made of rubber. If she happened to skin her knee, she'd limp along carefree as before until someone noticed the spreading bloodstain on her pants leg and forced her to disinfect the wound. She wasn't the kind of girl who'd weep and wail, the thought never occurred to her, there was always some other topic of fascination, far more interesting than her mere physical pain. But when it came to *the police*, that was quite another matter. Then she'd scream as if possessed by a demon.

"Olivia, cut it out, it's nothing but a scrape." And the nanny would give her a spanking.

But nothing the nanny could do or say would silence her, if either of those young men dared to approach her. She'd just scream louder: "Get away! Get away from me!"

Not me. I was delighted to go to the park with the police. I'd gaze at their uniforms and holsters in rapt admiration. I'd ask if those were real pistols, like the grandfather's Beretta.

"Can I touch one of them?" I never tired of asking.

"No."

"Please, just for a second."

"Valerio, I told you no."

Even in the gardens around the villa, we were closely guarded. No one actually followed us around, but Olivia was only allowed outside with a little gray device hanging around her neck. It was to summon the Carabinieri, she only needed to push a red button. The inventor of that device hadn't counted on the fact that we were tireless climbers of trees. Sure enough, the alarm went off pretty much every other day, summoning two or three squad cars, sirens wailing, while Olivia sat happily perched in the high branches of a fig tree. So a second device was designed and built, this one with two red buttons instead of one, to be pressed simultaneously. Olivia could wear that one around her neck without unleashing holy hell every time she moved.

These were the years of kidnappings in Italy and the Morgantis, a family of wealthy builders, were afraid. Especially after the grandfather's partner's son was taken. Although the story was a violent one, we'd been told all about it.

"They kept him in a walk-in refrigerator, with the power off, for six months..." Olivia's grandmother would punctuate the story with dramatic pauses, to heighten the suspense. "And for that matter the poor boy was actually lucky. They cut the ear off another boy."

We'd listen to the stories, gulping down saliva.

We were allowed to call Olivia's grandmother Nonna, but nobody did. Even her own children never called her Mama. She was known to one and all as Manon, pure and simple.

"Really, Manon?"

"Word of honor," and she'd put her hand over heart, covering her pearls with those long, perfectly squared-off nails, gleaming with transparent polish.

Then the snow would start falling, and we'd immediately forget about all that. We'd get out the sled and hurtle down the hill at top speed, arms wrapped around each other. We'd tumble off the sled at the bottom, and then climb back up the hill, out of breath, ready for another ride.

"Valerio, look!" Olivia's eyes were glittering with joy. "*It's snowing for us.*"

Even in the fall it was nice, though. When we went out in the woods, wearing rubber boots, we'd collect the thorny chestnut shells, pry them open with a stick, and carry home the smooth nuts inside. My mother would roast them in a pan with holes in the bottom, and we'd eat them for our midday snack.

In summer, we'd pick fruit with my father, climbing ladders to pluck cherries, plums, and apricots. Then we'd run to our favorite hiding place. It was a little wooden shed where Papa stored his gardening tools. No one could see us or spy on us in there. In that secret hiding place, Olivia and I exchanged our first kiss. It was 1980, and we were five years old.

2

THE BOMB

SUMMER at Forte dei Marmi was what we did. My mother had gone to the station to put our bicycles on the train. On the morning of August 2, at 10:25, that's where she was.

From the hillside, we heard a blast. No one knew what had happened. Then word reached us: there'd been an explosion at the station. And that's when the terrible anguish began to spread. There was a frantic dash in all directions at the house. My father immediately rushed down to the station, in his Fiat 126. Olivia's parents were glued to the phone. "The gardener's wife," they'd say. Or else "Our housekeeper."

That day, for the first time, I realized that I did not really belong to the Morganti family. I was worried about *my*

Mama. They were talking about their *gardener's wife* or their *housekeeper.* Naturally, I couldn't grasp the enormity of that tragedy, so instead I wept over this discovery.

My father had found my mother covered with dust, wandering through the rubble like a ghost. She wasn't injured, she was just in a state of shock. She didn't even recognize him. He'd embraced her, but my mother let herself be hugged as if he were just some stranger, a policeman or a nurse.

"Sonia? Sonia? Are you all right? It's me, it's Guido."

She was trembling, she practically couldn't speak, and she kept obsessively repeating my name, pointing at Track 1, as if I were still there. Valerio, Valerio, Valerio. Papa tried to explain to her that I wasn't at the station, that I was at home, but she just shook her head. She refused to leave until she'd found me. She scratched and kicked and tried to break free and run toward the second-class waiting room. My father tried asking the first responders to help him, but nobody had time to pay attention to his problems. They didn't have time to worry about a woman who wasn't even hurt. There was no more room in the hospitals, and they were still pulling people out of the rubble. In fact, as there weren't enough ambulances, one doctor had loaded two of the injured into my father's Fiat 126, since he was right there, and asked him to take them to the emergency room.

Mama, sitting in the front seat, stared straight ahead. In the back seat, a man was moaning. Next to him was a young woman. She kept saying that her boyfriend was on "the bus of the dead."

"The bus of the dead," she kept saying like a broken record, "the bus of the dead."

In the meantime, everyone had listened to the 11:35 morning news. The announcer reported that the authorities "only suspected" it had been a terrorist attack, though they made it clear enough that they were in fact certain it was, and then ended the news bulletin with the day's latest development: the court had just indicted the suspects in the Italicus train bombing. All the same, in the news report, there was mention of "a boiler," a boiler explosion. No one believed that for a moment. Word was that there were a hundred injured and a "substantial" number of dead.

While helicopters wheeled overhead and the city's historic center had been shut down to aid in rescue efforts, the call went out for people to donate blood. Come to the main hospital or the Red Cross office on Via Boldrini. The nanny, who was just twenty-two years old, shocked by events and her own youth, wanted to hurry in to donate blood after hearing the appeal on the radio. But Olivia's parents had forbidden her to go.

"It could be dangerous, Cecilia. Absolutely not."

Meanwhile, from the living room, unsettling rumors arrived. The nanny could shut the door all she liked, open up a colorful picture book, raise her voice, insist upon reading the story of Hansel and Gretel, but our hearing wasn't affected in the slightest. Olivia's parents were upset, very upset. The phone was ringing constantly, everyone was talking in frantic voices. The grandparents had come down from the villa.

Even Edoardo, Olivia's uncle, whom everyone called Dado, had come running up the stairs. The entire Morganti family had gathered together and were now talking at the top of their lungs.

"Boiler my foot, that was a terror attack," Gianni was saying.

"Those bastards," Manon was shouting.

And that's when the grandmother started throwing her tantrum, envisioning coming catastrophes, as always. Manon said they needed to pack their bags instantly, leave the country, maybe for France, because this was no way for people to live, with bombs going off like in wartime.

"Enough's enough," she shouted.

Olivia's father tried to calm her down, he even called her Mama, but she was in a raging fury.

"Mama, please, try not to get too upset."

"Oh, no, nothing doing. I survived the Fascists and the Germans," she replied, "I'm not going to let *the Communists* kill me." Meanwhile she called for the housekeeper, telling her to get out her luggage.

For the second time that day, I'd experienced the horrible sensation of realizing I wasn't a member of that family: I, Valerio Carnevale, might not be a Morganti at all. I just sat, grimly, in a corner, all by myself. I wouldn't even accept Olivia's company, not even when she came over with an orange plastic record player.

"Valerio, come over here! Let's put on some French music."

Olivia had been taking French lessons since she was three, just in case they really did decide to leave the country, if it looked like a Communist regime was about to take over. The only words I knew were the lyrics to her damned little ditties, like *bergère* or *gentil coquelicot*, you can imagine how useful.

"*You* listen. I don't feel like it."

I wondered whether they'd take me with them to Paris. I'd even forgotten about my mother. I just imagined Olivia wearing a navy-blue overcoat and a cap with a pom-pom, waving goodbye with her woolen gloves, telling me that sooner or later we'd meet again, somewhere in the world. I bit my lip and started banging my head against the wall, without making too much noise. As far as I was concerned, the Bologna train station wasn't the only thing that had just been blown to smithereens.

When I saw Papa, I ran to greet him. Suddenly, I remembered about my mother. My father was filthy, sweaty, and smelly, and most of all, there was a strange look in his eyes. He hugged me too tightly. She's dead, I thought. And now I'm an orphan, too.

But he gave me a light smack on the bottom: "Go on down to see her, she's downstairs. But be quiet, in case she's sleeping. She's exhausted, so don't wake her up."

I tiptoed into my parents' bedroom. My mother was asleep, sure enough, face down on the bed. I stood there for a little while and looked at her. Papa had cleaned her off with a washcloth, but her clothing, tossed carelessly on the floor, was still caked with dust. Her hair was wet and there was a dark halo of water on the pillow. At a certain point she moved one foot, kicking the sheet off. She was sweating and talking in her sleep. She was saying that my bicycle had been crushed under a taxi. That the bicycle was ruined. It scared me, and I turned and ran away. I knocked at Olivia's door with all the strength in my body. I wanted to be with Papa. But he wasn't there, he'd gone back to the station to try to lend a hand. Cecilia took me by the hand and led me into Olivia's room, where my friend sat playing in silence with her Legos, head bowed.

"Valerio, stay here. Your papa will be back this evening, and he'll pick you up then."

The last thing I felt like doing was playing with Legos, but I picked up a red cube and asked Olivia where it was supposed to go.

That evening, in the kitchen of the grandparents' villa, literally everyone was there. The cook, the chauffeur, Manon's housekeeper, the Eritrean maid. Even the nanny was there, though she usually ate with the Morganti family.

"The Fascists," said the chauffeur, who was considered to be an authority on the subject, "those damned Fascists."

Everyone agreed with him.

"Bastards."

After drinking a couple of glasses of wine, Papa had started telling what he'd seen, forgetting that I was there in the room with him. He was too tired, and he just needed to let off some steam after the day he'd had. He'd been back and forth, carrying people who'd been ravaged, people without legs, without feet, without arms.

"The things I saw," he would say. Dead children, men badly burned, fragments of bodies under the rubble. He'd helped shovel, extract, and transport. The seats of his Fiat 126 were smeared with blood. Everyone sat listening to him, mouths agape.

Then the nanny shyly reported what the grandmother was planning to do.

"Leave the country? Move to France?" The cook was worried, too. For a moment, the Bologna bombing had been forgotten.

But the chauffeur, the wise old sage of the group, smiled: "That's just the way the Signora is, you shouldn't take the things she says too seriously. She's the queen of this city, she's never going to move away."

And so, with a sigh of relief, everyone went back to the tale of the bloodbath.

ON AUGUST 4, 1980, two days after the bombing, we flew over the wreckage of the train station. No one was threatening to leave the country now. The time had come to leave for the seaside, in Versilia. We boarded Olivia's grandfather's private plane, which he piloted himself. Gianni had been an aviator during the war, and flying was what he loved best.

Usually, when we weren't flying, we left in a caravan. Manon led the way, in the biggest car, driven by the chauffeur. Riding with her were us children. In the next car back were Olivia's parents. Another car back was the nanny, who had just got her driver's license, and riding with her were the cook, Manon's housekeeper, and lots and lots of other people's luggage.

The grandfather would often join the rest of the family a few days later, from the sky. Everyone would go to the airport to wait for him. We'd look at the wind sock filling up with air, the blades of grass in the meadow trembling in the gusts. Wobbling on its landing gear, the *Fox-Trot* would make its final approach. The propellers would turn more and more slowly, a short set of stairs would be thrown down, and Gianni would step onto solid ground, together with his copilot. He'd come strolling toward his family, with a loose-limbed slouch and a dazzling smile. He bit Olivia on the cheek, he patted me on the head, he kissed his daughter-in-law, he slapped his son on the back, tossed off an affectionate wisecrack for the nanny and a compliment for the cook. Then he headed for the exit, followed by the procession. Manon was never there to meet him. Neither was Olivia's uncle, who was generally quite intolerant of the family's hierarchies, rituals, and ceremonies.

We were accustomed to traveling on the *Fox-Trot*. To our eyes, that airplane was like a tour bus. We even knew the technical terms, like "flap" and "landing gear." "The left flap doesn't seem to be responding, better fasten your seat belts." "The landing gear won't extend, we're going to try to touch down anyway, so let's all hope God's on our side." At these critical moments, Olivia's mother, breathing deeply, would distribute handfuls of candy. But we weren't afraid. We'd just sit there, contentedly drawing on the tables, blithely unaware of impending disaster.

But that day, August 4, 1980, was different. We flew over the ravaged station. We all looked down at the wreckage from high above. The nanny wept and apologized for her tears.

"Just awful," said Gianni, pulling the joystick toward him. He didn't know whether he should fly low, to get a better look, or climb above the cloud cover, to forget.

Even though he'd fought in the war and had seen more than his share of rubble and wreckage, even if he'd been perfectly capable of flying into battle as a young man with an unloaded machine gun because the Italian army didn't have enough money for ammunition, even considering that he'd become accustomed to ravaged corpses from an early age, he was still shaken by that sight: "Awful, it's just awful."

He'd been a Fascist, but so had everybody else. He'd had no political passions, though. All Gianni cared about was airplanes. His parents had inculcated in him a generic sense of duty, serviceable for the barracks: fight for your government, be a good soldier, those were his credos, and he didn't stop to ponder any deeper questions. After the armistice, given the oath he'd sworn, he was ready and willing to head north to Salò. But Manon, who had a far different history behind her and, most importantly, a Socialist father, had refused to let him go. She was ready to divorce him if he became a die-hard Fascist, a *repubblichino*. Manon was one of the most beautiful women in Bologna and Gianni would sooner dump Mussolini than run the risk of being dumped by Manon.

After the war, his indifference to any ideology only grew. Gianni had developed a certain contempt for politicians of any party, perhaps because he had to deal with them every single day. He was a real estate developer: contracts, buildings to construct, land to clear and develop. Politicians clustered around him like ravenous dogs.

"Olivia and Valerio," he announced from the cockpit, "don't get near the windows. Don't look out. Just keep drawing."

Olivia's mama stuffed us with candy, telling us it was important to swallow so we wouldn't get earaches. And Manon told us story after story, usually violent ones. She told us about when the Allies had bombed Bologna. She had been forced to step over the severed head of a deliveryman. And she'd seen a woman screaming, covered with dust, in an apartment building ripped half open by an explosion on Piazza Ravegnana.

Manon, like all the other high-society matrons, hated the Communists. But she'd never been a Fascist. She'd been named Manon precisely because her father was an atheist and a Socialist at the turn of the twentieth century, and he was determined he would not name his daughter after a saint: he much preferred opera to the gates of Heaven. She had always been the most beautiful girl in the city. When she was young, she'd even won a beauty contest, which brought money home to her parents. But she had much more than just beauty. Manon was one of the few women of the 1940s to have taken a university degree. Her real gift was pure mathematics, but she hadn't been able to afford that field of study. Her father owned a pharmacy, and she needed to work, so she was forced to opt for a more practical course. During the war, father and daughter lived and worked together. It was just the two of them and no one else, because Manon's father was divorced. One of the very few divorces in that period. He had been sent to prison twice: once because he was an anti-Fascist, and the second time because of his wife, who had reported him to the police for adultery. And so the two of them, father and daughter, had remained in Bologna even during the bombing raids. They couldn't afford to leave the pharmacy to join the other evacuees in the countryside. So she'd witnessed plenty of bloodbaths. And she hadn't viewed them from the sky.

Afterward, of course, she'd more than made up for it. She'd managed to marry the most eligible bachelor around. Though, let it be said, Gianni's family had turned up their noses at her, since Manon was neither wealthy nor born into nobility. What's more, her parents were divorced, a great source of shame. The fact that she was intelligent and a college graduate was of no interest to anyone.

In any case, Manon had taken revenge for that humiliation.

No one could have adapted better than she did to her new position as the wife of one of the city's leading businessmen.

And she was particularly adept at using her bottomless reading for life in high society. She traveled, she kept her eyes open, she studied, she enriched her mind, and she kept this vast patrimony of knowledge for herself. She would go out with her husband, well dressed and elegant, and she did her bourgeois duty, carefully measuring her words. An understated discussion of ancient art, well calibrated and worldly, perhaps anchored in a discussion of a trip she'd taken, just to offer her listeners an opportunity to take part in the conversation, but she never went beyond that. Woe betide anyone who dared to suggest that she appreciated Morandi or Burri, at a time when no one had been willing to pay a penny for their work.

There were things that could only be discussed within the family. Her husband's face turned bright red, his coronary arteries backing up: "Are you saying you want to hang a chunk of burnt plastic in the living room?"

Manon jutted her chin, with calm determination: "Yes."

Gianni started trembling with irritation: "Let me buy you a Chagall, how about that? Don't you want a Chagall?"

"I'd prefer a Balthus," she replied, with a grim smile.

"Who?"

Manon was only able to show off her culture with us, innocent children that we were. She could even read us Shakespeare. We hung from her lips. To our minds, Shakespeare's violence was no different from stories about the war: the poison poured into Claudius's ear was as shocking to us as the deliveryman's lopped-off head.

And so, that day, as we flew high above a tragedy that closely concerned us, as we traveled thousands of feet above the site of the Bologna massacre, toward the seashore and sweet forgetfulness, we listened to stories of bombing raids and *Hamlet*. Manon was a skilled storyteller.

As we passed over the train station, Olivia tried to peek down. I grabbed her arm and upbraided her.

"Gianni said not to look," I told her.

"I'll look at anything I want to, for your information."

When we disembarked from the airplane, one of the many suitcases tumbled to the tarmac. It burst open and a hundred or so apricots came rolling out. Everyone was bent over, gathering fruit, even the grandparents, determined not to let anyone see that they'd brought produce from their garden at home so they wouldn't have to buy it at the seashore, where it was more expensive.

3

WAR IN THE COURTYARD

MEANWHILE, for me, the world really was about to collapse, and the Years of Lead had nothing to do with it. Because in the meantime my mother had fallen in love with a Roman, and to be more exact, a *cravattaro* (that was slang for "loan shark," but he had assured her that he was a traveling salesman). Max happened to be in Bologna to collect a debt, and he wasn't happy with the debtor, who was doing his best to lie low. His meeting with my mother was a chance event. Mama had gone out to shop for groceries, at the market on Via Ugo Bassi. She was very nicely dressed because Manon gave her the outfits she no longer wore, and Mama liked putting on airs as if she were a grand lady, especially if her audience consisted of people who couldn't contradict her playacting. She chose an assortment of zucchini, rehearsing the usual fictions for the fruit-and-vegetable man's benefit.

"I'll be leaving for Cortina soon, my son's going to learn to ski," she was saying.

Max, who had happened to be at the market to buy some mortadella to eat with a loaf of bread, was struck by this woman. And at first he also thought he'd hit pay dirt. A rich woman, this is my lucky strike. He'd walked over to her. He'd started giving her suggestions about the vegetables, making her laugh. Then he'd offered to treat her to an espresso, and he'd told her a lot of ridiculous stories. He claimed to own a small villa "outside of Rome," as if he'd opted for the bucolic choice of living in the countryside, when in fact he was sleeping on his uncle's pull-out sofa, in the Quadraro neighborhood, a quarter that you actually might be right in considering "outside of Rome," for real. He told her that he was about to "go into business for himself," coming dangerously close to the truth because he did have a small pile of cash set aside, and he intended to use that money to make money, and had no intention of going halves with his friends. He told her that he was in love, and that Sonia was the most beautiful woman he'd ever laid eyes on, and about that, at least, he wasn't lying.

Mama wasn't accustomed to certain kinds of attention. She felt enormously flattered. My father was the silent type, a bit overweight, his hands rough and callused. In contrast, that ambitious, athletic, amusing man who was openly wooing her was an absolute novelty.

Max would catch the train north to Bologna on a weekly basis. My mother would dream up a bunch of errands to run. "I need to take Olivia's lace dress to the cleaners." "I'm just stepping out to buy a squash for tonight's risotto." "I'm taking the Signora to the beauty shop." She'd drive down off the hillside with her heart racing and spend a couple of intense hours in a two-star pensione. No one suspected a thing. That wasn't Papa's style, he didn't even have the imagination to be suspicious about certain things.

But the problems started when Mama began to air her grievances. She said that she was sick and tired of being "a scullery maid" and that before we knew it I was going to turn into a servant myself, and that was something she simply couldn't accept. She freely spoke of divorce, quitting her job, and demanding severance pay. She shouted all day long. Her unhappiness, hollered out at the top of her lungs, was sheer torture for Papa, who didn't know what to say. He'd sit in the kitchen, rubbing his eyes with fingers still caked with soil, trying to listen to her and understand, but the whole thing struck him as insurmountable. Usually, that just drove my mother even crazier, and she started firing off barrages of insults. She told him that he was ignorant, that he was "a loser." That she'd had her fill. And she dragged me into it, intentionally.

"They've taken Valerio, he's just become another one of their pieces of property," she'd say.

"But that isn't true. They treat him like a son, Sonia."

"Oh, certainly. They've turned him into a lady's companion! The little girl is just bored. Open your eyes, Guido, for God's sake. I don't think so, sorry. I'm not putting up with this."

I was putting my hands over my ears, trying not to listen. Then I caught a smack to the face. During that period my mother was absolutely out of control.

"Listen, you idiot. And *try to smarten up*. You don't want to grow up like your father, who's just a clueless asshole."

She was clearly tormented. She even argued with Manon, though no one else dared to talk back to the old woman. She'd take umbrage if anyone told her she'd ironed a shirt less than perfectly. And it was like taking your life in your hands to point out that she'd burned the countertop by setting down a scorching hot pot on a section of blond pine. It seemed as if everyone was conspiring against her.

My father was at his wits' end. He tried to interact with her, the poor man. She would talk about divorce and he would reply, "Don't be an *ass*." She would burst into tears, and he'd say, "Why don't you stop *zagnare*," stumbling over the *z* sound of the verb *zagnare*—to bust someone's balls— like the native-born Bolognese that he was. He'd come up with ways of pleasing her, but they were always the wrong thing. One day he'd bring her a ten-pound *culatello* ham that she would just pick at, making a show of having no appetite. Another day he'd suggest going out for a picnic along the banks of the Po to get some sun, but my mother would turn her nose up at the idea: too many mosquitoes. How about going to Rimini for a nice fish fry? His wife would shake her head, claiming she had a stomachache.

Finally he'd worked up the nerve to go ahead and have it out with her: "So, have you developed a *scuffia* on another man?"—using the dialect term for "crush."

Mama exploded. She started to confess. She talked about falling in love and contradictions, senses of guilt and lust. She used the word "laceration." Papa listened to her, aghast, without taking any explicit position on the matter. Finally, he got to his feet, unable to take any more ("You're *sgodevole*," he said, again in dialect: "unpleasant"), and smacked her hard in the face. At least he knew what he was doing when he made this mistake.

AND SO, in September 1981, I was taken away. The scene wasn't the way I'd imagined it. Olivia wasn't waving goodbye with woolen gloves because she had to leave for France. I was the one waving goodbye. I didn't want to. For that matter, neither did she.

One evening my mother took me around to say our farewells, and I followed, my head hanging low. First we went to the grandparents' villa. Gianni patted me on the head the way he usually did, then he handed me a check. He was a generous man, and he just wanted to give me something to help with my studies. But Mama was a proud woman, and she rejected the offer. She shook hands with Manon, her head held high, and a more arrogant glare in her eyes than even Manon could muster. She smiled with satisfaction. She shoved me toward the old woman: "Valerio, thank the Signora for telling you all the lovely fairy tales."

Manon raised an eyebrow. "They weren't *fairy tales*," she replied.

Right after that, we went to Olivia's house. Giulio Morganti was on the phone, Elena came to meet us. She was worried.

"Sonia, are you sure about this?"

"Yes, Signora, I'm absolutely certain. Thanks."

Elena wrapped her arms around me, she planted kisses on my cheeks. "Valerio, we'll expect you for summer vacation. Will you come to the seashore with us?"

I nodded my head, looking up at my mama as I did so. I was asking her permission. Then the nanny arrived. Cecilia was in tears, she practically couldn't speak.

"You'll always be my little boy," she said, "always and forever."

Not me, I wasn't crying. I was waiting for Olivia, holding my breath. But she refused to emerge from her bedroom.

"She's acting up," the nanny said. "I'm going to scold her now, this isn't the way to behave."

A stabbing pain pierced my heart, I could feel it sink into my body, as if it were about to poke all the way through and out my back.

Elena and the nanny had already set out on their mission. But Olivia had locked her door.

"Olivia! Open up! That's an order." Stern tone of voice.

From the other side of the door: silence.

"Olivia, come out this minute to say goodbye to Valerio. I'm warning you, there will be consequences. If you don't open this door immediately, I'm going to forbid you to sleep with the dog for a whole month."

Unbudgeable silence.

"Olivia? I'm going to call your father now." That was the most fearsome threat.

Not a word.

I wanted to find a door to hide behind, too, but Mama had a solid grip on my shoulder. She was waiting impassively, her back erect. At a certain point she leaned down, tucked my shirt into my trousers, and told me: "You see? Olivia *doesn't love you.*"

My father drove us to the station and helped us to load our luggage on the train. He didn't say a word. After getting us comfortably settled, he pulled me to him, pushing my face into his belly and holding the back of my neck.

"Then we're agreed. You'll spend the summer with me." I nodded my head.

My mother was perfectly dry-eyed, and she said nothing but "Excuse me, Guido, could you get my light sweater out of my suitcase for me?"

I'D NEVER SEEN Rome before. Max had come to meet us at the Termini Station, he'd even brought a present for me, a large box of Play-Doh. I held it in my hands, inert. We got out in front of a tall apartment building on Via Chiabrera, and we climbed up to the fourth floor. The apartment was practically empty. There was a table with a few chairs standing around it, there was a king-sized mattress lying on the floor. Max took me by the hand and showed me my room, which was furnished with a small cot. There was nothing else in the room.

"Do you like it, Valerio?"

I nodded my head, but I was overwhelmed. I turned around to ask my mother for an explanation. But she had already vanished.

Max gave me a pat on the back, gleeful and contented: "Great. If you go downstairs to the courtyard, you'll see there's lots of little kids."

I replied with another nod. I was terrified. My mother reappeared and walked me downstairs.

"Stay here, Valerio. That way you can make friends. I'll come and get you in an hour."

I found myself standing motionless in front of a crowd of kids who stared at me in silence. They'd even stopped playing their soccer game. As soon as my mother turned to go, they all burst out laughing. They looked at my clothing and rocked with laughter. I was standing there, head hanging low. They were mocking me, but I couldn't understand what they were saying. They were speaking in Roman dialect, *romanesco*.

I kept trying to figure out the drift of what they were shouting, all while keeping my eyes downcast. But it wasn't easy. There was too much noise and the words kept drowning each other out. Then a fat boy came over and took me by the hand. A general wall of silence ensued. Probably this boy counted for a lot in the group and they all resumed their previous activity, no longer paying any attention to me.

The boy was named Danilo, but everyone called him Er Faccia, because he had a fat face, like all the rest of his body, for that matter. He asked me what my nickname was. I shrugged. But he remained calm, it wasn't a problem. A nickname would come of its own accord, sooner or later. I thanked him.

IN THE FIRST FEW MONTHS I tended to be very quiet, maybe because I barely understood half of what they said. Even if I was only seven years old, I realized that I had had a different childhood than they had. Certainly, there was Er Faccia, who protected me, and that meant no one could make fun of me or beat me up. But his protection alone wasn't sufficient, there were plenty of things I needed to learn on my own. I understood that when the police arrived.

They were all living as squatters, so the police were public enemy number one. We lived in a tumbledown apartment building that was officially uninhabited because it had been condemned. It was leaning at such a sharp angle that when Mama was frying dinner, the potatoes would slide right out of the frying pan. Every now and then the police would come around to try to evict us, but that was just part of the routine.

Only I didn't know that. And I'd had a radically different experience. At last, something familiar, I thought to myself. Pleased and relieved, I went running toward the police with open arms. Maybe these boys are nicer than the other ones, and they'll let me hold their pistol, I told myself. And I ran and ran, happily. Will they have Berettas, too? At a certain point, I turned around and realized that I was all alone now. The other kids were all watching me from a distance, wondering what the hell I thought I was doing. Even Er Faccia was upset. I observed the scene, worried now. Even the police were feeling uncomfortable. A kid from Via Chiabrera running to hug us? I really had nobody on my side, now.

My friends called me a "rat fink."

"Rat fink! Rat fink! Valerio, you're a rat fink," they shouted.

I had no idea what that meant. Was it a compliment? An insult? My new nickname?

Anyway, something had happened. For a number of days, no one would speak to me. As if I no longer existed. I would try to get them to pass me the ball, but nothing doing. I'd ask a question and no one would answer. I'd offer to share my snack but no one wanted any.

Then, one Saturday, Er Faccia, with his splay-legged walk (with those fat thighs of his, he really had no other way to walk), pulled me off to one side. He sat me down on a step and then stood before me and asked questions. I wanted to be straight with him, I owed him that much. Plus, he was the only one there that I trusted. Er Faccia listened to what I had to say and scratched his cheek, perplexed. He clearly suspected that I was spouting lies.

"So, explain to me so I can understand this friendship you seem to have with the cops."

While I was explaining that the police had taught us to ride bicycles, Er Faccia furrowed his brow.

"With training wheels," I explained.

"You couldn't think straight even if you had training wheels for your brain."

After a pause, he stood up, tugged his T-shirt down over his belly, and gave me an affectionate smack on the back of my neck. He'd come up with a reasonable solution.

"Okay, you might be a little bit strange, but your father's still a loan shark. They'll respect you anyway."

"But he's not my father," I replied.

"Less said about that, the better."

No doubt about it, the place where I lived was an important center of operations in the neighborhood. People felt free to ring our doorbell at all hours of the day and night. And it wasn't just to ask for a loan. They brought food to eat, they shared whatever there was, they went ahead and took a seat even though there weren't enough chairs (often they'd bring chairs with them, from upstairs or downstairs), and they'd stay until the wee hours drinking and talking, all in our kitchen.

Some showed up with mussels freshly caught out at Ostia, others brought zucchini they'd grown on a code-violating terrace, or else they might happen along with a three-liter plastic jerrican full of wine from the Castelli Romani. Any excuse was a good enough reason to throw a party, with whatever provisions came to hand. Mama was so cheerful, finally she was the queen. She could forget about Manon.

I had learned how to do my homework in the midst of all that bedlam. I had no nanny to help me. I'd just lie down on the floor and do my best to concentrate. I was the best student in the class, something that made even Er Faccia proud. In his eyes I was a bizarre creature, but a fascinating one, as everyone freely admitted. In some odd fashion, I reinforced the group's charisma. But I could never mention Olivia's name: that was the way matters stood. My previous life had to remain as mysterious as possible. Er Faccia was determined to uphold my public image, which inevitably had a bearing on his. So I was required to forget about her, and that was that.

But Olivia hadn't forgotten me at all, and she wrote me letters regularly, at least once a week. They would arrive in a sky-blue envelope and I'd take care to hide them immediately. I'd write back to her at night, out of sight of prying eyes.

Every so often, my father would call me up. He'd tell me all about her. How she studied English and French on Mondays and Fridays with a young lady who was a native speaker, how she played tennis on Tuesdays and practiced gymnastics on Wednesdays and took piano lessons on Thursdays. And that on Saturdays they'd take her to parties and repurpose all the gifts she'd received on her birthday.

My father didn't want to know anything about my life in Rome, all he asked me was how I was doing.

"Fine," I replied. And then I'd hang up the phone.

THEN SUMMER CAME. While all the other little kids in the neighborhood had no choice but to stay home and sweat in the sweltering courtyard, I was going to have to leave. I didn't want anyone to know that I was going anyplace as fancy as Versilia, but my mother just didn't know how to keep her mouth shut. She boasted of it to everyone.

Er Faccia took it as an annoyance and even worse, this really wasn't anything he'd been expecting. He felt it was a slight to his honor. He'd worked so hard to force the others to accept me, as his personal protégé, and now he just couldn't begin to imagine how to justify the eccentricities I was guilty of. If only my mother had known how to be a little more discreet, there would have been no real difficulties. "Valerio has relatives in Bologna, he's going to stay with them," and that would have been that. But no, she felt called upon to tell people everything. He's leaving for Forte dei Marmi, she'd say. In a private airplane, she'd go on, exaggerating. He's going out in a sailboat. Even Er Faccia bade me farewell with nothing more than a curt nod, to keep from getting himself into hotter and deeper water.

THE HANGED MAN

We're reporting on a mystery genuinely befitting a film by Hitchcock. Several hours ago, Scotland Yard fished the corpse of a middle-aged man out of the river Thames. Practically unidentifiable, it appears to have been in the water for some considerable length of time, perhaps three or four days, or possibly even longer. What has really alarmed the authorities, however, is the fact that they found an Italian passport on the unidentified man's person, made out to the following strange name: Signor Gian Roberto Calvini. So far, neither Scotland Yard nor the Italian embassy has been willing to make any definitive statement concerning the identity of the corpse.

At first, the Italian ambassador in London sent an em-
ployee to identify the body, as far as was possible, and
ascertain the cause of death. Then, once this employee
got a good look at the strange passport, he rushed to the
morgue to take a look for himself, and as of this broad-
cast he has not yet returned. It is quite likely that we'll
all learn much more about this case in the next few . . .

IT WAS JUNE 18, 1982, and we'd already been at the seashore for a week. We were playing cowboys and Indians with
Olivia's mother, who'd painted our faces with lipstick. We'd
wrapped sashes around our foreheads, pulling them low over
our eyes, and glued seagulls' feathers to them. Elena had put
on a cowboy hat and was chasing us with a water pistol. We
ran excitedly in all directions.

"Mama, if you don't put down that Beretta, I'm going to
sound the alarm!"

"Sweetheart, you're an Indian. There aren't any alarms
to sound in the desert."

"Then I'll call the police!"

And I'd start chanting a new refrain that I'd just learned,
giving Olivia shoves as I sang it: *"Beat it, beat it, beat it, the
cops!"*

"What kind of song is that?" Olivia wanted to know,
convinced that she must have missed some fundamental episode of the Zecchino d'Oro show, an international children's
song festival.

Then the phone rang, Elena took off her hat, threw it on the ground, and ran inside to answer.

"Hello?" Panting.

We ran inside, drenched and dripping, shouting, slipping and sliding. We fought loudly: "Mama! Mama! Valerio doesn't want to give me the Beretta, now it's my turn."

"No it isn't. It's still my turn."

Elena scolded us both: "Silence! That's enough out of you two." She lit a cigarette, her hands trembling: "They *killed* him?"

We fell silent. We stood looking at her.

A short while later Manon arrived, fresh from the hairdresser's. She had a buoyant blond bouffant of hair, a coral necklace that looped three times around her neck, opentoed sandals, and bright red toenails. She and Elena spoke quietly, whispering into each other's ears.

Manon took a seat on the sofa. "We need to send a telegram. We need to express our condolences."

Naturally, a few evenings later, Manon, impassioned lover of atrocious stories that she was, told us the fairy tale of Calvi. In her opinion, children always had a right to know what was going on around them. The truth never needed to be a secret, it was *only a matter of narrative.*

"They hanged him at night, in London, beneath the Blackfriars Bridge. They put a brick in his pocket, as a warning. That brick was their way of saying: 'You knew we'd kill you, you should have been more careful.'"

We kids, sitting on the carpet with our legs crossed, stared at her, wide-eyed.

"He belonged to a mysterious secret society, where everyone wore a black hood over their head and white gloves."

Olivia and I huddled close in fear.

"They wanted him dead because he'd got his hands on the world's biggest treasure: he was God's banker."

Olivia raised a finger, in bafflement: "Grandma, is God rich?"

Manon broke out laughing: "God is very, very rich, little one. And like all rich people, He doesn't want to pay taxes." She suddenly realized she'd ventured onto a slippery slope: "But that's a little complicated to explain. It's also got a lot to do with tax havens and offshore banking, I'm afraid." Now she was starting to get things confused: "But lately, God owed a lot of money to people. He was actually on the verge of bankruptcy."

Olivia shook her head: "Wait, I don't get it: is He rich or is He in debt?"

"Well, sometimes there's no difference. I know, it's hard to understand. Let's forget about the motive." She sighed. "Let's move on to the story of the secretary."

"God's secretary?"

"No, Calvi's."

"Ah."

"I've shown you lots of Hitchcock movies, I feel sure you can follow me now..."

Manon never tired of stuffing us with information about Hitchcock movies. "I don't know what I was thinking," she'd say, getting up from the sofa and turning off the television as the end credits scrolled up on *Dial M for Murder* or *Rear Window*, "that's not a film for little kids." But we were in a state of utter ecstasy. Both of us head over heels in love with Grace Kelly. She called thrillers *giallacci*—literally, "nasty old yellows," a pejorative variation on the slang for detective novels, which customarily had yellow covers—a brutal term that gave a pretty good idea of the depth of her passion for violent stories, whatever the genre.

"The secretary jumped out of a fifth-floor window exactly one day before Calvi was found hanged under the bridge in London. So what would you guess? Murder or suicide?"

We exchanged a glance: *Elementary, my dear Watson.*

And we raced to see who could be the first to shout the word "murder," shoving each other as we did.

"I said it first."

"No, I did. Grandma, which of us is the investigator?"

Manon gave us each a mint chocolate candy, as a prize. "Now, that's enough, it's time for bed. It's nine-thirty, it's very late."

We refused to hear of it.

"So, Manon, did you know *the hanged man?*"

Olivia's grandmother, a natural-born storyteller, just couldn't resist: "I knew him, of course I did. Every now and then I'd run into him at a cocktail party. He was a very intelligent man, excellent company. When he was around, I was never bored, his conversation was witty and scintillating. He'd sit down beside me and tell me all about his return from Russia, during the war. He'd been in the infantry and he'd made his way back to Italy on foot. Just imagine walking for months and months, through the snow, with worn-out boots and frostbitten feet. But he made it."

Manon was a magician when it came to details. When a story lacked them, she would just make them up, unruffled, to keep her audience's attention riveted. We'd listen to her, captivated.

"Did I ever tell you about the Russian campaign, children? Oh, there are wonderful books about it. People froze solid the minute they stopped walking, and others ate their dead to survive the winter."

"Really?" We lifted our upper lips in horror, revealing our toothless gums.

"What do you think, if someone has the strength to get all the way back home like that, what do they do? Do they hang themselves?"

The goodnight kiss: "Sweet dreams, children."

SWEET DREAMS...if only. Back then there was definitely something funereal in the air and I couldn't seem to sleep at all. At Olivia's house, nobody talked about anything but a single letter and a single number, a *P* and a 2. At breakfast, lunch, and dinner. And we kept imagining people wearing hoods, everywhere we turned.

"How dare they call it suicide," the grandfather shouted at the dinner table, choking on a chicken wing. And then he'd switch off the television set, in annoyance.

I'd have nightmares and scream in the night. I no longer wanted to sleep at all: I was afraid that a hooded man would come and take me, and then hang me under a bridge. The nanny would walk into the bedroom, angry with me: "Valerio, cut it out. Olivia is already asleep, don't you see?"

As soon as Cecilia left, I'd start screaming again. I'd cry out for my father in despair: "Paaapaaa! Papa, *please*, come get me."

Olivia would sigh, turn onto her other side, and clamp the pillow over her ears. That was already something she did habitually, though, because ever since her grandmother had first told her the story of *Hamlet*, she had a deathly fear that someone might pour poison into her ear.

My father would walk softly into the bedroom, sit down on the bed, and stroke my hair: "Valerio, what on earth's wrong?"

I'd grab him by the arm, in sheer terror: "Save me, only you can save me."

He'd laugh: "Save you from what?"

I'd feel suddenly stupid. "Oh, nothing, Papa, sorry."

"Good boy. Now I'm going back to the kitchen, I have to help the others wash dishes. Think happy thoughts. You'll see, you'll fall asleep right away."

"All right."

I thought about breaking waves. When the sea was rough, the beach at Forte dei Marmi was just fantastic. Indifferent to the red warning flags and the scoldings that were sure to follow, we'd run into the surf and let ourselves be slammed down onto the sand by the violent, foamy breakers. When the sea was flat, on the other hand, we could take a pedal boat and ride out to the buoy, naturally with our nanny, who didn't know how to swim. We swore up and down that we'd help her, if she was drowning. Cecilia was young and a bit of a child, so she let herself be pulled along by the current.

Two weeks later we were at Calvi's niece's birthday party. The birthday girl was much younger than us, so we objected.

"She's only three years old."

Our nanny didn't want to hear our complaints. We were expected to stand still and let ourselves be dressed. Olivia was expected to wear a sky-blue dress, with a lace collar and pleats on her chest, an ample skirt, ruffled socks, and patent leather shoes with little straps.

"It itches," she said, scratching herself.

"Your mother said that you are to wear this dress. Come on, it doesn't itch."

"Does, too."

"Well, that just means you're going to have to feel itchy."

Olivia never threw tantrums. The few times she'd tried having her own way, it had turned out so badly that she'd run to throw her arms around her grandmother's knees (because Manon had once told her that that was how the ancient Greeks begged for forgiveness). She was instantly forgiven, of course. But from on high, haughtily, like the gods. It was handed down as a gracious amnesty and the corresponding humiliation received from Olympus was, frankly, intolerable. And so, as long as it meant avoiding the pardon, she was willing to refrain from tantrum-throwing entirely. She preferred to vent her rage against me.

She forgot about the itchy dress and pointed her finger at me: "Ha ha. You're funny dressed like that, you look like a stupid penguin."

I gave her the side-eye, offended and hurt, adjusting my bow tie on the collar of my shirt. I didn't even feel the need to respond, I just told myself that if my friends from Via Chiabrera had seen me tricked out like that, things would have gone much, much worse. They were capable of much more vicious wisecracks, things that would never have occurred to Olivia in a million years. There was a guy, for instance, who'd lost an ear in a motorcycle crash, and they'd nicknamed him Er Tazzina—the espresso cup—because he only had one handle on the side of his head.

Then we wound up at Calvi's niece's party and our complicity returned. They were playing piñata and hide-and-seek. The prizes were quails or baby chicks or turtles, prizes that no one knew what to do with. Helpless creatures slated for a horrible fate.

The birthday girl was sweet as could be: very skinny, with an enormous pair of eyeglasses. Her hair was so blond that it looked white and, all dressed up in pale pink, backlit, she seemed like a ghost. But she didn't scare us. In fact, we'd pick her up with a special sensation of tenderness, possibly because we knew that her uncle had been killed and it had been God's fault, because he didn't want to pay the taxes. Poor little thing, what did she have to do with choices that were made high above, in heaven.

There was another one of Olivia's classmates who prompted our empathy, because we knew his story. Jacopo's mother had been killed in the plane crash off the island of Ustica. He'd been at the beach with his aunt, and his mother was supposed to join him on Pantelleria, that very day.

Manon had explained to us that the plane had gone down, but not because of some mechanical malfunction. Everyone claimed that was why, but it wasn't true. It had caught fire in the sky, mysteriously. There were people who blamed it on a bomb, while others mentioned a missile. But we weren't allowed to say anything about it to Jacopo, who knew what lies they'd told him. We were just supposed to be nice to him and invite him to play with us.

That was hardly a chore: Jacopo was easy to like, my favorite in that little group. I had a certain influence over him, for that matter. No one else seemed to be even slightly interested in my life in Rome. He alone seemed fascinated and he'd listen to me rapturously.

"We put firecrackers in dog poops," I was explaining to him. "You should see how spectacularly the shit explodes. Just think how the *fruttarolo* gets pissed off, *mortacci*," I went on, slipping into Roman dialect, cursing as I invoked the fruit-and-vegetable vendor. "It gets all over his produce. He comes after us yelling at the top of his lungs, but we can run faster than him."

"Doesn't your nanny scold you?"

"They don't have nannies in Rome," I said with a world-weary sigh.

"You mean they let you go out all by yourself?"

"Yes, they do," I bragged. "Anyway, if you really want, I'll go find a firecracker and the next party we go to you and me can blow up a dog shit together."

"Really? You promise?"

"*Ce poi giurà.*" I told him he could count on it, in *romanesco*.

I usually spoke *romanesco* only at home. I would have been ashamed to talk that way in front of Olivia, with her I only spoke in proper Italian. But Jacopo liked it, so I wallowed in it a bit. Sometimes he wouldn't understand, and I really enjoyed that. I put him through what I had experienced the first few days, surrounded by the kids from Via Chiabrera. I was starting to recognize that my double life might be a real asset, if I used it right.

At that children's birthday party, for reasons unknown, there was also a veritable host of adolescents, between thirteen and eighteen years old. Naturally, we were curious about their presence. For one thing, they weren't wearing nice, fancy clothing like we were. We were decked out in lace and nice socks and patent leather shoes. They were dressed like the young people who congregated at the café downstairs from my apartment building: ripped jeans, running shoes, gel in their hair. Only these teenagers didn't have tattoos. And their clothing only looked like it was old and worn.

"My mother says that if I try to cut my Levi's with a pair of scissors again, she's going to stop buying me jeans."

"Mine stopped my allowance when she found out that I convinced our Filipina maid to bleach my Lacoste."

"I like your Superga sneakers, I wanted mine in blue. How did you get them to fade like that?"

They smoked lots of cigarettes where the parents couldn't see, and they were angry about things that seemed brilliant to us, so much so that I started to wonder whether they were playing the game where you say the exact opposite of what you really think.

"What a pain in the ass, spending the summer at Forte dei Marmi. I wanted to go spend the summer in America."

"What are *you* complaining about? I have to go spend time on my father's boat, on the Costa Smeralda, ugh."

Olivia and I were maneuvering to get in among them and try to win a prize that was more desirable than a quail. Naturally, we kept quiet, satisfied just that they weren't shooing us away. They were sitting on a low wall and passing back and forth a bottle of wine that someone had smuggled out of the kitchen. Obviously, they weren't about to start playing hide-and-seek or hitting the piñata.

"Hey, Selvaggia, how much did they pay you to come to this fucked-up party?" asked a boy who must have been fifteen or sixteen.

"My folks? Ten bucks," replied a girl who was clearly much younger. Everyone else laughed.

"Is that all? Wow, stingy. I made them give me fifty. It's such a pain in the ass, this time I decided to raise the price," said her girlfriend, who, feeling prettier and more self-confident, exhaled a mouthful of cigarette smoke.

"Oh, really? Then I'll ask for fifty myself next year," said the first girl, clearly feeling defensive.

They'd all been paid money by their parents to go to this party. But none of them talked about *the hanged man*. When evening came, they just headed home carrying a quail or with an extra banknote in their wallets, and that was that. Maybe no one had told them the story.

ANYWAY, that summer something else had happened that was rather important. Dado, Olivia's uncle, who almost never came to the beach with us, had shown up with an American friend, a guy named Stanley whom Dado had met while doing a master's degree at Yale. Gianni and Manon were delighted. They couldn't say much to Stanley because they didn't speak English, but their children acted as interpreters.

The guest, who was tall and handsome, brought a spirit of cheerfulness to the house, especially among the matrons who did their best to entertain him. His presence spread a wave of excitement among the family. No one wanted to spend the evening inside or just go to the beach for the day: it was all expensive restaurants, every night out to the Capannina club, outings in sailboats, an endless round of parties.

Even Olivia's grandfather seemed to have a soft spot for this muscular, healthy-looking young man. He told his wife more than once that such a charming friend might prove helpful to Dado, who just didn't seem able to find a girlfriend. Sly winks all around, behind Gianni's back.

"Stanley, let me lend you my car," Gianni told him. "The girls love it, I promise. Don't tell my wife how well it works, otherwise she'll make me sell it," and he gave the young American an affectionate slap on the back as he placed the keys to his Maserati Biturbo in Stanley's hand.

Even Manon gazed at Stanley adoringly, we'd never seen her so dazed and confused. She would say to him: "Has anyone ever told you that you look like Cary Grant?" Then she'd turn toward her son: "Dado, do me a favor and translate."

Only Olivia's father was being standoffish. When we went to play with her uncle and Stanley, Giulio got annoyed. He'd dream up any excuse to keep us from going.

"We're going out on the paddleboat with Stan!"

"No. You just ate," and he'd grab us by the arm.

"But Papa, it's four o'clock, we've digested," Olivia replied.

"I said no, and no means no."

Then one morning the tragedy unfolded. The house-keeper had stopped by the dry cleaners to pick up Dado's linen suit, and Manon decided to hang it up in his armoire, to keep the suit from getting wrinkled. In her dressing gown, she went up to Dado's bedroom, while he had left the house for an early morning swim.

Carrying the cellophane-wrapped suit in one hand, she gave the door a little shove. And there, in her son's bed, she found Stanley, fast asleep on his belly. His hair was wet in the morning light, his naked arm lay on the mattress, and his bronzed back was uncovered, the sheets having slid down to his waist. Manon went galloping down the stairs, fetching up in the living room with the gaunt, wide-eyed expression of Lady Macbeth.

"Woe is me, my son is *sick*," and she ran to the window: "Now I'm going to jump! I'm going to jump!"

It was typical of her, this sort of scene was a regular thing. Manon adored playing the victim, and she went for it with more than a little theatricality. Nobody was worried, the family was used to it. Plus, the living room was on a safely low mezzanine, at the very worst she might sprain her ankle. But she refused to stop her yelling.

"Oh, woe is me, woe is me."

Giulio and Gianni were forced to relinquish their hot espressos and marmalade and get up from the table with a

sigh; they trooped in to restrain her with sighs of exaspera-
tion, as usual. Deep down, Olivia's grandfather was grinning.
For once none of this was his fault.

"Darling, what on earth has happened?"

Manon could barely get out the words through her coughing. No way was she going to miss out on added fillips of drama:
"A glass of water, please—" cough, cough. She was surely determined to increase the suspense, the way she did with us
when she told us fairy tales. Meanwhile the Greek chorus was
questioning her, clustering around the sofa on which they had
managed to get her situated. Elena, too, had come running,
still dripping from the tub and wrapped in a bathrobe.

"That *pervert*."

"Who are you talking about?"

Elena tried clapping her hands over Olivia's and my ears,
a hopeful if utterly futile operation, seeing that together
the two of us had four ears and Elena only had two hands.
She made do by working in shifts: for a while she'd cover up
Olivia's ears, then she'd move to mine. After doing that for
a while, she resigned herself to the inevitable and decided
it was simpler just to send us to another part of the house:
"Children, take your cups and go into the kitchen. You can
finish your breakfast in there," she told us.

We left the room and headed for the kitchen at an intentionally slow pace: we didn't want to miss a thing. Olivia
kept turning to look at me, eyebrows raised questioningly.

I whispered, "Your uncle is…," and I scratched my ear
lobe, the Italian equivalent of flicking a limp wrist.

She continued not to understand.

"He's a faggot. A queer, a nancy. Where I live there's lots of them. And everyone makes fun of them."

"Ah," she said, but she was more bewildered than before.

So I waved for her to follow me into the kitchen. I sent the nanny away, telling her I'd forgotten the Nesquik in the dining room. Whereupon I started explaining. But she was having a hard time following my explanation.

"What does his ass have to do with it?"

In the meantime, Gianni had gone upstairs, to have a talk with Stanley. "Man to man," he'd told everybody, inartfully, setting Manon off on another round of hair-pulling and garment-rending. That little talk had been anything but peaceful, however: the family's hot Emilian blood wasn't prone to moderation. Gianni was shouting so loudly that we could hear him downstairs ourselves, from the kitchen. "In my own home! How dare you? Get out of here, right now!"

We were briskly deported to the beach ("Kids, get your swimsuits on pronto, we're going down to the water"), and we didn't even go home for lunch ("Surprise! Today we're going to eat focaccia right here, under the beach umbrella"), and they left us there to roast until six that evening. When we got back, there was no sign of either Uncle Dado or his friend Stanley.

At dinner, the family was no longer talking about Calvi. Maybe because they were exhausted, or else because they were angry, but the measures that had been adopted previously had been forgotten. We children were allowed to stay, as long as we pretended not to be listening. And so, concentrating intensely on our dishes and—after we were done eating—on a blank sheet of paper where we were supposed to be drawing something, our brows furrowed with the effort, Olivia and I did our best to assemble the scattered pieces and reconstruct what had happened.

Meanwhile Stanley had suddenly stopped being "a young man from an excellent family, the son of major industrialists from Boston" (the Morganti family introduced him to everyone in those terms) and had become "that American pederast," he was no longer someone who had "studied at Yale," but rather someone who had "led Dado astray," and most of all, no one talked about his physical attractiveness anymore.

"Papa, I'd always suspected as much," Giulio said, "after all, I've known Dado since he was born."

"Well, I myself have known him since he was born, if you'll give me that credit," his mother objected, in a faint, weary voice, her forehead propped up by her braced hand. Her eyes were puffy, her hair unkempt, her face unmade: we were face to face with an unprecedented Manon, who had no desire to engage in theatrics.

Elena said nothing, as usual, possibly because she had no opinion of her own. She was the most sensitive member of the family, but she was too insecure, and was incapable of making herself heard. She inwardly believed that her thoughts were worthless. All she knew how to do was ask, over and over again, in a reedy whisper, "How are you feeling, Manon?"

And then she'd accept without objection her mother-in-law's rude response, snappishly dealing out her usual sarcasm: "How on earth do you think I feel? What stupid questions you ask."

Gianni was still upset, his anxiety visible on his bald scalp, which glistened with sweat: "The problem is that Dado has always been a weakling," and as he said it he mopped his beet-red face with a handkerchief, "how can I entrust the company to his guidance? If anyone ever discovered his little *weakness*, he'd lose all authority."

Giulio, careful to stifle an over-brimming grin of contentment at having suddenly become an only son, did his best to appear noble: "Come on, Papa. Dado's good at what he does, he'll command respect, he even has one college degree more than I do."

"What matters most is character, Giulio. Being *men*."

5

SETTLING ACCOUNTS

IN ROME, a surprise awaited me. I'd wondered why Mama seemed so revved up, but I'd told myself that she was just happy to see me again. Another signal had been transmitted by the group of kids from the apartment building, who had all turned out to greet me en masse.

"Er Principe is back!" The Prince. That was my nickname.

But my mother was impatient to get me home: "Come on, Valerio, let's go. You can come down to the courtyard later."

When I walked in, my jaw dropped. The kitchen was brand-new, the sofa was brand-new, too, and there was an enormous television set, likewise brand-spanking-new. I turned to look at Mama. "Did you win the lottery?"

She started laughing and pushed me into the hallway: "Go take a look at your room."

My cot had disappeared, and in its place was a proper wicker bedstead. And a white desk with a green plastic chair. And new wallpaper. And a bamboo armoire. "Well? Do you like it?"

"Wow," I replied.

Max had stopped being a loan shark. He'd found a much more profitable line of business.

"And all this happened in just three months?" I asked, naively.

Mama always had an answer ready to fire back: "These days, people can make a fortune in the blink of an eye, Valerio, all you have to do is be smart. Not like that loser father of yours."

I couldn't stand hearing my mother talk that way about my papa, even if by now I was used to it. But there was nothing I could do about it, it had become an obsession with her: she was terrified that I might turn out like him.

"You know, in life you need to be elastic, a little bit flexible. If you dot every i and cross every t, you're always going to wind up being a loser," she'd say. "Get that into your head. Take a look at your father, who's always been a stickler. What good has it done him? He paid all his traffic tickets, for instance. But there's no need to pay your tickets, people like us have nothing to repossess. Do you have any idea of how much money he basically threw in the trash?"

My mother would go on for an hour to list all the stupid things my father had done, it was one of her favorite topics. But I got out of there, down to the courtyard—I couldn't take it anymore.

Everyone was waiting for me. They wanted to hear all about it. But I was embarrassed.

"It was nothing, I just went to the seashore. Same as you all."

"Come on, tell us."

"Just like Ostia, what do you think?"

Since I wasn't giving out much information, they stopped questioning me then and there. They started to talk amongst themselves. But the topic, unfortunately, was still me. They told me the story of Max's rise to power, something they'd been tracking with their own eyes and ears. They told me that he'd worked his way into the right network, thanks to one of the young men who patronized the bar on Via Chiabrera (a guy whom we had actually personally watched get rich in a hurry: his wife, who lived on the second floor, by now went everywhere in a fur coat). They were all proud of Max and weren't shy about letting me know that, as if he were my father. I responded with a tight, faint smile, and nothing more. Then, in the midst of the general state of excitement, Roscia—"Red"—so dubbed for her copper-colored hair, let slip a phrase that she might better have kept to herself: "But with the baby..."

"What baby?" I asked.

The consternation was universal. My mother hadn't told me that she was pregnant.

I ONLY EVER SPOKE to the kids on Via Chiabrera in dialect. I couldn't say whether speaking in dialect was just a tactical move to help me fit in, or whether that new idiom dialect was actually starting to feel like home, a welcome achievement. For instance, when I wrote to Olivia, it was a pure, clean Italian. And at school I always got A's on my papers, because I was the only one in the class who out of eleven lines didn't produce at least ten in *romanesco*.

Dear Olivia,

My newborn sister is very hairy and cries all night long. Still, I like her, she's nice and she makes me laugh. I've learned how to change diapers because where we live there's no such thing as nannies. Mama is getting hysterical because she can't get a wink of sleep. Max is never around because he wants to get rich. Marta is the only member of the family who stays in one place.

Now Olivia had letterhead stationery and I had been obliged to persuade the mailman to deliver her letters to me personally, in concealment, without letting the others see, for God's sake. ("Valerio Carnevale?" He'd shoot me a wink and then I'd hide the envelope under my T-shirt, stuffed down my pants.) If my friends had even managed to lay their hands on those sheets of paper with a Florentine motif and her initials in fancy calligraphy, I would have been mocked mercilessly. So I hid them under my mattress and I'd read them at night. After all, Marta wasn't old enough yet to make fun of me.

> *Dear Valerio,*
>
> *I'm in Cortina with my grandparents. They give me a Smurf every time I do a black run. You know, sports are super-important to them. I'm skiing with an instructor and another little boy from Padua. Our motto is: "Through Staunies, the Forcella Rossa, and the Canalone, either a Smurf or a medal!" Gianni says that we're willing to get ourselves killed for very little, all things considered. Two afternoons a week, they make me do figure skating, too, but I'm not very good at it, maybe because I'm a little fat. I see all these other little girls, incredibly skinny, in leotards and tights, and they look like butterflies, basically. They really get on my nerves. I go skating in my ski suit, I lift one leg to do a camel spin, and I fall flat on my face on the ice. I'm covered with bruises. Every time it snows, I miss you. Tell me, how are you doing?*

Just for starters, I was jealous of the boy from Padua. And then I had no idea what a "black run" even was. My mother didn't give a damn about sports. All right, I played soccer down in the courtyard, but no one ever thought of calling it a "sport." And Mama seriously didn't care whether I was good or not. At the very most, she'd give me a tongue-lashing for coming home all dirty. "Filthy pig," she'd say. And that was that.

EVERY NOW AND THEN my father would come down to Rome to see me. He'd rent a room in the apartment of an old woman who lived by the train station and spend two or three days with me. The only time I ever went to the center of town was when he'd come. I looked around and it seemed to me I was in a completely different Rome from the one I lived in. We usually had no idea what to do, so we'd go for walks in Villa Borghese and then head over to Piazza del Popolo for a gelato.

We didn't know what to talk about, either, as far as that went. He'd ask me how things were going at school and I'd tell him that I was getting "Outstanding" in all my subjects. Then he'd want to know if my mother was all right. I'd tell him yes. When I tried to tell him about my little sister, though, he'd get all sad, so I just tended to skip the subject entirely.

The only possible subject that still allowed us to feel united was the inevitable one: the Morganti family. My father had been living with them for twenty years now, and basically there'd never been anything but them in his life. And, for obvious reasons, I cared very much about being informed. I was so deeply interested that the afternoons with Papa flew by. He treated me like an adult, we'd laugh together, commenting on events and words with the same degree of engagement. Sometimes he'd buy me bags of popcorn, pointing out that keeping up with the affairs of that family was like going to the movies, and you didn't even have to buy a ticket.

"Does Manon still pretend she's about to throw herself out the window?"

"What do you think?" my papa responded with a laugh.

He told me that Manon had just discovered that Gianni had a new lover ("a *gran penna*, a young *ragazòla*, just a young thing," using dialect terms for an underage sweetheart). And, even worse, the fact that Gianni was writing check after check for millions of lire ("She makes sure he gives her plenty of *pilla*, you get me?"). *Pilla* meant cold hard cash.

Gianni's affair had come to light because one day, the young lady in question, her dander up about some supposed wrong Gianni had done her, had returned to sender no fewer than ten mink coats, both short and long. Manon stood aghast as all ten were delivered *to her own home*.

"You could see her counting up the numbers in her head, she was always gifted at math, Manon."

I was chortling in amusement: "And then what happened?"

"*Mo niente*," he replied in dialect. "Not a thing. The rich are always happy to make peace in a hurry, as long as the numbers add up. Signor Gianni gave Signora Manon a modernist painting that she'd been longing for, a nasty-looking thing that, when we opened it, we all assumed had been damaged in shipping, there was a cut right across the middle of it— search me. But she was delighted, and she stopped all her *zagnare* and let him be. Good for her: *bona lè*."

"Seriously, that was the end of it?"

Actually, of course, that wasn't the end of it, because now Manon realized that she was going to have to deal with a young woman far more dangerous than the stock market (Olivia's grandfather regularly lost large amounts on stocks). So the very next day Manon made sure every penny of their personal fortune was put in her name.

"For the past few weeks now, Signor Gianni has become a penniless pauper, a *puvràt* just like me. The Signora gives him a daily allowance, and she isn't even especially generous. Last Saturday I drove him to the golf course, and he asked me to lend him fifty thousand lire so he could have lunch with a friend, because his wife had gone out for a manicure, forgetting to give him his daily walking-around money."

I was having some trouble understanding these last details. "But doesn't he still earn all the money?"

My father smiled at me, amiably: "Eh, Valerio, you have a good point, it's not a stupid question at all."

I respected my father, and I was happy to have conversations with him. In my eyes, he was neither an asshole nor a loser. He was somebody who didn't care much about social rankings. Someone who did what he was supposed to do, and in the meantime, took the opportunity to look around him. A patient, decent, humane person.

All things considered, my papa had more personal conversations with Manon than she had with her own children.

"She confides in me, you know."

And he explained to me that when he was alone with her, whether because he was driving her to the hairdresser or they were pruning roses together, she'd tell him lots of things. Manon was a beautiful woman, but she'd come to realize that her beauty was pointless, her husband had stopped desiring her after several years of marriage, and they'd been sleeping in separate rooms since 1953. She was an intelligent woman, but she'd come to realize that her intelligence also was pointless: she couldn't even manage to have a conversation with her own sons. She was a cultivated woman, but in the final analysis, all that culture served no purpose other than to let her acquire gifts that were a bit more elegant than others. When all was said and done, her only true happiness ("that one thing, so fulfilling and intense, that you need to have every so often in life," she used to say) was her granddaughter, Olivia.

I was touched to the quick by that mention: "So what did you say?"

"I told her that Olivia is a *brava cinna*, a good girl. I didn't have the heart to tell her that when Olivia grows up, she'll be no better or worse than her parents."

I'd never thought of that. I furrowed my brow. "How do you mean?"

Papa shrugged a shoulder. "What can you expect, she'll get some college degree or other, something like law or business, but she'll never get a job because she'll marry one of those rich boys that surround her. They'll build a third villa on the grounds and they'll stick Olivia, her husband, and their children in it, so that she can be within easy reach for her parents and grandparents. All those people, they're a *clan*, it's an English word, or maybe French, anyway, that's what you call that. And Manon won't be able to read her *Hamlet*, don't kid yourself. She'll have to just say the usual things. So who was there at the party? Why, look at how you're dressed, darling! Are you going to Cortina for the Christmas holidays or not?"

I dropped my eyes: "But she's different."

My father shook his head: "*Brisa vaira*—not true. In a few years you'll realize for yourself."

ACTUALLY, these worlds, apparently light-years apart, did touch each other. Even on Via Chiabrera, people talked about Calvi, for instance. No one was personally acquainted with God's banker, much less his niece, of course, but through twisted and intricate connections, that man was involved in the bar across the street from our building and, by very lateral links, the parents of a young friend of mine, a girl who played in the courtyard with me. The name of the Magliana Gang wasn't circulating yet, but everyone who lived around us knew what that gang was, no one needed to say its name.

That was where all the money that had suddenly show-ered into our apartment came from. Because the young guys from that bar would occasionally offer jobs from the building across the way. Little jobs, nothing special, okay, but they paid very well. Considering the risk.

Certainly, in our apartment building, we had nothing to do with the kneecapping of the deputy chairman of the Banco Ambrosiano. And we knew nothing about the con-tacts between De Pedis and Flavio Carboni and the Vatican, and all those things. Just as we never imagined that there could be any links between the young men in the café and the Mafia, and if they had told us, we would have laughed, because we thought of them as next-door neighbors and the Mafia as something very far away that couldn't possibly be of any concern to us. But a part of the money earned from those criminal pursuits, looming so much larger than any-thing we could possibly imagine, flowed into my home. That money became my new bamboo armoire as well as what Max and my mother were hiding inside it. A great deal of that money, of course, was invested and—through a long and meandering path, extraneous even to its origins—so Calvi in some sense came back into my bedroom, but this time in the form of heroin.

"Valerio? You are absolutely not to put your hands on this bag, is that clear? You'll be in trouble deep if I catch you rum-maging around in it. I'll beat you silly, are we understood?"

Every now and then my mother would raid my room to make sure I wasn't disobeying instructions.

"Now listen carefully. If the police come around, you have to get the bag and flush everything that's in it down the toilet. And don't pull the chain, use the bucket that's under sink, and plenty of water. Right away. And fast. Do I make myself clear?"

"Yes, Mama."

Secretly, I dreamed of the day the police would finally arrive, so I could perform my thrilling task (*the police*, what an ancient obsession!). But it never seemed to happen. The one time the cops came around, I wasn't at home. Darn my luck, I was at school. The narcotics in the bag wound up flushed down the toilet anyway (I believe that my mother tended to that chore), but that's not what they'd been looking for. They were looking for Max.

MAX, like everyone else in the *borgata*, had a perfectly respectable history of small-time crime behind him. Strictly petty misdeeds, however, that were on the borderline with the law. He did a little loan-sharking and what was generally known as "debt collection" (which meant he'd beat people up and take fifty percent of whatever cash he could convince them to cough up). Sure, no question, every so often he'd also deal narcotics, just to make ends meet. Or he'd go out with friends on their scooters and snatch purses or gold chains (they'd often grab gold chains off old ladies strictly for fun, to bet on the weight of the gold. It was like going to the horse track. "How much did yours turn out to be?

Twenty grams? Mine's thirty!" "Here's my end"). But he'd never slipped into actual organized crime. Not that. Even around where we lived, there were people who were considered just too dangerous.

In fact, when one of the young guys from the bar on Via Chiabrera had come around to his place to offer him in on the job, Max had turned him down at first.

"What, are you joking? Those people are just going to keep asking you for favors," he explained to my mother, "and then you can never get shed of them. Then you're a guy who knows things, and who could talk, and they'll kill for much less."

My mother was ambitious and would literally stop at nothing. Operating completely outside the protocols and customs of the *borgata*, she was incapable of recognizing the thin red line that separated respectable small-time criminal activity (shared in a way as a social value) from straight-up organized crime, and kept busting his balls.

"Hey, though, we could definitely use a little extra money..."

Sure, these might not exactly be reputable people we were talking about, but what did that have to do with *them*, after all? It wasn't like they were being asked to hurt anybody. All they had to do was keep a shipment of narcotics or weapons hidden in their home, big deal. I mean, it wasn't as if anybody had asked them to use the weapons, to shoot anybody. In that case, certainly, they'd have had to turn down the offer. But this was just a trifle. This was easy money, after all, not the kind of thing you just turn your back on without a second thought. Especially not with two children to raise.

"I want them to be able to study," my mother would say, "I want to send them to private schools."

Torn, Max consulted with his relatives. Nonna Ettorina, the owner of five gambling dens, who still drank grappa like it was milk at age seventy-two, because she'd spent her life in pool halls surrounded by drunken men, was strongly opposed. She had it in for my mother. She said that it was easy for her to push her boyfriend into serious trouble, after all, the only one who was going to be shot dead as a result would be Max.

"Don't pay any mind to that floozy, you're betting on a counterfeit card, listen to your aged grandmother," she'd say in heavy dialect, and then spit on the floor, in an open gesture of contempt.

Zio Vittorio, who had been a highly respected apartment burglar, not only in Italy but abroad as well (he'd served time in France, too, he proudly boasted: he worked on an international level, just sayin'), and had only retired due to old age, because it's tough on the body to do that work after age fifty—climbing, running, jumping: at a certain point, you just have to give up *clambering*, like any other accomplished athlete—was every bit as concerned.

Max's father had died young in a work-related accident (shows you what happens, if you're going to work construction) and Vittorio had raised him as if he were his own son. Sensitive as he was, he didn't want to lay down the law, but rather lead him to an understanding of the problem. So Vittorio had sat down and told him a story.

"When I was just getting started, behind bars, in Lucca, a *carceretto*—a little two-bit prison—in the provinces," and he emphasized the setting to make it clear to his nephew that very important experiences might be had even in some of the less prestigious locales, you don't necessarily have to be in one of the top-flight maximum security prisons like, say, Regina Coeli in Rome or San Vittore in Milan, "there was a guy there who'd murdered his wife's lover. Well, these things happen. He'd pretend he was deaf. But since we'd figured it out, to show what a bullshitter he was, we called out to him: 'Hey, think quick, catch this coffee pot,' which was steaming hot. Obviously, he immediately started yelling and that's when we all chimed in, 'So you see, you can hear just fine.'"

Max smiled at him, and then confessed he'd been unable to figure out the meaning of the story. At that point, his uncle explained to him that when that story had unfolded, he'd realized that you never stop learning the codes of conduct of a world, and that we're often at risk of making missteps for the sole reason that we never fully understand the language spoken in that world.

What he was trying to make clear to his nephew is just how easy it is to set your foot wrong, when you get caught up in a game whose rules you really don't know. And there are so many games, and the rules to them all are countless. He told him that the language of organized crime is very different from the language of two-bit *borgata* crime, which is what Max was accustomed to. The message was simple: *They aren't stand-up people like we are.*

"Stay on the lookout, 'cause if you eat snails, you're going to shit out horns," Zio Vittorio concluded, in his heavy dialect.

IN THE END, though, Max let himself be swept along by my mother's insistence and his own damned ignorance. Over time, even as our own quality of life improved noticeably, Max was increasingly concerned. At the dinner table, he'd hunch over his food, elbow propped against the table, the palm of his hand flat against his forehead, staring at his bowl of rigatoni.

"They're already pushing me to do them other favors," he was saying.

My mother lost her temper and immediately started shrilling at him: "Well well well, so I've found another coward. It's just my fate, after all, then!"

When I tried to ask questions, I got the flat of her hand straight to my cheek. Mama glared daggers at me: "Now don't you start in, too, Valerio. Just eat your food and shut up. In fact, why don't you go change your sister's diaper, that way you can make yourself useful for a change."

I gave my chair a kick and headed off to do what my mother'd told me to do, head bowed.

In no more than a few months' time, we had become the wealthiest family in the whole apartment building, after the people on the second floor. Er Faccia was proud, he kept saying that he'd known from the start that I was bound to make something of myself, he put it down to personal intuition. My nickname, Er Principe, had been perfectly suited.

But for Max the change hadn't been much of an improvement, he seemed to get worse and worse. One evening I crossed paths with him in the courtyard, he was all alone, sitting in a rusty rocking chair with a beer in one hand. He was drunk, I think. He'd probably snorted some coke while he was at it, because he was lucid and restless. I was coming home from a soccer match, sweaty from head to foot. He called out to me, "Hey, Valè? Come here, take a seat."

I sat down.

"Did you win again tonight?" He ran his hand through my wet hair.

"They kicked our asses."

I was about to get back up, but he stopped me and gripped my wrist.

"Swear something to me," he said.

"What?" I was frightened now.

Max was serious, continuing to drink and staring into the darkness before him: "You take care of your sister, if anything happens to me."

I nodded my head. But I was worried: "What's going to happen to you?"

Max turned and put his hands on either side of my face: "Swear to me that you'll always do the right thing."

I will always have this immense regret: instead of hugging him, I was so upset that I jerked away from him. And I didn't promise him a thing.

When the police arrived, I wasn't there. They took Max off to prison, and two days later, he was murdered.

Enough time to hold his funeral, and we were whisked off to another neighborhood. Nonna Ettorina and Zio Vittorio took us to live in Cinecittà: me, my mother, and my sister, his only legacy. Max had left them a last will and testament that was as terse as it was clear: "If anything bad happens to me, you two take them."

Once again, my lodestar had shifted. The end of my story on Via Chiabrera. Now I'd need to learn to navigate through another constellation: Lamaro, Tuscolana, Quadraro Vecchio, Don Bosco, Ceccafumo. Luckily, right across the street was the lovely Parco degli Acquedotti—the Aqueduct Park—teeming with child molesters.

6

THE END OF A WORLD

IT WAS FALL and the hills around Bologna were slippery, the curves in the roads were kept secret by the fog. Olivia's grandfather had gone to play tennis like every Thursday, but he hadn't yet arrived at the club.

His best friend, Mario, invited for a doubles match—an important game in a small informal tournament among former university classmates, played for the stakes of a lavish banquet to be paid for by the losers—waited awhile for him, then made up his mind to call. At the office, they told Mario that Gianni had already been gone for an hour. Worried now, Mario tried to reach him at home.

Manon was even rude to him. Ah, tennis, the usual excuse. She hung up brusquely, convinced that her husband was in the arms of one of his lovers. And immediately after that she got out the car to go to the hairdresser's: she bided her time, ready to let fly when Gianni came home well before seven that evening, because they were invited to dinner at the Rangoni home, to celebrate their thirtieth anniversary. What a grind, thirty years of marriage. Meanwhile she prepared herself mentally for the scene she planned to make when he showed up, insufficiently sweaty and without a speck of red clay on his rubber soles. Well? Who won the match? Let's hear all about it. She even considered what gift to demand, when the time came to pardon her wayward husband. Another emerald collier? She'd seen one at Bulgari that she'd liked well enough. But maybe she'd rather have a painting. If she played the tragedy to the hilt, she might even be able to wangle a contemporary painter out of him, the kind that made his coronary arteries swell. After all, Mario's phone call had put Gianni with his back against the wall: he no longer had a shred of an alibi, and now she could even dare to demand a Burri. Burnt plastic in the living room: hooray.

But then Gianni didn't even come home when seven o'clock rolled around. Manon, in her dressing gown, seated facing her mirror, tried to make up her face without losing her temper, otherwise she'd apply her eyebrow mascara crooked. Late, this time unforgivably late. A formal dinner, for eighty, she'd even reminded him about it at lunch. He's going to make her look like a boor, damn it. As if all the rest of it wasn't enough. Which hussy could it be this time? None of his lady friends had ever been capable of keeping him out past seven, especially when there was a formal invitation at stake. An invitation that had come in the mail months before, by the way. Gianni knew the rules of the game perfectly well, and he'd never dreamed of breaking them, not even for the lust of his life, a well-known slut. Could there be a new one on the horizon? More dangerous than any of the others?

A suspicion suddenly sprang up that her husband might have opened a new checking account, without saying a word to her about it. Manon got up and went to search the dresser drawers to see whether there were any checkbooks lying around he might have overlooked. Nothing to be found. Cunningly hidden? At the office? Perhaps his longtime secretary was holding on to them, to supply him with as needed. Oh, but she'd get to the bottom of it. At the bank there wasn't a clerk or officer who dared to defy her, seeing that the entire family fortune was in her name. And she was free and willing to move the entire sum at her whim, leaving the bank with a devastating gap in their capital base from one day to the next: she need only put her pen to paper, a signature would do it. She jotted down the names of two or three people in her diary, making a note to call them the very next day. She'd go over the account balance, transaction by transaction. There were sluts out there who'd already made off with enough of her money, enough was enough.

At eight that evening she called Giulio in tears. Annoyed, her son was quick to dismiss her fears.

"The Rangonis' dinner, big deal. He probably just forgot. Don't torment him, Mama, take it easy on him. He's been working so hard lately, he has a lot on his mind."

So she reached out to Dado, who could be a little more sensitive at times.

"Aren't you happy, Mama? Come on, we'll go together to pick out your new Burri."

"But I don't want a Burri, I want *him*."

By eight-thirty, Manon was inconsolable. She was convinced that something had happened to him, something serious. She could sense it. Maybe a car crash. She slipped a lorazepam under her tongue and started calling around to all the hospitals. No results. My father, sitting beside her, leafed through the phone book and dictated the numbers. As always, at moments of crisis, he was the only one she could rely on.

"Try not to get too upset, Signora, maybe he just had a mechanical problem. The Fiat Ritmo isn't reliable, you need a new car, it wouldn't run last Sunday, either. I had to call a tow truck."

Manon shook her head: "No, I have a bad feeling about this, Guido. I know my husband far too well, he would have found a way to let me know. He always has phone tokens in his pocket. He would never willingly worry me, he's *such a dear man*."

At ten that night, the two sons agreed it was time to have a chat with the police. And the alert went out. All cars were on the lookout. At twenty minutes past midnight, they found the grandfather's car. But it was empty.

He'd vanished into thin air, he of all people, the one who lived in constant fear of everyone else vanishing. He who drove his granddaughter to school every morning, with an armor-plated car and a Beretta in the glove compartment. The pistol was right where it was supposed to be: only its owner was out of place. Clearly, Gianni hadn't had a chance to draw the gun.

THE FOLLOWING MORNING, Olivia went off to school as on any other day. My father drove her, since he regularly took her grandfather's place when he was away on business. Nothing really strange, therefore. Certainly, Olivia asked what had become of the Fiat Ritmo with its bulletproof glass, but it was easy to come up with a convincing answer: "It's at the shop."

"And when will Grandfather be back?"

"Soon. But don't call him Grandfather, you'll hurt his feelings."

For lunch, she ate a cutlet with her nanny, who was less chatty than usual, though again, that was the sort of thing that happened. Every now and then her boyfriend would dump her, it was a volatile relationship. Olivia had learned not to put too much stock in these minor dramas, and so she'd trotted off to do her homework without asking too many questions.

While she was studying geography, Giulio walked into her bedroom. Olivia looked up from the map she was copying, a shade of concern on her face. What was her father doing home, in the middle of the afternoon? Something must have happened, she decided.

"We have *some problems*, Olivia. It's nothing serious, just work matters," he told her.

She nodded her head. But she still didn't understand. Why was he coming around to talk to *her* about such things?

"So we've decided to send you to do some skiing," he went on. "What do you say?"

Olivia looked at him in bewilderment. "Skiing?"

"Well, you've always enjoyed skiing, right? I promise we're not going to make you do figure skating."

"But it's November, Papa."

"But it snowed."

Elena had come up with the idea, and she'd put her foot down during the family meeting. "I don't want the child to get the slightest hint of what's going on," she'd announced, with firm determination, in sharp contrast with her habitual demeanor in the presence of the Morganti clan, accustomed to seeing her submissive and eternally grateful, if only for the privilege of having been ushered into their Halls of Olympus.

Everyone had turned to stare, stunned. That iron tone was a new development.

"I've decided to send her up to Cortina with Cecilia for a while," she'd continued, shoulders thrown back and chin jutting out. "I know that she's your only source of joy, but I can't allow her to be used for that purpose."

Manon had jerked to her feet and, in response, knocked over a Louis XIV chair. "What an ingrate," she said, pretending to be talking to herself. "The minute we have a moment of tragedy, *she starts deciding things.*"

Elena didn't blink an eye. "She's leaving Saturday. I've already made reservations with the ski instructor."

Giulio stared at her, stunned. His wife had never dared to take initiatives without checking with him. He'd never felt so fragile in his life, and he hardly knew what to say. He limited himself to asking, with a stammer, "What about her school?"

"I don't give a damn about her school," Elena had replied, with great firmness.

Meanwhile Manon grumbled: "Look at her, taking advantage without a moment's hesitation."

But Olivia's mother didn't even glance in the older woman's direction. Still, no one had taken into account Olivia's opposition; in fact, she wouldn't hear of it.

"I don't want to go skiing, it's too cold," she said, arms crossed and brow furrowed.

Her father did his best to cajole her: "Well, you could phone that friend of yours from Padua, maybe he could come, too."

Olivia shook her head: "I don't feel like it."

Then Giulio had an idea: "What if you invited Valerio?" Olivia snapped her head around, eyes sparkling. "Valerio Carnevale?"

"Why? Do you know any other boys named Valerio?"

She was finally willing to give it some consideration. A moment later, she threw herself into her father's arms. "But he lives in Rome! Can I go see him? *Pleeeaase*, Papa."

Olivia had been to Rome once before, when she was five. She'd gone with her grandmother. Manon naturally had come up with an ordeal by fire that more closely resembled an initiation ceremony than a tour of Italy's capital. First day: a stroll to see all the notable works by Caravaggio. Second day: Hadrian's Villa, in Tivoli, to kiss the head of Antinous (Manon might be incapable of accepting her own son's homosexuality, but when it came to her favorite emperor, his sexual preferences demanded veneration). Third day: the Capitoline Hill, and not to enjoy the panorama, but to visit the Capitoline museums. And so on and so forth.

"Rome, oh, Rome...It's my favorite city, Papa. *I'm begging you*."

AND SO, that same evening, Olivia called me, all excited: "I'm coming over to your house to play! Aren't you happy?"

I didn't get a wink of sleep all night, and not because of any delight. I was very worried at the thought of trying to fit her into my world. I was ashamed of her. I far preferred worming my way into her world, which at least I had some familiarity with.

First of all, she'd be coming with her nanny, and just explaining that detail to the other kids was a challenge. Then, there was the fact that she'd be staying in a hotel on the

Via Veneto, like an American starlet. I had a reputation to defend, damn it.

When I moved from Via Chiabrera to Lamaro, I already had a few years of living in the *borgata* under my belt. What's more, I'd fetched up in the new courtyard trailing clouds of heroic glory: the son of Max, who'd died behind bars (I wasn't about to explain that Max wasn't even my father, it was far more convenient to batten off his fame and say nothing).

I tossed and turned in my bed, in a state of anguish. What would she wear when she came to our courtyard? Would she be dressed in lace, with her ample skirts and her cunning little collars? Oh my God. Surrounded by all the rest of us, shaved bald, boys and girls alike, because just one child in the apartment building had contracted lice and none of the parents wanted the hassle, so they'd just made a clean sweep. All of us, heads shorn, gazing at her pigtails, her braids, her headband with a plastic flower stuck to her temple. Why did this kind of thing always happen to me? We, with our knees perennially skinned and our trousers tattered and full of holes, free to run and trade punches, without nannies to bust our asses and outfits too stiff and uncomfortable for brawling. We in our T-shirts, which the neighbor kids outgrew so they wound up in our dressers, but only on a provisional basis, because they were still destined to be handed down to somebody else one day. And just how would Olivia react, when my friends, taking advantage of a game of hide-and-seek, asked her to take off her panties and let them have a look?

Suddenly, my face lit up. Maybe this was my big opportunity. I could keep her hidden, as my secret companion. I even thought through the strategies: I could slip into the apartment of Lungo's grandmother, who was blind, after all. And there I'd teach her the panty game, I'd teach her myself, personally, before the other boys even got a chance to try. And I'd see her naked. I pondered further about how I'd go about keeping her from showing off her private parts to the others. I was already jealous: she was to be mine and mine alone. Deep down, it was in my best interest for the others to hate her. That way, Olivia could play with me and nobody else. And pull down her panties just for me, because no one else wanted her. I was getting worked up again.

Olivia's highly exotic allure in that setting made everything pretty unpredictable. They might reject her out of hand, or acclaim her in showers of glory, with the grandmothers all grating tomatoes on the *panzanelle*, the scraps of stale bread, for her to taste and her alone, and too bad if they were then expected to provide snacks for ten other kids. Oh my God, oh my God. Strange as she was, there was every risk that she'd become the star of the *borgata*. Oh, no.

———

AT FIRST, it was a pretty cold reception. To start with, Olivia arrived in a taxi, and it wasn't like we see many of those in our neighborhood. A taxi that had been summoned by the doorman at the Excelsior, and the man had asked her nanny to repeat the address three times because he was sure he'd misunderstood ("Via Togliatti, did you say? Are you quite certain, Signora?"). The nanny, who was making her first visit to the Italian capital, had even removed the thin gold chain with a cross that an aunt had given her for her baptism, because she'd been told that "they steal in Rome."

A small crowd of curious kids quickly assembled. Wise-cracks hailed down: *romanesco* decidedly lent itself to this purpose, ironic and world-weary as it was, the language of people who've lived through everything you could think of and have a word for everything ("*Ao', ma che ha fatto questa? 'A comunione?*" was one catcall: "Hey, where's she coming from? Her first communion?" And then: "*A Scirli Templeee!*" to represent the exaggerated Italianization of the American child actress Shirley Temple, evoking a resemblance).

Olivia got out of the car wearing a cute dress that might not have been what she'd wear to say, Calvi's niece's birthday party, but it was at that general level. To make things worse, she was carrying a present for me, which I was ashamed to open. Who knew what the devil her parents had bought for me? I walked along with the gift wrapped package hidden behind my back and a line of children following behind me, tugging on the ribbon. Olivia looked around, a little bewil-dered. She understood the difference perfectly clearly, and hardly knew what to say. With considerable intelligence, she'd decided that for the moment, the best thing she could do was keep her mouth shut.

Meanwhile, I acted as her tour guide, explaining how we played in the courtyard, that here in our building everybody's apartment door was wide open to everyone else, without locked gates, burglar alarms, and police, that we all ate noonday snacks together, one day at one person's grandmother's house, and the next day at someone else's, that they'd shaved our heads because Er Vetraro's son had lice, and so on and so forth. The other kids were all hypnotized by my explanations, they weren't accustomed to looking at their own world from the outside, much less to hearing it described in a running patter. They followed us, fascinated. Before you knew it, they were acting as her tour guides themselves. They'd point to a balcony and tell her that Er Cipolla lived on the third floor (his name was "the Onion," because he was a notorious gigolo, and had been dubbed that because he "made women cry") and that his apartment was empty because he was "behind bars." And that they went there to play when it was raining and the courtyard couldn't be used.

Olivia's eyes sparkled, she'd immediately understood that in Rome she could do things she'd never have been able to dream of back home. She didn't know exactly how to behave, but she was dying to have fun, that much was clear.

And so, when she saw three little girls playing with a jump rope, she went straight over to them. At first, she watched them from a distance, hesitantly touching her skirt, too long and puffy to think of jumping rope in it, trying to figure out how she could hike it up. Er Biondo (Blondie) and Er Fregnetto (Shorty), who had fallen in love with this new female outsider, stood awkwardly behind her. They told her that one of the girls was Gelatina's sister, that they'd known her since she was born, and that if she wanted, they'd be glad to introduce her to them. They told her that *I* was the newcomer there, the last one to arrive, little bastards that they were. I objected, retorting that actually I was friends with the brunette, and warning them not to underestimate me. Olivia let us go on and argue, preening and showing off for her, because she was too busy shooting flirtatious glances at the other girls, whom she was dying to play with. She had plenty of jump ropes of her own, probably tossed and forgotten in a basket somewhere, but she wanted *that* one in a way that she had never longed for any other, because she wanted the little girls who were turning that rope, ignoring her (but with one eye on her the whole time).

At a certain point, the little girl who was jumping at the center of the rope collapsed to the asphalt. She leaped right up again, without yelling or crying, worried as she was about losing her place, but the two other girls immediately seized on this opportunity to be rid of her. Oh, no, now you need to take a rest, look at your knees, they're bleeding. The little one stoically tried to clean her knees with gobs of saliva, spitting on them, but she didn't have a chance, her two friends were already gazing in Olivia's direction. It was a clipped conversation, made up of extended pauses and things left unsaid, and it was up to the outsider to make her move, they would never stoop so low as to extend an invitation.

Olivia ventured still closer, with the excuse of getting a better look at the rope. She told them that she had one that, instead of ordinary wooden handles, had two ice cream cones. But her story didn't have the desired effect. The little girls jutted their chins out contemptuously: *So what? Who the fuck cares?* And so Olivia realized that her best bet was to jump rope and keep her mouth shut, without a lot of preliminary chitchat. Before half an hour had passed, she was out of control, inventing bizarre jumping routines to be performed in shifts and rounds, and everyone wanted to jump like idiots alongside her. She'd done it.

Before the sun set that day, Olivia had won over the entire courtyard, and not just the little girls with the jump rope but also their parents, because she'd asked for the loan of more comfortable clothing. As if she even had to ask. The concept of the loan in the *borgata* is a crucial one: people were competing to offer her a faded sweatshirt and a patched pair of shorts. All the mothers and grandmothers and aunts in the apartment building wanted to dress her, and feel as if she belonged to *them.* A girl who gladly tossed her expensive clothing aside—in a heap atop a low wall, a thousand times happier with clothing that was generously given to her, clothing that was made for this, to be handed down from brother to brother, from sister to sister, from neighbor to neighbor, happy to repay the favor the next time the need arose—was irresistible to them.

That evening, as she prepared to leave, sweaty and red-faced, Olivia asked whether she could keep those trousers and that sweatshirt, and just leave her little dress there for someone else—she had already fully mastered the new underlying logic—proud of the tomato stain on the chest, her own personal contribution to the garment's history, after a memorable chomp into the *panzanella* offered to her by Er Negro's grandmother.

She said goodbye to this child and that—"Well, then, ciao, I'll be back tomorrow, ciao"—clearly contented with how the day had gone.

Before climbing into the taxi, she took my hand. "This was the most wonderful afternoon of my life, Valerio." Then she remembered the customary expression, which they'd drilled into her every time she left a party. "Thanks so much for inviting me."

BACK AT THE HOTEL, in the evening, Olivia dined in the Excelsior's restaurant with her nanny, while the pianist played a tune or two from *Cats* for an American couple. Humming a few bars from "Memory," she returned to her room and, before dropping off to sleep, she drew sketches for her grandparents, to be delivered the following day to the desk clerk, with instructions to mail them to Bologna.

At the top left of one, she'd written: *Nonna Ettorina and the Gambling Dens.* Beneath that caption appeared a little old lady walking around a pool table with a bottle in hand. For another, titled *Zio Vittorio and the Swag,* she patiently colored a figure bent over a bag with the word "swag" written on it. In another, *Er Cipolla in Prison,* you saw a fair-haired young man behind bars and lots of women standing around him, tears spouting from their eyes like the jets of water from a fountain (Olivia was convinced that women wept because he was in prison).

Manon would open the envelopes and pause, baffled, when she saw evidence of her granddaughter's new style. But she had plenty of other things to worry about, in that period, so she'd just put up the drawing in her dressing room with a thumb tack and avoid wasting too much time on it. Children, the imaginations they have!

One evening, at dinner—in part to cut the tension which had, by now, become intolerable—Manon handed around her granddaughter's Roman creations.

Uncle Dado was enthusiastic: "I just love *Nonna Ettorina and the Gambling Dens,* can I keep it? It reminds me of you, Mama, when you play bridge with your girlfriends."

Manon replied that a sketch of her friends playing bridge had already been done, and it had gone down in history because Olivia, in order to make clear just how heavily bedecked with jewelry they were, had done a depiction of Pinuccia in profile, with a large ring wrapped around her nose—a nose that served as an eleventh finger to be bejeweled, just in case the other ten weren't sufficient. The sketch in question, which had brought much laughter to the lips of Pinuccia's fellow bridge players but had ruined Pinuccia's own reputation for all time, had wound up, framed, on the wall of the billiards room (which more closely resembled the murder scene in an Agatha Christie mystery novel than it did the gambling dens of Nonna Ettorina). And this one would have to be framed to hang alongside it, as its companion piece.

Giulio Morganti, bent over the portrait of *Er Cipolla in Prison*, was more baffled. He kept turning to look at his wife and asking: "So have you heard from her this evening? Did she call you? Are you sure that she's all right?"

"She's fine, sweetheart," Elena replied. "She's in such a good mood."

Manon, who just hoped that her granddaughter would soon be returned to her—the only source of joy in that grief-stricken household—was a little disappointed. She therefore reached out for the little silver handbell and shook it tensely, summoning the housekeeper: "What about dessert? We've been waiting for half an hour."

THE FINEST LAWYERS of the time, specialists in kidnappings, were all on retainer. And private detectives were on the case, too. But they made sure to keep the reporters at a safe distance, thank God.

"Don't let those snooping reporters get anywhere near my house," Manon would shout. "I don't want to see even one of them around here. I swear I'll take my husband's Beretta and shoot every last one of them that strays within range."

The police were less of a concern: in fact, all that was required was to make the right acquaintances aware of the sensitive issues at hand. Ever since the first phone call had come in, in fact, no one ruled out the hypothesis that a ransom would have to be paid. We'll pay, they said, if we have to. Name the price. In the budget for expected outlays, there was also a slush fund for bribes. A politician here, a public official there. There was no price before which they quailed. But, as it turned out, there really was no money to be spent. The Morgantis, this time, couldn't buy a thing: neither the life of the loved one, nor the law itself.

The long-feared kidnapping turned out to have been a tawdry setup, an idea that came after the fact. Gianni's killer was every bit as bourgeois as he was. After killing him, caught in a wave of panic, he'd decided to act promptly and do his best to muddy the waters. Stage a kidnapping: What else was there to try? There was no other way out. The killer was an industrialist and a conservative, exactly like his victim, and therefore a man with the exact same set of fears: the Communists, the Red Brigades, the Sardinian gangsters. And the only thing that had popped into his mind, in the swirl of confusion, had been that very idea: his fears, so deep-rooted and atavistic that they were able to withstand the great and dizzying panic that comes in the wake of an un-premeditated murder.

Gianni knew the man, he knew that his company had slid into bankruptcy, and he'd even expressed his condo-lences: "I'm sorry to hear about it." They'd played tennis to-gether more than once, at the same club where Gianni had never arrived that day.

Gianni unfortunately had the reputation of being a gen-erous man, willing and able to lend money to his friends if they were in dire straits, which was actually something Gianni had done before, and more than once, but before

Manon had the entire estate put in her name for fear that his lovers, one promissory note after another, might leave him with nothing but his boxer shorts. And so, when the future killer went to beg his future victim for a loan, in the name of who knows what friendship (I mean, let's be frank, they might at most have hit a few balls back and forth on the clay court), Gianni had candidly shrugged his shoulders and proffered, with a laugh, the pure and simple truth.

"I'd be delighted to give you a hand, but my wife found out I have a girlfriend on the side and now she's had every penny put in her name. You know the way women can be," and then he laughed, wry and self-mocking as usual.

The other man, pushed to his wit's end by his mounting debts, the collapse of his social standing—as well as his marriage, because his wife had dumped him the day he'd declared bankruptcy, forget about any loving scenes of jealousy—was in no mood for laughter. He'd proceeded to ask Gianni for a ride somewhere and then, as soon as they were far out on an isolated stretch of hillside road, he'd pulled out his pistol (back then, there were Communists, Red Brigades, Sardinian mobsters, and so on and so forth, so people tended to carry concealed weapons). He'd leveled the gun at his host and driver, his hand shaking.

"Stop the car. Pull over and park right here, and then get out."

Gianni had immediately stopped kidding around, because he'd realized that he had a lunatic on his hands. But he hadn't taken fright. After all, Gianni was a man who had gone off to war at age twenty, flying a plane in the face of enemy aviation, with an unloaded machine gun because the Italian state had no money for ammunition. Someone who had found himself burdened beneath his father's mountain of debt—if it was really necessary to talk about debt—and who had not only single-handedly restored that small company, languishing at death's door, to robust good health all by himself, when he was little more than a kid, rather than letting it collapse into bankruptcy. In fact, he had turned that small activity into an empire.

Instinctively, he did his best to instill a little calm. Even in that situation, with a gun barrel aimed at his face, Gianni thought that it was possible to talk sense. His mistake was to imagine that the pistol in question was a friendly one. Better than a fanatical Communist, he thought, because there was no way to establish a dialogue with them. Better than a half-feral Sardinian, who would never be able to understand me. This is a man like me, he's just desperate and he's lost his bearings. So he was talking and talking, the poor guy. He was utterly human, and Gianni knew it. And at the crucial moment, he tried to use his finest qualities.

"Listen," he told the man, "just drive me home and we can talk to my wife, Manon is only afraid of other women, and she's not wrong, I won't bore you with stories of the bloodsucking women I've run into. I'll arrange for her to write you a check. Trust me, we can take care of this."

OLIVIA HAD REMAINED in Rome for a long time, because the agony of the kidnapping had dragged on forever. It wasn't until a month later that her grandfather's corpse was finally unearthed, in the woods a few miles from his house. He, who had always dreamed of dying in some heroic fashion—preferably smashing to earth in his airplane, hurtling downward, that's how he'd imagined his demise: something going wrong on high, in the sky, the element in which he felt most intimately at his ease—had instead been found filthy, on the ground, wrapped in a moth-eaten blanket. Manon, summoned to identify the body, refused to do so.

"There's no way that's my husband," she kept repeating, in defiance of the hard facts. Stunned and grieving, she fiddled with Gianni's wedding band, upon which were unequivocally etched both their names and the date of their wedding, June 24, 1945, the end of the war and the beginning of a new era, a world they were going to rebuild—together.

They hadn't celebrated that day, their wedding day. But they threw parties afterward: lots of them, and memorable ones. Maybe to make up for it. They'd gone to church, just the two of them, alone, with two witnesses, dressed in their only good outfits and carrying a bouquet of flowers. Gianni's parents disapproved, Manon's parents were divorced and couldn't be invited, the city was a heap of rubble and there was no money for celebrations: what else could they have done? Still, it had been nice just the way it was. They walked out of the church arm in arm and had nowhere to go.

Neither a restaurant for lunch nor a home of their own. So now what? Now we invent ourselves a life.

And they'd invented it very well indeed, no two ways about that. For a couple of years, they'd scrimped and saved, and then the company had taken off. Gianni's father died, barely a year after their wedding, and Gianni had found himself the owner of a farming operation that was strictly dead weight. But he'd managed to revive it and then promptly sell it off so he could invest in another sector, a far more profitable line of business: construction. *Cement*. Italy had been razed to the ground, and walls had to be built in all directions.

While they built appalling oversized apartment buildings together, dotting the landscape, Manon was busy renovating the loveliest villa in Bologna. An eighteenth-century villa with a magnificent view of the city and frescoes on the walls that would have made Catherine II of Russia blanch with envy. Manon was a well-read, educated woman and she wasn't going to settle for mere wealth.

For thirty-nine years she had instructed her husband in the ways of beauty, and she'd never stopped studying. Travel? She wasn't satisfied with a luxury hotel. There were better uses for their money. So she took him to Cappadocia, Petra, and Granada. In Paris, there was only one place to stay, the Hôtel Plaza Athénée, but Olivia's grandfather, whether or not he wanted to, wasn't going to be allowed to settle in comfortably. There'd be hell to pay if he failed to squire her around to all the exhibitions, from the Grand Palais to the Pompidou.

"Manon," he had told her once, "you taught me how to see."

She'd smiled at those words, gratified by his acknowledgment. She hadn't succeeded in convincing him to open a single book, because he wasn't capable of sitting quietly "in front of a stack of paper," but she had managed to transform her husband's daily labors into an intelligent joie de vivre. There was no splendid spectacle on earth they'd denied themselves, from China to Patagonia. There wasn't a room in their home that wasn't attentively curated, detail after precious detail carefully chosen. There wasn't a table that hadn't been set to perfection, whether for friends or for family, with silver chargers, magnificent glasses, embroidered tablecloths, and color-coordinated flowers. Not a single dinner without special recipes that she'd gone personally in search of, patiently leafing through dozens of cookbooks (Manon didn't know how to boil an egg herself, but she gave instructions on how to make a champagne risotto or an orange buttercream frosting, and it was worth as much as your life to try to contradict her about portions and cooking times), naturally, with just the right wines accompanying them.

Every couple rests its foundations on a secret pact. There are a thousand nuances to the relationship, but the underlying pact is singular, and it can never be betrayed. There are those who base all their complicity on ambition, others who focus entirely on the children, some who seek protection, or establish their identity in their socializing, or who care only about money (a pact based on sex within marriage is less common, but if the darker shadows happen to intertwine, then it can be every bit as powerful as any of the others). There are countless arrays of possible pacts, and in a way, these pacts are forms of love.

Manon and Gianni's pact was beauty. They'd stuck it out together for forty years that way: he had to guarantee that she had the means to obtain beauty, and in return she had to guarantee the successful outcome. That was why Manon refused to identify his corpse. Their pact had been nullified in death. The problem wasn't the violence, the forehead ravaged by a pistol shot. Nor was it the putrefying body. No. It was the sight of her husband, reduced to that state, filthy, wrapped in a tattered, ripped blanket, like some hobo.

"That's not him," she kept insisting.

BUT 1984 hadn't just been the year of Olivia's grandfather's death. The end of that year happened to coincide with the end of a world—that verged on mythology—at least for the Morgantis. There are people who take an era with them when they die. And those who are left behind are forced to resign themselves to a twofold loss. Everyone guessed that now they'd be looking at a lengthy decline, with the occasional false recovery along the way. The golden age had ended.

I went back to Bologna for Gianni's funeral. Dressed in high regalia (my mother had spent every last penny of her savings to make sure my appearance was up to the occasion),

I was back in the villa where I'd been born nine years before. Standing in front of the main entrance, half hidden behind the baroque fountain, I kept a tight grip on my father's hand while they carried out the grandfather's coffin, draped in flowers. The exit from the stage contained within it the following act. He's leaving his home: What now? What will happen now that he's gone?

Every so often I'd shoot a glance at Olivia, who returned my glances, head bowed, her hand gripping Manon's long fingers. The casket hadn't passed through the front door more than a few seconds before the sons were already quarreling about the order in which they would arrive at the church. One of them wanted to ride ahead of the hearse, the other wanted to be sure that all the cars in the procession came directly after him in line.

"I'll lead the procession, that way no one will interfere with the others. Then Mama, with the chauffeur, will ride directly behind the hearse, the first of the mourners."

"Who the hell cares," Dado objected. "It's a funeral, not a goddamned fashion show. This kind of bullshit drives me crazy. I won't do it."

"You never learn," Giulio replied. "Papa cared about form. Even now, you can't show him the most basic respect."

Manon, who had managed to maintain her self-control even at the most trying, awful moments, burst into tears (that was her all over: to be calm and collected while bombs were raining from the sky, and then burst into hysteria over a broken drinking glass).

"Stop it, stop it! Quit your arguing, please! You're both causing us enormous pain." She was referring to herself, in the plural, as though still part of a couple.

This was just a prelude to the battles over the inheritance that would follow, and those were waged to the last drop of blood. Olivia and I still didn't know it, but our own relationship would be just one of the many victims. We weren't witnessing the burial of her grandfather's body alone.

A few months later, in the huge big bang unleashed by the reading of the will, my father was going to be swept away in the wreckage, too, a victim of the brothers' reciprocal hatred.

Manon had urged him to stay, but to no avail. My father was mortally offended, he just wanted to collect his severance pay and leave the Morganti family to its fate. He had come to Rome expressly to inform me of his decision in person.

"I mean, *porco giuda*," he swore, his eyes bloodshot in rage, "I gave my heart and soul to that family. I lived with them for twenty years. And now they accuse me of being a *lader* (a thief, in dialect) and kick me out just because a stupid watch has gone missing. What on earth would I even do with that piece of *baggage*, would you tell me that? I have a watch, and it works just fine."

He explained that actually the watch had been nothing but an excuse. Giulio was angry because he'd refused to testify in the case against his brother. All this was happening because Dado, kicked out of the company, had received as his inheritance more cash and more real estate in compensation for that expulsion. Both of them claimed that the outcome had been inequitable, each convinced that they'd been the victim of a rank injustice, and by now they only communicated through their legal counselors.

"Well, *ben ben*," he tutted, "I didn't want to have any part of that *brutto lavoro*—that nasty business. Those were Olivia's grandfather's decisions, it had been his money, he had every right to do exactly as he pleased with it, as far as I'm concerned. He'd taken one thing away from one of the boys, and something else from the other. That's justice, too, after all."

I listened to him breathlessly, horrified at the thought of the collateral damage. What was this going to mean? No more vacations with Olivia? That I'll actually never see her again, *as long as I live*? I wanted to interrupt him and ask questions, but I just couldn't do it.

"Maybe I'll take my severance pay and buy a taxi, I don't know. We'll wait and see. But I'm saying farewell to them, *at salùt*."

My father just stopped talking all at once, the way he did. A brusque silence and a burst of coughing. He stroked my hair, looking elsewhere, toward the wrongs that had been done to him.

"You understand, Valerio?"

There was going to be another separation. Sure, I understood.

PART TWO

1993–1994

JUDICIAL INDICTMENT
AND SUMMONS:
RSVP

RÉPONDEZ S'IL VOUS PLAÎT. It was May 1993 and I hadn't seen Olivia again for nine long years. I certainly wasn't expecting to receive that invitation. At first I was tempted to toss the little rectangle of hard cardboard into the trash, without a second thought. *Manon Morganti is pleased to invite.* I read and reread my name written beneath—*Valerio Carnevale*—in lovely calligraphy, with a fountain pen. *For her granddaughter's eighteenth birthday.* And at the center, in garishly oversized characters: *Olivia.* I didn't know how to picture her to myself, this young woman just about to reach her majority.

Olivia had always forced me to reckon with my sense of time. Every time I saw her, I somehow felt obliged to deal with a piece of history, together with her. The diagram laid out by our distancings and renewed proximities, who knows why, always seemed to entail a settling of accounts of some sort, and sometimes it wasn't even especially personal.

My simplest doubts were bound up with two words printed at the bottom of the card, on the right: *Black Tie.* I knew exactly what they meant, because my mother had worked her fingers to the bone so that she could enroll me in the classical high school, and to be exact, one of the finest schools in Rome, where she informed me that I'd have the opportunity to rub shoulders with the city's crème de la crème. And in fact, that's exactly what had happened, though in point of fact that crème turned out to be dregs, people who were only interested, when all was said and done, in narcotics, even worse than back in the *borgata*, but that's just how that went. To make a long story short, invitations like that one were common enough in my own class at school. Just not ones that were addressed to me.

"But I don't own a tuxedo."

"I'll lend you mine." Costantino Bernasconi, my classmate, was urging me to go. "Who can say, maybe she's turned into a complete babe."

He, too, was the scion of a great and wealthy family of builders and, more or less like Olivia Morganti, he had chosen me above all the others. A coincidence? I was convinced that it wasn't one. In all likelihood, without even realizing it, it had been I who chose him. After all, deep down, the magnetic laws that attract human beings are always somewhat mysterious.

Certainly, it had been Costantino Bernasconi who came over to *me* on that September morning, when no one knew anyone and everyone was entering a completely new and unfamiliar place, still free of names and all the baggage they carry with them, when—for a vanishingly brief time—everyone is just a face, fear in the eyes or flashes of enthusiasm, alive and real and open to the possible, before society can force us into a role that we frequently haven't even decided on for ourselves. It had been Costantino who'd asked me if he could sit next to me. But out of the thirty classmates, perhaps I had been the one who'd invited him with a special glint in my eyes.

For that matter, it's true that our desires have subterranean powers that often override our more conscious intentions. Sometimes they can see farther than we can, they can recognize what we fail to, and without bothering to check with us, they just go ahead and make decisions on our behalf. After all, that first day of school, I was returning with a lurch from the *borgata* to a decidedly bourgeois world. What else could I be hoping for, if not to meet a second Olivia Morganti, capable of rendering the transition sweet for me?

If, that first day of school, Costantino Bernasconi had decided to sit, say, next to Rebecca Antinori or Gaetano Cavallari, I would have been unable to tell you this story today. We all know how the great wheel of fortune, spinning past deeds done and undone, works in life, and it's always a slightly stunning exercise to review its revolutions, working backward. Now, however, as I write, a doubt seizes me: But did I already want this story to unfold back then? And did I want it so deeply that I unleashed my desire into the air, making it explode into thousands of microparticles capable of surrounding another person and their desires, themselves in search of a destiny? Perhaps my future was so powerfully designed in my imagination that Costantino Bernasconi could never have taken a seat next to Rebecca Antinori or Gaetano Cavallari, because he had no choice but to meet me and change my own future path.

A man's imagination is his destiny. If you ask me, character doesn't matter, it's not enough to say: I'll do one thing and another thing will happen, because life goes where it will and tricks you endlessly, and you do one thing and another ninety-nine things will happen, but not the thing that you were expecting, so there's little or no reason to trust in your own character or the character of other people. If, on the other hand, you *imagine* being someone, through some very twisted path—through the ninety-nine things that you neither wanted nor foresaw—you actually will arrive at the hundredth thing, the one that you had in mind in the first place.

"So? Do you or don't you want my tuxedo?"

"Sure, but you have to come, too."

I didn't want to go to that party all alone. I wouldn't know anyone there. And most of all, I didn't want to go back into that world—the world I came from?—without the support of my new world, and all its everyday reassurances. When people talk about equilibrium as something internal, sometimes it makes me feel like laughing. Maybe so. There exists a kind of equilibrium, very delicate and complex (perhaps because it doesn't depend on us alone), but there's absolutely nothing internal about it: it's the equilibrium of the worlds we belong to. And that's what I was worrying about.

"Are you kidding? To the Morganti home? Papa would kill me," Costantino laughed, "*it's their fault* he's under house arrest."

Nothing could have surprised me more. What role had the Morgantis played in the arrest of Beppe Bernasconi? Among other things, it was a topic that Costantino never talked about, as if it had never happened. In fact, at first I hadn't even realized that his father was under house arrest. I went over to his house practically every weekend, but precisely because it was the weekend it wasn't strange to see Signor Bernasconi sitting in his bathrobe in front of the TV or in a terry-cloth robe lying by the pool. No one had explained to me that this was different. Most of all, no one seemed especially concerned about things. The aperitif was served at seven in the evening, on the dot, as usual, champagne and salted peanuts and a few expensive cheeses, or else a selection of fresh vegetables and olive oil dip—crudités or *pinzimonio*, when the *Cavaliere* was on a diet, because Signor Bernasconi was an engineer by education but Cavaliere del Lavoro, literally, a knight of labor, by honorific, as

Costantino's mother never tired of reminding us, especially when we both brought home failing grades in ancient Greek. And immediately afterward dinner was served, a frugal meal but only because it was important to stay light at the evening meal. Carbohydrates at lunch and proteins for dinner, ideally lean meat or fish, and lots and lots of vegetables. Not like at my house, where we'd be served a steamer trunk full of pasta just to prove the opposite, that there was plenty of food so everything was all right and dinner was supposed to be a moment of satisfaction for us all. That same steamer trunk full of pasta was certainly welcome to my friend Costantino, tall and skinny and muscular, "a growing boy," as my mother often said, and he invariably and willingly polished it off whenever he came to my house, with a ravenous appetite. It took him five seconds to empty two bowls of spaghetti *aglio e olio*, which my mama would set before him with a wink, knowing she was making him happy, since at our house no one ever worried about bad breath or excess calories. And the sweet young wine—the vinello—that Zio Vittorio brought us by the plastic jerrican from a vineyard in the Castelli Romani was easy and delightful to drink, with no need for all the complicated ceremonies involved in extracting and sniffing the cork.

"Of course! Wait, don't tell me you didn't know?" Costantino chomped relaxedly on his chewing gum while he copied off the blackboard two dates that our history teacher had felt the need to underline, with a certain hint of emphasis in her voice ("'89 and '93, guys, you need to learn those dates, they're *crucial*, they changed the history...of the eighteenth century").

I shook my head: "No, I never knew that."

"It happened when they scooped up Giulio Morganti. You know the way the magistrates in the Clean Hands investigation did things, right? Tell me other names, and I'll reduce your sentence. You talk and I'll make deals. Anyway, when he received his indictment, that turncoat named us. There's no way I can go to his daughter's birthday party. My father would not only stop my allowance, he'd garnish my pension."

In the meantime, the teacher called out for us all to turn the page. After a collective rustling of pages, we all sat staring at Jacques-Louis David's *Death of Marat*. The painting had unleashed a stormy debate. One young woman had raised her hand. The usual teacher's pet, top of the class, who always wanted to have her say. Which would have been reasonable enough if not for the fact that her father was a member of parliament, up to his neck in the recent scandals inasmuch as a member of the proverbially corrupt Socialist Party.

"Teacher? This painting makes me think of Bettino Craxi as he leaves the Hotel Raphael and people throw a hail of coins at him." Bettino Craxi was the leader of the Socialist Party.

"Only a deep-seated anger is capable of producing epic images, so in a certain sense, I sort of agree," the teacher ventured to respond, uncomfortably. "These are acts that out of the depths of history ultimately sublimate themselves into *a perfect composition*. But epic images have one defect: they're so clean and simple that they can muddle the mind. A vendetta, precise in its trajectory, is so easy to memorize that it condemns us to remember for all time itself, and not the mile after mile of subsequent smoking rubble. Only because certain ruins are too filthy and too dusty and too vast to fit *inside a perfect composition*."

We didn't know it yet, but she was right. My class, which graduated in 1993, would remember forever the crowd that scornfully tossed coins at Craxi but would quickly forget the fact that his friend Berlusconi had tossed millions at him, even though we had him around for the twenty years that followed. My class would remember the collapse of the Twin Towers—precise in its trajectory, to a fault—but would forget the square blocks of smoking rubble that ensued. But I was too taken up with my own private affairs to lend any real attention to this topic.

"Giulio Morganti was arrested? Really? What for?"

Eventually, Costantino started to get a little annoyed at my questions: "What are you so astonished about? The Morgantis weren't a bit better than anybody else. If you wanted to be awarded contracts, you had to pay bribes, there was no other way of obtaining work, and everyone knew that. It was the way things worked, on a normal basis. Then, all at once, they all started treating us like criminals. As if we'd invented that system ourselves." Then he turned around: "What are you doing, moralizing? You, with your father who was killed in prison?"

I was about to retort: *He wasn't my father,* but come to think of it, this wasn't right either, not only because Max remained a sort of hero in my eyes, albeit a slightly irregular one, but also because he had been a sort of father to me, and in any case, he was my sister's father, my sister whom I adored and would never dream of offending. Ah, the family: that enormous cluster of worrisome concerns and tacit protections, especially a soul as Italian as mine.

"No, I wouldn't dream of it. I was just asking."

"Well, listen, take it from me, when you come over on Saturday, don't start asking my papa questions. He's already sick of spending all day every day in the pool"—at that he laughed. "He refers to this as his involuntary vacation. It might have been a rotten system, but he preferred working to doing nothing."

Costantino explained to me that Beppe Bernasconi had even managed to bribe the court-appointed physician and obtain house arrest for an imaginary problem with his heart. The Biondi law did not yet exist, a measure stitched as if by a compliant tailor to fit people like him by the brand-new Berlusconi administration, not even a year later. During preventive detention for those charged with crimes of corruption, they weren't going to let you get away with house arrest. You waited for your trial behind bars. In fact, that's where Giulio Morganti was waiting for his. But Beppe Bernasconi, as usual, had outfoxed everybody else, which meant he wasn't living in a prison cell of a few dozen square feet. No, he was living in a bathrobe, lazing by the pool or in the comfort of his living room, in front of a video cassette recorder (and his wife was happy to turn a blind eye if she stumbled across a few pornographic cassettes lying around).

At this point, the fancy little engraved invitation presented another problem, more complicated than the small *Black Tie* written at the bottom right, which had been tormenting me until an hour before. I was starting to wonder if it was *right* to turn down an invitation, now of all times, now that the Morgantis had fallen into disgrace, reviled both by the legal system and the press. I wondered how Manon was handling this. What an unacceptable injury to her pride, what a low blow to her perennially upthrust chin, what an intolerable humiliation to see her son's photograph in all the papers. *Judicial indictment and summons*: it wasn't hard for me to imagine her calf clad in a fine silk stocking, thrust halfway out the window, with a shout of Now-I'm-going-to-jump, and everyone trying to restrain her, laying firm hold on her arm tinkling to the sound of her forty Cartier gold bracelets, gifts from her late husband, one for each anniversary of their wedding, testament to a marriage perhaps not always happy, but glorious, no question about that ("It's just a good thing that your father is dead and isn't forced to experience this mortification").

Another doubt flashed through my mind: Are they seriously throwing a party while the master of the house is behind bars? That, however, was a doubt that I pushed off to one side, it didn't strike me as entirely legitimate. Perhaps this was simply normal, like paying bribes to be awarded a public works contract. Maybe everyone did it, throwing parties while fathers and husbands were under arrest—who could say? After all, we too, in our small way, were doing it. Half of my class was over at the Bernasconi home on Saturday evenings, ordering pizzas and renting movies, twenty or thirty at a time up in Costantino's mansard, carefree and cheerful and blithely indifferent to the fact that there was a gentleman downstairs, invariably in his bathrobe, who was actually serving time.

Or perhaps the party was just a superb act of defiance and provocation on Manon's part. After all, she'd been through war and starvation and death and was determined to accord minor human mishaps no more than their due, considering them as little more than petty tragedies, whoever might be to blame. Passing misfortunes that would just have to step aside and leave the limelight to the one and only truly important event, by no means passing and transitory, because a recurrence is a recurrence, and you only become a grown-up once, and that date never rolls around again: her beloved granddaughter's birthday. A birthday that was to be commemorated and observed in grand style, if only to ward off misfortune, because while things might not have gone as wished for the rest of the family, such was *not* to be the case for her Olivia: that girl had a golden future ahead of her, to be inaugurated with streams of champagne and lots of fireworks. And dark times were not to be allowed to dim the splendor foreseen for her.

But panic had engulfed me when I came to the third and final doubt, when I'd started to wonder if it was *right* to go to the home of the Morgantis after they'd accused my father of being a thief. All because of a watch.

"And he didn't even know the difference between a Patek Philippe and a Swatch, that half-baked fool, that *lesso*," Mama would say, and immediately after that she'd start off on one of her usual tirades about how my father never let her have enough money. She was angry with him because in the end, Papa hadn't bought a taxi at all, he'd just gone on working as a gardener at a hospice for the elderly, where he wouldn't even be able to end his days, because being godforsaken and forgotten in that hospice was just too darned expensive. Here my mother would take advantage of the opportunity to remind me that I must never become "a loser like your father," her eternal refrain. And I would froth in rage because this story about winners and losers was an obsession with her, a sort of ongoing, perennial sword over my head.

After Max's death, my mother had also gone back "to working as a scullery maid" (she used that phrase intentionally, to make me feel the burden of her sacrifices, and the corresponding importance of redemption, which of course was my responsibility). Except that she hadn't wound up surrounded by old people, godforsaken and soon to die, like my Papa, because she was more conniving. Her old people weren't hospice bums, but a couple that lived in a beautiful apartment in Trinità dei Monti, a property that they were still trying to decide whom or which charitable agency to leave to, seeing that they had no heirs.

My mother had buttered them up to within an inch of their lives. She, who constantly preached pride, had for years taken me every Sunday to eat lunch with them, leaving my sister at home because Marta, the daughter of a *borgata* criminal, had in her DNA a ferocity quite different from mine, and was unwilling to kiss anyone's ass, even when she was small.

When the two old people finally died, Mama had discovered that the apartment hadn't been left to us at all, in spite of their promises, but instead to a religious institute, because a parish priest had worked harder than she had. Thanks to a small bequest, however—twenty million lire in the money of the time, which was hardly a trifle—her efforts hadn't gone entirely unrewarded and she'd been able to keep me in school, up to university.

Répondez s'il vous plaît. Perhaps the only sensible thing to do was to phone my father and ask him for advice. He might very well be a loser and an asshole and a beaten man, as my mother always said, but he was also the only person I could trust.

"Papa? Do you have five minutes?" I'd just come home from school, I still had my backpack slung over my shoulders.

I would need to be sensitive in laying out this matter, but at the same time thoroughly sincere, and careful not to be tempted into convenient omissions, otherwise my doubts would seem ridiculous, when they were actually deadly serious, and even somewhat grievous. The result of that effort was a tangled welter of explanations and suppositions in which I, too, completely lost my way. Still, my father understood all the same. And he replied with two brusque sentences.

"Don't worry about me. You go ahead to that party."

I was touched. Still, that wasn't enough. What about all the rest?

"When all is said and done, people are who they are, and there's nothing you can do about it."

This is a summary, in all his simplicity, of all the justice and injustice in the world. Something to be accepted, "when all is said and done," as he always liked to say, about anything and everything, to the extent that it had become a regular interjection. When all is said and done, I ate the mortadella. When all is said and done, old people are courteous, that's just a fact of life. When all is said and done, I have my pension. Then there was "what can you do?" another typical interjection of his, which was useful in retrenching a set of demands or expectations. It was midway between his "what can you do about it?" and his "what more do you expect?" The Emilian accent gave it a good-natured fillip, but it remained an unconditional surrender. It's raining, what do you expect. I have a backache, what do you expect. I'm all alone, what do you expect.

And *when all is said and done*, I went to the party. What can you do?

2

BLACK TIE

COSTANTINO'S TUXEDO was a bit big and loose on me, at age eighteen I was skinny as a sardine and my trousers flapped around my spindly legs. The jacket, on the other hand, fit me comfortably, fairly snug. I had well-turned biceps because often, on Saturdays and Sundays, to make ends meet, I would work at the Ceccafumo market. I loaded and unloaded crates of fruit for five thousand lire a day. That was my gymnasium.

"Have it taken in, don't worry. After all, I can't fit in that tuxedo anymore."

"Are you sure about that, Costa?"

"Positive."

In front of the mirror in the hallway, my mother, with a pin in her mouth, was taking measurements.

"Stand up straight, Valerio. Straighten your fucking shoulders, that's right. I'm not letting you go over to see the Morganti family dressed like a clown. That would make me look good, wouldn't it? Not on your life. I told you to stand up straight"—a flat-handed smack to my lumbar vertebrae. "Up!"

She had me try it on every other day, that damned tuxedo. She stitched it onto me, with something approaching viciousness, poking me here and there.

"Ouch, Mama!"

She frequently lost her temper: "It's your fault, you can't keep still."

One leg of mine would always shoot forward, irritable and unwilling to put up with her obsessions—"The cuff has to fall right there on the shoe"—as if giving a small kick to her tightly clenched, otherwise occupied jaw. This whole issue of the party was turning into a nightmare.

"So what gift am I going to take her?"

"I bought one for you. I got her a silver frame. The Morgantis gave silver frames to everyone they knew. They had industrial quantities, and they'd ask me to wrap them. 'Sonia, would you please gift wrap a silver frame, thank you.' They even regifted them. There was a steady flow of them, incoming and outgoing. Sheer madness."

"Perfect."

"And I used it to frame a photo of the two of you when you were little. You and Olivia on the sled, in the snow."

"Have you lost your mind? No, I can't let that go. Take it out, immediately."

"But why? You were so cute."

"Mama! We're not five years old anymore. I'd be embarrassed. I'm begging you, please. Not the photo."

"I've very sorry, but the package has been wrapped." She wouldn't budge. "You'll see, she'll like it. You'll both have a laugh."

We'll have a *laugh*? I was terrified of this Olivia Morganti whom I couldn't even begin to imagine. Maybe she'd become a snobbish and arrogant young woman, no different from many of my female classmates, sullen and fashion-obsessed, always sporting just the right shoes, whispering into her girlfriends' ears in the hallways, with a smirk. Someone who was constantly moving and twisting her feet, like a ballerina, just to give herself a certain tone when she was otherwise standing still. Someone who pursed her lips when she smoked, with a superior air about her. Someone with well-tended fingernails and transparent polish, a pair of tiny pearl earrings on her lobes, with gold bracelets on her slender birdlike wrist, and wearing a quart of perfume, to make up for the light layering of makeup, never sluttish, heaven forfend. With a ponytail that tossed as she walked, slapping the air with every confident footstep. Someone who crossed her legs, even when seated on her Vespa. Oh Lord.

———

ALL THINGS CONSIDERED, I didn't really know her any-more. When we were in middle school, we were still exchanging letters. But by high school, we'd stopped, and we hadn't heard anything about each other for at least the past five years. For that matter, it was a senseless correspondence, between worlds that didn't have much to say to each other.

Olivia would write to inform me of the most absurd kinds of things, such as, for instance, that she'd won a prize for The Best Manger Scene of the School: she'd stuck Jesus, Joseph, and Mary into an aquarium and, in place of the Ass and the Ox, an orange goldfish "*as wrinkled as Reagan*" and a white goldfish "*with a birthmark on its forehead like Gorbachev's.*" It was 1986, it was a quick fix. In a private school, of course. The awards panel, made up of Jesuits, had simply dissolved in ecstasy, out of the hundred submissions they'd chosen hers because it was "a relevant and timely work of art, a celebration of Peace on Earth." Even though the fish in question had died horrible deaths, poor things. Unfortunately the fishbowl was heavy, she had to change the water every day, and one morning the whole manger scene had slipped through her fingers, just as the bell was ringing, while the students were rushing out of the classrooms, and that was the end of the two heroes of the Cold War. A massacre, no two ways about it. Reagan, gasping, had skidded along the marble floor to the door of the principal's office, and none other than the principal himself had crushed it underfoot ("*Squish, flattened by his loafer*"). Gorbachev had tumbled down the stairs, trampled beneath the feet of a horde of elementary-grade kids, rushing to meet their mothers ("*And we'll never know the name of Gorbachev's killer*").

In other letters, she'd tell me that now Manon took her on holiday to Monte Carlo, Versilia was too crowded with memories. After her grandfather's death, they'd sold the house and bought a new one on the Côte d'Azur.

Olivia filled page after page with her thoughts about Arabs, a topic that seemed to be of special interest to her. "*The Arabs are ALL extremely wealthy,*" she explained to me, "*they have 100-meter yachts, with helicopters on deck and gold faucets in the bathrooms. My grandmother says that even though they're absolutely swimming in crude oil, they're still just jumped-up hicks. She's all for the Persians, who are descendants of Cyrus and Darius, and there's no mistaking the fact, because they're so much more elegant. She says that the Persians are right to call the Arabs rat-eaters.*" Olivia was somewhat confused about it all and couldn't seem to reconcile the stories that Manon told her about the war between Iran and Iraq, being waged furiously in those years, with the port of Monte Carlo that lay before her ("*But to me, actually, the Persians seem worse, because they send children out to fight the enemy with the keys to Paradise around their necks. The others might be unlettered oafs, but they send their children on vacation aboard yachts*").

With the same degree of focus and commitment she described the matrons that she met at the Beach Club, "*with an emerald ring on one finger, curlers in their hair covered with a Dior silk scarf, and sequin-spangled swimsuits,*" women whose faces were frozen into immobility because they'd had too many face-lifts (*"Manon says that they'd be willing to have their belly buttons stitched to their ears"*), capable of pulling a diamond necklace out of their purse while searching for a pack of cigarettes (*"Oh, how do you like that, there it is after all! I thought I'd lost it on the beach yesterday"*). Ladies who gambled from dawn to dusk every day out of boredom (*"Manon doesn't like to gamble, she'd rather read. But her girlfriends are actually sick. Last week, Carlina spent 48 hours sitting in front of a slot machine: her husband, not seeing her return home, was about to call the police. Signora Talamoni forgot her poodle, just left it sitting on the sidewalk in front of the casino. Poor dog, it was about to die of thirst"*).

The world of the Côte d'Azur inspired her to write very long letters, perhaps in part because she felt so alone there. She talked to me about little girls who lived on a large, three-masted yacht.

"They looked like two angels, fair-haired, with headbands and little white dresses. They invited me to play on their boat and then proceeded to torture me for the rest of the afternoon. They took me to see their aquarium, then they told me it was full of piranhas and forced me to stick my hand in the water. Then they threw me into the netting that's wrapped around the tip of the boat. I tossed and turned under the bowsprit like a trapped tuna, until one of the crew came to free me. My grandmother says they're bad little children because they're the daughters of a gentleman who sells arms. Manon hates people who sell arms,

*she refuses even to say hello to them. Sometimes they try to in-
vite her to a party, but she won't go."*

Every so often she'd give me the latest news about her
family. She'd tell me that her uncle and her father were no
longer speaking *"on account of the inheritance."* That her
uncle had bought a chocolate factory (*"Last month he invited
my class to come tour his factory. My classmates vomited the
whole time, the smell was so strong"*). She didn't seem especially worried about the quarrel between them (*"I mean, can
you believe it? Now I can have all the chocolate I want for free"*)
even though at the end of one letter, she did confess, a bit
sadly: *"You know, ever since my grandfather died, absolutely
everything has changed."*

But Manon pretended everything was perfectly normal.
She asked for very little from her sons, after all: Giulio and
Dado were free to communicate exclusively through their lawyers if they wished, but not on Sundays. When they were at
their mother's house, they were expected to reel it in, and say:
"Why, this risotto is delicious, Mama." Or else "What a lovely
spring day, when are we going to open the swimming pool?"

In the same spirit, Manon would pretend that she'd completely forgotten that Dado was a homosexual (*"Papa says
that my uncle is a queer and Mama gets mad at him because
you're supposed to say that they're gay. But in front of my grandmother, we're not supposed refer to the subject at all"*). Manon
had constructed a complicated theater piece on the subject
with her son, a bit of playacting so intricate and complex

that it supposedly made up for the absence of any genuine intimacy: every time she saw Dado she'd ask if he'd finally found a girlfriend. This persistence was so imbued with caricature that it verged on playfulness. A perverse game, somewhat sadistic, smacking of the exchanges of a couple: closer to a form of erotic foreplay than genuine, full-blown torture.

"*Every now and then Manon will introduce him to a young woman, usually the daughter of friends of hers. 'That girl is a catch, you should marry her,' she'll say. And Dado will invite her out to dinner, just to make Manon happy. The next day he'll call her on the phone and make her laugh and laugh, telling her all the things that are wrong with the girl he took out the night before. 'The whole evening was a disaster, Mama. You have no idea. She absolutely reeked . . . She must have some kind of a problem with her sweat glands, the poor thing.' 'Why, no! Anna's daughter? Dado, don't be a fool.' 'I swear it.' Manon has the time of her life.*"

I could perfectly imagine Manon's low-timbred laugh, similar to an elegant, masked cough, and Dado's flattened, drawn-out vowels, the way he loved to stretch out a word ("She *reeeked*. I *sweeeaaar*").

The same technique was used to deny the marital crisis then unfolding between Giulio and Elena ("*Mama is always traveling. Right now she's in Indonesia with her girlfriends. If you ask me, she's bored in Bologna. I have a sneaking suspicion that Papa has a lover because, when he's at home, he spends hours on the phone in the evening. And not with my mother, though that's the way he tells it, because both of them are far too stingy. When they talk to each other in my presence, the whole conversation lasts two minutes tops, they're just afraid of spending money"*). Given Manon's lack of warmth toward Elena, it would have been simple to imagine an intervention of some sort on her part, or at least a stinging comment or two. But no, Manon took great care not to utter a word on the subject. For one very simple reason: she was afraid that a divorce might create a gulf between Olivia and Giulio, and therefore between Olivia and Manon. Her granddaughter absolutely had to remain in the villa next door to hers until she was married. Then—she had already thought it through—they could even divide the big villa into two apartments, one for her, who, having reached and passed her seventieth year, certainly had no need of tens of thousands of square feet, and the other for Olivia and her children. So for now, Manon was throwing water on the flames. Whenever Giulio complained to her about his wife, testing the terrain to see if there was an opening, Manon, without batting an eyelash, would play the role of the wise old woman, with a series of undisputable pat phrases. "Sweetheart, marriages require patience," or else "You should give each other some personal space, if you think that might help." That sort of thing, idle conversational gambits that could easily be interrupted with trivial excuses. "There's too much egg in this pastry cream," or else "That green sweater suits you perfectly."

BUT I HAD the hardest time writing back. What could I tell her about in exchange? That I'd set up a snack racket of my own and it was thriving? The littler kids offered me their Girella cookies, in exchange for my protection. So what? How would she ever be able to understand that this was a major achievement? And if I'd told her that I wound up caught between the bars of a wrought-iron fence, luckily my arm and not my whole body, while I was trying to steal roses from the neighbors for my mother's birthday, what on earth would she think of me? How could I explain to her that they sent me out to wash dishes at Pippanera's pizzeria to help make ends meet? She'd never be able to understand that I was proud of the fact that I was now a member of a band of older boys, known as the Vicolo dei Persi—the Alley of the Wrecked—because everyone there got high from morning to night. Or explain to her that the guy who sits next to me in class regularly brings hash to school, and that when I got in a fight with the Italian literature teacher, I broke two of his ribs while trying to protect this friend of mine who was trading punches with him: no, too complicated. So I'd tear a sheet of paper out of my notebook, and start a letter—"*Dear Olivia*"—and before I knew it I was crumpling the paper in my fist, transforming it into a tight little ball that I could toss into the wastepaper basket from around the room: a perfect shot, nothing but net.

At a certain point, I just gave up trying. The Berlin Wall had only recently come down, but in my mind that year marked another turning point, almost more important, because I'd just changed schools, leaving behind me middle school and a crumbling educational institution on the outskirts of town, and transferring to a high school with a prestigious name, inside the Aurelian Walls. The transition, by no means a gentle one, forced me to evolve, and to summon all my energy. I no longer had either the time or the inclination to look back.

What's more, Olivia's last letter, which dated back to the Christmas holidays of 1989, had greatly irritated me. Suddenly, Olivia was no longer a little girl, and she'd put on an annoying, typically adolescent tone, which no longer amused me in the slightest.

"Hey, how's it going? I'm doing great. I'm in Cortina and I'm having the time of my life. I like a guy who's older than me. He's a paninaro and he's in high school. He doesn't even know I exist, but I can live with that. He's horrible looking, his hair is smeared with gel and he has an enormous nose, my grandmother shuddered with disgust when she saw him. I go every afternoon to the video arcade to meet him, but it's pointless. Unfortunately, he already has a gorgeous girlfriend who's seventeen. I don't have a chance."

Why was she bothering to tell me these things? What else could she still want from me?

3

FIREWORKS

THE ROAD LEADING UP to the villa was illuminated by candles, though I'd have preferred pitch darkness. In front of me there was a procession of convertibles and sporty two-seaters. Fuck, I'd told my father. Better to show up in a taxi. No, not at all, he had insisted. You can use my car, what do you need a taxi for? Sure, a beat-up old Fiat Uno, with the bumper half hanging off because a next-door neighbor didn't know how to park. One time she'd crushed his side door, another time his trunk. And my father, incapable of showing anger to the world at large, had practically apologized to her. Oh, no, don't think twice, it hardly matters. ("What can you do, it breaks my heart, she insists on continuing to drive, even though her eyesight is basically gone." "I under-stand, Papa, but she must have an insurance policy." "With all the damage she does, they keep raising her premiums, poor thing. I don't want to take it out on her.")

A gentleman in uniform, standing in the middle of the lawn, was showing the guests where to park. When he waved to me to come on ahead, a wave of shame swept over me. Oh my God, what must he think of me, with this beat-up old Fiat. In certain situations, you might be more afraid of the servants than of the masters. Because you can't fool them. I rolled down my window and smiled at him.

"Is this all right?" My elbow stuck out of the car window, and I was trying to make up for my inadequacy with a brash manner. I revved the engine of my little car, just for the plea-sure of the noise it made, as if I were pressing down on the accelerator of a Ferrari.

He tried to get a better bearing on me, bending severely forward and turning a flashlight straight into my face—a party crasher? Nervously, I tugged at the bow tie of my tuxedo. There's something about me that's not adding up, I decided.

"Valerio?"

I stuck my neck out the car window. He was the Mor-ganti family chauffeur, whom we had dubbed the Authority, because he would spout out his opinions during our dinners in the kitchen, hypnotizing one and all with his stories over-flowing with plots and conspiracy theories.

He was a hardline Communist, and he'd churn out pro-paganda, even to us four-year-old kids. After the elections in June 1979, when the Socialists gained in credibility and the Communists took a historic shellacking, he'd decided to focus all his energy on the younger generations. "Communism is super-simple, children," he'd explain to us, "if you have two swimsuits, then you just give one to someone who doesn't have any." Olivia just loved these kind of lectures, which we were also treated to at the parish church. Only she was very particular about hygiene and, especially, obsessed with other people's saliva. In fact, she wouldn't even drink from her own mother's glass without first wiping off the edge of the glass with a napkin. Therefore, before promising that she would vote for Berlinguer, she'd done her best to get more detailed information: "So, if I have an ice cream cone, do I have to let everyone else lick it?" Her own personal fear of Communism, which took the form of a series of wet tongues authorized to slobber all over a pistachio ice cream cone, had greatly amused the grown-ups, domestics, and homeowners, militants and Christian Democrats. They all laughed, with broad and shared understanding.

I got out and threw my arms around him: "Ugo! It's been such a long time..."

"Let me take a look at you, Valerio. Jesus Christ, you've become a man!" He walked around me, contented.

"A man, huh? You may be overstating the case. And how about you? You haven't changed a bit."

"*Mo va' là*," he replied dismissively in dialect, "I've put on a gut—*una buzza*," slapping both hands on his belly. "I'm almost seventy years old, you know. How is your father?"

"He's in good shape," I replied through clenched teeth. I'd just seen him, looking run-down, fat, and puffy, drinking cheap wine every evening in front of the television set to keep from feeling too miserably lonely.

"Give him my regards and tell him to come visit us in Budrio, I have a Nocino that my wife makes that's just spectacular. And if he comes on a Sunday, Marisa will make *tagliatelle al ragù*. Do you remember Marisa's *tagliatelle*?"

"Of course I do."

"Oh, now you're a grown-up, too. So make sure you vote. I'm serious."

"Certainly!" I replied, and gave him a wink.

My first experience voting, actually, wouldn't come until the next year, in the spring of 1994, when the Italian people would overwhelmingly acclaim the candidacy of Silvio Berlusconi, inaugurating the Second Italian Republic. But no one could have known that that's the way it would go. Aside from my Emilian childhood and education, with a bright red, leftist political preference by very definition, I had grown up in the only Roman *borgata* that was historically and traditionally left-wing, and I had no need to be told how to vote.

"Well, now you'd better run along, Valerio. You're late, you know. They've already served the buffet, if you don't get moving you won't have a bite to eat, those locusts won't leave a crumb for you. You're so skinny, you're all skin and bones. If my wife could only see you."

In fact it was ten o'clock. Because before I could work up the nerve to drive through that gate, I'd driven the circuit of the hills above Bologna not once but four times, listening to Lucio Battisti and using up all the gas in my father's Fiat Uno's tank. As I drove, I sang out loud like an idiot, too. *A fari spenti nella note . . . Tu chiamale se vuoi emozioni, mmm.* (With my headlights out, driving through the night . . . You can call them emotions, mm-hmm.)

"All right then, I'd better get going. Ciao. It was a pleasure to see you." I couldn't seem to drag myself away.

"Go." He waved his hand in a broad sweep. "And vote the right way!"

But I wasn't destined to arrive until much later. Because at the entrance I ran into the cook, who was manning the coat check that evening. She would take your overcoat and give you a number in exchange, just like at the discotheque. But I didn't have a coat of any kind, because it was May. Only the young women were handing her shawls and scarves, which had to be carefully stowed away, to keep from ruining their décolleté.

"Valerio?" Incredulous.

I was a little annoyed: I'd hoped that I'd become a grown-up, and therefore radically different. But everyone recognized me at first glance. There really was no getting away from myself.

"Nana?" I hugged her back.

Nana would heap a burst of words all over you and with her Tuscan accent she'd aspirate you away, with all those breathy *h* sounds, in a whirlwind of quite tangled chitchat. She was allergic to names and nouns, preferring to use

"whatsit" or "whosis" or "what's-her-name," all fairly indis-
criminately. And you'd be forced to guess from the context.
The "whatsit upstairs" was the party. "Whosis over there"
was the chauffeur. The "what's-her-name who watched you
grow up" could have been either the nanny or Manon herself.

"Give me the whatsit." I handed her the gift. "Is there a
card? If not, I'll have to write your name on the giftwrap, because what's-her-name won't open her gifts till tomorrow and
she wants to be sure she can thank everyone." She pulled a
felt-tip pen out of her pocket. "So how's whosis?"

"My papa? He's fine, thanks."

Christ, I really had come home. My legs were shaking.
Luckily my mother hadn't taken in Costantino's tuxedo too
much, and she'd left some room for my excitement.

While I was climbing the stairs, a woman came running down in the opposite direction, slightly out of breath,
and bumped into me. At first we both apologized, hastily.
Then she looked up: she studied me, trying to place my
face, remember where she'd seen me before. I recognized
her, even if she was now an attractive thirty-year-old, rather
sophisticated.

"Nanny?"

Cecilia narrowed her eyes, as if she were nearsighted,
trying to summon up my identity. Was I someone who had
attended elementary school with Olivia? A long-lost cousin?

"It's me, Valerio," I stammered.

"Valerio who?"

Now my feelings were hurt.

"Olivia's Valerio?" she asked me a moment later.

Irritated by that definition of my person, I hardly knew what to say. In the course of a few seconds, Cecilia had already thrown both arms around my neck and was kissing me on the cheeks.

"Oh my God, Valerio! How handsome you've become," and she looked me up and down, from head to foot. "So you came after all, we'd really given up hoping."

Oh, hell. *Répondez s'il vous plaît*: I'd completely forgotten.

Caught in the anguish of responding, actually seriously responding, I hadn't so much as made a phone call.

Cecilia took me by the hand and dragged me to the kitchen, she wanted me to come with her so we could make a phone call to her husband. Her daughter had a fever of 104. She certainly couldn't miss Olivia's birthday party, another daughter of hers in a certain sense, but she was still anxious and concerned.

"I married a physician. And still I can't stop worrying."

She gripped me tight by the arm, she wanted to know all the latest news, and that with a certain frantic quality: about her daughter and about me, at the same time, and with the same urgency.

"Has she already taken the drops?" She held the receiver away from her head for a moment. "Which high school are you attending, Valerio?" She listened to both answers simultaneously and then immediately fired back: "Classical high school? Well, good for you. Did she eat the pablum? And are you going to enroll at the university? Majoring in what?"

The topic was of keen interest to her, maybe because she identified with my prospects. She, too, had managed to secure her high school diploma, by attending night school. And while she was pregnant, she'd made up her mind to enroll in the university, even though she was already thirty years old.

"To become a teacher myself," she told me, with pride in her voice. "A degree from teacher's college might not be particularly useful, but it doesn't matter to me. I haven't taken a lot of exams, because with a daughter of my own, you can imagine. But it's so nice to study."

After the phone call we went up together, using the back stairs that ran out to the garden, more or less by the portico. Cecilia sat down on an Etruscan sarcophagus that Manon had filled with cyclamens, and we started chatting.

"You could at least have sent me a postcard, Valerio."

I explained that in the past nine years, I hadn't gone anywhere to send a postcard from.

Then she rummaged through her purse and pulled out a picture of her daughter, to show me.

In the background of that picture, I saw Manon's unforgettable boudoir and was more captivated by that than by the sight of the little girl. You could see the eighteenth-century table upon which Manon kept her lipsticks and rouges, the large mirror framed in gilt scrollwork, the blond wall-to-wall carpeting, the wallpaper with its busy flowered pattern, and the ottoman where she'd sit, erect and focused, with a hairnet on her head, doing her makeup. Olivia and I, when we

were small, would watch hypnotized by her preparations, rapt
and motionless, finally budging only when Manon threw a
light cape over her shoulders to keep from getting smudges
on her dress, and then proceeded to tease her hair with an
ivory comb. The smell of hairspray meant that the elaborate
operation we found so utterly seductive was finally over and
she was ready to leave the house.

I was dying to hear news about the Morganti family.
Perhaps Cecilia knew something, since she still saw them
regularly.

She lit a cigarette and explained that, leaving aside the
spectacular celebrations, these were difficult times for the
Morgantis.

"Yes, I heard."

"We're waiting for the trial. But Signor Morganti is still
behind bars, to prevent any chance of manipulating the evidence, they say. That came as a tough blow to Olivia. And
her mother is next to no help at all, obviously."

"Why not? Isn't she well?"

Cecilia shook her head. "She has that drinking problem."

"Elena?" Incredulously, I asked, "She's an alcoholic?"

In a low voice, she told me that Elena was in the other
room, unfortunately, and that it was her job to look after her.
Olivia had asked her this favor.

"Let's hope she's not already drunk. She's capable of
dancing on the dining room tables with a boy her daughter's
age, if I don't keep a constant watch on her."

I listened to her, eyes wide open. I really was having a hard time picturing Elena as some latter-day Zelda Fitzgerald. Elena, always so silent and composed, so compliant and conformist and fearful of what other people might think of her. What had happened to her? But Cecilia had no time to talk.

"I'm sorry, I have to get back to her." Again, frantic and out of breath, she gathered purse and shawl. "Let's hope things go smoothly, at least this evening."

I stood up alongside her. Maybe the time had come to wade into the fray.

"Olivia is going to be happy to see you. It wouldn't have been the party she's been dreaming of, if you weren't here."

In the living room, Manon enjoyed dominant pride of place. Standing in the doorway, I looked at her. How pretty she was. She could even afford to wear a white dress, just like her debutante granddaughter. She was seventy years old, and she cast a shadow over the fresh-faced young does that clustered around her, all of them struck dumb with admiration and anxious to learn the mysteries of seduction that she had so completely mastered. They even stood very erect, shoulders thrown back, in an effort to rival her regal bearing. The young men, intimidated, buzzed around her at a safe distance. The most shameless among them tried to kiss the back of her hand, and Manon laughed, though with a hint of annoyance. Good heavens, what buffoons. I could read that thought in her cocked eyebrow.

I slowly approached her, cautiously extending my hand. I was a little scared. What if she doesn't recognize me? Instead her face lit up.

"Valerio?"

Eminently courteous, amiable, she lavished me with attention, far more than anything I'd been expecting. With a half-turn from the waist, she abandoned the little crowd that had been boring her and instead spoke directly to me.

"Tell me everything, I'm all ears," she said. She was happy to learn that my mother had enrolled me in the classical high school. "So they'll let you study the *Divine Comedy*. Excellent, that's excellent. Do you remember when I made little puppets for you with the characters out of Dante?"

How could I ever forget that little cardboard puppet theater and Manon on her knees on the hardwood floor, hidden behind it, both arms raised, staging the story of Paolo and Francesca.

"Of course I remember."

Her enthusiasm for me was understandable; after all, I was an eyewitness to that golden age to which I often and willingly harkened back in my thoughts. When her husband was still alive and we all vacationed together in Versilia, when Olivia was small and always turned to her for help, when her sons were still speaking to each other, and Giulio was a young industrialist on the rise and Dado was studying in America, letting his parents imagine who could say what future, and Elena was still staying in her place, trying to learn from Manon how to behave. I really hadn't been looking to make her cry.

"I'm such a fool, I'm starting to tear up. What a stupid old woman I am."

Had she become so fragile? Manon apologized, dabbing at her eyes and trying to laugh it off, to make fun of herself a little, but it was no good. Without at all meaning to, I had unleashed an inferno inside her. So much so that she'd been forced to hurry upstairs, to redo her makeup. I stood there, frozen. I was uneasy because people were looking at me, wondering who I was and what I'd done to make Signora Morganti burst into tears like that.

At that exact moment, Olivia appeared. She was striding briskly toward the portico, holding hands with a girlfriend. Suddenly she stopped and turned her head in my direction.

"Astrid," she said. "It's the little boy I fell in love with. I have to introduce you."

Her friend, yanked unexpectedly in my direction, barely kept from tripping over her high heels.

I raised a hand in greeting.

"Ciao, Astrid."

I looked at Olivia and Olivia looked at me. I still couldn't say exactly what flashed between our eyes in those few seconds. Neither one of us seemed capable of opening our mouths. Then she broke out laughing, loudly.

"Aren't you cute in a tuxedo, you still look like a fool, the way you did when you used to go to Calvi's niece's birthday parties." Another burst of noisy laughter. She lifted a swatch of cloth with two fingers, calling my attention to her Pauline Bonaparte dress: "You can't begin to imagine how badly this fucking thing *itches*."

She turned her back on poor Astrid, who still hadn't managed to get out a word, and took me by the hand.

"Come on, let's take a spin around the party. I'll introduce you to some folks. Tonight everybody must have fun."

She hadn't changed all that much, actually. Her hairstyle made her look a bit like a bride, and it had certainly cost her hours and hours at the hairdresser's, bobby pin after bobby pin—but it was already half collapsed, dangling askew down the back of her neck. Despite the refined elegance of her dress, she hardly seemed to have stepped out of a painting by Gérard or a sculpture by Canova: she strode with determination, taking long steps, but also with a certain lack of coordination, as if she were wearing a pair of mountain hiking boots and not a pair of sandals made to measure, with the same material and the same embroidery as her dress. Every so often she'd adjust the collier necklace her grandmother had given her for the occasion, the way a dog scratches its collar. And she often shook her head, because she had no idea how to manage the weight of her earrings, which dangled to her shoulders.

"Look, there's Calvi's niece. She's turned into quite the babe, so I'm not going to introduce you, because I'm jealous. And look, there's Jacopo, remember him? He's the kid you taught how to blow up dog shit."

With one excuse or another, she didn't introduce me to anyone, or else she'd drag me into the midst of a small knot of people, quickly rattling off a series of names, often strange ones, or names assembled with a perverse burst of imagination—Esmeralda, Olimpia, Gianbattista, Pierfrancesco, Mariasole, Guiberto, Lucetta, Orsetta, Altea—and then she'd quickly say: "This is my friend, Valerio" and suddenly whisk me off toward some new Ginevramaria or a Simonluca.

I would just say to each, "Ciao."

That alone was enough to make me feel like a trained monkey, but still, I was a happy young man. Because Olivia continued holding me by the hand.

"But my real friend is Astrid. Huh, what became of her, anyway?"

"You dumped her in the other room."

"Oh, yeah, you're right, poor thing. Let's go see if we can find her."

But the search for Astrid was just an excuse: a short while later we fetched up in the garden. Far from the lights of the portico and even of the torches, Olivia continued walking on the lawn, her fingers intertwined with mine. Now she wanted to sit down on a bench amongst the lemon trees and take off her shoes for a moment, because she couldn't stand wearing high heels any longer. My heart was thumping, racing. What did she expect? A kiss? Or was I supposed to act like an old friend? Bent over, as she rubbed her feet, I didn't know what to say. *Valerio, what kind of a man are you?*

I'd only had one girlfriend, and come to think of it, maybe she hadn't even really been a proper girlfriend because, the next day, she'd pretended she didn't remember a thing. That was the full and complete extent of my experience: this Ludovica, who, during a party in Costantino's house in Fregene, with the excuse that she was deliriously drunk after downing one rum and Coke, had kissed me in the room where we'd all left our overcoats. And so, sprawled out on down coats and hats and scarves, I'd managed to get a hand inside her panties and then I'd even got my mouth down there, licking her for a little while, even though she laughed the whole time as if I was tickling her. Something I'd masturbated to for months afterward, as if who knows what had happened. We hadn't gone any further than that because Ludovica had a steady boyfriend. She'd confessed that to me, while she was searching for her panties, which had vanished under a mountain of jackets.

"You know, I'm still a virgin," Olivia told me, still massaging her feet. "In theory, I have a boyfriend, we've been dating for a few months and I promised him that after I turned eighteen we could make love, but I really don't feel like it. I don't feel like doing it with him, is what I mean."

"Starting *tomorrow*, you mean to say," I stammered with legalistic precision, worried about the deadline, unable to focus on any other details of the conversation.

"That's right, starting tomorrow. But maybe he figures midnight is technically the starting point, I couldn't say."

"So you're saying you have another half-hour of virginity, right?"

"Right," she replied, shooting me a glance.

I'd understood, but I didn't know how to handle the situation. I rocked my shoulders back and forth, twisting my fingers in embarrassment. Then Olivia turned around and stroked my nose.

"Could you do it without ruining my dress? Afterward, I'm going to have to cut the cake and dance waltzes."

This challenge, I mean, keeping the dress intact, worried me greatly.

"What if we stain it?"

"Oh, we just have to be careful. We could lie down on your jacket, for instance. After all, it's black."

"Ah, good point."

Instead of kissing her immediately, I sat there thinking how glad I was that I didn't have to return the tuxedo to Costantino and other things like that. While waiting to hear what I had to say, Olivia was humming the Beatles' "I Want to Hold Your Hand." A song that would later become our personal soundtrack, in the cover by Cathy Berberian.

Olivia had a nice voice. She wasn't off-key like Manon, who even butchered the *Hallelujah* when she took us to Mass on Sunday morning, beautiful, erect, in her mink coat, always in the front pew as if it were the royal box at the opera. She'd remove her leather gloves and take our hands—her long fingers with the well-tended nails were icy, but we held them all the same and sang with her, doing our best to cover up her flat notes.

Suddenly I remembered the task that had been set me. With a certain solemnity I placed a hand on the back of her neck, where various hair clips hung, and I bent over to give her a kiss. But then the fireworks went off. Olivia leaped to her feet.

"Oh, Jesus, I'd better get going. They must be looking for me. Manon has prepared some insanely grandiose production, she's willing to burn the villa to the ground for me. If I miss the show, her feelings will be hurt. Oh, Jesus, oh, Jesus, there's no time to waste."

And while the spectacular fountains of light were bursting over the three-century-old cedars of Lebanon, charring a few branches that had survived all the various wars but not Olivia's birthday party, I thought to myself that I'd just missed my great opportunity.

I HAD MINGLED with the crowd, watching Olivia as she got ready to blow out eighteen birthday candles surrounded by her girlfriends, holding hands with the usual Astrid, her favorite. Then someone touched my shoulder. I whipped around, in part because I was scared. That touch didn't seem like a greeting, and the person in question was leaning on me with all their weight. It was Elena, and she could barely stay up on her feet.

I was trying to contain my astonishment at seeing the condition she'd been reduced to, but I probably didn't do much of a job of it, because she mumbled out a series of phrases, as if angered.

"What, don't you recognize me? So I got fat, so what? The Morganti family always has to be attractive, slender, and youthful, believe me, I know. But I'm not really one of them."

"Signora, you are always, invariably..." I couldn't think of a single nice thing to say to her.

Her face was so puffy that her features were distorted. Her eyes were a pair of bubbles wobbling around narrow slits, and every so often her hair would slide over them, no longer blond as honey, but stringy and dyed. She was only fifty, but she looked at least ten years older.

I struggled to put a smile on my face and tried to encourage her to look at the cake, as everyone else was doing, to take in her daughter as she blew out the candles, possibly making a wish as she did so. But that sideshow was of no interest to her.

"I know, I know," she kept saying, "I'm ruining their reputation, looking fat like this. Winding up behind bars is nothing in comparison, believe me. Everyone still thinks the world of my husband, for example. Much worse to be overweight, you know?" And she staggered and swayed, sloshing her glass of red wine all over the other guests, who moved away from her in annoyance.

I was very embarrassed, and I didn't know what to say.

"I did it on purpose, though," she was saying. "I got fat because I knew how it would annoy the Morgantis. I wanted to shame them." She laughed, unsteady on her feet.

Meanwhile Olivia, to a round of applause, was cutting the cake. Champagne corks popped in the air. And the birthday girl's friends, bottles in hand, were spraying people like Grand Prix champions celebrating on the podium.

"Aren't they wonderful?" Elena cheered sarcastically, spilling more wine on her neighbors' shoulders. "I think they're little assholes, don't you? They think they're proving some point by using champagne bottles as if they were lawn sprinklers. They think of themselves as gods who've been exonerated by their very fall. I put the blame entirely on their mothers, for raising them this way. I've always told my daughter the way things are, loud and clear. Life isn't . . ."

But just then "The Blue Danube Waltz" started up, summoning the guests into the living room, and she veered away from that line of conversation.

"Humph, time to start dancing," she laughed. "The debutante is bound to follow tradition, far be it from me to interfere. Even if she has to dance a waltz with that queer uncle of hers because her father is in prison, and doesn't exactly enjoy full freedom of movement. Well, it is what it is." She wheeled around, mimicking the steps of a waltz. "One-two-three, tra-la-la."

I was upset to see her looking so angry and disputatious, as if she were the one who'd just turned eighteen.

"Valerio, would you take me home, please?"

Maybe Olivia had taken it badly, Elena hadn't even gone over to give her a kiss or wish her happy birthday, not a single kind gesture. Or maybe that was just a relief for her daughter; at least this way, Olivia wasn't worried she might have to watch her mother dance drunkenly with her classmates or find her vomiting in some bathroom, being helped to her feet by some of Olivia's girlfriends from school.

"Well, actually I—"

"It's just a matter of getting across the grounds, but it's dark out and these high heels are hurting my feet."

I was at my wit's end, this was certainly the last thing I'd expected. The clock had just struck midnight, and I had a small piece of unfinished business to tend to, rather time-sensitive.

"Don't be mean, Valerio. After you drop me off you can hurry back to the party and have all the fun you want."

Meanwhile she was dragging me toward the door, without leaving me time to wish Olivia a happy birthday and explain that I'd be right back, just a matter of minutes.

It ought to have taken no time at all, there and back in a flash, in my beat-up old Fiat Uno. Two minutes to get to the end of the road, two more minutes to get Olivia's mother out of the car and up her front steps, and then another minute and a half to get back, in fifth gear. I'd never have dreamed that Elena would pass out, sick to her stomach, just as she was unlocking the door, and that I'd be spending the rest of the night at the emergency room.

When I realized that she'd stopped breathing, that she was pale, her eyes rolling up out of sight and her eyelids trembling, I was seized by a wave of panic. I tried to shake her, bring her out of it with little slaps in the face, but it was no good. What was I supposed to do now? Disappoint Olivia by failing to keep that promise, or let her mother die? I couldn't even speed her over to the hospital and drop her off and then rush back to the party as if nothing had happened. Phone her daughter and ruin her birthday party? It was probably better to call her later, once the danger had passed.

"Are you a relative?" the doctors asked me.

"Why, uh, no. No, no I'm not, oh, I mean, listen," I answered in annoyance, and then I tried to clarify the situation.

To be perfectly frank, I wasn't much worried about Elena's state of health, seeing that she'd decided to choose Olivia's birthday party to bloom as a hardened alcoholic. Though I guess we owed her a debt of gratitude for not fainting a few minutes earlier, while the cake was being cut, in front of three hundred guests. She could just kick the bucket, as far as I was concerned. I rested my face in both hands, my jaw clenched in rage, my teeth cutting into my lip, in search of any kind of pain that would be easier to take than jealousy.

"Please just keep me posted on how the signora is doing. I'll be waiting out here."

Hunched over in a plastic chair, under the fluorescent lights of the Sant'Orsola Hospital, surrounded by people on gurneys who had been injured in car crashes and dying old men moaning and complaining, I listened to the noise of the fireworks still lighting up the hill, explosions that could be heard all the way out here, and I thought to myself that Olivia, not having found me, would by now have thrown herself into the arms of her official boyfriend, if only for revenge. And I would no longer be the first man in her life, I wouldn't get a chance to kiss her and make love to her in a dark corner of that beautiful garden illuminated by candles, while the DJ put an LP of a cover version of "Over the Rainbow" on the turntable.

4

THE PRESENT

I'D SPENT the whole rest of the night at the hospital, so the morning after I was a wreck. Luckily, my father had gone to work and couldn't ask me how the party had gone. I woke up around two in the afternoon, when the doorbell rang. I went to open the door, eyes half closed, scratching my underwear. Standing in front of me, with an embarrassed smile, was Olivia.

"Did I wake you up?"

"No, no, of course not."

"Am I intruding?"

In jeans, wearing a baggy sweater, her hair all tousled and still poufy from the hairspray that had been holding together

her elaborate updo, she looked very different from the night before. I almost hadn't recognized her. I have always been captivated by women's ability to change appearance and—with their appearance—their personalities to some extent as well, as if their spirits somehow matched their hairstyle. I wondered whether there was some subtle message I was expected to understand in all that sloppiness. Today I don't want you anymore? Sometimes one's soul is the master of one's attire, rather than the other way around. She hadn't even bothered to brush her hair, and that detail offended me, if ever so slightly. Not even the minimum effort of dabbing a bit of mascara on her eyelashes.

"Come right in."

Suddenly I realized I was standing there in my boxer shorts. There was very little to connect her disheveled state to some veiled rejection of me and the promises made the night before. I was naked: perhaps that also had some meaning.

"Let me go... I need to put on a pair of... hold on, I'll be right back."

"Certainly."

Olivia looked around, in search of a place to sit down. I was more ashamed of my father's apartment than I was of the fact that I'd opened the door to her in my underwear. The sofa was cluttered with a fruit crate, there was dirty laundry occupying the armchair, tossed there in the living room rather than in the hamper, one chair was stacked with old newspapers, and the stool was clearly unusable because one of the legs was stuck on with shiny brown moving tape.

"Sorry, here, let me clear a place for you." I lifted the crate full of yellow plums. "Go ahead, have a seat."

"Thanks." Meanwhile she was twisting her fingers, working at them, ferociously picking at the skin around her nails.

Sliding along on the floor in my socks—though the floor was anything but shiny and slippery, because my father wasn't much when it came to cleaning—I disappeared into the bathroom. As quick as I could, I washed my armpits and gave my shirt a quick sniff before putting it back on.

"Okay, here I am."

"No, it's just that, excuse me...I just wanted to thank you."

"For the picture frame?"

Olivia burst out laughing. "Oh, sure, I love that picture. I've already put it on my bedside table."

"Really?"

"Yes." She gazed at me sweetly. "You picked it specially, didn't you?"

I didn't have the nerve to tell her that it was my mother's work. "*It Snows for Us.*"

She laughed, and then silence descended over us. We were having a little difficulty getting in sync. We were teenagers, so we'd oscillate in an almost schizophrenic fashion between the most absolute aloofness and total verbal violence, between the fear of putting a name to anything and the desire to write our every last thought on a wall.

Sometimes I have the impression that the ages of our lives remain inside us for all time, and that maturity is nothing but the ability to recognize them inside us, those ages that never really pass, that will never belong to the past, ages that accumulate in the soul for the sheer pleasure of confusing us even more.

"It was very nice of you to take care of her," Olivia murmured, after a while. Women are always much braver than we men. She kept her eyes downcast, though, and she seemed unable to utter the word, either "Mother" or "Mama." Incapable of euphemisms or elliptical statements, she used her tongue primarily to run over her gums.

"Is she feeling any better today?" This wasn't the civility of good manners. It took just an ounce of common sense to understand that I could hurt her badly, if I used the wrong word.

"Yes, she is, thanks," still with her head bowed, still without looking at me. "I've just come from the hospital, they're going to keep her there for observation a few more days, that might give her a chance to rest up and give her liver a break."

"Would you like an espresso?"

Olivia shook her head: "Oh, it doesn't matter, I should really go now."

Suddenly I had a hunch. Sometimes you just need to stick your neck out. Poetic delicacy is no doubt a lovely thing, but it can tie your hands. When you dare, you may come off less elegantly, but you may get much farther.

"What if you and I got drunk right now, ourselves? After all, yesterday we didn't even get a chance to drink a toast."

She smiled, suddenly her face lit up. "Sure."

"Let me see what my father's got in his cabinets."

I got up, opened the sideboard, and pulled out a bottle of grappa, the only thing I found. Certainly, at two in the afternoon, it was hardly the ideal drink. Especially on an empty stomach. But it didn't really matter. I set it down on the table, with a thud to highlight the implied challenge, and I handed her a dull, opaque drinking glass that had never enjoyed the privilege of the sparkle induced by a rinse aid. Maybe the grappa would help us to converse more freely, and possibly about more intimate matters.

She looked at me curiously, without uttering a word.

At first, just to get loosened up, we talked about school and the subjects we would be tested on for our final high school exam. We had both skipped a year, so the time had finally come. She liked history and was a little worried about her ancient Greek translation, because she did better with modern languages.

"Me, too! Me, too!" I kept saying, contentedly. "I love history, too. So what period are you getting tested on?"

The enthusiasm that kids show whenever they can say "me, too" is heartbreaking. They're desperately trying to establish a personality all their own, unlike others, if possible entirely unique, and then they burst into frenzies of happiness as soon as they can unite with someone else their age.

"The French Revolution."

"I picked a revolution, too! The Russian Revolution, though."

Olivia had run her hands through her hair and she was supporting her temples like that, her hands tugging and stretching the flesh around her eyes. I so desired to kiss her. But instead I offered her a cigarette.

"I have my own, thanks. I keep them hidden inside my sanitary pads. You know, they really give me a hard time, if I try to smoke."

She reached into her bag and pulled out a crumpled Stayfree pad, inside of which was wrapped a Marlboro ten-pack. She seemed very proud of her little stratagem.

Just to shatter as many taboos as possible, she asked me for another dollop of grappa. She was starting to relax.

"I sure hope I don't wind up an alcoholic like my mother," she laughed. "People say it's hereditary."

"What on earth happened to her?"

"She just didn't know how to roll with the punches. My father's arrest was the crowning blow. But it all dates back earlier. Papa has been cheating on her ruthlessly for years, and she has a hard time overlooking it."

"Why doesn't she just divorce him?"

"That would certainly make more sense. A healthier re-action. Instead she started down this self-destructive path. As a way of destroying him, if you ask me. She realized that her weakness was the only power within reach."

Olivia had come to this conclusion: in order to humiliate the rest of them, Elena could only humiliate herself. She did everything within her power to make herself *unpresentable*, because all that was expected of her was *pure presence*.

"It's just a way of saying, 'No, I don't want this,' you un-derstand? I don't want to be a wife there for purposes of show, strictly useful for the formalities of succession. I don't want to be here for the sake of appearances, so I'm going to destroy everything that has to do with them. I'm going to become fat and ugly and I'm going to vomit in front of polite company. My psychologist tells me that this theory holds up, all things considered, but I don't know if she's right."

Elena simply couldn't resign herself to the absence of love, something that was becoming more unmistakable with the passing years. She talked to her husband about it, she did her best, but Giulio didn't know how to respond. ("What do you mean by love?" he'd ask her.)

"That's just the way my father is put together. There are some things he doesn't know how to talk about."

"Haven't you tried taking her to rehab?"

"If only it was that easy. She won't hear of it. But enough of that, I'm tired of talking about her. Did you have fun at my party?"

I burst out laughing. "It was nice enough, I guess."

"Oh, right, I guess I forgot," she laughed along with me.

I half-shrugged. "So did you keep your promise?"

"Not at all, I dumped him. While we were dancing the waltz, that way he couldn't make a scene."

"But why?"

"Because I was reminded of an old proverb: what you do on your birthday, you'll keep doing for the rest of the year."

"That's a proverb about New Year's Eve, not birthdays."

"That doesn't really matter: just to be safe, I decided not to run that risk. Especially if it's your eighteenth birthday, then I'd have to do something I don't want to for the rest of my years as an adult."

She was superstitious, like the rest of the Morgantis, who'd held university degrees as a generations-old tradition, whose very DNA was university-educated and certified, but who still could not tolerate hangers or hats on the bed, who stood frozen in place if a black cat crossed their path, and if salt happened to spill on the table, would toss three pinches hysterically over their shoulder. I kissed her.

But I was too worked up to fully enjoy the moment. I was afraid I wasn't kissing her well enough, not rising to her expectations. And the more I worried, the worse my teeth banged against hers. My panic lasted until the moment that she placed her hand between my legs. At that point, something odd happened: Olivia was no longer the little girl with whom I used to sit naked in the bathtub at age three, nor was she the attractive young woman from the night before, offering me her virginity with the same nonchalance as someone offering an ice cream cone, exciting me terribly. Suddenly, she was nothing. Because she was *everything*. She was all the countless women I would love in my life, good or bad, icy or sweet, absent or passionate, she was one person and a thousand people, both reality and fantasy: in short, an erection.

I tried to undo her jeans, tight and stiff, taken out of a washing machine without fabric softener just hours before. Olivia got to her feet: with a great effort, sighing as she strained, she managed to push her jeans down her hips, and then over her thighs. She was very sensual at that moment, perhaps because she was forgetting to be sensual in the face of a larger, logistical problem. When her jeans finally dropped to her ankles, the relief that I saw stamped on her face was so naive and pure and clean that I became even more aroused.

For a moment I was worried that the blanket my father had tossed onto the sofa, more like a blanket for dogs than anything else, was bothering her skin.

"Is that itchy for you?"

"No."

Maybe she had fears of her own, but I was becoming a man and I felt it clearly and urgently. I touched her with an assurance I'd never even suspected I could possess, my fingers endowed me with a new confidence, my first confidence as an adult male. Intoxicated by this discovery, I was determined to give her an unforgettable moment, even though I had no idea how.

"Can I do this? Do you want me to?"

"Yes."

I looked her in the eyes. It wasn't a gaze eager for possession, it was a gaze in search of something. But what? For a moment I was frightened: my instinct was already more complicated than I was. Then I calmed down and realized—by some visceral instinct, certainly not by knowledge and rational understanding—that the object of our love is just that way: the sum of elusive phantoms which you'd do best not to examine too closely. The correct sum at a given moment, no more and no less.

5

THE COUNTRY THAT I LOVE

"ITALY IS THE COUNTRY *that I love. Here I have my roots, my hopes, my horizons. Here I learned my profession as a business-man, from my father and from life. Here I obtained my passion for liberty . . ."*

"Oh fuck off."

A slipper in the forehead. A terry-cloth slipper, luckily. It was January 26, 1994. While Berlusconi was speaking to the Italians, launching his first famous video message, Olivia and I were having a fight. The television set in the living room was playing, but we weren't listening to it. We were too caught up in other matters.

"All right, then, go to Paris. Go right ahead. Ciao."

I waited for her to leave my room, arms folded across my chest. I had enrolled in the University of Bologna so I could be with her, at nights I worked in a downtown pub to pay the rent on an apartment I shared with other students. And now she wanted to leave for France.

"Don't be like this, Valerio. Please don't. We're twenty years old, if we expect to spend the rest of our lives together, we need to give each other some space."

"Hey, I'm not objecting to you having a night out with your girlfriends. You're talking about going to live in another country, I don't know if I make my point. This isn't taking a little space, this is a thousand kilometers. Listen, it's possible to study art here, too, you know. Just because you want to change your major doesn't mean you necessarily have to emigrate."

At first, Olivia had battled fiercely to make it clear to her father that her future belonged to her, and that she had every right to choose it for herself, but it had never really taken. Giulio refused to argue the point. He had a very specific plan in mind and no one could change his plotted course, not even Manon. "Just let her study whatever she wants," his mother would tell him, "after all, she's a woman, she'll find a husband capable of looking after our business." But Giulio didn't trust strangers, least of all any hypothetical husband of Olivia's, certainly not a husband who didn't yet exist. He was basing himself on established facts: he had no son, and that meant the girl was going to have to live up to her responsibilities and stand ready to take over as successor to the company, which he was determined not to turn over to that queer brother of his, even if it killed him.

For a few months, Olivia had obeyed and she'd enrolled in the Economics Department. She went to class, got bored, and pretended to study for a major oral exam. Then a minor event, which had nothing to do with her future as a businesswoman, finally convinced her to rebel.

Giulio had left prison apparently unchanged from when he went in. But only apparently. He was the same highly controlled, chilly man as before, utterly devoted to his work, to which he had returned as if nothing had happened. He hadn't changed any of his habits. Two espressos and a freshly squeezed orange juice in the morning, then off to the office in a dark blue car with a driver. Meetings, conferences, phone calls, banks, and construction sites, discussions with the labor unions, business lunches, appointments with politicians, planes and trains, but only for the day, because he didn't like sleeping in hotels. And then, in the evening, society dinners and cocktail parties, to cultivate the right business relationships, parties he went to alone now, because his wife, already completely drunk by midafternoon, was usually fast asleep, snoring sloppily, by eight o'clock.

The only thing about Giulio that was new was a different glimmer in his eyes. It was the need to fall in love. In less than ten years, he'd lost his father, then his brother, because he'd refused to speak a word to him since the day of his father's funeral, and in many ways, his wife, too, because the woman he'd married no longer really existed. And when someone feels the need to fall in love, they usually succeed.

This time, Giulio wanted a divorce. Naturally Elena's condition had gotten still worse, even she had realized that this wasn't just another of his many betrayals, more cheating to be taken resignedly in stride. One evening, blind drunk, she'd fallen asleep with a lit cigarette and had set the house on fire. In the space of a month she'd managed to wreck no fewer than three of the Morganti family cars; it was pointless to try to hide the keys from her, she always managed to find them. People were constantly calling at midnight to ask us to come pick her up at some party or other where she'd gotten totally smashed on martinis ("Olivia? Your mother wants to go home on her own, but she's in no condition to drive. Do you want us to just let her sleep here? Sorry to call so late, but you understand"), whereupon we'd have to say good night to our friends, get in the car, drive through the fog to some sixteenth-century villa in the hills, throw her over our shoulders while the guests in evening attire watched us sorrowfully, and then drive back through the night with the windows open in the icy chill, because she was about to vomit.

Olivia, exasperated, dreamed of running away. And, as long as she was at it, of a liberation that might prove to be somewhat more definitive, namely, an emancipation from a life that could never really belong to her.

Manon, heartbroken at the idea of being separated from her granddaughter but well aware of the problem, had finally managed to impose her will. And so it was established that, *for everybody's welfare*, Olivia was to be left free to go wherever she pleased. The Morgantis had an apartment in Paris, so why not there? A change of scenery could only do her good, that was an accepted truth. The only remaining stumbling block was me.

Once again, I was facing up to the nightmare of my childhood. Only Olivia wasn't leaving for France on account of a Communist regime. In fact, that very same evening we were entering the two-decade era of Silvio Berlusconi.

"I DON'T WANT TO *live in an illiberal country, governed by immature political forces*," Berlusconi was saying.

"Just come with me. We can leave Italy together."

We'd calmed down a little. Now Olivia was sitting on the bed, legs crossed, waiting for an answer.

With a hint of sadness, I mused on the fact that it hadn't even occurred to her to move into my tiny bedroom, where her parents certainly couldn't come bother her. Far better to live in an apartment in Saint-Germain-des-Prés, obviously.

I looked around and realized that I couldn't force her to adjust to such squalor. The apartment was little more than a dump for the furniture and household objects that the landlady didn't know what else to do with. The single bed was actually a wire-mesh cot with a mattress, atop which the landlady had arranged a faded red duvet with a series of absurd patterns, resembling tops and balloons, that had clearly come from her children's bedrooms from when they were very small. So it had come to us; after all, everyone knows that college students don't expect much. Why waste money on a brand-new quilt? The Formica desk was already a substantial outlay, and who could guess how much time she'd spent driving through the fog to some big box store on the outskirts of town where she could buy a cheap piece of furniture for a pittance. The office chair, which sat slightly askew on its swiveling wheels, certainly came from her husband's office—he was a well-known accountant. Crushed under the weight of a neurotic secretary, possibly with a fat ass, who had swayed and tilted too aggressively between one phone call and the next, it was basically useless now. But for us, who spent our entire day sitting there studying and paid three hundred thousand lire a month for that whole disgusting mess, it could still work. As for the rustic armoire, which had nothing to do with any of the rest of the place, I still sometimes wondered. From a country home that had belonged to recently deceased grandparents? Other furniture and bric-a-brac did seem to confirm the hypothesis of an unwelcome inheritance, poor relatives who had left them nothing but the inconvenience of having to clear out a couple of rooms. The sofas and armchairs in the living room, for instance, and everything that filled up the common area, all lace doilies and statuettes that you couldn't even have foisted off on a junk dealer for the Sunday street market. The same provenance for the round table, a fake antique, as grim and dark as the old age and poverty of whoever had once owned it. Did I seriously expect Olivia Morganti to come live here? With a Calabrian student who never cleaned the toilet and a Livornese student who farted in the kitchen? For the first time, I clearly understood that I was inadequate, Paris or no Paris. Maybe, once I had my degree, I'd make some progress. But for the time being, in spite of all my best efforts, there was seriously nothing I could offer her. And the idea of taking what she was offering me was completely out of the question. I would have felt humiliated. The only thing I could present in the face of sorrow was my pride.

"I'd like to remind you that I've chosen to study the law, and French jurisprudence is simply not the same as ours. I'm sorry, I won't change my plans for your whims."

To our minds, high school students who managed to obtain their diplomas during the Tangentopoli scandal and the season of Mafia bombings and massacres, while Judge Falcone and Judge Borsellino and the investigative pool in Milan brought an entire political class to its knees, all our heroic fantasies, our ideals and enthusiastic ambitions were focused on a single, sought-after profession, more thrilling than dreams of being an astronaut: becoming a magistrate. And that's what I hoped to do. Once I took my degree in law, I wanted to sit for the civil service exam and place high enough to win a position.

"Sure. But why do we have to break up? I can come back here once a month, and you can come to Paris and visit me."

"Forget about it. I'm already struggling to pay for this shithole of an apartment. The airplane is too expensive."

"I'll pay for your ticket."

"I don't want your money."

"...*the old Italian political class has been swept aside by events and overcome by changing times...crushed beneath the sheer weight of the public debt burden and the illegal system of party financing, leaving the country ill-prepared and uncertain*..."

I gave her a slap on the hand because she'd been biting her nails. I was very protective with her, there were times when I treated her like a little sister. I'd get mad at her if one evening she had too much to drink. I'd yell at her if she rode her scooter without a helmet. She was only authorized to smoke a joint in my presence, because I was afraid that it might make her sick. And if she went out to a disco with her friends, I'd expect her to call me as soon as she got home. ("Astrid is a terrible driver, plus she's nearsighted: tell me when you get home." "What a pain you are.")

"Do you really want to break up with me?" She was crying. Deep down, after all, she was still just a girl.

"Look, I came to Bologna just so I could see you. Now you're the one who wants to leave me to go to Paris."

She's too spoiled, I was thinking to myself, I'll never be able to make her happy. She wants everything and its opposite, people that have been raised the way she has are just that way. Maybe my father had a point when he said that Olivia would turn out exactly like her parents.

"Valerio, I feel like I'm losing my mind here, I just can't take it anymore," she sobbed.

She was so adorable as she rooted through her backpack in search of a Kleenex, focused on extracting absolutely useless objects from internal and external pockets, pen caps without the pen, empty chewing gum packs, lighters that were out of fluid, as if she could magically pluck a solution out of that glorified trash bag.

"Use some toilet paper."

Olivia stood up and went into the bathroom, sniffing loudly and rubbing her nostrils with the back of her hand, sliding along on her white terry-cloth socks that had immediately turned black because the apartment I lived in, inhabited by three young men, was a complete pigsty.

For a moment, in the silence, I could hear Berlusconi's voice, loud and clear: "*Italy, which rightly mistrusts prophets and saviors, needs people with their heads screwed on straight . . .*"

"Well, what if I just went to Paris for a few months?" She had come back with the whole roll of toilet paper in her hand, "By then things might have calmed down at my house."

"I won't wait for you."

With deep and abiding bitterness, I thought to myself that at long last, her family had managed to separate us. Let it be clear, no one had been so stupid as to oppose our relationship, which the Morgantis had actually sort of treated as a laughing matter. Our youth, after all, had reassured them that the ties between us would be of limited duration, nothing that was likely to get in the way of an actual marriage with all the bells and whistles of officialdom, which would come along in the fullness of time. No, Manon was certainly no fool, and she knew that trying to get in our way would only have prompted Olivia to be more stubborn, made her think of me as a weapon to turn against her family in the midst of what was already an age of protest and defiance, the supreme form of spite. They would have transformed me into a martyr, our love into a cause for which she would be determined to battle with all her might, and her into a romantic heroine, a figure that was always just a bit too attractive in the eyes of any young girl. Heaven forfend. No, it was far smarter to welcome me with smiles on their lips, as if they were delighted with this new twist. If no one got in the way, Manon felt certain, Olivia would realize of her own volition that I didn't know how to ski, that I didn't own a house at the beach where I could invite her to spend her holidays, that spending the summers camping in sleeping bags was far less relaxing, in the long run, than spending them on a yacht, and that it was more enjoyable to dine in a fine restaurant than to rely on take-out pizzas that arrived at your home stone cold. Confident in what they considered to be the natural outcome of things, never quite as poetic as you imagine them when you're twenty, they'd invite me over for Sunday lunch as if I were the Prince of Wales.

Manon was very careful not to express any of her misgivings. When we told her about the time in Prague that we'd caught crabs, in the youth hostel next door to a sex shop, she just howled with laughter. And she pretended to be highly amused when we called her from the campground to tell her that the tent had collapsed, swept away by a small wall of mud.

Giulio, who was less subtle and conniving than his mother, and in any case less strategic, like all men, often put us in awkward situations without even meaning to. "Aren't you going to participate in the tennis tournament that the Martinellis are holding in the countryside?" "Papa, Valerio doesn't play tennis." "Oh, right, that's true. What a pity." He'd forget that I wasn't a member of the golf club, he seemed vexed that I knew nothing about vintage cars, and when he took me out on his sailboat, he was scandalized to discover that I didn't know what a mainsail was, and was utterly aghast when he saw see me trip over the sheets, as clumsy as any person who wasn't accustomed to the ways of sailing.

To Giulio, I was "a loser." Certainly he never said so to my face, but he offered so many elucidations and commentaries on that particular category that I was forced into the awareness that I belonged to it by rights. To be a loser was to be the opposite of a man who had become powerful or rich, in short successful; another word for it was, frequently, "poor." But the term could also be used to describe someone who failed to take satisfaction from the same things he found satisfying, and pretty much all intellectuals were members of the category. Someone like me, who instead of going to a party preferred to stay at home and read a book, for instance, was definitely "a loser." But the term could also refer to someone's appearance, and here it became even more insidious, because it was no longer limited just to the surface of things or one's personal tastes. "A loser" might be someone who dressed poorly, and therefore someone who lacked the money to do better (and there, once again, "poor"), or else someone who didn't give a damn about clothing (such as, for instance, an intellectual, once again), or else someone who was a bad, bad person, who intentionally dressed poorly in order to annoy other people, and therefore a "Communist." Every single definition that he offered I felt I could check off: yep, that describes me, and so does this. I've passed the loser test.

OLIVIA HAD STOPPED crying now, she just looked at me without a word. She didn't have to say a thing, I knew what she was thinking. As if you hadn't seen these things with your own eyes, she was telling me, with that glance.

In fact I had seen them, and I didn't know what to hope for her. If her folks stayed together, it was hell on earth, guaranteed. Giulio was getting increasingly aggressive because he felt trapped, and Elena just kept getting drunker all the time. But then again, a divorce was hardly a happy solution. What would become of her mother? Who was going to have to manage that problem?

And the young woman with whom Giulio was head over heels in love only promised far worse trouble to come. Talking to her friends and acquaintances, Manon had gathered information and quickly reconstructed the woman's brief biography. It hadn't taken her long to get a clear read on her rival. One Sunday, at lunch, she'd told us everything she knew about her. And I had learned that a product of the midlevel bourgeoisie of the province (her father had a little ceramics factory, a two-story detached villa in Imola with pretentious furnishings, and a little apartment at the beach on the Romagna riviera) could be far more insidious in her social climbing than a *borgataro* like me, who'd just happened to fetch up in a family like Olivia's.

She called herself Marilù, to cover up the awkward name they'd given her (Maria Luciana, after her grandmother), and she looked upon Bologna as a glittering metropolis and the Morgantis as a royal family, but always with a smirk, as if that promised land that she was longing to reach actually left her indifferent.

Her relentless climb to the top had been planned all the way back to her time at university, when she had left her parents' home in search of a more glorious future. Her college studies were of little interest to her—mediocre grades and tests taken far behind schedule. She was probably using the School of Law strictly as a venue where she could meet the better sort of people. She'd immediately latched onto a girl in her class who was a frequent guest in the settings to which she aspired, a fragile young woman who needed a person just like Marilù, someone willing to accompany her to any dinner party and serve as her sidekick. She was no fool, Marilù: she knew how to stand out of the spotlight, act humble, and keep out from underfoot to avoid upsetting the precarious ego of her all-too-useful girlfriend. And then she knew how to dart forward like a snake when her moment came. She was very cute, no doubt about it, but her calculations were so subtle that she did her best to keep even her beauty at bay, and assumed a dowdy, nondescript appearance, lest she be seen as an irritant by the other women in the environment she'd managed to wangle herself into. Courteous to a fault, amiable and winning, she went so far as to feign fears she'd never experienced, to keep from frightening others. And she was careful to keep from succumbing to the flattery of the men buzzing around her. Her reputation had to be kept spotless. She knew what she wanted, and if she hoped to secure a marriage that would offer her all the guarantees she was seeking, at a time when people were perfectly happy to cohabit, she needed to construct an ironclad persona. If she'd come from a lower social class, she would have been less dangerous. Instead she knew exactly what she wanted, she knew the codes of the world to which she aspired like the back of her hand, and she was capable of mingling in that world, vanishing as if camouflaged, and seducing without any appearance of cool calculation. She always dressed nicely, with a certain element of style, sober and tasteful, and appeared to be nothing other than a well-brought-up young lady, harmless and even highly principled.

Once she'd taken her degree, her useful friend invited her to start a company together. The plan was to organize conferences and trade shows, a profession perfectly suited to her purposes. Then, when she finally met Giulio Morganti, doing the numbers quickly in her head, she realized that she'd hit pay dirt. Here he was. Evaluating risks and the flukes of fate, her best bet was to welcome the courtship of one of the most powerful industrialists in the city (modestly, reluctantly, letting things fall into place around her, as if unasked for), and who cares if the man is married.

"...*the best of a clean, reasonable, modern country*," Berlusconi was saying.

Manon had remained supremely unmoved in the face of Giulio's descriptions, as he referred to her variously as "an extraordinary young woman," "lovely both inside and out," "sunny, generous, and caring," and many other overused words of that sort. She'd instantly realized that that woman was far more dangerous than Elena, who was basically only capable of doing harm to herself, chugging down alcohol the way you might pour gasoline over your head if you wanted to set yourself on fire. But there was very little she could do, by now her son was already head over heels.

Dado was in seventh heaven: at this point his brother's misdeeds were beginning to become legion. Meanwhile, he might be a queer, but his legal record was clean as a whistle. And if being put under arrest hadn't been enough to besmirch the pure escutcheon of the shining firstborn in his mother's eyes, well, now the parvenue would take care of the rest of the job. Naturally Dado enjoyed needling Manon about it ("If you ask me, that girl's going to get herself pregnant," he cackled, "she's already savoring the blackmail she's got cooking in her belly"). But those were bitter vindications, and his mother continued treating him like the son who had turned out *wrong*, even if he was more accomplished professionally than his elder brother and he'd never let himself be lassoed like a naive fool by a fortune hunter (he personally preferred to waste money on rent boys).

Starting with that little chocolate factory, over the years Dado had built an empire that rivaled his father's, sensing that with food and Italian style it was possible to make his fortune. And without having to get his hands as dirty as he would if he were working with cement.

Dado had always been very kind to me, I have to admit it. When Olivia told everyone that she was going to be moving to Paris, he'd been the only one to ask: "What about Valerio?" Maybe he identified with his niece's mistakes; after all, he too had lost the man he loved because of his family's meddling. From the day that Stanley left, he'd never fallen in love with anyone else. And for fear of annoying his mother, he didn't even try to find a partner with whom to share his life. He condemned himself to loneliness, a torment that, to his eyes, wasn't as fearsome as the horrors of coming out in the provinces, in the gilded world he'd grown up in, a world he didn't have the courage to turn his back on.

"AREN'T YOU GOING to do anything to save our relationship?"

"What am I supposed to do?" I replied.

From my time in the Roman *borgata* I'd learned that apathy is the other face of pride. It seems like passivity to outside eyes. But it's not. It's the flaunting of superiority. So I can't do anything about it? Then I'll decide that the object of discussion means nothing to me, because if there's one thing I won't put up with, it's humiliations.

My family, for that matter, had been no more thrilled than hers had. There are unions, evidently, that make no one happy. My mother, for instance, had taken great umbrage at this passion of mine for Olivia. As if having her as my girlfriend had undercut all her efforts, making redemption impossible. The Bologna Law School was one of the finest and most respected institutions of legal learning, but you'd think I'd chosen to attend the University of Tirana in Albania. "You're moving *to that place* just for her," she hissed, contemptuously. "And I worked myself to death for all those years so you could study."

When I went back to Rome to see her, she never had anything nice to say: "What about your girlfriend? Are you ashamed of bringing her here?" It was pointless to explain that Olivia would have been delighted to come but that I'd discouraged her because I was afraid that my mother would mistreat her if she did. Usually I just tried to change the subject, but my mother was obsessed, so she'd get up from the table and go into the kitchen to wash dishes, muttering ill-omened imprecations ("Sooner or later she'll dump you").

My papa of course wasn't the type to object, but it was clear that he wasn't especially happy about this either. Meanwhile his feelings had been hurt a little because I'd refused to sleep on his sofa bed and I was willing to work in a pub to earn the three hundred thousand lire I needed to rent a room. He didn't understand the logic. "There's room here, you know," he grumbled, "why would you want to flush away all that money?" It never occurred to him that I might want a certain shred of privacy, especially with my girlfriend. Apart from that, he made no comments. He limited himself to rebuffing any invitations Olivia or I might extend to him. "Come to dinner with the two of you? Why, I'm an old man, *what can you do,*" was how he got out of it.

Only my sister was rooting for us. Marta had just met Olivia twice, but that was all that she needed. Since I cared very much about introducing Olivia to her, one weekend we went to Rome specifically so they could meet. Naturally, I hadn't chosen just any old Saturday and Sunday for the occasion, I knew that on that weekend my mother had been invited to Ladispoli to stay with a girlfriend. Perfect: it was just us three. Olivia, raised at Manon's knee, had immediately taken my sister to see the newly restored Sistine Chapel. Marta wasn't accustomed to doing certain things, and that day in the Vatican was emblazoned in her memory for the rest of her life (she kept asking us: "But is all of Rome like that? Where have I lived for the past ten years?").

They'd later seen each other again in Bologna. Marta had managed to get herself put aboard a train ("If you insist,"

Mama said) and had joined us for a couple of days. To celebrate her arrival, Olivia had taken her up into the hills to eat *tigelle*—flatbreads with cheeses and cold cuts. The *tigelle* had stunned Marta every bit as much as had Michelangelo. "You need to marry her, Valerio," she kept telling me, "and I want to be there as bridesmaid."

MEANWHILE, Olivia had started biting her nails again, only this time I no longer felt like slapping her hands.

"I'm sorry, Valerio. I have to run, try to understand."

"*The history of Italy is at a turning point.*"

"Good luck," I replied.

"Same to you." She got to her feet.

"*. . . together we can build a great dream . . .*"

"After all, we're bound to see each other again," she said, picking up her backpack.

"*. . . a new Italian miracle . . .*"

I shrugged. "Who can say."

PART THREE

2001

1

THE BEST OF ALL
POSSIBLE BOURGEOISIES

It was August 2001 and I was on Ponza, on the Berna-cconi family yacht. While we were mooring—clumsy and intrusive as always, because Costantino didn't really know how to pilot the boat and he just revved the engine, kicking up black smoke and churning foam, only to slam against other boats here and there, randomly—we almost rammed a sailboat.

It was dark, and I didn't even recognize the sailboat at first. I was in the bow, hard at work pushing away from the hulls of my neighbors' boats, like a human fender, while they shouted at us, heaping insults upon us ("Would you look at these bumpkins! They spend millions to buy that piece of plastic junk, and they don't even know how to pilot it. Hey, hey, stop right there! You're going to hit our hull! And they don't even apologize. Oh, what oafs, oh, what bumpkins!"), when I suddenly found myself facing a boat hook, pointed right at my belly, like a sword.

"You idiot," I shouted at the blurry feminine presence I had before me, "look out or you'll rip me open."

Laughter in the darkness: "Well, as far as that goes, you ripped me open yourself, you know."

Olivia's voice? I raised the flashlight and aimed it right in her face. She stuck out her tongue at me. I was about to untangle myself and leap to the other side, indifferent to the collision—as far as I was concerned, they could all go straight to the bottom—when Costantino bumped into them again, knocking us both to the deck.

Olivia, on all fours down on the teak deck, just laughed and laughed: "*Welcome back,* eh?"

Meanwhile, the others were cursing. The code of etiquette of the regatta was long since forgotten.

"Oh, then you really are an asshole!"

Olivia, who couldn't seem to stop laughing, tried to get to her feet, still waving the boat hook in all directions, dangerously.

"Put that thing away. You could knock the Cyclops's eye out."

Olivia was struggling to talk, because her laughing jag wouldn't seem to stop. Bent forward, hugging her belly, she made an effort: "My husband kept wondering...ha ha ha...

who those...ha ha ha...those bumpkins...ha ha ha...But it was you the whole time, ha ha ha..."

I wasn't laughing at all. She'd married? I felt a terrible stab of pain, somewhere deep inside—I, too, put my hand on my belly—as if I really had been stabbed and run through.

But we had more urgent issues: her husband and my friend were duking it out on the pier. Benedetta, Costantino's younger sister, had charged in and was trying to separate them, shouting loudly.

"Help! Help!"

An hour later, we were on Olivia's boat, having a drink in the cockpit, all together: background music and the caressing sound of water lapping against hull and dock. Olivia had put a bottle of champagne on the table.

"It's a magnum of Cristal, I found it in the galley. My father will never notice that it's gone. Who'll open it?"

Enrico, Olivia's husband, was ironically singing the refrain to the Peppino di Capri song, while untwisting the muselet: "*Champagne, per brindare a un incontro...*"

It was past midnight and the port was silent, all you could hear were our voices and our laughter. Costantino was clowning around as usual, he was the life of the party. The enemy boat was full of cute young women, better to make peace and offer some money to pay for the scratch on their hull, after all, the boat was insured.

Only Benedetta still had a pout on her sulky face, continuing to tug on the sleeve of my sweatshirt and whisper to me in a low voice: "It was the Morgantis who sent our father to prison, we shouldn't be here. Valerio, can we go?"

Of course I had no intention of leaving. You couldn't have budged me from there.

I was all caught up with observing, for the moment. Olivia's husband had a delicate face, light-colored eyes, and fair hair, rather long. He had a sweet, kind manner, perhaps even fragile, but he put on too much of a show of being a dandy. The linen shirt left unbuttoned to reveal the hairless chest, the vanilla-colored shorts, perfectly ironed even if he'd just been in a bit of a brawl on the dock, and the soles of his feet black with dirt because it was chic to go barefoot even on dry land. He held his flute of champagne perched upon a book by Foucault, as if he were about to open it and start reading.

From what I was able to gather, stitching together scattered phrases and snatches of sentences tossed back and forth in the conversation, they'd met in Paris. Olivia, who was feeling a little lonely, had decided at a certain point to rent out a room of her apartment in Saint-Germain-des-Prés. And she'd wound up with him as a tenant: Enrico, a young man from Turin, the friend of friends. The rest had just come of its own accord. After a couple of years (neither one of the two had finished their studies), they'd gone back to Italy and married. They preferred to live in Rome, where they'd opened an art gallery together.

I, too, had gone back to Rome after taking my degree. So now we live in the same city again, I thought to myself. And my heart was beating hard and fast: I was afraid she could tell it was racing under my T-shirt. I gulped down one glass after another to soothe my nerves.

"We've finished the champagne. If you like, I have some port," Olivia was speaking to everyone, but she looked only at me.

"Just a little, sure, thanks."

"I'll go get it, I really feel like getting drunk tonight," and as she stood up, she touched my shoulder. The touch of her fingers made me start.

Benedetta dug her fingers into my forearm: "Please, don't. It's late. We need to get up early to go to Ventotene."

At that point her brother snapped, because he had no intention of going to bed and abandoning the girls he saw all around him. "Don't be a pain, Bebè." He shooed her away as if she were a fly, slapping at the air. "Where do you all go to swim?"

"To swim?" A girl, already completely drunk, lurched unsteadily to her feet. "Let's go swimming *now*."

It was the kind of idea that was likely to get us all drowned, the state we were in. But Costantino was totally enthusiastic about the idea.

"Yes, let's go find a place! We'll sail to a bay, and then we can sleep at anchor."

"Oh, riiight," Enrico shook his head, "do you really think it's a good idea to take the boat out at this time of night? You of all people? Drunk as you are, you'd be capable of ramming and sinking an entire fleet. Believe me, other people aren't as understanding as we are, they're not going to invite you aboard for champagne *afterward*."

In response, Costantino, euphoric as ever, suggested lowering the inflatable dinghies and sailing to the beach behind the port.

"Let's go to the Frontone!"

The girls all acclaimed the suggestion with a shout: "Yes!"

Benedetta, increasingly out of sorts, grunted: "I'm going to bed, ciao all."

"'Night," we called back in chorus, without even turning our heads to look. No one else wanted to sleep.

ON THE SURFACE of the black sea, the two rubber dinghies tore over the waves at full speed, bumping each other spitefully, as if they were bumper cars at a carnival. It was a dangerous little game; it would be the easiest thing in the world for a person to tumble over into the water and be ravaged by the propeller in some idiotic duel, but we never gave that a second thought. We felt invincible, with the world at our feet, and that world included the sea. I actually have very little in common with their invincibility, and yet it was catching. I held tight to the rope lines, to keep from flying away, happy and self-confident: that evening the sea belonged to me, too, it was mine by right just as it belonged to all the others.

THE YEAR OF OUR LOVE

Olivia's husband had leaped into the water fully dressed and he hauled us all in toward the beach. The girls, who didn't want to get wet to their waist, let themselves be carried to shore, one by one, by Costantino, who couldn't have asked for anything better. Olivia was still in the dinghy.

"Valerio? Will you help me?"

Why hadn't she asked her husband? Maybe it was because he was busy planting an anchor among the rocks, to make sure the dinghies weren't swept away by the current. I took her in my arms and set her down on the shore.

The beach was a real nightmare: music at full volume, discotheque lighting, a sweaty crowd swaying and jumping with both hands in the air. Costantino plunged right into the fray, dragging the rest of the female crew with him. The Dandy, as I'd already dubbed Olivia's husband, with an indifferent, nonchalant demeanor, had already found himself a rock by the water, shrouded in shadows, where he could roll himself a joint in blessed peace and quiet.

Olivia, dressed more or less like a sailor in uniform, with navy blue shorts, a white T-shirt, and flip-flops, very different from her friends who had all jumped into the inflated dinghy wearing six-inch heels and fluttering skirts, stood there at the water's edge, her feet lapped by the waves.

"Ah, no. I'm not going over there. What an inferno."

I shrugged. I assumed she wanted to go join her husband and I wondered what I should do now. Those rocks appealed to me, too, better than the open-air discotheque, no doubt about it, but maybe that wasn't the best idea. I had no interest in being the third who makes an uncomfortable crowd.

But Olivia had other plans: "Why don't we go back to the boat?"

The Dandy shook his head: "I like it here just fine, I'll get someone to bring me a mojito. You go on ahead."

Olivia took me by the arm. "Valerio? Come away with me!"

I ran after her, a little worried: "Won't your husband be jealous?"

"Don't be silly. He'd find that utterly *petty bourgeois*."

"Ah."

I can't remember a more thrilling sea journey in my life. It was nothing more than a matter of passing from one bay to another, but I felt as if we were challenging the broad Atlantic. Olivia was piloting the dinghy and she was playing the fool. The chop had kicked up a bit and she loved taking the waves head on. She shouted with delight every time we landed with a thud and an icy spray splashed all over us. I recognized that laugh. It was the same as the little girl's who plunged into the huge breakers, the intoxicating thrill of letting herself be tumbled over by the spray. Olivia loved to let herself be swept away by things.

"Ahh, this is great. Hold on tight, Valerio."

When we got back to port, on the smooth, dark water, amidst the dim lights of the boats, she started singing "I Want to Hold Your Hand." And she took my hand.

"Ponza is so beautiful. All this noise, all these crowds just ruin it. We should come here in the low season."

I didn't know what to say. Was she making plans with me? I felt a little awkward.

"Beautiful, no doubt about it," I replied. "But I like Ventotene even better, maybe because it's more human and more peaceful. Have you ever been?"

She shook her head: "No. But I'd love to go. Will you take me?"

Even if I had to swim the whole way, I'd have taken her. But I didn't say a word.

WHEN WE BOARDED her yacht again, she tossed me a towel with a large M embroidered in the terry cloth. This mania that rich people have for their initials verges on the pathological, if you ask me, it's a caste disease, just like tattoos in the *borgata*. They all seem to feel the need to stamp a logo on themselves, the poor do it on their flesh and the rich on everything that covers their flesh and surrounds it. Who can say why?

"Dry off, Valerio. Otherwise you'll get diarrhea," she told me with a wink.

Such intimacy was upsetting, I stammered out my thanks.

We got comfortable at the bow, our legs dangling over the side of the hull, like a couple of figureheads. We could forget about the stars, there were only clouds overhead.

"It's going to rain soon. Those poor saps who stayed on the beach are going to be caught in a downpour. We were smart to get out of there."

Meanwhile she was smoking, bent forward to hold the cigarette low, making sure not to set her father's sailboat on fire through some carelessness in a gust of wind.

"Wait, though, are you sure this won't bother your husband? You just dumped him there, we're here all alone, just the two of us...I mean, if it was me, I wouldn't be all that happy. If I were him, *I'd beat you black and blue.*"

She burst out laughing loud and clear, until she choked on the smoke.

"Oh Valerio, you're such a sweetheart. But I already told you, we don't have a *petty bourgeois* marriage."

Again with that term, how annoying. It struck me as an obnoxious conceit, something that she'd learned in my absence and that she tended to parrot, to show me how grown-up she had become. I still hadn't understood that her tragedy lay right there, in that irritating definition.

"Forgive me, I'm not much of an expert on the bourgeoisie," I replied sarcastically. That know-it-all tone needed to be punished.

She bowed her head: "You're right, it's stupid."

Meanwhile she was biting her nails and picking viciously at the skin around them, but it was no longer my job to stop her.

"You know, my husband likes guys, too. In fact, he especially likes guys. And as far as that goes, whatever."

"What do you mean, 'whatever'? Then why is he married to you?"

"Well, these days we're *all* bisexual."

Her voice actually changed when she issued these axioms, I had the suspicion that acting arrogant helped her to conquer her bewilderment.

"You're bisexual?" I asked.

"I've tried it, but I didn't especially like it, so I don't think so." She turned to see how I'd reacted. "Maybe I was more attracted by the idea than the act itself. But then, when you're actually in the middle of it, it changes. I did my best, you know? But I couldn't really experience any pleasure. So I started to have my doubts."

It turned out that their living conditions were rather complex. A routine that seemed too complicated to manage over the long term. The Dandy blithely brought young boys into their home, right under her eyes, because he was only interested in creatures under twenty-one. And she, the morning after, made espresso for everyone.

"It's not cheating, if it happens in full view," she said. "The lies that my grandfather invented to tell Manon were much more humiliating, if you stop to think about it. And my parents, who forgave each other for everything without ever offering an explanation, finally broke up in the end."

I nodded my head dutifully, but I couldn't really say that I thought the third-generation solution was much healthier than the others.

"I don't like the idea of suppressing other people's desires, I'd rather share them."

"What do you mean, share them?"

"Oh, I don't know, a few times, to make him happy, I let them talk me into joining in. But they're actually pretty extreme experiences, and they can leave a scar. So it became clear that it was better to avoid that path. Now all we do is enjoy breakfast together. With whoever it happens to be, I mean. We have our laughs. We gossip ruthlessly about the latest boy, *like a pair of young girl cousins*," she laughed.

Red alarm. I didn't know whether I should ask the final big question. She was already trying to get another cigarette lit, maybe she could feel it coming.

"Forgive me for asking, but do you...the two of you, I mean...you and your husband, in other words..."

"Do we what?"

"Do you have sex?"

Olivia smiled, the filter in her mouth: "Don't you know that unconsummated marriages are the ones that last longest?" But she immediately screamed because the flame had burned her eyebrows.

I decided not to take it out on her, even though I ran no risk of being considered "petty bourgeois" because I belonged to a social class that was many rungs below the much-derided bourgeoisie, whether petty or grand.

Where I come from it's all much less complicated, I thought to myself. You're a queer or you aren't a queer. If you cheat on your husband, you're a slut and if you cheat on your wife, you're a piece of shit. If you have orgies, then you have orgies, and that's that, without a lot of theoretical constructions.

"And doesn't that bother you?"

"Well, they're delicate equilibriums, and sometimes they get out of hand."

Now she was scratching a scab on her knee, in search of blood. I was tempted to give her a light slap on the back of her hand, but I restrained myself.

"Am I talking too much?"

I shook my head, with a fond smile. Certain courteous pat phrases were by now an intrinsic part of her, an ineluctable toll that she paid to all the bourgeoisies that she'd traveled through in her life, more or less transgressive as they'd been. I couldn't possibly expect to find her immune to her experiences.

"They get out of hand," she repeated, raptly, staring at the monotonous water of the port. "In fact, something happened that no one could have foreseen. *Something really bad.*"

There, she was finally using a simple adjective. And she wasn't trying to elevate the matter with sophisticated theories, cadged or overheard during her brief experience of the world. Something really bad, full stop.

"Namely?"

"What can you do?" she sighed.

Was she using one of my father's expressions? When she was little, Olivia had spent lots of time with him, especially after I moved away. She was constantly buzzing around him, always ready to help gather fruit, prune rose bushes, or groom the lawn, on the seat of his lawn mower. And now, in a moment of fragility, the contamination leaped to the fore. It was only natural for her to say, "What can you do?" She'd even recovered a hint of her Bolognese accent.

SHE TOLD ME that one evening, his mind fogged with excitement or alcohol or narcotics or perhaps all three things blended together, her husband had raped a young man. To make things worse, a minor. There was no point trying to conceal the mess, a trial is open to the public, so they'd decided they'd be better off asking their parents for help. It hadn't been "pleasant" (she actually used that word), but she'd had no alternatives ("But then a criminal trial isn't *pleasant*, either," she said). Naturally the two families had acted in concert to hush the matter up, and the victim, in the face of a generous cash offer, had come to the realization that it might be in his best interest to withdraw the criminal complaint. Which meant everything had been taken care of.

"As if nothing had ever happened, only..."

"Only?"

"Only *it had happened*, for fuck's sake." And she looked at me, seeking understanding, as if that wasn't a commodity that had been easy to find.

I mean, fair enough, the whole matter had been laid to rest without triggering consequences. All the same, there actually had been a few consequences, because it really had pissed her off to no small degree and she had simply been incapable of swallowing her pride in silence for the mere consideration that getting pissed off is typical of the *petty bourgeoisie*. She explained that this rage of hers—visceral, profound, and increasingly unrestrained—had prompted great embarrassment and awkwardness for both families, especially her husband's family.

"To hear them tell it, you have to be *civil*, no matter what happens. You have to try to understand the reason why and the secondary factors and talk it over and over, with self-restraint, and blah blah blah. But I realized that it wasn't going to work. Because now, these days, I wake up in the morning, go into the kitchen, make my espresso, and I can't help but vomit. I vomit every morning, Valerio. Like little children who don't want to go to school."

In a certain sense, the price had been paid, but the sum that they'd personally delivered into the hands of the victim's family still didn't allow her to put her mind at rest. Olivia couldn't quite manage to forget the odor of that apartment, the odor of fried foods in the dining nook, the odor of sweat from the younger brothers, the odor of beer from the father's mouth, the harsh odor of shampoo from the mother's hair. The young man hadn't been there that day, luckily.

"They were all too polite," she told me, "as if we'd brought them a gift. But it wasn't a *gift*, it was a *crime*."

While she talked to me, she hunched her shoulders shut, protectively, as if the only possible defense was that solitary curve.

"I feel sorry for him, you know that? My husband, I mean. He's so changed. Sometimes I feel guilty toward him. But this anger is stronger than me. Sometimes I treat him badly for no reason, just to get shed of a little bit of the anger."

Now and again she'd turn and look, monitoring my reactions. But I didn't say a word, I'd just sit and listen.

"So what does Manon have to say?"

"She says to run," Olivia replied. "She says: Honey, just *run*."

Olivia was about to burst into tears. She threw her arms around my neck and buried her forehead in my shoulder for a moment. Then she sat up straight, heaving a deep sigh.

I softly stroked her hair. It was full of sand, maybe that afternoon she'd gone to some beach to lie in the sun and hadn't shampooed her hair since. I really hoped she was going to ask me to run away with her. But Olivia was too caught up in her story.

THE MISTAKE LAY even deeper, she felt sure. It dated back earlier: when she'd first met her husband's family, and she'd fallen in love with them. She'd let herself be influenced by them to far too great a degree. She'd fallen under the illusion of discovering a "far more enlightened" bourgeoisie than the one she'd been born into, and everything they did or said struck her as wonderful.

"They weren't provincial like my folks, even if they lived in Turin, which certainly isn't a world capital. It was all so different. I was so captivated. You understand?"

No, I didn't understand. But I was still perfectly happy to listen to her.

Enrico's mother was even more cultured than Manon, and possessed tastes that were even more refined than hers. Or at least different. The underlying wealth was roughly equivalent, the source of the money largely similar, she explained, businessmen just like the Morgantis, but the coding was entirely different. These people just spoke a different language, among other things, different in terms of the objects with which they surrounded themselves.

Their jewelry, for instance. None of them would have dreamed of buying the garish collier necklaces that Manon made Olivia's grandfather buy her. They would have been ashamed just to wear them around their necks. *Understatement*, first and foremost, using the English word even when speaking Italian. Enrico's mother never wore anything but discreet antique cameos or high-design necklaces, fine one-offs that she bought in other countries. There were bargains to be made with unhappiness there, too, but she wasn't about to have a screaming match for the prize of a Burri or a Fontana. These weren't courageous choices, they were *obligatory*. "Feel free to humiliate me, but let everyone see that I hang the finest works of the avant-garde on my walls." One chic humiliation after another, in strict keeping with the times, and in the seventies her husband's parents had become the most prominent collectors of Arte Povera, for instance. Only to wind up with a shark swimming through formaldehyde in the living room, in exchange for a young woman, thirty years her junior, to whom she would turn a blind eye.

"If I'd just been a little more clear-eyed, I might have realized that I was actually at home. But their weapons were so much more subtle."

Even if only because no one entertained the rest of them with jokes. The way Giulio Morganti did, since he couldn't come up with any better way of making himself liked. Instead, at the dinner table, they would talk about the latest book or the latest film by...Or they'd knowledgeably comment upon an exhibition they'd just seen in London or Paris. And Enrico's sister would lard her sentences with English words, often every other word, it seemed, because she'd been studying in New York for the past few months and she wanted to make everyone believe that she'd forgotten her Italian ("It was some pretty ridiculous stuff, but I wasn't capable of grasping the laughable side of their behavior, which was too new for me").

At their home there were no satin curtains, no silverware with baroque flourishes, the only lines allowed were minimalist bits of fine design, even when it came to antiques, if possible by Le Corbusier. The friends who moved in their social circle weren't licensed professionals who drew a blank the minute you stepped outside of their field of expertise.

No, they were fashionable economists who'd come back from Brussels with some hot piece of news about the European Union. At their parties no matron ever showed up in a fur coat, that utter vulgarity. And sitting at the dinner table was always the editor in chief of some newspaper or else an artist who had a monographic show in a major gallery. It was a steady procession of writers, psychoanalysts, professors, musicians, and theatrical directors.

What's more, they were "leftists" (and if they hadn't been so wealthy, that fact would have made Olivia's father and grandmother foam at the mouth with rage, but none of the Morgantis dared to call them "Communists"). Modern, openminded, always a bit formal, but more amusing. In fact, even capable of self-deprecating irony. At least, apparently. Enrico's mother never tried to jump out the window when a potential rival appeared on the horizon. Instead she'd invite her along to dinner and delighted in embarrassing her if she sensed the other woman might not be quite up to the situation ("Seriously, you've never heard of Stockhausen, sweetheart?").

Olivia realized it: maybe she'd fallen in love with her husband's family more than with him. Enrico took himself much more seriously than his parents did, didn't know as much as they did (she'd fallen under his spell for no better reason than that at age twenty he went around with a book by Borges in his backpack), and often tended to boast learning that he didn't possess. Her adherence to the lifestyle of *that family*, though, had seemed to her the most subtle of all possible rebellions, at least at that time.

Manon had tried to warn her ("Honey, have you ever wondered why they don't read Herodotus at bedtime? Because you can't talk about Herodotus with anyone during a dinner party") but Olivia acted all superior even with her grandmother, who wore emerald rings the size of dates ("I'll leave them all to you when I die." "Oh, I don't wear those, but thanks"). From the lofty vantage point of Olivia's new experience—intellectuals are just another matter, completely a different thing—she was even willing to humiliate her grandmother. Until she finally realized that the best of all possible bourgeoisies wasn't Enrico's family, and perhaps didn't even exist. And she'd gone back to sob in the arms of the one person who simply and truly loved her ("Nonna, what a con game it turned out to be. Forgive me").

The only reason they hadn't struck her as conformists was that they were conformists in another fashion, a fashion she hadn't yet learned about. And learning is always a thrill, it doesn't matter what's being learned. They didn't seem unethical to her because they were unethical in a different way, that too just awaiting discovery. In short, as long as the initiation process continued, Olivia was too busy absorbing the new codes of conduct to perceive their limitations. And once she started digesting them, those new codes of conduct—and maybe she was ready to keep the best and dismiss what she felt she didn't need—what happened just happened, sticking a wrench in the spokes of her bildungsroman once and for all.

Manon, who had silently tolerated her granddaughter's arrogant glare, even though she had taught the girl who Shakespeare and Caravaggio were, could finally enjoy her moral victories. But she chose not to ("I understand that it's a disappointment, honey. But you have your whole life ahead of you, at your age, mistakes aren't irretrievable yet, don't forget that").

I listened, hypnotized. And all the while I asked myself question after question. Just how many bourgeoisies are there in Italy? We complain in our country about the regional fragmentation, our shattered history, but maybe there are things that keep us disunited and prevent us from being a genuine nation, like France or England. My incursions into the ruling class helped me understand that perhaps it wasn't *one class*. More like a thousand classes, and no single class. Olivia's world was different from Costantino's and different again from her husband's. How could these different ruling classes even talk to each other if they didn't share a common language?

"Enrico's parents convinced us to spend one last vacation together, to see if things can get worked out. They say that, all things considered, he hasn't done *me* any harm yet. Unfortunately, they have a point. He hasn't done anything *to me*. Still..."

"Still?"

"Still, I'm not really happy, Valerio."

I was about to kiss her, her and all her efforts to seek out the best of all possible bourgeoisies. But Olivia suddenly leaped to her feet, adjusting her trousers on her bottom with a gesture that neither of her two families, the one she'd been born into and the one she was now part of, would have approved.

"They're coming back, we'd better continue this conversation tomorrow," she said.

2

A MIDSUMMER NIGHT'S
NIGHTMARE

THE NEXT DAY, since the weather had turned nasty, we rented little electric cars to take a tour of the island. They were two-seaters: Benedetta was stuck to me like glue, she wanted to get in the car with me, at all costs, but Olivia, with an insolent toot of the horn, summoned me imperiously to hers.

"Valerio? Come on! I'm driving, are you afraid?"

Bebè objected, announcing that she didn't feel safe driving her car all alone, she didn't even have a driver's license, but I didn't want to drag her around after me, and I pushed her to take the car driven by Olivia's husband, who was waiting for a passenger.

Olivia drove at high speed, narrowly missing precipices at every curve with a carefree laugh. Holding tight to the door handle, I was happy as that first night in the inflatable dinghy. As long as I could be with her, I would gladly have hurtled down to crash at the bottom of a ravine. In the space of half an hour, we'd lost the others.

Now Olivia was driving slowly, her sunglasses perched on her nose, searching for a parking spot.

"Let's go down to the pools, what do you say? They want to find a restaurant and get a bite to eat, they won't bother us for a while."

The rocky shores, because of the impending threat of a rainstorm, were practically deserted. Olivia leaped from one rock to another like a chamois. I, more cautious and much clumsier, followed her at a distance, taking care where I set my feet. We had stopped to buy a couple of sandwiches and two beers, delighted to go for a picnic all on our own.

We sat down and remained utterly silent for the moment, because an immense rainbow had just appeared over the sea.

"Make a wish, Valerio. When you see a rainbow, you're supposed to wish for something. But you can't tell me, or it won't come true."

I had no doubts: my wish was the same as it ever had been. I wondered what her wish might be. I looked at her as she closed her eyes, all focused, and hoped that she might be wishing the same thing as me. Who could say?

Olivia turned toward me and burst out laughing: "There are more tears shed over prayers answered than unanswered. It's a phrase from St. Teresa of Avila."

She'd learned it from reading a novel by Truman Capote. For a while, we talked about all the most important books we'd discovered in recent years.

"*The Bonfire of the Vanities*, God, it's wonderful," she was saying.

"Really? I'll have to get it."

"By the way, are you still determined to become a magistrate?"

I told her that immediately after taking my degree, I'd won a scholarship to continue my studies, and while I was preparing for the civil service exam to become a magistrate, I was helping out at the university. To my immense good fortune, that very same year, my adviser won a competition for a full professorship, and he'd transferred to the University of Rome "La Sapienza," which meant I had gone back to Rome with him, to work as his assistant. A very convenient solution for me, because it meant I no longer had to pay rent in Bologna. I could simply stay at my mother's home. Here, I was taking pleasure in laying it on a little thick. Reminding her that the only reason I'd even moved to Bologna had been for her, and her alone, only to watch her up and leave for Paris.

"So you're supervising exams for the students?"

"I'm their worst nightmare," I replied with a smug smile. "And I teach, too. The professor takes care of the deep dives, and I do the survey material."

"Impressive."

"And fun, too. I even clown it up a little, to keep the kids awake. Criminal law has no shortage of great stories to tell."

I hadn't come back to Rome before that, because in the end I liked living in Bologna, at least as far as my studies were concerned. At the university I'd met many professors who thought highly of me and asked me to choose them as my thesis advisers. I didn't want to give up what I'd built and start over again from scratch. I was afraid I wouldn't be able to find the same opportunities elsewhere.

After she left, I could have moved to my father's apartment and slept on his sofa bed if I wanted to save money. But the sense of frustration was so great when I went to stay with my papa that instead I'd just kept working at the pub to be able to pay for my room. A room where I could bring all the girls that I wanted, but which in fact I only used as a place to study, because when she'd abandoned me it had been a devastating gut punch (but I wasn't about to tell her that).

The only girl I'd taken to that rented room, the only one I'd had sex with on that disgusting cot that I paid three hundred thousand lire a month to sleep on, had been her girlfriend Astrid. Who hadn't hesitated for a second when I'd come on to her—was spite all that I had left?—and in fact she'd immediately opened her legs wide for me, as if she hadn't been waiting for anything else for months now, happy to steal something from her girlfriend who, in her opinion, had far too many things, "and didn't even know how to appreciate them" (her own words). But I certainly wasn't about to tell her that story, either.

"Well, I haven't accomplished a thing." Olivia was taking off her T-shirt, remaining in just her swimsuit, because the sun had returned. "I gave up studying art history after two months, I tried to get into a *grande école* but I failed the admission test, and then I enrolled in an industrial design school, but I quit that a year later because I'd decided to go back to Italy."

"You could always take up your studies again."

"I'm twenty-six, Valerio. I'm *too old*."

While a crab scrambled onto our rock, we continued our catch-up. A lot of things can happen in seven years.

"So your folks finally got a divorce."

"Papa has remarried."

"With that lady?"

"Yes, I'm afraid so."

The fortune hunter had got exactly what she'd had her heart set on snagging, even though nature hadn't come to her assistance. She'd done everything she could think of to get pregnant, but it hadn't taken. A case of polycystic ovary syndrome had prevented her from giving an heir to the Morgantis and she'd had to settle for a wedding at city hall.

"What about your mother?"

"She's reborn. She moved to the countryside, where she's found another dimension all her own, far from a world that clearly oppressed her and nothing more. She's always outside, she gathers fruit and makes jams and marmalades, cares for her vegetable garden, and eats the eggs that her hens lay. She's taking care of abandoned dogs now. She's founded an association for it, with some girlfriends of hers."

"Has she stopped drinking?"

"The problem vanished in a flash, the minute she broke up with my father. It turned out to be a malaise connected to her relationship with him, after all."

"Is she alone?"

"No, no. She's found a partner. A guy who makes wine and breeds horses. He's a decent fellow. They go everywhere wearing rubber boots and sweaters that stink of sweaty animals, and they're happy with that."

"Good, I'm happy for her."

"So am I." She took a bite out of her panino and, with her mouth full, asked me: "What about your folks? What have they been up to?"

Stumped, I knew there wasn't much I could say. My father was where he'd been for a while, in that hospice for the elderly. No women in his life. My mother, certainly less at peace, continued her tireless hunt for happiness. Without finding it. For several years now, she'd been dating a gentleman much older than her, the owner of a little hotel in the neighborhood by the Pantheon. A gentleman who was quite comfortable. He took her on vacations, out to dinner, to the movies. Mama wasn't exactly in love with him, but that comfortable life was agreeable enough, as far as she was concerned. Thanks to him, she'd been able to quit her heavy chores. She'd taken up a perch at his hotel, at the reception desk. And now she ordered the housekeepers around.

The news about my sister was a little more fun to tell. Marta had just finished her degree as a civil engineer and wanted to join the fire department. To think that we'd laughed when she was little and told us she wanted to grow up to become a firefighter. And now there she was.

Shortly before the start of summer, the civil service exam had been held. This was the first important event in her life, and so I'd done my best to be close to her. As part of the admissions process, they checked her criminal record, and Marta was afraid they might discover that her father had died in prison ("You never committed any crimes yourself, though," I pointed out). Since she had applied as a "brick mason," to prepare for the exam, which consisted of a technical challenge, she had gone for several months to work on a construction site. In spite of the many days she'd spent in the baking sun, braving the dust, alongside the other construction workers, the cross-bond wall that she'd erected in front of the judging panel hadn't turned out that well, because she'd allowed herself to get flustered. Luckily, there was the physical fitness test, and that had helped her to raise her average. She'd really put a lot of effort into learning the routine: sprint, three somersaults, balance beam, climbing a rope, descending a pole without using her legs, climbing over a barrier. She'd trained for it with a huge bodybuilder, simply bursting with steroids, a tough guy covered with tattoos who'd burst into tears while she was doing the test.

According to the psycho-attitudinal test, based on a series of standard questions such as "Do you like flowers?" my sister was found to be excessively sensitive, and for a number of weeks she was very worried ("What do you think, is being sensitive really such a bad thing for a firefighter?"). But in the end, she prevailed: she'd managed to get a passing score and was well within the ranking.

After the results were posted, we went out to celebrate. But my mother ruined the evening's festivities. She was by no means pleased with the decision Marta had made ("Couldn't you have found a more feminine profession?"). She'd hoped Marta might undertake a more brilliant career, perhaps as an actress. Naturally, by the end of the dinner, they'd broken into an open fight and my sister had stalked out of the restaurant, leaving us all looking at each other, aghast ("Why don't you take a good look at yourself, willing to settle for that Porky Pig just to get a job as desk clerk in a hotel!").

"Say hello to her for me," Olivia said. "She was such a cute little girl."

"Little girl? She's as tall as I am now. These days, she's in Germany, with a friend of hers who's a long-haul trucker. She wants to get a commercial license to drive semitrailers, so she's practicing."

"What a character."

"You can say that again."

Olivia was very curious to know what I was doing with a friend like Costantino Bernasconi ("with *that beast*," she'd say). I often wondered the same thing.

As she knew perfectly well, Costantino and I had sat next to each other in school. And after I went back to Rome, I ran into him again at the university, this time however as a student, because he'd fallen behind the rest of his class. With an average of barely 18 on his exams (17 out of 30 being a failing grade), he was having a hard time getting his degree. At first, I wasn't at all pleased to be back in touch with him. In high school, you still don't know what the world has to offer, and you're much more tolerant. At age twenty, however, you get to know the world all at once, but you're not used to swallowing it, this newly discovered world, gulping it down without complaint, so you're much more severe in your judgments than at any other age. And so, to make a long story short, I kept my distance. Me and Costantino Bernasconi? Sweet Jesus forgive me. A misstep of my youth.

But—and here I was really making an effort to be sincere—my Italian side was kicking like a baby in the womb, eager to get out into the light. Even if I felt contempt for Costantino, and even if that contempt extended from his person to the array of decisions he'd made in the years that had separated us—his stupid, trivial, consequence-free life, while I was studying hard and working my ass off—I couldn't help but treat him as a bit of a friend. After all, he'd always been very fond of me, or at least acted like he was.

He was running the serious risk of flunking out, once and for all, and that was the real problem. The desire to do him "a favor" burned in my trachea like a sore throat, it was actually a concrete pain, persistent, relentless. When would

I not give a friend a hand? I wasn't capable of asking myself whether or not he really was a friend, what prevailed inside me was an entirely Italian urgency—finally trans-sectional, yes, this time: identical in the *borgata* as in any bourgeoisie, high or low as it might be—to be different with him, to favor him in some way.

I started out by correcting one of his written exams. It was riddled with ridiculous answers and even simple spelling mistakes, so giving him a passing grade was truly a scandalous act, but still the temptation was overwhelming. After all, I wasn't running the slightest risk, my professor trusted me implicitly, he never double-checked the exams and papers he entrusted to me. Partly because doing so would have been a waste of time and he didn't feel like it, and partly because he knew that I was more rigorous and demanding than he was, with my self-righteous twenty years of age and my recent studies, still so fresh in my mind. When all was said and done, Costantino Bernasconi's written exams were just a drop in the bucket; no, a drop in the deep blue sea, a minuscule and invisible infraction weighed in the balance against a thousand far more serious ones, such as the ones he regularly committed—my professor, I mean—when he failed to show up for a class or a party, because other, far more profitable career moves were demanding greater efforts on his part. So you can be sure that he gave not a single damn about a stupid written exam submitted by a friend of mine. In other words, I could rest easy. But easy wasn't how I was resting. Because I knew that I'd now wandered into a subterfuge which could be very difficult to get out of. Costantino, seeing manna falling from heaven, immediately wanted more. Much, much more.

"So what did he want?"

"He wanted me to write his thesis."

"And did you?"

"Yes."

"Did he pay you?"

"I refused to let him. I think that he invited me here, to vacation on his boat, to make up for it. To thank me." I felt like a worm. So I clarified: "Actually, Costantino was always inviting me anyway, even before that, when we were at school together and I wasn't doing anything for him except letting him copy my classwork."

"That is, what he needed from you at that moment," Olivia pointed out to me.

"Well, true."

It didn't matter a bit to me that I was on Ponza on a hundred-foot yacht, dining out every night in fashionable restaurants at his expense, truth be told. In fact, I felt uneasy with them, I couldn't wait to get back home and eat a big platter of mixed fried seafood at Ostia. But I'd accepted the invitation because I was alone.

"No girlfriend?"

"None," I replied, with downcast eyes.

I was a little envious because she'd managed to do so many more things than I had, such as get married and commit a crime. While I'd done nothing. Not even a girlfriend for a few months. So I preferred talking about the Bernasconi clan.

"Costa is what he is, you've seen him for yourself. All he cares about is buying cars and getting laid. We don't have that much in common. And his sister is even worse. She's twenty-four but she thinks like a sixteen-year-old. The sailor is pretty nice, though. And he'd even be capable of steering the boat without ramming the neighboring yachts if only Costantino would leave him alone and let him do his job."

WITH ONE EXCUSE or another, Olivia and I were always sneaking off and spending most of our time together. Evenings at the discotheque were boring and just moving off to a secluded sofa wasn't much of a solution, because the music was too loud and you couldn't hear yourself think, much less talk, so we'd tiptoe off for an hour or so in some cute bar down by the port to drink a mojito. And even when we were on the yacht, anchored in a bay somewhere and couldn't get away, we still found a way to get some privacy. While the others were playing cards or baking in the sun or showing off on the jet skis that we'd rented, she and I would get masks and fins and swim off, far away, in search of a grotto.

Every so often, Benedetta, keenly jealous, would try to follow us, if for no other reason than to spoil our fun.

"I'm coming to the Lucia Rosa sea stacks, too!" she'd shout.

But long before she could get her mask on, we'd already splashed into the water and swum off.

The same thing happened in the evening, when we said goodbye to the others. Bebè would invent a sudden headache and ask us for a ride to the port, with a begging expression. But we would shrug, cruelly: "So sorry, we're on a scooter."

"The little Bernasconi sister is such a pest," Olivia said. "Is she in love with you or something?"

Frankly, the thought had never even occurred to me, that whiny girl was of so little interest to me that I wasn't even willing to waste time on analyzing her behavior.

But then, one night, I was forced to become fully alive to the problem. It was well past midnight, Benedetta came into my cabin and, without uttering a word, bent over me, pulled down my boxer shorts, and took my penis into her mouth. I was so stunned that I froze, paralyzed. She was licking and sucking awkwardly, clearly inexperienced, coughing and gagging if it slid too far down her throat, scratching it with her teeth, moving her hand jerkily and hurting me a little, actually.

"Bebè?" I whispered gently to her. "Thanks, but that's enough."

She lifted her head and burst into tears. "Did I do something wrong? Didn't you like it?"

I took her in my arms. I rocked her gently and spoke softly in her ear: "Listen, the normal thing to do is to start with a kiss, on the lips."

She started crying even harder: "I wanted to make a big impression on you."

"You did make a big impression on me, believe me. But you should only do this sort of thing with a man who's in love with you."

Now she was sobbing hard: "Don't you think I'm *cute* enough?"

"Of course you're cute. But that's not the point."

She started pounding me in the chest with both fists, angrily: "You're still in love with that Morganti bitch, aren't you?"

I froze, growing rigid: "What did you say?"

Through her tears, her eyes half shut and saliva wetting her mouth, she leveled her forefinger straight at me: "You tag after her like a lapdog! You're still her servant boy!"

I slapped her in the face. Silence. Benedetta touched her cheek, which was flaming red. She was no longer crying now. She got to her feet, adjusted her skirt which had hiked up a bit on her derriere, and then told me: "Well, you should know that she already has a lover, and it's not you. I eavesdropped on one of her phone calls. She thought she was alone on the boat, but I was still in the cabin, the porthole was open, and I heard every word. He's a foreigner. I don't understand English all that well, but I know enough to understand what I overheard."

She turned and left. I didn't get a wink of sleep all night.

———

THE NEXT DAY, I was different. Olivia asked me to take her to the market and I replied that it was too hot out and I'd rather read a book in the shade. At lunchtime, she took me by the hand, utterly confident that I'd follow her to a grotto in search of a moray eel that someone had spotted, but I was curt in my dismissal. I told her I had no desire to go swimming. In the afternoon, while we were under sail, she sat down beside me: I put in my earpods and turned up my music.

That evening, when I refused to leave the discotheque in favor of the usual mojito down at the port, dancing instead as I'd never danced in my life, sweaty and crazed, with the air of someone having the time of their life kicking up their heels, Olivia took me to one side.

"Hey, what's come over you? Do you have it in for me?" She was shouting because the noise was infernal. "Did you just hear me?"

Thumpa thumpa

"What?"

Thumpa-thumpa.

"I'm asking whether you're mad at me about something."

Thumpa-thumpa.

"What?"

She heaved a sigh of impatience, turned on her heel, and left. Benedetta watched the scene from a distance, smiling through clenched teeth. I sang the inevitable song of that summer, both hands in the air like I was at a concert: "*Cos'è successo sei cambiata, non sei più la stessa cosa, o sei ancora quella che è cresciuta insieme a me?*"

Even Costantino, the most insensitive creature in this world, was worried to see me so caught up with the music of Lunapop.

"*Fratè*, brother—everything all right?"

"Never been better, thanks."

That evening, everyone was strange. Even the Dandy was, for once, not stalking through the club with a cocktail in his hand, in search of prey, if only for his eyes to feast on. Instead, he sat in a corner, in the dark, uneasy and lost in thought, constantly checking the time. Then he disappeared.

We headed back to the harbor around four, crowding into a small jitney. The girls, all of them drunk, were sprawled over Costantino, who pulled them on top of him, one at a time. Benedetta had the hiccups and was lurching with each spasm, hand held in front of her mouth. And I continued singing the lyrics to Lunapop's hit ("*Ma c'è qualcosa di grande tra di noi, che non potrai cambiare mai, nemmeno se lo vuoi!*").

On the darkened dock, there was no missing our neighbors' yacht lit up bright. I could hear the voices of Olivia and her husband. They were going at it hammer and tongs, fighting loudly.

"Uh-oh, there's a gale kicking up," said Costantino, turning on his heel. "Let's leave them alone, girls. What if we all went and got a nice hot breakfast bun?"

I just announced that I was sleepy and headed for the boat. Benedetta watched me. I knew perfectly well what she was thinking: "You want to listen to what they're saying, I know that. You just can't get free of her."

I reached the gangway at a single lunge, took off my shoes, and went into the galley. I got ice out of the fridge, selected a large glass, and filled it with whiskey. I got settled in the cockpit, sprawled out comfortably in a director's chair, feet up. Like someone simply drinking in the moonlight.

The topic of discussion was as simple as could be. Olivia was packing her suitcase and said that she wanted to leave. And not just leave Ponza. She said that she was going back to Rome, she'd already made a reservation on the hydrofoil, and on the train after that. She was saying that in Rome she'd pack another suitcase, gather up all her things, and leave the apartment where she lived with him. The Dandy was sobbing like a child.

"Do you have another man? Tell me, I have a right to know. Are you going to be with him? Is he expecting you?"

Icy-voiced, she said only: "Please don't be so *petty bourgeois.*"

"I'm hurting, goddamn it I'm suffering, you bitch. If you dump me for another man, I'll kill myself. And I'll kill him, too. I'll unleash a blood bath."

I was laughing softly. Damn, what a show of aplomb. Long live civilization. The Dandy, suddenly, had won my respect. Teetering on the rear legs of the director's chair, pleasantly drunk, I enjoyed the radio drama.

That is, until I heard Olivia scream. Was he beating her? I leaped to my feet and jumped over onto the neighbors' boat, practically ran down the stairs, and burst into the dinette, where I found them both. She was on the floor, one hand clutching her nose, shouting. Her fingers were dripping with blood.

"I'm going to report you to the police! And no one's going to be able to keep this quiet!"

The Dandy, also seated on the floor, was holding his head in both hands: "Forgive me, darling, I apologize. I'm sorry, I'm sorry. *I didn't mean to.*"

I helped Olivia to her feet: "Come on, let me take you to the hospital."

"I think he broke my nose. Fuck, it really hurts," she said through her tears, occasionally laughing. "After all, my nose wasn't my best feature, I was going to have to get it redone sooner or later anyway. Manon always said so: 'Honey, you need to get that little bump sanded down.'" She laughed and laughed, twisting and squirming with the pain. Then she leaned against me: "My head is spinning, I think I'm going to faint."

And she fell backward, luckily onto the sofa. Everything else that happened was a natural succession. She was rushed to the hospital for an emergency operation, but the bump on her nose was there to stay. A moment before shutting her eyes under anesthesia, she told the surgeon: "I don't want a face like everybody else's. Please just leave my cosmetic defects." The police were never called on the Dandy. Olivia preferred just to say it had been an accident. That she'd slipped and fallen on the wet teak decking. You know, the humidity.

3

HIDDEN FROM HISTORY

AT THE END of September, with a bandaged nose, Olivia had already moved out. She'd decided to stay in Rome all the same, because she liked the city. She'd just moved to a different neighborhood. She'd found a nice little apartment, cute and sunny, in Monti, with exposed wooden beams and a little terrace she could fill up with plants.

It was a Sunday afternoon, and I was helping her to open boxes and shelve her books. I'd rather have been doing it in a place of our own, finally starting something together. But Olivia said that she was delighted to live alone, and in particular, she was treating me like a childhood friend, making it clear that the Valerio that really belonged to her was the little boy that had played with her, not the boyfriend that she'd had at age eighteen.

"Well? How are things going with your new job?" She was speaking to me from high atop a ladder.

"Okay, I guess." I was opening a moving box with a box cutter. "Yesterday, I had a meeting with the union representatives, and they were all *decrepit*. I asked Costantino why they were all so ancient and he told me, with a laugh, 'That way they can't send them to prison.' So we're starting out great."

After the vacation on Ponza, Costantino offered me a job at his father's construction company. Old man Bernasconi had cancer, and he'd soon be forced to hand over the reins to his son, who didn't really feel that he was cut out for running such an entrepreneurial business, or really for any kind of business or work ("I'm begging you, don't leave me flat on my ass here. I can't do this on my own, and you know it. I really need you. This will make you rich, give it some thought. You won't have to live on a magistrate's miserable salary!").

"Look out, Valerio," Olivia was saying. "Those are dangerous people: the original capital is laundered money. That's how Costantino's father made his money in the first place. Everyone knows it."

"But I'm not going to stay with the Bernasconi operation long," I told her. "I just want a chance to put aside a little money. I don't know when I'll be able to pass the civil service exam, and with scholarships you can't make ends meet."

I explained to her that I wasn't sure I was going to succeed in becoming a magistrate, and that I was starting to feel the need of a parachute. If things went sideways, I could use my savings to set up a law office, for instance. I was already a lawyer, I'd passed the bar, and one way or another, I'd mastered the material.

I told her my plans, gasping out the details so fast I could barely breathe, just hoping she'd get the message. Deep down, I was trying to tell her that soon I'd be able to offer her a life worthy of her expectations. Certainly not as luxurious as the life to which she'd become accustomed, but she'd be able to hold her head up. A house of her own (with a mortgage), a husband with a profession, a couple of good-looking children (I was happy to offer the best chromosomes at my disposal), and a devoted lover. I gulped at the thought of this last offer, the fantasy vision of me, the "devoted lover," thrilled me more than any of the rest of it. I could imagine myself bringing her to ecstasy every night before falling asleep and every morning upon reawakening: I even thought I could glimpse her smile.

"Your mother, eh?" she replied, still talking from her perch atop the ladder, while I handed her detective novels to be shelved on high.

"What does my mother have to do with any of this?"

"I imagine she had a few things to say about it."

With the excuse of picking a couple of books up off the floor, I looked down. "Well, she advised me not to let an opportunity of this kind slip through my fingers." I hunkered down, bent over, on the defensive. I only stood up when it was time to change the subject: "What about you? What are you going to do now?"

Together with her husband, Olivia had been forced out of the art gallery where she'd been working, but it hadn't been much of a loss, to hear her tell it.

"Believe me. We lost money and that's all. It was the opposite of a job, which theoretically ought to give you a living. I read a bunch of novels there—after all, no one ever came through the door."

Olivia was a professional squanderer of her intelligence. If she had any talents, she tossed them away freely, frequently in service of some nutty idea she'd come up with. The pleasure of running through a fortune was irresistible to her.

She had a magnificent voice, for instance. Manon, who'd been taking her to the opera since she was small and taught her arias from *Don Giovanni* since she was in nursery school, insisted constantly that she cultivate that gift. "My nightingale," Manon called her. But any effort to push her to attend conservatory had been in vain.

"You'll find something more interesting, don't worry."

"I don't have any talents, Valerio."

"That's not true."

She had climbed down off the ladder and was biting her nails, unconcerned at sticking her dirty fingers in her mouth, covered with all the dust that only books are capable of accumulating.

"You're swallowing mites and keratin. Tasty?"

I had decided to take the part of the solicitous friend helping her to unpack her moving boxes, hang paintings on the wall, driving her to Ikea or else to the drapery shop, after taking measurements with her for the windows. It wasn't an especially gratifying role, but I was happy to settle for it.

But then, one October evening, after an exhausting day at the city housing registry to change her official residence and then over to the tax office to take care of certain issues paying social security contributions for her cleaning woman, while we were sprawled on the sofa watching a TV series— she was already in her pajamas, what's more with a pair of socks on her feet that had anti-skid pads on the soles—I couldn't resist and I kissed her.

Olivia burst out laughing: "You're *tickling me*, Valerio."

I jerked my hand away from her and stopped caressing her hip. I went on kissing, but I did so while tormented by my bafflement. Olivia wasn't recoiling from my lips, but she only seemed to be moving her tongue out of affection or, worse still, to keep from disappointing me. As if she didn't want to reject the tenderness of a close friend who had stood by her in a moment of great need. All at once, I stopped.

Olivia bent forward, toward the table where she'd been resting her feet, and filled her fist with pistachios.

"Want some?" Her eyes focused on the TV set and her arm extended to her left, she was offering me nothing but a handful of empty shells.

"Are you with anyone?"

"Sort of."

What did "sort of" mean? What the hell kind of an answer was that? I was twenty-six years old, and I still expected answers to be answers. I grabbed my backpack, I unzipped one of its pockets, I pulled out a tin can and laid out on the table: tobacco, rolling papers, a chunk of hash, and a sky-blue lighter. Just for starters, I needed to soothe my nerves. Plus, it might prove helpful to her: if she could just relax, she might be able to tell me something more.

After a couple of drags, Olivia was already resting her head listlessly on my shoulder and was willing to confide all her secrets to me, from age four on (except for the dark secret of where she'd hidden my Rubik's Cube, in August 1981, when she'd discovered that in order to make all the faces look the same, I'd detached the color stickers).

"Who is he?"

"It's a complicated story. Maybe I could tell you some other time, what do you say?"

"In that case, tell me where you put the cube."

She laughed and laughed, sounding like a pony, partly on account of the hashish.

"*Never, I'd sooner die.*"

"All right: either the cube or your lover. If you continue to refuse to talk, I won't take you tomorrow to the tax office to request your health care card. And you can also forget about me driving you to the department of motor vehicles to get the duplicate of your scooter's registration, which you lost."

"All right," she said, hands up. "I surrender."

"Well?"

"Well, then, I'll give up the lover." Olivia had tossed back a gulp of beer from the can and she was licking a mustache of white foam off her upper lip. "I'll take the truth about the cube to the grave with me."

In our conversation, there was still a childish tone that could pop out at the most unexpected moments. We let ourselves plunge back into time, arms open wide, not worrying about the ensuing splash and floating there with smiles on our faces.

"You bitch."

"You stripped off the stickers, never forget it. *That was unforgivable.*" She wanted me to understand that the pain hadn't yet subsided.

Meanwhile I was crumbling more hashish between my fingertips and licking the second cigarette paper. A few more drags and Olivia would tell me everything, to the last detail. Maybe even what had become of the cube.

"Well?"

"His name is Mehdi."

"What kind of name is that?"

"He's Iranian. Mehdi is the name of the Hidden Imam. The story is complicated, I warned you."

"YOU'RE A TWENTY-FIVE-YEAR-OLD WOMAN, favored with good fortune, all things considered, but with neither skills nor talents," Olivia was saying. "You've tossed aside all your finest opportunities, and you're well aware of the fact. You haven't studied, and you haven't pursued any of your interests: it's too late for you to dream of anything spectacular. You can only try to be reasonable and settle for what happens next. Anything would be better than this pointlessness.

"You're married, but your marriage isn't an occupation because your husband, affectionate and kind though he may be, doesn't think much about you. You have no children, and not just because you make love only rarely, but also because he has a low sperm count." Here Olivia, having just taken off her socks, wiggled and stretched her toes, as if that would help her to think more clearly. "You've lived in three cities, too many for such a short span of years, and you haven't managed to create lasting ties of friendship in any of them. So there's really no one to turn to, to confide in.

"Your husband, a child of privilege and as confused as you are, has been unable to come up with anything better in twenty-eight years of life. You've started an art gallery together, even though neither of you knows anything about art, and that was because the only thing you don't lack is money. Almost immediately, though, you realized that it wasn't a solution. He's chewing through his inheritance without results and you're bored to death."

Olivia tossed back another gulp of beer and threw her head back. An amber drop slid sensually down the side of her neck.

"So every now and then the two of you go over to someone's house, but you're actually both quite antisocial, you never know what to say to people," she went on. "So, when the woman who lives next door asks if you want to become a contributor to a women's publication, where she writes herself, you can't believe your good fortune. It's a glossy magazine, certainly much more frivolous than what you think of yourself—you might be useless, but you don't have those kinds of weaknesses—and yet you find that you're excited at the prospect. At last you can enter the world, you don't so much care what kind of world it actually is. At the art gallery you're always alone, and ditto at home. You nourish your intelligence by reading magnificent novels, but still, it's a somewhat self-centered activity, which you seem incapable of sharing with anyone else. You dearly hope they'll ask you to write some book reviews. You'd even be satisfied with a capsule review. But that's not how it works out."

Olivia turned toward me for a moment and smiled, but not really, her eyes half shut. She was using this engaging, welcoming "you," but she wasn't really talking to me at all. She was really talking, though. Maybe the second person was helping her get out of herself. In the garb of an interlocutor, she somehow felt liberated.

"So you show up for the interview and they ask you to give them two hundred words or so about a couple of trendy diets. The book column has already been assigned to a young woman who's your same age but while you were fooling around and wasting time, she's already published at least four novels. Writing, after all, isn't exactly your strong suit, you weren't even very good at writing papers back in school, but you roll up your sleeves and you get to work, editing and re-editing your article. No one tells you whether it's any good, they just publish it and move on. They're not particularly selective, that much becomes clear immediately. The next assignment, they send you to cover a concept store, and off you go. You already realize you're never going to make it onto a serious publication, they're not going to give you interesting topics to write about, but still, you're happy to be working. You do your best to hold on to that profession by the skin of your teeth, without throwing any sharp elbows because you're not used to that kind of maneuvering, no one ever taught you how to be aggressive in pursuit of something, you've always been too lucky from the outset. It's nothing much, you're not telling yourself any lies, but that work gives you a sense of identity. They pay you next to nothing, but you've always subsisted on the kindness of others anyway, supported by your family or your husband, and you realize that it gives you a feeling of satisfaction to earn money, even if it's just two hundred euros. When people ask you what you do, you finally have an answer. It's not much, but at long last it's something that belongs to you. Now you're engaged and you've hit your stride, you willingly write about nail polish and spas, royal weddings and spring collections—whatever. If the opportunity presents, you'll even write about recipes, though you know nothing about cooking. And everyone else appreciates you precisely because you don't shy away, no matter the topic. You've managed to make your contributions matter, in some sense. You're valued: you who are so fickle, you who've never finished a single thing in your life."

Olivia stopped for a moment to calmly shell a couple of pistachios. She chewed on them in silence, without looking at me.

"Then one day they ask you to go to a press conference for an Iranian film director, they want an interview right away, by this evening. And here you finally waver. This is the big chance you've been dreaming of, you've always wanted to write about bigger things, but you're too scrupulous. You know exactly who this director is, but you've never seen his movies. You don't want to show up for your big opportunity unprepared. This time, you'd prefer to let someone else do the article." She quickly jabbed a pencil into her head of curls and tucked up her hair. Now I could see her profile better.

"But no one gives a good goddamn about your scruples. The woman who writes about film is at Cannes and there's no one else in the newsroom who can do it, one guy's grandfather is in the hospital, another guy has to go pick up his son from soccer practice because he's in the middle of a full-blown court battle with his ex-wife, who's threatening to take custody away from him entirely. They even make fun of you. 'It's not like we need a film critic to do this, you know,' they tell you. One of them, a little more sensitive than the rest, takes you aside and explains it to you: all you need to do is ask a couple of questions, the first things that pop into your mind, and turn in five hundred words in time to put the issue to bed."

She drank another sip of her beer, lost in thought. Then she started talking again, but this time her voice had changed. Now, suddenly, it was the voice of a grown-up woman.

"So, you find yourself in a packed press conference room, there's not an empty seat in the place. You take notes like a college student, your back against a column. You look more like a student than a journalist, by the way. Not only because you put on a pair of loose-fitting trousers, spangled with pockets, and a faded T-shirt. But also because, the whole time, you're standing with your head bowed over your notebook, as if you were in class. But when you look up, you realize that someone's staring at you. All around you are five hundred people listening attentively, but the Iranian is talking to you and *you alone*. Then and there, you're knocked for a loop, you press your back harder against the column. But then you start to enjoy the game, you stop taking notes and you stare back at him."

Olivia heaved a deep sigh. "It seems like a movie where the dialogue's not synced up right to the action: he utters these awful, portentous phrases, but his eyes are saying the exact opposite. He speaks into the microphone, saying: 'The whole film is set in a bunker, what I wanted was to vividly render the claustrophobia of any war.' But to you, and only to you: 'I don't know who you are, but I want you. And what I need above all else is this desire, because desire is life.'

"He's evoking worlds light-years away from yours, and you can't imagine why he's chosen you. When he was a soldier, you didn't know a thing about the war between Iran and

Iraq, you were a little girl vacationing in Monte Carlo, and the only Persians you knew about were friends of the Shah, safely ensconced in their hundred-foot yachts, certainly not in a bunker. You're roiling inside. No one's ever made love to you with their eyes. This contrast between funereal and luminous messages hypnotizes you," and she smiled to herself, with her eyes shut. She had shut me out, once and for all. This was a story that belonged to her, and her alone, and she was clearly telling me so with her body as well as her voice.

"After the press conference, everyone gets up. You turn to head for the exit and think to yourself: 'Okay, well, the game ends here.' Yes, you thought of it as a game, *between history and your own story*. Even though you've stopped taking notes, you'll have no difficulty writing up five hundred words. They can forget about the interview, you certainly can't approach this Iranian director with your tape recorder after everything that's happened (in silence) between you. For the first time, you don't give a damn about the magazine anymore. Then you turn your head and you realize that he's walking rapidly in your direction, pushing his way through the crowd. He's coming after you. You get scared. And so you run away."

At last, Olivia turned to look at me, but her gaze was distant. She had remained where that man had taken her.

"You enter the house with your heart bursting, you can't even get the key into the lock, your hands are shaking so badly, the keys fall to the floor. You pick them up and think: 'It's a good thing my husband is in London.' You never even touched that man, he doesn't know your name, but to you, it's already perfectly clear: this is cheating, plain and simple."

Olivia pulled a cigarette out of her pack, and her hands were trembling the way they did back then.

"You take a bath and you make yourself an herbal tea. Now that you've calmed down, you can sit at your desk and turn on your computer. But you just wilt. You can't even conjugate verbs properly. Come on, it's just five hundred words. It's no good though—you're looking at the watery sky-blue screen saver, blankly. You get up and walk into the kitchen and gulp down four pieces of chocolate without hesitation. You're hoping that a shot of sugar will jump-start your brain. You're ready to demolish a box of cookies crammed with butter and a pack of whole-wheat breadsticks, while you're at it. You have the scissors in hand, and you're about to cut open the packaging, when you realize that you're not trying to nourish your neurons, but your anxiety. That's when you burst into tears. I can't do it, *I can't do it*. You angrily toss your laptop computer at the couch (it's taken worse falls in its time than that, actually). Then you pull out your cell phone and turn it off, pressing down hard on the power button."

She was laughing to herself now: "You know that they're going to call you a hundred times from the newsroom, damning you in absentia because it's your fault that they can't put the paper to bed, and after you stand them up like this, they're never going to call you back for work, but none of that matters. Just as it doesn't matter to you if your husband has to call the doorman to find out if you're still alive ('My wife hasn't answered the phone since yesterday evening, I'm a little worried, would you mind knocking on her door, please?')."

She leaned back, against the cushions. She grabbed a fleece blanket and covered her legs. "For a couple of months, thinking back on what happened, you convince yourself that you did the right thing. Your husband has certainly never been a saint, but with you, after his fashion, he's always been faithful. He's never lied to you. And you know that passions like the one you just sidestepped can only be experienced in utter secrecy. What's more, you've asked around a little bit and learned that the man who was looking at you like that is married and has two young daughters. Sure, you could have just indulged in a night of illicit sex without really hurting anyone. But, even if you've never experienced anything of the sort, you know that trying to place prior limits on these things is pointless, relationships just get out of hand. You've lost the job you cared so much about, but still, you're happy with yourself."

I stand up, I don't feel like listening anymore. But Olivia turns around and takes me by the arm. Please, she says with her eyes. "Please, stay here." So I sit down again.

"BUT THEN, one night you come home and find your husband in tears. You don't even have time to ask him what's happened. As soon as you approach him, he confesses everything. You don't even bother to ask about the hapless victim.

The only thing you're capable of telling yourself is: 'What a cretin.' And in that first moment of confusion, your fate is set." She gazed directly at me now; at last she was looking me in the eyes.

"Ever since you first digested the news, over the course of just a few months, you're already a different woman. You've even bribed someone, you've committed a crime. You behave the same as you always have, but you're different. You don't worry anymore about your husband, who's changed even more than you have. You realize that he's fragile, but your empathy has run out and your compassion has become routine, there's not an extra gram of your soul for him. He often turns aggressive and you shout at each other and fight, but that's convenient for you, at least you have a pretext for unleashing your resentment." She sighed. An all-too-human sigh, that smacked of cigarette smoke and beer. All the air that left her mouth took oxygen away from me: I was starting to realize that she really was in love.

"Then the Iranian comes back, because his film is in competition in Venice. After the festival, he's even going to swing through Rome. And you read in the newspaper when and where. If you want, you have another shot at it. You think about it for a day—should I do this or shouldn't I?—even though you focus on only the most trivial aspects (In that case, what would I wear?). This time you really don't want to let him see you in a faded T-shirt."

Olivia scratched her temple, as if trying to root out a thought.

"When you walk into the theater, on the strength of an assignment from a publication that no longer wants anything to do with you, teetering on a pair of heels you don't even know how to wear, you feel a little ridiculous. But you're certain you're not making a mistake. He was looking at you and only you, there can be no doubt about that. You trust his intuition more than you do your own, seeing that yours has failed you." And she laughed, with a liberating laugh, because she'd never allowed herself to laugh that way before.

"When you see him on the stage, so far away, you feel like even more of a fool. Why on earth should he even remember who I am, you think to yourself. After all, he never even found out your identity. You listen to the discussion absentmindedly, curled up tensely in your seat. You're tempted to turn and run again. But something happens, and it's the last thing you were expecting: he was hoping to see you the whole time. It takes him a second to recognize you, even if this time you're dressed like a fancy lady, and not like a college student. From a distance—and it's certainly a distance—he raises his arm and waves at you."

A woman who feels precious changes her expression. And that's the way Olivia was right now, her eyes speaking: *Excuse me, I'm precious.* I found her stunningly beautiful, even if it wasn't me she'd become more beautiful for.

"And so, unsteady on heels you don't belong in, claiming a profession you don't belong to, you walk into the cocktail party and enter a world that doesn't belong to you (to approach a man who will certainly never belong to you).

"You reach out a hand and you grab a glass, shyly. You try to mingle with the crowd, hoping that he doesn't miss you in it, though. While you look around, feeling a little marooned—where am I, anyway?—you feel a hand touch your shoulder. And you recognize that touch, even if you've never felt it before. You turn around and you stagger even further." Olivia raised a shoulder, as if her resignation to that destiny was the most joyful thing that ever happened to her. "You don't know what to say. Luckily, he goes ahead and starts talking. You're too on edge, so you have a hard time understanding his English, with its Middle Eastern accent. All those summers spent at boarding schools in London, from age twelve on, are proving useless. But it doesn't matter. Your eyes know how to travel the worlds that you yourself don't know how to traverse."

She was thinking about something, but she wouldn't tell me what it was. She had an unattainable smile on her lips. And that smile was much worse than all the words she'd said to me until then. Because it was the smile of a woman who had been, for at least a fleeting moment, happy.

"You go back home in a state of euphoria, even if you can't remember a word of what was said. You fell back on made-up words and ungrammatical expressions, and yet you succeeded in confirming an appointment for the following day, at Piazza del Popolo. Your English studies fail you once again during the walk you take together in Villa Borghese, you stammer and trip yourself up with your wording, but you aren't worried, your pact is based on mystery: you know full well that, leaving aside this language or that, the two of you will never understand each other. The distance between your worlds transcends you, the limitations of words pale in comparison with this reality. But here you discover another power, that you couldn't have known, much less studied."

She took what seemed like a strategic pause, as Manon did when she told stories. It wasn't a calculated thing, it was simply hereditary. But perhaps these were suppositions on my part, maybe Olivia just needed to take a little extra time to tell me something indecent, in other words, something that was too authentic.

"When the barrier is so high, the body reacts with a knowledge all its own, which transcends any efforts and impetus. The body cares nothing about history, whether on a grand scale or a small, personal dimension, the body has no fear of any babel: it speaks for itself. And then you surrender to his slow Middle Eastern caresses."

I was pretending not to hear her, but she insisted, refusing to spare me.

"This physical intimacy expands well beyond your expectations: now that you're calm and profoundly satisfied, you even manage to communicate and perceive truths, both yours and his, to which you previously had no access. Your mind opens up, your ideas expand, as you pass through the choke point of a limited vocabulary. Now it's you who expand words. The two of you are by no means confined to a bunker or a principality out of an operetta. You're no longer prisoners of your affair."

She suddenly leaped to her feet and rummaged through the CDs, looking for an album by the fado-influenced Portuguese folk ensemble Madredeus, the only gift Mehdi had ever given her. By now, she was talking freely, completely unleashed.

"You're riding a license that gave you the freedom of darkness," she was saying, "and your hands always know how to find each other's bodies. And this groping affinity, too human to be usurped by everything that exists around you, makes you feel all-powerful."

Then she sat back down, and all we could hear was the music of Madredeus, in the background.

"But you're not all-powerful. You both start to feel it the first time you're separated, when each of you returns home. He leaves and you don't feel ready to return to the inferno that you've built with your husband ('Nonna, help, I'm in love. Can I stay at your place for a few days?')."

Here, Olivia went back to speaking to me directly, because she knew that I understood. I was the only one to have the keys to her story—her history—in hand, the Iranian couldn't compete.

"When you come back home to the house you grew up in, you are no longer capable of saying what distance is. You don't know if it's a matter of space or of time. Your father, your mother, your uncle: they all seem farther away than he does. Only Manon can help you to shorten the distances ('What Arabs are you talking about, honey? What boats? You mean Khashoggi?' 'Yes, that was his name.' 'He

worked as a middleman to sell American weapons to Iran.'
'Then those people weren't that distant from war after all.'
'No, certainly not, war was what made their fortunes. But I
think that Khashoggi lost it all at the casinos. A few years
ago I remember reading that the High Court in London
demanded he pay back twenty-two billion lire he lost gambling at the Ritz'). You realize that you'd lived in a world
that really wasn't that walled off from his. It's just that
you'd never known it."

And she looked at me again, but bewildered. Her eyes
were wide open, her eyebrows were raised, she was biting her
lips.

"At this point, you can't seem to stop digging deeper.
You are determined to find all the points of contact, whatever the cost, even where there can't be any such points of
contact. You search for answers everywhere, even from your
friend Astrid, whom you haven't seen in so long, perhaps
not since her wedding, where you were her maid of honor,
but then, there were at least three hundred people in that
villa, you barely had a chance to give her a kiss on the cheek.
Unlike you, she took her degree in business and economics, with a GPA of 4.0, summa cum laude, and now she has
a job, she's the administrative director of her father's company, she accomplished everything you failed to do, and yet,
all the same, her ignorance bewilders you ('What war are
you talking about? The Gulf War?' 'Why, no, Astrid, that
has nothing to do with it. The war between Iran and Iraq:
it lasted from 1980 to 1988.' 'I was too young to read the

newspapers back then.' 'What about Khomeini?' 'Oh, right, that fanatical Arab…' 'He wasn't an *Arab*.'). You try to turn a blind eye, convinced that between human beings, there is no gap too wide to bridge. But you walk away from the bar, thanking her only for the aperitif."

I swallowed a mouthful of saliva. Even if her story upset me, I had no intention of confessing that her dear friend Astrid had thrown herself at me, the minute Olivia had left for Paris. I would have liked to let her know that there were other women without qualities, but I held back.

"You return to your life, without resolution. But you can't think of anything but the words that Mehdi used to whisper in your ear, in a guttural language, full of aspirated sounds, sounds you couldn't even understand. He taught you only a few words: 'kitty-cat,' 'life of my own,' and 'good night.' *Gorbeh, joonam, shab bekheyr.* And yet that little snippet of code was all you needed. You can't afford to act like a teenager, this much at least you've learned. You can wait for him and be patient."

Olivia slowly lifted her eyes to look at me and there was something truly intimate in her gaze: I understood that she trusted me.

"Then you realize it one afternoon, while you try on a pair of shoes," she went on. "You're collateral damage in the war, you of all people, you who walk through an intact world. This time you can't play with the shadows of others, there's too much darkness around you. Not even by accident can you add blood to blood, or fanaticism to fanaticism, all you're allowed to do is touch each other ever so gently. This is the only way you can love him, *in hiding from history*."

Meanwhile I was thinking that we two had always loved each other that way, "in hiding from history." But I said nothing.

"You continue seeing each other, for a year, roughly once a month, every time he can find an excuse to come back to Italy. Enclosed in a bubble, a light airy bubble that doesn't cause claustrophobia, the way a bunker or a principality does, but still: locked up in it. Until 9/11." She nervously slid a ring off her finger, turning it over and over in her hand. "On September 11 you are together and the coincidence strikes you as something sinister. You both understand that that day something more than the Twin Towers collapsed. The Middle East is going to have to pay for that rubble, Iran is branded a 'rogue state,' and Mehdi has to return immediately to Tehran. At a time like that, he certainly can't abandon his family. You don't know what's going to happen, what the consequences are going to be, you know only that history has overtaken you."

"I'M PREGNANT, Valerio," she told me, suddenly abandoning that *you*, so engaging, that I had finally had a hard time putting up with.

"Pregnant?"

"Yes." She lifted the joint out of the ashtray and lit it. "But we broke up, the only right thing to do now. So I have no intention of telling him anything, I'll decide what to do on my own."

I took the joint out of her fingers, for starters. Maybe it wasn't such a good idea to smoke weed, especially not in the form of hashish. Then I put my arms around her and hugged her tight, because that's what Olivia expected of me. But my embrace wasn't an act of consolation, it was a farewell.

PART FOUR

2005

1

THE REACTIONARIES

FOUR YEARS LATER. February 2005, a week of skiing, Cortina d'Ampezzo. I'm in the bathroom of our chalet, and I'm having an argument with my son, who thinks he can pee without taking off his ski suit. Given the fact that this is the first day of vacation, and I really don't want to start things off with a spanking, I let him keep on his helmet and goggles. I hold him up, both hands under his armpits, begging him to aim into the toilet bowl. But Filippo can't stay still, he kicks and throws his head back. The helmet slams into my lips, I taste a surge of blood in my mouth. It's inevitable that a struggle ensues, during which his penis naturally slips out of his hand. I head back onto the slopes, my trousers drenched, in a black rage.

I leave the chalet, I look up, and there she is, right in front of the ski lift, bent over the skis of a little girl, working on the bindings. She's gained some weight, but that broad derriere, that slight double chin that's most notable when she bends over, the belly that pokes out under the form-fitting fleece, do nothing to make her any less desirable to my eyes than she was.

I'm deeply tempted to venture closer to get a better look. I wonder if that vertical crease between her eyebrows has become more accentuated. I wonder if she's still capable of shifting the tone of her gaze in a split second. I wonder if she's learned a new smile. Better steer clear.

Better to take the stairs and vanish into the café. I suggest to my son that we go together to buy some chocolate, certain I won't encounter any resistance on that front, and I don my sunglasses, to ward off the risk of being recognized.

"Valerio! Valerio! Wait!"

SHOULD I HAVE pretended I didn't hear? Out of the corner of my eye, I saw her come running toward me, legs slightly splayed and knees bent, because of the ski boots she was wearing.

"Oh, ciao. I hadn't noticed you. How are things going?"

"Oh, fine, just fine, thanks," and she seemed disappointed. Understandably, after all I hadn't even given her a peck on the cheek.

She was looking at my son. She pointed at him, finger leveled, with a look of disbelief.

"Is this little fellow yours?"

Then she caught her breath, having just remembered that she'd abandoned her daughter in front of the ski lift. The little girl was sobbing in despair.

"Just a second, sweetheart!" Before taking off at a run in her ski boots, she grabbed my hand: "I'll be right back. Don't move. Don't you dare."

Filippo tugged at my windbreaker: "Who is she, Papa?"

"No one, just a woman I know."

Even more unsteady on her feet, Olivia returned with the little girl in her arms. She was breathing hard and a curl, wet with sweat, was glued to her forehead.

"This is Sara." Then, to her girl: "Darling, say hello to this gentleman. He's a great... great friend of Mama's."

Now it was my turn. I laid a hand on my son's helmet, and with a smile said, "This is Filippo."

Filippo lisped out a ciao. Neither of us touched the other one's child, not even a good-mannered pat on the head. As if they were radioactive.

"Well, so I heard that you married Bebè," she cackled, slightly insolently.

"Yes, she's his mother," I replied flatly.

"And where *is* she?" Olivia turned her head back and forth, searching among the people basking in the sun on the terrace.

"She couldn't come, she had to go to the hairdresser's. Tonight we're invited over to friends' for dinner, they've rented a hut up in Tofana."

Olivia gave me a punch in the shoulder. "You sound like my father, oh my God, what a laugh!" She mocked me: "'Tonight we're invited over to friends' for dinner'...*Just listen to him.*"

"Don't make fun of me. You know how sensitive I am."

Had we already regained all our old-time intimacy? Then I noticed that while Olivia was talking to me, she was holding one hand on her chest to cover up a jam stain on her white windbreaker. I was immediately reminded of my pee-damp trousers. I wondered if they smelled. If she'd still been five years old, Olivia would surely have teased me: "You wet your pants, ha ha ha." But she wasn't five years old anymore, so she pretended not to notice the wet patch on my leg.

We didn't know what else to say to each other. Embarrassed by our role as parents, tangled up in emotions from our childhood, we were having a hard time finding a practicable path.

"Well, it's noon. The lesson's about to start, I'd better go see whether the instructor has arrived," I said.

"Maybe they're in the same class." Olivia jutted her chin in the direction of a group of children lined up in front of the ski lift. "Is that where you're supposed to meet, too?"

Considering that our children were going to be skiing together, we decided we might as well ski together ourselves. After all, we were going to have to wait until two for them to be done. It was almost an involuntary choice. We'll run a couple of slopes together, just to kill time. And maybe we'll have a beer together, on the snow.

From the very first curve, the competition was on. I couldn't stand the idea of Olivia going faster than me. I was willing to hurtle down headlong without once braking.

"You feel like skiing a black run?" Olivia asked, pulling a woolen headband down over her ears.

"Why not?" I replied.

"A single shot all the way to the first chairlift?" she asked with a note of challenge in her voice.

"Single shot, how?"

"Without stopping."

"As long as I don't have a heart attack."

"Well, then, ready, set... *goooooo!*"

She was already ahead of me. She curved fast, bent low on her knees, her ponytail bouncing on the back of her neck. She was leaving a high spray of snow in her wake, like a speedboat. I could feel the wind in my face, the chill of the speed, and it seemed to me that I could feel the time I was moving through, that thing we rush through so quickly.

But then, without warning, Olivia braked to a halt.

"Would you just look at that," she shouted, pointing with her glove at the peaks before us.

The sun was shining brightly and the glare forced me to squint. But I could see, and very clearly: the Dolomites spread out before us in all their vast, airy beauty. These are generous mountains, which extend well beyond the span of your gaze. You see them, and you see so much more, as if someone had installed a wide-angle lens in your eye. Was life giving us another chance?

"Valerio? Valerio?"

Olivia, who had stopped a little farther down, was calling to me, waving a ski pole. Then she started climbing quickly back up, doing a herringbone. She reached me and kissed me.

When she pulled away from my mouth, she licked her lips in some bewilderment. "Wait, you're bleeding. Did you get in a fistfight with someone?"

OUR GOOD LUCK wasn't limited to a ski school in Cortina. The second sign of destiny came from a bathtub in Rome. Parioli neighborhood, 6:30 p.m.: my mother-in-law slipped in her jacuzzi and broke a hip. Benedetta was forced to return home immediately. Costantino was in China on business, so someone would have to look after their mother.

Naturally, I was willing to go, too, but Bebè insisted I stay in Cortina. Not out of any sense of generosity, let's make that clear from the start. She just wanted to have an excuse to use on her mother, so she could quickly leave her to her own devices, after putting on a show of daughterly duty ("If

I tell her I need to get back to be with my boy, she can't really argue with that"). As soon as I was alone, I immediately reached out to a blonde named Natasha, willing to look after my son for thirty-nine euros an hour. I paid the ransom in advance and left them both in the hotel restaurant. And I invited Olivia out to dinner.

To avoid any risks, I chose an out-of-the-way gourmet restaurant, in Corvara. It didn't matter that it was a long drive and we'd have to climb through the Falzarego Pass. After all, we had plenty of things to say to each other.

The drive up lent itself to increasingly intimate conversations, and every hairpin curve eliminated another layer of shyness. From what I was able to deduce, Olivia had kept her little girl.

"And what became of the Iranian?" I was trying to keep my eyes glued to the road, as if that question didn't really matter much to me.

"I never saw him or heard from him again."

For that matter, that's exactly what Olivia had promised him: silence. So she had limited herself to giving her daughter a biblical name that went well with the surname Morganti. A silence of this sort could only be broken by a story out of the *Arabian Nights*, she said, a story that she would invent the day that Sara finally started asking her questions.

"So now you're all alone."

"No, I remarried."

"Oh, you did?" Unruffled.

In her seventh month of pregnancy, Olivia had taken something of a fright. She wasn't so sure anymore that she could stick to that courageous decision. And it was in Cortina, of all places, three years earlier, during a week of skiing, that she'd met Piero, a hematologist, very caring and kind and very much in love with her, happy to take her on, even pregnant as she was. In her eighth month, without a lot of careful thought, she'd moved north and set up house with him, because he worked in a hospital in Milan.

"What about your grandmother?"

I just wanted to change the subject. But Olivia had misunderstood the question.

"Manon? She took the news pretty hard."

At least the "Communist queer" had been as handsome as a Greek god, so the mistake was an understandable one. A moment's silence and indulgence for that latter-day fall of Icarus. And the "Iranian" (Manon never referred to anyone by their name) truly was an intelligent man, possibly even rising to the level of genius, whose allure was not to be denied. But . . . this guy . . . *this* was one Manon couldn't accept. A nondescript, unremarkable doctor. Not even chief physician at a hospital. Not even professor at a school of medicine. Nothing noteworthy about him. Someone who said little and tended to sweat heavily. ("Honey, you're just settling. Life will file away your expectations, it happens to everyone. But in order to avoid that slippery slope, you've at least got to start out *big*.")

But Olivia wasn't listening. She wanted to get married again, and right away. Even if her divorce hadn't yet been finalized. The only solution to this legal problem was a morganatic marriage. With the "Communist queer," naturally, she had opted for a secular ceremony, at town hall. That meant the Church could still welcome them into its arms. All they had to do was pretend to be devout Catholics, a bureaucracy like any other. And then there'd be plenty of time to get things straightened out later. Manon didn't know what else to do or say to put a halt to this folly ("Honey, there *is* such a thing as cohabitation"), but Olivia seemed utterly possessed.

Naturally, her second wedding had been arranged and held in the villa, bedecked with flowers to celebrate for the third time some wonderful future or other for Olivia. Though she might have refused to wear a white dress at her first wedding, in a show of contempt for conformist norms, at her second she not only went back to the traditional color, but even to the style she would have adopted at age eighteen: an Empire-waist dress, perfect for accommodating her swelling belly.

But Manon was increasingly weary, it was a tremendous effort for her to organize perfect parties these days. She was no longer the tireless Mrs. Dalloway she had once been. She felt the crushing weight of time in the very details of things, when she realized that she no longer cared whether there were lilies of the valley or tulips at the center of the table. And any old frosting would do, even custardy frostings with far too much egg, after all she didn't even bother to taste them anymore. The half-hearted, slovenly manner in which she'd selected the glasses for the wedding banquet made it clear to Manon that her era had finally come to an end, from here on she could only hope to age without inconveniencing others, as she watched her granddaughter grow old more quickly than she at the side of a man who could never bring her happiness ("Honey, you're making a mistake. And that's my last word on the matter").

"And *are* you happy?"

"Well, he's a good man."

Actually, though, for the first few months in Milan, Olivia just wept all the time. She blamed the fog, and her grandmother laughed right in her face ("You grew up in the Po Valley, you know, not in Sicily, sweetheart"), or else the diet she'd been following after her pregnancy ("If you'd only drink less, my little chickadee"), or the apartment she was living in, which she thought didn't get enough sunlight. She went on to such an extent about possible reasons for her tears that her grandmother had ventured to trot out a question she'd been holding in reserve: "Permit me a momentary indiscretion, honey: Do you have regular intercourse *with that gentleman?*"

Olivia had found a perfect definition for the malaise that afflicted her: postpartum depression. It hits twenty percent of all mothers. And with that formulation she felt suddenly authorized to spend her days smearing ointments on her newborn daughter's ass and chatting about recipes with the

butcher and the fruit vendor. "You know, you get to a certain point in life when sex isn't that important anymore,"
she'd explained to Manon, "or anyway it's not a priority."
Her grandmother, annoyed at being preached at, stood up
brusquely from the table: "Oh, really?" Though she immediately afterward regretted that harsh and dismissive lurch—
after all, Olivia was acting the know-it-all only because she
wasn't capable of giving a name to the mysterious thing that
made her so melancholy—and therefore circled back to give
her a more complete answer, along with a kiss on Olivia's
forehead: "Not at age thirty, little mouse."

A year later, Olivia, not entirely deaf to that wisdom,
had realized that the time had come to take a lover.

"And who is it?" I was driving, impassively: just me and
the curves of the Falzarego Pass. By now, I was ready for as-
cents and descents.

"Oh, there's lots of them. I'm not interested in getting
involved with any of them."

She told me that, just to keep up her morale, she'd set
out to amass a collection of short-term relationships, because
within the first few months, they all inevitably fell in love,
which meant all sorts of needless complications. There were
those who became morbidly jealous, others who showed
signs of dependency, and others who couldn't sleep and
slipped into depression.

"I'm just hurting people left and right, lately."

Olivia unquestionably possessed an unhappy gift: she
was capable of drawing out people's dark sides. It wasn't

something she did on purpose. In part because it's impossible to capture shadows, depths, hidden follies, by means of any conscious strategy. They will only rise up spontaneously, attracted by a glitter on the surface, like barracudas drawn by shimmering jewelry.

When I was a boy, I thought this ill-favored gift of hers was a problem that affected only me. Then I watched her live her life, one husband after another, lover after lover, and I realized that it was a much broader issue. A person's dark side is always something very exclusive, for obvious reasons. It's already difficult to accept in and of itself, but it's much harder to accept the fact that it's not really even all that unusual, and that everyone has a dark side.

Her diabolical ability not only to tolerate but actually to love the shadows in other people tended to produce chain reactions. Like opening a Pandora's box.

Sometimes, she even made me laugh. She was incapable of doing things conventionally, like everyone else. And she didn't even seem to realize it. Often, relationships are deals. I'll give you this and you give me that, and if the underlying pact is respected, we can just turn a blind eye to everything else. Not for her. It didn't even occur to her to *negotiate*.

"I mean, to get what you want," I felt obliged to explain to her.

Olivia opened her eyes wide: "But I don't want anything! *Which is exactly why* these guys fall in love."

I was talking to a woman who did things without ever considering the consequences. The women who negotiated and gnawed away ("What sort of privileges are we talking about, after all," she said) were too far from her mindset.

MANON WAS STARTING to think that that unfaithful husband of hers, whose betrayals she'd been unable to forgive even once he was dead, might not have been that bad after all. Manon, who used to go to the cemetery to make scenes and throw tantrums, slamming the bunch of roses she'd brought down on the marble and changing the water in his flowers the way you'd change the adult diaper on an invalid relative, finally free to unleash all the resentments of a lifetime, had all at once turned softer and kinder. Now she'd bring a stool with her and sit down next to Gianni's vault, dusting off his photograph and thanking him. For having treated her like a queen, for his generosity and his ability to give her his love, for always having put the family first, for the moments of happiness, the travel, the world that he'd opened her eyes to, and for the joy of being together in the middle of so many beautiful things, lucky couple that they'd been. One afternoon she'd burst into tears as if she'd lost her husband the week before, and not twenty years ago. She dabbed at her eyes with a forefinger wrapped in an embroidered hanky, poked in under her sunglasses, talking to herself all the while ("Do something for *your granddaughter*, dear boy. Come on now").

Neither Dado nor Giulio were doing particularly well, but there were priorities, and she had to be cautious about asking for favors, because Gianni didn't like being maneuvered and she would need to lead him where she wanted him to go without making it obvious that she was pushing him ("What do you think of *that man*? If Olivia would only meet the right person...").

For the Morgantis, this was a period of great retrenching. The companies that made up the group were shuttering their operations one after another and Giulio was drowning in problems as well as in debt. Increasingly fragile, by now utterly in thrall to his wife, who openly mistreated him. "Well, what a bargain *he'd* turned out to be," Marilù threw relentlessly into his face on a daily basis: she never should have married him. There were evenings—Giulio confessed to his daughter—when the new Signora Morganti was complaining about the state into which she'd fallen, for instance, after she'd been forced to sell the house in Sardinia that she'd so lovingly furnished, evenings when he was even beginning to miss Elena ("After all, your mother was so affectionate").

"So why doesn't he divorce her?"

"I ask him the same thing. But, you know, he's sixty years old, and he doesn't feel like turning his life upside down again. And if he did, she'd leave him without a pot to piss in, he didn't do a thing to protect himself, not a prenup, nothing. I think that's what he's afraid of, in part: losing what little he has left."

Dado wasn't doing all that much better. He'd sold the company trademark to the Chinese, a company he'd founded himself, proving to the rest of the family that he knew how to be a successful businessman, too, even if he was the outsider, and in fact that he was more farsighted than any of them, seeing that at this point Italian style—what the Italians themselves called, sounding the English words with their accent, "*il Made in Italy*"—was going great guns. And if he was now handing everything he'd created over to the Chinese, he was only doing it because—successful businessman, in fact, that he was—he'd sensed that this was the right time to do it. He was still in time to *sell* to the Chinese, and later he'd surely have been forced to *give* the company to the Chinese, free and clear, as a gift, so he'd decided to sit himself down and have a frank little conversation with himself, practical and concise. He'd told himself that he'd much rather die of boredom sprawled on a mountain of cash destined to become scrap paper, rather than rotting under continual stress chasing after money that was being systematically taken from him, like what was happening to Giulio. "Rotting" was the right term, because Dado was starting to feel his age, the Viagra- and cocaine-fueled parties were starting to weigh on his reflexes, to say nothing of the alcohol that had built up like a fatty sediment around his belly and his hips, a jolly life preserver. His agitated life, his continual quest for excitement, and his overarching loneliness, all this cumulative strain—luxuriant thrilling effort—was starting to bow his back a little.

I UPDATED HER periodically, but Olivia already knew everything. Manon clipped any article that mentioned me and sent it to her ("The Bernasconis launch a takeover move," "The Age of Bernasconi: Another Real Estate Tycoon on the Stock Exchange," "Bernasconi Group at 3.7%: 180 Million Euro Investment," "The Rising Star Leads the Iron Axis. Small Shareholders Counterattack, a Clash on the Newly Established Board of Directors," "Summit Meeting of the Big Guns: the Bernasconis Lean In with Their Purchases, Up to 5%," "The End of an Era in Italian Capitalism: the Bernasconis Run the Table, the Country's Last Grand Old Man Shuffles Offstage").

"Of course, I know all these things about you," she laughed, "you're a notorious speculator and profiteer. And to think that you wanted to be a magistrate, not a real estate developer."

"Well, you know how it is, life kind of makes decisions for you," I replied evasively.

At the hairdresser's, in a gossip magazine, Olivia had even seen pictures of my wedding. Bebè's garish wedding gown, specially designed for her by Roberto Cavalli, politicians standing up as witnesses, even the arrival of Silvio Berlusconi by helicopter. She'd seen my mother, who'd put on plenty of weight over the years, sheathed in a Versace dress, trying to smile, stiffly, at the photographers, even as she stifled her rage at my sister who'd been seized with a giggling fit right there in the church, during the ceremony.

"You did things in style, didn't you?" Olivia's irony was starting to irritate me.

Who knows how much she'd laughed with her grandmother at all the gaudy excesses my wife had come up with to make her dream come true ("I want *the party of the century*"), with the guidance of a Famous Wedding Planner who indulged in even more delirious outbursts of kitsch than usual, specifically in her honor. Bebè had managed to render ridiculous a perfectly dignified Baroque church, already overadorned on its own account, by covering the seventeenth-century floor with *an actual grass lawn*, laid all the way to the altar like a red carpet ("It's so romantic to get married in a garden"). And there had been no way to restrain her when it came to the candle arrangements, which you found hanging in flower vases or floating in the swimming pool, even clustered around the wedding cake, at the serious risk of setting fire to the newlyweds when the cake-slicing ensued (a seven-story cake that weighed in at 350 pounds, with genuine pearls studding the frosting, and it was up to the guests not to swallow them).

I was hoping that Olivia would never get a glimpse of my home, with the tiger-stripe and leopard-spot fabrics, the round bed with the mink fur blanket, the pools and pools on top of pools, with and without hydromassage, and those gadgets that let you switch on the lights by snapping your fingers, which drove me crazy every time because the switches never seemed to want to listen to me.

For that matter, Benedetta never asked me when the time came to make decisions: "things" were her territory. If

I dared to object, she silenced me instantly telling me that I was always at the office, that she *worked* all day long *for me*, and that all I knew was how to complain ("And here I am, killing myself with work. You're never satisfied with anything." "No, no, that's not true. I was saying that a round bed strikes me as not particularly comfortable, I'd just prefer a normal bed, that's all").

"Well, your mother got what she wanted," Olivia added.

It was a cruel cut, but also the truth. I couldn't seriously disagree. If my mother hadn't insisted so adamantly, maybe I would never have agreed to accept a position in the Bernasconi Group. After all, I had other plans ("Remember the sacrifices that I've made for you, Valerio. And now you're thinking of turning down an opportunity like this one? You're every bit as much of an asshole as your father").

Mama had also worked tirelessly to persuade me to start going out with young Bebè. "Such a fine young lady," she'd say, "the way she calls you every day, poor thing. Why don't you take her out to see a movie?"

But then we were interrupted by a ping from her cell phone, a text had come in.

"Your husband?"

"No, no, don't worry about that. One of my lovers. He has a weak spot for trans women, so one night I went with him. They're really too ambiguous, at least for my tastes, so I didn't do anything more than stay with him while he made his selection. You know, I was sorry to leave him all alone with his obsessions. But now I can't stop him: every time he goes out to see them, he feels the absolute need for me to go with him. He texts me, he sends me pictures, he tells me all about how it went. I'm sick and tired of it."

Her tone was neutral, she mentioned other people's perversions with the same nonchalance with which she would read a menu.

"I'm very torn. Cavatelli pasta with porcini mushroom, shellfish, and vanilla? Or black-tea scampi with potato spaghetti?"

AFTER DINNER, I went upstairs to her place. It really stunned me to see that apartment where we'd played as children and made love as students. It hadn't changed a bit. Wooden walls, the large sky-blue *stube*, and the panoramic view of all the mountains, from the Cristallo to the Tofana to Cinque Torri.

"Regular grappa or licorice?"

"Just regular, thanks."

The lights were low, because Olivia had only turned on a single lamp in the corner of the room, and we were talking softly to avoid waking up the little girl. The sofa was a big one, but she had chosen to sit right next to me, and her knee was pressed against my leg. We were talking about our marriages.

"I'm not very faithful, but I'd never leave him. He offers me security, you understand that?

I, too, defended my relationship, which I described as "solid and tranquil."

"Benedetta is a little childish and she can be capricious, but she's starting to mature. It's done her good to have had Filippo, she's a good mother. She lives for him."

I didn't know what else to add. So I looked out the window and noticed that it had started to snow. We both thought the same thing, at the same time. We looked at each other.

OUR LOVE was an underground river, but the sensation was always that of a new beginning. We were no longer two children gauging the shapes and sizes of each other's bodies, as we rolled and tumbled, nor were we even two young people mythologizing sex and not daring to play. No, we were two fully conscious adults, with a certain amount of experience, and we realized that we had something precious in our possession—namely a distant and mysterious familiarity. Something that we could truly call intimacy.

But our troubles began when the holiday ended. Managing the relationship was complicated ("I'm running into difficulties, the meeting is going on much later than expected, I may only be able to spend an hour or so with you." "But you realize that I came to Rome especially for this..." "And I'd like to remind you that I've just purchased land zoned for construction in Gallarate especially so we could celebrate your birthday together"). After two months, we were both at the ends of our respective ropes.

I even went to conferences on sustainable construction, just so I could spend a couple of days with her. I would move meetings from Campania to Lombardy like pieces on a Monopoly board. To carve out a day I could spend with Olivia, I'd pretend to be interested in parcels of land I wouldn't have dreamed of buying, not even to bury toxic waste in.

My wife hadn't noticed a thing, but my brother-in-law was worried, he thought I seemed "distracted" ("You need to get some rest, Valerio. Take a trip, go somewhere with Bebè." "God, not that! Oh, I meant to say...I absolutely can't. I have too much work, Costantino, you know that").

Meanwhile Olivia was subconsciously doing everything within her power to confess to her husband that she'd been cheating on him, but he stubbornly ignored any and all provocations. One day, she'd even managed to leave her computer turned on and unguarded, with the screen open to her email and a deeply emotional message addressed to me in prominent view. No reaction. Piero had managed to drain the laptop's battery. His wife never let her cell phone leave her hand, not even when she went to the bathroom, and without warning she'd started to lose weight, and instead of buying artichokes at the grocery store, she'd return home with bags full of new negligees and panties. But he asked no questions.

Manon recommended that Olivia just tell him the truth ("Honey, there are times when the suspicion begins to arise that you might not really be in love with that gentleman anymore." "Nonna, what can you be thinking?"). Maybe Manon wasn't so much rooting for me as against him. But it worked just fine for me all the same.

And so, one evening in Bologna (the official excuse was a ceramics fair) I invited her out to dinner, too. I hadn't seen Manon in ten years, and I was worried that this dinner together would force my whole mythological system into a state of crisis. But that was not at all the case. Manon was now a magnificent eighty-year-old woman with a long neck that would still do honor to a thousand glittering necklaces. She came striding toward me, her skirt barely revealing an agile knee, locking arms with her granddaughter, more as a reminder to me that if I wanted to harm a hair on her head I'd have to stride over her dead body to do it than out of any need to rely on the support of a young creature, not actually that much more robust than she was. She was waving a glove in the air—hey there!

How I had missed her. The Bernasconi grandmother couldn't begin to compare. I'd been struck dumb when Costantino and Benedetta introduced me to an old woman wearing an apron and her hair up in a bun, as if she'd walked straight off the screen and out of any of a thousand movies about southern Italy. Nonna Rosetta was barely capable of signing her name (even if she was the queen of documents, since her granddaughter, in a vigorous campaign to avoid paying taxes, had put a fortune in her name, as well as a Ferrari convertible), and she could only converse in dialect. The only thing that old woman had in common with Manon, aside from her age—born the same year? how could that even *be*?—was her unmistakable demeanor of *command*.

Bebè and Costa pushed me toward her ("Don't let her *intimidate* you, Valerio") and I had to stifle a laugh. At her age, Nonna Ettorina was still running five gambling dens and regularly drinking her customers under the table. And at the age of seventy-nine she'd filed for divorce from her husband ("I don't want to die still married to that man"), with a team of lawyers and an agreement for a regular alimony check made out to her name ("He owed me so much money for years, this way he'll finally have to start paying me back"). Me, who'd grown up in the Roman *borgata* and up in the Bologna hills: *intimidated* by a woman like her? A woman who looked mentally unsound and who'd gone, in her youth, from harvesting tomatoes to the frenzy of construction in the 1970s, without ever advancing beyond that. Deported to Rome by a husband certainly far more clever than her, she'd lived right up to the end behind the shutters of an apartment on the outskirts of town, while her sons built towering apartment buildings in all directions around her. There'd been no way to persuade her to move, and in fact they'd even struggled to convince her to let them renovate her bathroom. She didn't like changes, and *that* was what she had to say about that.

And while I was hugging Manon the way you'd embrace your own history, I was considering how it is that the history of other people never manages to stir you the way your own does. I was proud to be able to take her out to dinner myself, since I was happily a member of that 8.5 percent of young

people who, according to the data of the social survey institute, ISTAT, prove the existence of a certain social mobility
even in Italy. I told her that she was beautiful as always, and
I bent over her hand to plant a kiss.

"Don't talk nonsense, you scoundrel."

We had let her choose the restaurant, to avoid making
some calamitous error. This was the most secretive family
dinner in the world, which only made us rock with laughter.
After a bowl of *tagliatelle al ragù* (when Manon had guests,
she served exceedingly refined risottos, but the minute she
set foot in a dining establishment, she went for a menu
straight out of a country tavern) and a glass of champagne
(she wasn't a drinker: she'd only drink vintage bubbly), we
began to talk about more serious matters.

"Well? How is the soap opera proceeding? Have we
reached the happily-ever-after yet, or not? Don't drag it out
too long, kids, I'm not getting any younger."

Olivia and I insisted that we couldn't ask for divorces
because the children were too young, and Manon told us we
were wrong, saying that it made no sense to cling stubbornly
to relationships that had so clearly failed.

"Good heavens, you're more reactionary even than your
parents. And you can't seem to understand the choices your
grandparents made. What a strange generation you are."

Without sparing us her sarcasm, she pointed out to Olivia
that Sara might very well consider *that man* to be like a father to her, but he most certainly wasn't ("Thank heavens").

"Nonna…"

"Oh, the way you go on. Get busy, if you want you can get married at my house."

That's when I remembered how, when I was small, watching *The Leopard* with her, I'd turned and said to her: "These seem like the parties that you throw, Manon. Will you throw one for me someday?"

BUT NO ONE BOTHERED to speculate about what would happen if we were found out. One evening I returned home (from a weekend with Olivia in Barcelona, where I'd gone with the excuse of a meeting with a "starchitect," who was suddenly interested in building glass-clad eco-skyscrapers studded with gardens) and I was greeted by the entire Bernasconi family arrayed in my living room. Costantino, his mother, and even an uncle and aunt, Zio Silvio and Zia Alberta. Someone must have died, I thought. Nonna Rosetta? Then I realized that the only person missing was my wife and I understood. The dearly departed was me.

Olivia's husband, after pretending he hadn't noticed a thing for months, had finally run out of patience and had picked up the phone and called Benedetta, who was now weeping behind closed doors in her bedroom. If I'd had anything like a normal marriage, a moment of confrontation would eventually have ensued. But this wasn't a normal marriage, and the Bernasconi clan were afraid of losing a trusted and capable CEO much more than they were worried about any son-in-law and brother-in-law.

"Think of the boy," they said. But the subtext was: "You're not going to dream of leaving us now that Costantino has managed to win the contract to build the new Olympic village" (over two million square feet of construction to be carried out in an area subject to extremely strict environmental, architectural, and archeological zoning ordinances, to say nothing of the fact that it was a flood zone as well as a surface characterized by crumbly soil).

Olivia's husband, for his part in things, was no less combative. He was living in a two-story apartment in the Brera district, with an internal courtyard and a very convenient parking place. And he had no intention of letting me have the parking place.

Roughly a week later, Olivia and I arranged to meet "for our farewell." We said things like "Maybe it's better this way." Heads bowed. It was raining hard, and at times it was even hailing, it almost seemed as if the elements were opposed to our separation, which had been decided at something like a drawing table. We were in the car, and pellets of hail were dropping from the sky so violently that they threatened to shatter the windshield, so we'd pulled over in a tunnel. We didn't know exactly what to say, we'd used up our whole store of clichés, all we had left was the truth, but it seemed better not to delve into that.

"This is an *ethically* correct decision, Valerio. And someday we'll both be proud that we made it."

"Certainly."

As always, when we indulged in noble-minded statements, we were tempted to make love. But that was a mistake, because making love like this—in a car, in a tunnel, during a storm, thinking that this would be the last time—summons up a final power that sex already contains within itself. And when we were done, there was nothing we could come up with to justify the separation that we'd just agreed upon.

"I saw my parents' divorce, I know what it means," I said.

"Yes, same for me."

Suddenly, however, we understood the reasons for what they did. Suddenly we were no longer the children of divorced parents, but parents helplessly in love. And this shift in status, sudden as it was, stunned us, to a certain extent. When you stop blaming your family for all the mistakes you've made, it means you're getting older. This phase is called maturity, but only to sweeten the concept.

What's more, we knew perfectly well that certain frustrations are inflicted first and foremost on your children. But we were playing the role we'd been assigned, convinced that it was best to stick to the script, to avoid giving rise to excessively risky improvisations.

"We, too, will feel calmer, more at peace, wait and see." Olivia was trying to comfort herself.

"Certainly. It's been scientifically proven that sudden coital death tends to occur more often with a lover than a wife. I read it in the newspaper just a few days ago."

Olivia burst into gales of laughter.

"Listen, I'm not kidding about that. For starters, the systolic and diastolic pressure increases substantially during orgasm"—and here I was even wagging my finger at her—"thereby increasing the risk of both ischemia and myocardial infarction."

She laughed and laughed.

"Coital angina occurs during the minutes following sexual activity and it constitutes on average nearly five percent of all angina attacks, don't kid yourself."

How she laughed.

We couldn't even keep serious faces during our final farewell. And so we said goodbye like two former classmates who once sat together, forced to part because they're changing schools. A slap on the back, and so long.

HISTOIRE D'O?

STILL, we went on writing each other: lengthy, extremely lengthy emails. It was like trying to quit smoking but taking a drag every so often. Which meant not quitting at all.

Our lives, far away from each other, seemed pointless to us both. We even chanced, at times, to put it down, black on white, perhaps involuntarily.

Ding-dong, guess who this is? It's raining here. But it's not sleeting sufficiently to pull over under an overpass. Whatever. I came to Bologna for a week because my husband is at a hematology conference in Florida, all excited for the past two months because he's going to get a chance to have his say on I'm-not-sure-anymore-which etiopathogenetic mechanisms. In other words, he's going to have to explain certain phenomena: why they occur. Lucky him, if he can do it.

I'm trying to keep Papa's morale up, his wife has left him. He's taking it pretty hard. I tell him that he should really be celebrating, but he just looks up at me, dejected. I just hope he doesn't slip into a complete funk. You know, he says the strangest things: that he hasn't been able to build anything, that all he's been able to do is lose everything that his father left him.

I'm also very worried about Manon, who until recently could recite Dante to you by heart, and now she forgets things she just said to you a second ago. Yesterday was her birthday. I wanted to set off fireworks for her. The two cedars of Lebanon, which survived all the bombardments from the Napoleonic Wars to the present day, have no idea how close they came to danger. But she, who's spent her whole life throwing lavish parties, wanted this one, which might be her last one, to be calm and sober-sided instead.

So there we were, just the four of us and her. Granddaughter, great-granddaughter, and her two sons. An explosive combination, considering that my father and

my uncle hadn't exchanged a civil word since 1984. Ka-
boom! Like the model trains I used to blow into the air
back in the seventies. And the song by Charles Trenet
that I sang to my grandmother while she was blow-
ing out the birthday candles: "Quand notre coeur fait
Boum . . ." Manon was clapping her hands, the way she
did when she went to La Scala, elbows stuck tight to her
ribs and wrists moving frantically. Then she lifted her
chin, jutting it slightly: "How you've wasted your talent,
honey."

It was all so sad that my uncle and my father, after more
than twenty years, actually spoke to each other. They
retreated into the kitchen, with the excuse of putting
candles on the cake ("Do you think this is Alzheimer's?"
"Senility." "You always make it sound so simple." "You'd
like it if it was Alzheimer's, wouldn't you? No, she can
still judge you clearly." "Cut it out, stop spouting bullshit
and light that candle, it's gone out." "This lighter is too
hot, it's scorching my hand." "Give it here, I'll do it").

But I was the only one who made my grandmother
cry. Because of a stupid gift, which wasn't even one of
those ridiculous objects we bought, silly things to make
a woman laugh who has already received everything in
life, and lost everything in life. It was a homemade CD
with every available version of her favorite song, the one

she asked them to play in every hotel and restaurant she went to. Manon, who had such refined tastes, here sank happily into sheer saccharine sentiment. She'd sit and listen to Wagner for five hours at a time, and she understood that in her day, the difference was more between Luciano Berio and Cathy Berberian than Maria Callas, but still, she was thrilled to listen to "Memory" from the musical Cats, played in just any old piano bar.

What a mistake to slip that CD into the stereo. Manon wept as she sat facing her cake. My father and I held hands under the table. "I remember the time I knew what happiness was, let the memory live again," bump-a-thump-a-thump. Orchestra. She apologized over and over again, poor thing, but she just couldn't stop.

But Sara livened up the atmosphere, aiming my grand-father's Beretta at us all. Luckily, it wasn't loaded. We had just gone to the police station to report it had been lost. Instead, no one seems to know how or why, it had found its way into her toy chest.

I told her about my forbidden evenings out, which consisted of clandestine visits back to the *borgata*. Benedetta wasn't happy to have me socializing with certain people, so I did it without her knowing. I'd dream up business dinners and then go back to see my old friends. "I continue to feel like I'm a stranger in my new life: the transition was just too fast, my head is still spinning," I wrote her. Yes, certainly, I was vacationing in the Maldives, but when all was said and done I was more at my ease on the beach at Ostia, tucking into a bowl of spaghetti with clam sauce at Zagaja. I was taking tennis lessons, but I could only truly feel the endorphins circulating in my bloodstream when I went to lift weights in a Cinecittà gym.

On Friday I went to a seafood restaurant in Fiumicino, to celebrate Er Faccia's release from prison. Twenty men and two Cuban whores, respectively the girl-friends of Er Lungo and Er Biondo. Toward the end of the meal, drunk as dogs, we started singing songs by Franco Califano. "L'urtimo amico va via" ("Our last friend is leaving"), that kind of thing. Or "Te la ricordi Lella" ("Do you remember Lella") by Lando Fiorini. I don't know if it was the wine, but I had tears in my eyes. And so, on Sunday, with the excuse that I had to go see my mother, I joined them again to watch an MMA match (mixed martial arts, people beating each other silly in a cage, a typical sport of the borgata). I realize that this world of tattoos, jokes in romanesco, and men singing in chorus is just too much a part of me, I can't tear myself away from it. When it comes to having fun, you can't lie: that's where your true nature is found. And when I stop to think that my son will

*never know what it means to light a firecracker jammed
into dog shit, I feel a twinge of regret.*

In the meantime, all our good intentions proved to be pointless because, roughly a year later, Olivia was already getting
a divorce. And not on my account.

*When the judicial indictment and summons arrived, I
didn't want to believe it. I later learned many of the details from reading the papers. If my husband came home
with a new computer or a sophisticated stereo, it never
would have occurred to me that a pharmaceutical company might be behind it. I had a far more elevated concept of corruption, if you don't mind my saying so. I'll
just say that the most valuable gift was an all-expenses-
paid trip to Florida, for a conference, and I didn't even
go. Now I understand why he was so persistent about
Sara and me going with him. The company had paid for
the whole family to go. But it was hurricane season, so I
really had no interest.*

*I didn't even want to know how many bad prescriptions
he'd written in exchange for so little. Apparently, he was
even writing prescriptions for the dead. I recommended
that he hire two lawyers. He'd need one to defend a
clever little weasel on charges of criminal conspiracy,
and he'd need the other to defend a man whose wife*

considers him to be an obtuse asshole: one person alone couldn't handle both tasks.

My daughter still doesn't know a thing. It seems useless to me to bring it up at this point, after all, he hasn't made up his mind to get out. Not even out of bed, last night I went and slept in the guest room. I just hope they'll go ahead and put him in jail, that way I'll be able to use my bedroom again.

My marriage, too, was starting to crumble, and in fact I'd asked Benedetta to let me have some space to think things over. But she responded to the crisis by making sure she got pregnant again.

Couldn't she have told me that she'd stopped taking the pill? Tomorrow I'm taking her to the gynecologist for her first sonogram. I'd already made a reservation at a residential hotel, planning to spend some time away, until I could come to a final decision. My sister says that she did it on purpose. She might be right. That's her style, for sure. And I've been a tremendous idiot.

The baby was born, it's a girl [I wrote her a few months later—this was in 2007]. *We've named her Flavia. I hope that she's not as energetic as my sister. When Marta was little, we had to write our phone number*

on her arm with a felt-tip pen because the minute you
looked away for a second, she'd head out the door. And
I hope she's not as ambitious as my mother, because am-
bition keeps you from enjoying the things you have. I
hope that she's more curious than my wife, who never
wonders what other people are feeling. And less sensual
than you, otherwise I'll die of jealousy.

Olivia must not have welcomed the news, because she never did answer my email. She vanished for almost two years, and then reappeared, all of a sudden, in 2009, as if it were the most natural thing in the world. Without the slightest comment on my news. An ongoing correspondence between good friends, talking about this and that. Even if her intention of needling me was fairly unmistakable.

I've discovered that life as a single parent is a job. Ex-
cept, instead of earning, you spend. I'm trying to get out
regularly, but I already need a vacation, my God, I'm
so tired. Yours truly, Olivia, is very popular on the dat-
ing market, did you know that? Fat ass and all. But the
guys circling around me are all completely unacceptable.
Monday, at Nobu, I met your brother-in-law. He was
coming on to me shamelessly, I'm not kidding. For a mo-
ment, I was tempted to go to bed with him, just to play a
little trick on you. But Costantino is just such a repulsive
creature, I couldn't bring myself to do it. Anyway, we
talked about you, just so you know.

He told me that you've managed to secure contracts for rebuilding in L'Aquila. He was all delighted about the earthquake, laughing like a preacher who was finally face-to-face with the Apocalypse. He told me that you come to Milan regularly, to get your hands on your share of the construction business around the 2015 Expo. Sure, if there was a tsunami in the Milan Navigli canal system, that would bring in even more business, but you can't just snap your fingers and summon up tragedies on command, so you're going to have to settle for this little block party coming up in 2015. I get that. Oy, oy, Valerio, the sadness that settles over me on certain evenings. I swear to you, it's a struggle to smear on the lipstick to make my smile credible.

Then, one day, again without warning, she announced to me that we were going to have to stop communicating. That was that, it's just the way life is, it made no sense to go on.

I spent a weekend at my mother's house. Her boyfriend's niece was there, too, and she has a little boy the same age as Sara. The two little ones simply fell head over heels in love. For three days, they played, slept, and ate together. Then, on the last evening, there was an accident. The boy was down on all fours, and Sara was riding on his back, tugging on his suspenders like he was her little pony. Someone called her name, maybe it was because dinner was ready, and she let go of the suspenders all at once, snapping them sharply on his back. Naturally the little boy started yelling, because it really hurt. He was furious, he thought she'd done it on purpose, and he refused to speak to her. So Sara came to talk to me, and she told me: "Mama, I think I've lost the love of my life." I burst into tears, I swear to you. It was a phrase I should have laughed at, you have no idea how ashamed I was afterward.

Luckily, that accident was quickly overshadowed by another accident, because my mother set fire to the tablecloth when she knocked over a candle with her elbow. We were trying to put out the fire with a blanket, and as I gazed at the flames I realized that everything about us still burns hot. I need to forget you, Valerio. I beg you, don't write me again.

Underneath there was a link, she'd added to her farewell a song, and in fact, to be precise, *our* song, the Beatles' "I Want to Hold Your Hand," in a cover by Cathy Berberian. I listened to it every day.

TARALLUCCI E VINO

As soon as I got rich, I naturally thought about my own family. I immediately bought an apartment for my mother. An apartment that was soon put on the market and sold, because it wasn't right for her.

At first Mama thought that she'd get a long-yearned-for satisfaction by buying an apartment in the Parioli neighborhood, like her son's mother-in-law. Her wish was my command. Renovation work began immediately, and Mama went wild choosing all manner of delights. Renovation continued for nearly a year, because the new owner was enjoying herself. She came to the construction site every morning, and it was whims on a regular basis. They laid down the hardwood floor and she had them take it back up because she realized she preferred broad planks. The light of a spring sunset made her realize that the bathroom mosaic tiles were too yellow, so it all had to be ripped out. She leafed through a magazine and decided she wanted an open-space kitchen, so they had to tear down the wall separating it from the breakfast nook and redo the flooring there as well, in order to put in an island.

Struggling forward, it was finally time for her to move in. Six months later, my mother was in a state of crisis. She didn't know a soul in the new neighborhood. She was glad that her new neighbors had no idea that all her life she'd had to "slave as a housekeeper" (words that she still utters with resentment), and yet she was still unable to make friends, she really wasn't considered friend material. She missed the *borgata*, where she could have invited her girlfriends into her beautiful, newly renovated apartment and been treated by one and all like a queen. What a mistake she'd made. Changing neighborhoods in Rome is like moving to a new country.

One day, she screwed up her nerve and came to me and confided her problem ("I feel like I'm living overseas, Valerio").

Such a large apartment, in an equally prestigious apartment building, was, of course, impossible to find on the Via Tuscolana. But Mama was heartbreaking: you could clearly sense all her happiness at the idea of returning to a smaller place. Still, she wasn't used to having even that much square footage at her disposal: she wound up spending all her time in just one room. The rest of the apartment was left empty, and it filled her with sadness.

She didn't even have the interest to keep after the new renovations. In the bathroom, any old ceramic tiles would do just fine. And maybe, just maybe, she was happy to have a more contained, less sprawling kitchen, with a perfectly normal table where you could eat dinner while watching TV. The island with a stove top, all things considered, was something for chefs ("people who get their kicks by cooking all sorts of weird things").

As soon as I'd made my money, Mama had dumped her old boyfriend then and there ("I don't need to work at a reception desk anymore," she would say, her voice dripping with contempt), and suddenly she was all alone. She'd gotten grandiose ideas into her head, unfortunately. I could overhear her talking with her girlfriends on the phone, and I was ashamed for her. "I'd like to find a man more on my level, you understand," she would say.

And so she'd glued herself, like some unwanted appendage, to my mother-in-law, a woman who, in Mama's mind, frequented "a world that was suited" to her, in hopes of meeting a man. I was ashamed of this, too. Not only because she hadn't the slightest notion that Bebè's mother had no desire whatsoever to have her underfoot, but also because my mother had failed entirely to realize that Bebè's mother never saw anyone. She just stayed home, tidying her possessions, and only ever went out to buy more of them.

One evening, Mama did something that even melted my heart a little. I was at dinner at her house, just the two of us because my sister was in Amsterdam with a friend, touring coffee shops, and my wife was at her tango lessons. The only other person in the apartment was a Filipina, a housekeeper who, really, was strictly there for show, because Mama didn't trust her and wouldn't let her do a thing.

At a certain point, she looked up from her food and said to me: "Valerio, thank for you helping me to live the life that I've always wanted."

It was the first time she'd thanked me for anything. Everything had always been taken for granted, and that was that.

I replied that I was happy to see her happy. Meanwhile I thought to myself that in reality I was paying for her happiness with my own unhappiness, but never mind about that. I never would have dreamed of saying that to her.

A second later, though, she smiled at me, bitterly: "But this isn't how I imagined it, the life that I wanted. I have a hard time understanding how it works."

"How do you mean, Mama?"

"For instance, your mother-in-law. She has plenty of money and could do whatever she wants. Instead she just stays put, behind locked doors, in her apartment. And when she does go out, she just buys more useless possessions, a bunch of bric-a-brac, I get bored to death shopping with her."

I smiled.

"No, I'm perfectly serious, Valerio. A person makes it, and then what?"

MY FATHER, of course, had refused any help whatsoever. He continued working as a gardener in that hospice for the elderly, and it was trouble if I tried to intervene. For a while I'd insisted that I wanted to buy him a car and a taxi medallion: after all, that had been his dream. Nothing doing, though, he wouldn't hear of it ("You know, taxi drivers are always out on the street, driving around." "Well, that's what the job consists of").

And he of all people, a person of great honor and dignity, who'd never felt intimidated by any of the Morgantis, for who knows what reason, seemed to feel deeply uncomfortable around the Bernasconis. As if he felt out of place ("Papa, why are you so formal with your daughter-in-law? Just address her as Bebè, please").

The day of our wedding he had made up an excuse at the last minute and hadn't come ("It's just my cervical arthritis acting up, what do you expect? I'll come some other time..." "But there's not going to be another time, Papa"). Was he afraid that I was ashamed of him? Did he not want to see my mother again? Did he disapprove of the wife I had chosen? Never did find out.

As a grandfather, too, he was something of an absentee. He was less familiar with his grandchildren than he had been with Olivia when she was little, and when I pointed it out to him, he'd shrug his shoulders ("Well, when all is said and done, that *cinna* grew up with me. What can I say?" "Why don't you come see us?" "You're so far away").

And as for the work I was doing, he never wanted to hear about it. I would come through Bologna, stop by to have lunch with him, and try to have a conversation. I'd tell him that I was building a whole new subdevelopment, that it was practically the size of a city all on its own, and to capture his interest, I'd show him plans on the computer. But he seemed rather cool on the subject ("I like old houses, I could never go and live there." "No, I wasn't saying this is for you, no one wants to get you to move there." "Well, then, why do you talk about it so much?").

In the meantime, though, he'd modernized, too, and he'd even learned to use email. He sent me very brief messages, just to show me that he knew how ("How's everything there?"). I'd reply with a short, two-line email, complimenting him effusively for his progress. One time, though, he really surprised me. He sent me a link to an article about the Bernasconi fortune, without any further comment. The headline read: "The Empire Built on Money-Laundering." That time I was the one who failed to reply.

MY SISTER WAS, without a doubt, the person I cared about most in the world. In the end, she never did enroll in the national corps of firefighters. The queue for admission was lengthy, and before her name had come to the top, I had been able to completely change my own life, as well as hers.

There was a small trattoria—in local parlance, an *osteria*—in the San Giovanni neighborhood, where Max spent nearly all his evenings. It was a place with a floor plan of less than 450 square feet, with a microscopic kitchen in the back, and not exactly up to code, seeing that it had been built with Coleman camp stoves as a range. But the allure of that place was simply irresistible. Not a single detail had changed since 1952, when the clientele consisted largely of *fagottari*, literally, packed-lunchers, who brought food from home and only paid for wine tapped straight from the barrel or demijohn. There were bunches of artificial grapes dangling from the ceiling, surrounding the slow-turning fans, red-and-white-checked tablecloths and curtains, wooden chairs and tables dating back to the fifties, copper pots and pans hanging on the walls, and arrangements of garlic and chili peppers decorating the doors. And a huge wooden barrel from which they served the house wine, decked out with old promotional signs (GLASS OF VERMOUTH, 100 LIRE).

But Tarallucci e Vino wasn't just a vehicle that sent you back in time, to a small-town Rome that no longer existed: it was a mythical place, charged with memories of all sorts, including personal ones, because Max used to go there to get drunk with his friends, playing poker until daybreak or watching soccer matches of the home team, A.S. Roma. And it had become clear to me that there was only one way to keep my sister from throwing herself into the flames. I had to buy her that osteria. After all, if there was one thing she loved to do, it was to cook.

The owners weren't interested in selling, so I made up my mind to give them a shove or two. One day I'd send the health inspectors to pay a call, the next it would be the tax auditors. Finally, they came back to see me and said that they'd come around to my way of thinking. At that point, I stopped being an asshole. I highballed them with a generous offer, much higher than the actual value, whereupon their jaws dropped. I didn't want my gift to Marta to be some cheap trinket, that was part of it.

My sister was so contented that she'd already forgotten she'd ever felt the calling to be a firefighter. She felt as if she was working with her father beside her, she would tell me. She would be grateful for the rest of her life.

There was nothing else she needed. She scolded me if I ventured so much as to give her a designer handbag ("It's cute, thanks, but what am I supposed to do with it? The Chinese street vendors sell the same thing"). She'd bought herself a used car, financing it and paying monthly installments, and refused to accept mine, even though I was about to buy a new one ("That SUV, the kind of thing a *cassamortaro* would drive?" She'd used the dialect term for undertaker, calling my SUV a hearse. "For God's sake, no way. Where would I park it?"). And she'd taken out a mortgage to buy herself a little apartment in Cinecittà, with the money she was making at the restaurant.

Every morning she went and shopped for groceries at the Ceccafumo market, where I used to load and unload crates as a kid, and she drove the Via Tuscolana to the San Giovanni neighborhood. She cleaned the *puntarelle* chicory and the artichokes, chopped the parsley with a mezzaluna rocker knife, making tomato sauce for her meatballs and manhandling crates of beer with all the ease and power of a longshoreman.

SHE WAS THE ONLY PERSON I could talk to about Olivia. In part because the one thing that my sister wished for with all her heart was for me to finally dump Benedetta. Things had never been idyllic between my sister and my wife, but for the past few months they weren't even on speaking terms. All on account of a restaurant receipt.

We'd gone out to dinner at a trattoria near the Castelli Romani, a place in the countryside that Marta really liked a lot and, frankly, so did I, but my wife complained all evening long. Up to that point, a bit of unpleasantness. Then the check came, or anyway the owner handed us a scrap of paper with a row of numbers added up by hand instead of a proper, official receipt. Whereupon Benedetta threw a fit (and not because she was against tax evasion, not out of any sense of civic propriety, but strictly because she wanted to claim even that Sunday meal out with family as a business expense, for a handful of change as a tax deduction). The owner was a friend of my sister's, and he'd even taken a discount off the price of our dinner: naturally my wife's outraged tone had hurt and offended him. And at that point Marta had lost it. She stood up abruptly and said: "Well, just listen to her. She's got a hell of a lot of nerve, the little Bernasconi girl, daughter and granddaughter and sister of large-scale, serial tax evaders, people who've been defacing the beauty of half of Rome for generations now, one unsightly apartment building after another, but the one building they've managed to steer clear of is the almighty Hall of Justice." My wife stared at her, eyes round as saucers. My sister burst into loud peals of laughter—laughter as angry as it was loud—and slammed down on the table the official invoice that had just been brought at Bebè's rude insistence: "Congratulations, you've just saved thirty-seven euros that tomorrow you can deposit in your tax haven bank account in the Cayman Islands." From that day forward, it had been impossible to patch things up between them. Neither one of them wanted to hear a word about the other.

We'd only discussed that episode once, because I was tormented by a nagging doubt ("So, wait, do you think the same thing about me?" "What do you have to do with it?" "Well, I certainly have *something* to do with it..." But she didn't want to talk about it anymore, she preferred to change the subject).

On the other hand, Marta had been very fond of Olivia ever since she was a little girl. During our illicit affair, Marta had also proved very useful to us. Not only was she on my side, but she even kept Olivia company when she came to see me in Rome. In the evening, when I had to go home to be with my wife, the two of them would go out on the town. Olivia would eat at Tarallucci e Vino, and then, as soon as the osteria was done for the evening, they'd roam the city, far and wide.

I was painfully jealous of their nights out, in part because they didn't get back until dawn. My sister would take Olivia out dancing in plenty of places of ill-repute that she really loved, fond as she was of dives for *frociarole* (a term in *romanesco* that translates far more elegantly into English: "gay friendly"). They got drunk together, they'd smoke up all the grass that Marta grew on her little terrace in Cinecittà, and then they'd stride out into the night teetering on high heels befitting a fetishist. "The only thing she doesn't have is a tattoo on her ass," Marta commented, with satisfaction, the morning after.

ONE EVENING, when I was feeling sadder than usual, taking advantage of my wife's absence—she was at the Saturnia thermal baths with a girlfriend—I went to have dinner with my sister. Only Tarallucci e Vino could console me.

Outside the front door, I ran into L'Avvocà, who'd stepped out for a smoke. He was a regular customer, because you always ran into the same people in that osteria, which had become a sort of second family for Marta.

For starters, L'Avvocà wasn't a lawyer at all, as his nickname might otherwise have suggested: he was a retiree who had worked all his life for the Italian state railways. But everyone called him that because "he got people to get along." He lived in Garbatella with his ninety-year-old mother. His existence was punctuated by very precise habits, which verged on rituals. He woke up every day around noon, and then he'd catch a bus to Porta Metronia, always arriving at Tarallucci e Vino around two in the afternoon. He'd take a seat at a small table, right in front of the cheese counter, to avoid interfering with paying customers, seeing that at that time of day he wasn't eating, just leafing through one of those commuter newspapers they hand out on the subway and drinking a bottle of water. He'd stay there until the restaurant closed for its afternoon break, at four o'clock. Then he'd catch another bus and move operations to another osteria, in Testaccio. And there he'd remain, comfortably ensconced, until eight o'clock, playing cards and drinking a glass or two of the house wine. That was just a lead-up to his return to my sister's osteria for dinner, readying for the evening's culminating event, when he'd head over to his favorite bar in the Celio district and take a seat at one of those little round tables with a view of the Colosseum, downing one whiskey after another, into the wee hours. L'Avvocà was the reigning king of Rome's Gay Street.

But he wasn't a homosexual, he'd just carved out a different space for himself: instead he was the protector of all the lesbians out on the street, who all called him *zio* (uncle) and every now and then, amidst the general state of drunkenness, accidentally wound up in bed with him, usually in the feminine plural. Wild nights that never carried any real consequences because the next day his "girlfriends" were looking for him again to ask advice on their fights with their *actual* girlfriends. It wasn't until three or four in the morning that L'Avvocà finally relaxed: that's when he returned home and ate the pasta that his ninety-year-old mother left for him in the fridge, in a plastic container, which he heated up in the microwave. He and his mother lived together and never saw each other: they were in different time zones. It was a perfect coexistence, he used to say. He wasn't built for marriage, even though he had two children and a wife from whom he was happily divorced.

With the wrinkled face of someone who never says no, his skin reddened by alcohol rather than sunlight, a necklace of sky-blue beads around his neck, and a panama hat perched on his head, L'Avvocà was adored by one and all. I shook hands with him.

"Hey, how are things?"

"Valerio, haven't seen you around for a while now. Just think, yesterday I asked someone for your number. I wanted to call you because my son is about to buy a little apartment in the new neighborhood the Bernasconis just built. Do you think it's a good investment? It is a good one, right?"

"Oh, Jesus, tell him not to do it."

"But those are buildings that you constructed."

I was tempted to explain to him that when you want to build more structures but you aren't allowed to by the zoning ordinance, there are other ways of getting around the restrictions and obtaining the building permits. This dodge is called "a zoning agreement." You have to pretend that your extremely private interests as a builder actually coincide with the interests of the public, at least technically. In exchange for this concession, you have to pay money to the city government, to allow them to do something like, I don't know, build a new road or another section of the subway system, which of course no one will ever do. So you kick in some cash, but it's always a fee that's a hundredth of what is actually required to build the major public work. You obtain permits and the city gets cash, both parties are satisfied, and the people who discover that they have to live in a district without public services will just have to find other solutions. But I couldn't tell him that.

"Well . . . there were problems we weren't expecting."

"Problems you weren't expecting?"

"Well, maybe they won't be able to build a subway station after all, in spite of what they'd promised. You know how it is here in Rome: you excavate, you find ruins, and then you have to seal the hole right back up, because it's too expensive to try to get the ruins and artifacts out of the ground. Better to just leave them buried for another stretch. But then any projects are frozen in place. It's not like you can toss that stuff in a dumpster just to make room for a subway tunnel."

"Yes, okay, but how does a person get around town if they live there?"

About fifty thousand people had been left high and dry on account of the project I'd masterminded, but I hated to rip off one of my sister's friends.

"Exactly. I wouldn't recommend it."

"Well, thanks for warning me. My son was about to take out a thirty-year mortgage."

"Don't mention it."

My sister's osteria really did resemble a tiny theater: everyone knew everyone else, people would chatter away from one table to another. The groups were fixed, well established, especially for lunch. There were the *vivaisti*—nursery employees taking a break from their greenhouses, the secretaries from the nearby CPA's office, people who worked at the ministry, *er Cassamortaro* (the undertaker) and the other employees from the funeral parlor, directors and screenwriters who worked at an editing studio nearby and left their autographs on the paper tablecloths, doctors and nurses from the neighboring hospital, and a varied and haphazard stream of humanity that would never have come together if it hadn't been for Tarallucci e Vino.

The "Table of the Four Marys"—four gay men who lived one street over—was my sister's favorite, and she'd spend whole evenings sitting and chatting with them. So I stopped to say hello. One of them in particular, a very attractive and sophisticated guy in his early forties, who was widely considered to be the queen of the osteria, leaped to his feet. His short, cropped sweater revealed his midriff and abdominals ("Cover up your belly or you'll get a case of diarrhea," whispered his boyfriend, but he just ignored him). "Oh, Valerio! We haven't seen you around much lately. Come here, let me introduce you to my twin. We don't resemble each other much, because we're heterozygotic twins. It's the only thing hetero about me," he laughed.

He explained that his twin had come to Rome to see him on his birthday, and he showed me, with great satisfaction, the gift that he'd just unwrapped (a pair of push-up underpants, to boost his butt cheeks).

"Happy birthday."

"Come on, sit down, raise a glass with us."

"Thanks. Maybe later, I'm not really in the mood tonight."

"To WHAT do I owe this honor?" My sister walked toward me, looking magnificent.

She had become a gorgeous woman, who'd have ever thought it, from the hairy little baby girl she'd once been. She was tall and dark, with the same dancing eyes and luminous smile as Max. The only thing she'd inherited from our mother, fortunately, was the straight nose. Definitely not her personality. Marta was a free soul, unfettered by the conditioning of society. She was the healthiest person I knew.

"I'm here in search of political asylum. I need to have a chat with you."

Marta helped me take off my jacket and fooled around with the collar of my shirt to loosen and remove my tie, which she then rolled up quickly with her agile hands and slipped in the blink of an eye into the pocket of my overcoat

("There, that way you won't forget and leave it here"). Then she seated me. Singing, she grabbed a pitcher, filled it with white wine from the tap, directly out of the barrel, and then slammed it down on the table, a bit loudly, truth be told.

"Have a drop of wine, Pisè."

She continued to call me Pisello ("little pea," but Pisè for short), and a thousand times I'd tried to explain to her that (a) I was no longer a kid, and (b) I had become an important man, with a reputation to defend. But she didn't hear a word I said.

"So you miss her, eh?" She sat down across from me, resting her chin on one hand.

"A little."

My sister had one distinctive feature: she was fast, at everything. She came to conclusions rapidly and directly, usually much faster than I did.

"How can I do it? I have two children."

"Who are probably riddled with complexes because their parents aren't divorced like everybody else's."

A hair clip had come undone, and it dangled over her forehead, still clinging to a lock of hair. Marta restored it swiftly to its proper place with her quick hands. Then she stood up.

"What'll you have? Spaghetti *all'amatriciana* or a breaded fried cutlet with a mixed *misticanza* salad? Oh, listen, I'll decide for you. A small portion of each? And a side of poached chicory."

"No, that's too much, I'll get fat."

"*Magna e statte zitto.*" She suggested I eat and shut my trap.

She vanished for a moment. The sauce was her domain, and the cutlet was dipped in egg and then breadcrumbs, personally, with her own two hands, but in the microscopic kitchen in the back of the osteria there was a cook who was responsible for the actual cooking (still on the camp stove burners). My sister was the owner of the place, and she spent her time in the dining room.

That evening, however, perhaps on account of the rain that was paralyzing Rome, as rain usually did, the restaurant was practically empty. Aside from the Table of the Four Marys and L'Avvocà, there were just a few American tourists, whom she had taken care of on the strength of a highly improbable English, just the basics necessary to communicate ("How you say, *fusilli?*" And she reached into the pocket of her apron for a sample of dry pasta to show them: "This with tomato?").

She sat down across from me again, took my glass, and tossed back a gulp of wine. Then she popped a piece of pizza into her mouth. She chewed and looked at me, a level gaze, waiting.

"Well?"

"She's even stopped writing me. I've really lost her this time."

"Don't be ridiculous. You two have been running into each other by sheer chance all your lives. You just need to wait for the next coincidence. *Nun annà a cercà Maria pe' Rome...*"

It had been Max's favorite proverb, and I even remembered when he'd taught it to me. *Don't go searching for Maria in Rome.* I'd arrived in the city only a short while before, and I was seated on my bed because it was the only stick of furniture in the room, it was two or three in the afternoon and my mother had just finished a shouting quarrel over the phone with my father about money, threatening to keep me from going on vacation with him. As a result, I was sinking into a pool of despair, because I felt certain that I'd never have another opportunity to see Olivia Morganti. At that point, Max, who had glimpsed and understood my sadness, sat down beside me and said: *"Nun annà a cercà Maria pe' Rome."* I was baffled. So he'd proceeded to explain to me that if a guy sets out to find a gal named Maria in Rome, out of millions of people, he'll never succeed. He just has to wait for her to come walking toward him.

Was this the age-old, indolent Roman fatalism? Perhaps, but perhaps not. After all, it was a proverb that helped to reduce by some measure all the pointless words and deeds that frantic pursuits bring with them. Lightning-quick but relaxed, bold, and self-deprecating, to my mind that's how the deepest forms of Romanness operated: with stretches of apparent slowness, and then sudden lunges. I carried its lesson within me, and it felt as if I had a cat in my belly, at once lithe and lazy, capable of seducing you with both its slumbers and its scratching claws.

"Maybe you're right."

"It's your destiny, Pisè. It can't just come to an end like that. I can feel it."

"Please stop calling me Pisè."

"Aw, I can't help it." Marta stuck a fork into my bowl and tasted the pasta. "I bought a first-rate pork jowl at the market, let me try it and see how it tastes."

Then she stood up (she was incapable of staying in one place for long), shot a glance over to the table of Americans to make sure they weren't in need of anything, and headed over to the cheese and salami counter, cut a slice of pecorino, and came back to me with her mouth full.

"So what's your next move?"

"That's enough, now tell me all about you," I smiled at her. She was drawing daisies on the paper tablecloth with her head bowed, like a little girl.

"Oh, but I don't have any stories as interesting as you do. I'm so faithful to my boyfriend that I can't even bring myself to masturbate. It would still be doing it with someone else, and I don't want to do that. Even if that someone else happens to be me."

We laughed. I pushed my glass across the table and touched it against hers.

"Thanks, you always manage to put me in a good mood."

PART FIVE

2011–2013

1

A VERY PRIVATE PUBLIC ACT

BUT THE REAL TROUBLE began in 2011, when I went back to the Morgantis' villa "as a winner," as my mother liked to say. They'd put it up for sale? Fine, I'd make sure I made the highest offer. Officially, the purchaser was a company headquartered in Antigua, but rumors had spread, so Giulio called me in person. His excuse was Manon, who was dying. Perhaps I'd like to say goodbye to her? Of course I would.

For a moment, the minute I walked in the door, before climbing up to the third floor, I was tempted to stick my nose in the kitchen, to see if the marble table was still there, the table I used to eat dinner on with my father and all the others. But I was there for a different purpose, and I needed to remember that. Now I was entering that house, so familiar to me, as a real estate professional. I was a builder—a *palazzinaro*, as those who wished me ill described me, using a term that combined "profiteer" and "land-grabber"—every bit as much as the Morgantis. And even to a greater extent, because the Morgantis were teetering on the brink of bankruptcy, while I was comfortably perched atop an empire. So I couldn't afford to risk any falls. I even pretended not to know my way around. I followed Giulio as if that house had never been my home, too.

"Manon will be happy to see you, I'm sure of it. Let's surprise her," Olivia's father said, striding briskly.

His quick step reminded me that when we were small we'd go running through those rooms. The long hallways scared us, possibly because Manon had filled our heads with ghost stories.

She used to tell us that during the war, the villa had been occupied by the SS. "The Germans always chose the nicest places, children," she'd say, "more or less like Napoleon, who, understandably, chose to sleep here when he was in Bologna." And she'd point to the marble plaque with Bonaparte's name and the date in Roman numerals. "But there was a secret tunnel that led from the city center to our garden, and the partisans discovered it. They sent a young woman to explore it, a courier, who successfully traveled its entire length, during the night, all alone. So brave, poor thing. She came up in the avenue of the boxwood hedges, surrounded by the busts of the Roman emperors. What a magnificent place, she must have thought to herself, good gracious. In the twenty years she'd been on this earth, she'd never seen a place like this. But it was the last place she'd live to see. Because the Germans had dogs, and they immediately caught the scent of an outside presence. The young woman was caught and executed by firing squad in the grotto." "In the grotto where we keep our rabbits?" We shivered with fear. "That's right," Manon replied. We were no longer sure we wanted to go back there.

Manon told us that in the early years, just after the end of the war, when she and Gianni first bought the villa, abandoned in horrible condition, first by the SS and then by the evacuees ("They burned the painted doors from the eighteenth century just to stay warm"), she would wake up at midnight because she could hear someone *digging*. She'd go to the window and look down, over to where the centuries-old cedars of Lebanon stood, because that's where the sound was coming from, but she could see no one.

"Someone digging a grave: that was the sound," she said, "the problem is that they were doing it every night and we couldn't get a wink of sleep." Manon was so exasperated that one day, knowing the story of the partisan courier girl, like everyone else, she had stepped out onto the balcony in her nightgown to negotiate with the unquiet spirit. "I told the girl: 'Listen, I admire you. After all, I was an anti-Fascist just like you. My father was a Socialist and they threw him in prison. We were just lucky that no one ever found out we were hiding a Jewish couple in the attic. So, really, my hat's off to you. But it's just that I'm pregnant and I need to get my rest. So can we make a deal? I'll send someone to look for your bones in the grotto and I'll give you a decent burial. Then would you stop that digging?'" The appeal, according to her, worked. The partisan girl's skeleton was in fact found and immediately buried in a cemetery, with a very nice headstone, and the ghost had stopped digging at midnight.

When I got to Manon's bedroom, I felt a pang in my heart. Probably, back in the days of Napoleon or the SS, it had been a living room or a dining room, considering the imposing scale of the frescoes, the loveliest ones in the whole house. In the panels between the grotesques, Basoli, a Neoclassical Bolognese painter, had depicted the story of Daphnis and Chloe by Longus the Sophist ("A Greek novel, children," she explained to us as we jumped on her bed, "one of the first romantic novels ever written"). But Olivia's grandfather had made the decision: this would be the bedroom of his wife, his queen. It wasn't really all that necessary to let everyone see it, the important thing was that *she* should enjoy it, every night, as she shut her eyes, and every morning, when she opened them.

The second pang came when I saw her. Haggard, skinny, mouth hanging open, chin trembling, and eyes half shut: Manon was looking out the window. She was unrecognizable, but still she sat regally on her throne of an armchair, where she was dragged, arms wrapped around the shoulders of her caregiver. She continued to survey her domain: the city that had always lain at her feet.

"There's a fly," she said when I walked in.

A fly caught in the mosquito netting was troubling her vision. The fly was immediately swatted and killed by a butler in white gloves.

At times she was lucid, but at others less so. When she was raving, she said, "How can I take my things with me?" Her things, she still wanted her things. That's when I decided that maybe she ought to be buried like a pharaoh. Probably the pharaohs just felt more relaxed with all their things around them. I could already see that she was upset because they'd moved a piece of furniture out of her room. She looked around in alarm: oh my God, there's an object missing. The sofa had been moved out for the sake of convenience, but she was suffering at its absence. She was constantly asking what had become of it, why had it been taken away. Because we need to make room for your thousand caregivers, that was the answer. What about the Empire bed? No, because it couldn't be adjusted, because it didn't have an air mattress, because they needed a hospital bed. Dying is hard, it takes plenty of room. Luckily, Bologna wasn't budging, the city still lay there, spread out at her feet. And Manon could still look down on it from on high. In silence.

"Mama? It's Valerio. You want to say hello to him, don't you?"

Giulio, bent over her, turned toward me reassuringly. As if to say, Just wait a moment, she's a little confused.

"No," Manon replied, not confused in the slightest.

I started coughing nervously. I wanted to leave, but Giulio insisted, he gestured for me to wait.

"Mama? Don't you want to say anything to him at all?"

Manon, a little annoyed, waved to the nurse with her hand. She wanted a drop of fruit juice. The straw was immediately brought near her mouth and proffered. She sipped the juice, cheeks hollow, looking around. After a moment, she fluttered her fingers impatiently, as if to say, *Let him draw near, if he absolutely must.* Giulio summoned me.

"Come over here, Valerio, come on."

I stepped closer, holding my breath. Manon slowly turned her eyes to me, wearily lifted a bony finger, and leveled it straight at me: "If you make my granddaughter suffer any longer, I'll come and *dig* every night in your garden."

Not another word. After that, she turned toward the window and went back to her deliriums.

"My things. How am I going to collect my things?"

Manon wasn't a greedy woman. She liked to surround herself with luxuries, no doubt about it, but the deeper reason for her attachment to her things might have had more to do with her sense of status, the role she played, her vindication and her humiliation, than with the possessions in and of themselves. After all, that notorious barter, which had seemed so mysterious to me when I was little—a painting in exchange for every betrayal, and over the years her house had become a museum—told you all you needed to know. Her things were precious to her because they served to fill in a wound.

Then another fly appeared and she summoned the butler again, impatiently, as if this were his fault. She had people to massage her feet, to spoon-feed her, by now she could barely whisper. But when it was a matter of upbraiding "the serving folk," as she called them, Manon could raise her voice, and then some.

"It isn't dead, you know." She was talking about an insect, but there was a subtext. She was actually saying, *I'm the boss and I'm still around, so don't you forget it.*

She was no longer in control of her body, she never had been in control of her affections, but her domestic help still existed and stood there at her beck and call, and that meant there was still at least one thing she could domineer. With a shiver running down my back, I remembered certain scenes that she'd made, dressing down my mother after striding into the kitchen with the gait of a commanding general. And now I was about to buy her home. Me, of all people.

I felt as if I were Lopakhin buying Lyuba's dacha. When Manon took us to see *The Cherry Orchard*, one of her favorite theatrical works, Olivia and I were just two students with not the faintest idea that twenty years later we'd live through something similar. It was a Sunday afternoon and the actors were a little tired, their performance was unremarkable, just waiting for the curtain to drop so they could go out to dinner. But we were stunned. Manon was wiping at her tears and saying that Chekhov insisted it was a comedy, but *that* was a drama, a tragedy—what else could you call it?

Luckily, she had no idea that her house had been put up for sale and that I was there to buy it. For that matter, it hadn't been necessary to inform her. By now, she signed anything that was put before her, biddable and quavering, all the papers that her children put under her nose ("This is so we don't have to pay inheritance taxes, Mama"). But with a mocking glint in her eyes, though. She knew, oh, she knew. Her beloved things would force everyone else to remember her forever, no matter how venomously. Her things would dominate the others far more than she'd ever been able to do. Faintly pharaonic even in her curse, she was letting go of her estate with an ambiguous, somehow triumphant smile.

I gazed at her beauty, stolen away by death. Her yellowish skin, her milky eyes, her skeletal arms. Her elegance, her wit, her memory, her learning: the end of it all was a process of theft. And she was worrying about her things? I said goodbye to her with a caress. Manon turned away. She had no wish to offer me any more significant farewell than that.

DURING THAT VISIT, Olivia gave no sign of being around. Her father brought me her greetings, but I knew that he'd invented them in a show of manners. Because Olivia had written me an email, two days earlier, and it carried a tang of bitterness. She was very angry.

My dear Antigua-based corporation,

Unfortunately, this dirty world is also a small one, and
we learned immediately that you were behind this. Did
you really need to come up with this pathetic contriv-
ance, this offshore company? Especially when dealing
with us, of all people. I will admit that right now you're
somewhat reminding me of God, and how He hadn't
wanted to pay taxes. But that's your business (or the
government's business). It becomes my business as soon
as you start deploying Chinese boxes to buy my grandparents' villa. You know how these things are, there are
times when you'd like to know who's really making the
purchase. This isn't some real estate transaction involving the Morganti Group.

Does the idea of bringing your wife into my home ex-
cite you somehow? Perhaps we're attracted by such per-
versely intersecting dovetails because we feel the need to
somehow master the great contrasts that tear at us. Who
can say. Or was it your mother who came up with this
lovely idea? I bet that she can't wait to come back here as
the mistress of the house.

Anyway, you're lucky this time, because I can't afford to
be a sentimentalist. As you know, it's not all that easy
to sell a heavily frescoed eighteenth-century villa. The

Russians prefer to buy elsewhere, the Po Valley doesn't exactly drip with glam. And a historic residence is under a number of different restrictions, not the easiest place to turn into a wellness spa. So let me ask you to do this. Go right ahead and TOUR THE VILLA.

I'm not kidding, I've never felt the slightest wish to live there. I'd rather give my daughter a normal life, let her grow up in a normal apartment and watch her go out to play in a public park, not on 75 acres of verdant grounds with a swimming pool. The excesses of wealth are dangerous. Be careful, Valerio Carnevale. It's a dimension that can swallow you whole. My grandparents' generation was sturdier than ours, they could afford certain luxuries. But we can't. We're too fragile, and we're at risk of being knocked overboard. We're at risk of being swindled and left penniless by wealth. It takes quite a sense of balance to know how to bear it.

That said, I apologize if I won't be there on Wednesday. My father will be glad to show you around the house, if by some chance you've forgotten what it looks like.

> *My kindest regards,*
> *O*

Giulio insisted on driving me back to the hotel, he really wouldn't take no for an answer. It seemed rude to reject the offer, so I said yes. And after all, it was part of my vindication. Look how he treats me, *now*.

When I was a boy, Giulio just told me jokes. He didn't know any other way of interacting. There is nothing more self-centered in this world than a joke: your listeners are held captive to your performance, they're forced to laugh at things they'd never laugh at otherwise. Because that role—the role established by the rules of a joke—is assigned to them: one person talks and everyone else laughs. But not now. Now he was asking me questions and listening to my answers.

When we arrived, I asked him in to share an aperitif.

"Gladly," he smiled.

For a while we talked about the economic downturn, to steer clear of personal matters. But after a round of Campari spritzes, we relaxed a bit.

"You know, Valerio," he said, "it's really painful for me to have to sell this house. It means that I haven't been able to hold on to it. You've built so much out of nothing and I've just lost everything my father left me. It's an immense humiliation, you know?"

Skinny, with his prominent nose and a white tufting of fuzz on his cranium, as light as dew on a meadow, he was looking down and toying with an olive.

"I've been fortunate," I replied.

"No. You've done a great job. And I sometimes think that if I'd had a son like you, things might have gone very differently. I should have realized it back then, when you were spending all that time in my home. I should have offered you a job myself. Gianni realized it, even though you were just a boy. He had plans for you. He used to say, 'That kid has something special, when he grows up, we'll take him in to work with us. He's the future of our family.'"

"Really?" I was touched.

"I swear to you. But on principle, I wanted to do everything exactly the opposite of how my father thought it should be done. And you see the results before you."

"Come on now, you're just going through a tough period. You'll overcome it."

"No, it's all gone to hell. And do you know what I envy him most? That my father was able to protect us. I can't protect anyone now."

I saw Giulio again, several months later, at Manon's funeral. He gave me a powerful hug, clearly an affectionate one ("Thanks for coming." "She's part of my history, Manon…") Everyone was there, of course. Elena was there, Cecilia was there, all the people who had worked in that house with my father were there, the cook, the chauffeur, now old and unsteady on their feet, come to bid farewell to a world that had also been their world. And Dado, of course, who felt lost without his mother, but not so much so that he didn't still make a show of sitting far away from his brother. And everyone treated me like a member of the family. Only Olivia barely grasped my hand, like any old acquaintance. And then she quickly turned to greet another person.

But she and I did have an appointment to meet: at the notary's office, for the closing on the house. It wasn't very romantic, but I was seething with excitement. Since the two brothers were fighting over everything, even their mother's silverware, Olivia had collected their proxies and had been assigned to resolve the problem of the villa, ideally as quickly as possible.

And so, that afternoon, I was waiting for her in an office in the center of town, seated in a Poltrona Frau office chair. I had managed to persuade my wife not to come to Bologna with me, with a shameful excuse that played on her sense of guilt about the children ("I'm afraid not, they're giving out Filippo's report card, someone has to go. At least one of the parents," with the clear innuendo that the parent in question would absolutely have to be her). It hadn't been easy, because Benedetta was fiercely jealous of Olivia and terrified at the idea of the two of us being in the same room together, but I'd employed all my skills to convince her. I'd explained to her that I wouldn't even see her, Olivia Morganti. "There are some kinds of business that you don't do with ladies, you know that for yourself, Bebè." Benedetta, who wouldn't even have known how to pay an electric bill, accustomed as she was to entrusting all financial matters to me or to her brother, had simply nodded her head. That statement rang credible to her ears.

But Olivia was late. And while I waited, I was eating all the mint candies sitting on the table, next to the magazines. I kept checking the hour, slightly worried by now.

After ten minutes or so, Olivia's lawyer appeared in her place. He was out of breath, in a frantic rush. He must have galloped up the stairs. We shook hands. I would have preferred other fingers, more slender than his, and with perhaps a whiff of that unmistakable scent of jasmine, but this concerned millions of euros.

"Is there some problem?"

"I'm afraid so. I came instead, and I apologize for the delay, but I was only informed half an hour ago." He was embarrassed. Not a good sign.

"Has she changed her mind?" I turned beet red with anger. What does she think she's doing? Humiliating me to amuse herself? This was intolerable. To make things worse, I had just disinvested a very substantial sum of money. In my mind, I rapidly totted up all the interest I was losing as a result.

"Valerio, don't take this the wrong way. You know her, this is just the way Olivia is. Now she says that this is her grandmother's house, and that she can't sell it to you of all people. That it would be a mistake *for both of you*."

Her friend the lawyer was rather uneasy, and he was clearly aware of all our history. I tried gazing into his eyes, to get a better understanding: Had they had an affair? Was he snickering behind my back, too? After all, Olivia had known him for so many years, maybe in a moment of weakness, she'd let him cuddle with her comfortingly. It was the kind of thing she'd do. Then perhaps she'd said to him: "Please forgive me." And that poor wretch had been left standing there, yearning for her like so many others—that damned woman, whom no one seemed able to possess nonchalantly, for thirty years or three days.

I leaped to my feet: "Where is she? I want to speak to her."

"No, no, no." The lawyer was clearly upset. "That's exactly why she asked me to come."

"I don't give a damn. I want to talk to her right now. This very instant."

"But she doesn't want to—"

"Tell me where she is, stop stalling."

"She's at her grandmother's house." He dropped his eyes. "She's packing boxes, taking away some of Manon's books. But she doesn't want... she doesn't..."

"Thank you."

To me that villa was more important than all the apartment buildings and subdevelopments that I'd built in my career. To own it meant, in my head, stitching back together the two worlds I'd lived in. It felt as if I'd worked my whole life for this and this alone, the money I'd made could serve no other purpose. That's just the way I was: I wanted to belong to all worlds and I wanted everyone to belong to mine, I couldn't accept any substitutions or losses. And I was every bit as ravenous, as insatiable when it came to time: I was always trying to hold it tight, all of it, in defiance of every law of nature. Maybe the reason I continued to be so in love with Olivia was this: because she *was* time, she was the worlds of other people.

I was so upset that I rang the doorbell at the tradesmen's entrance. Force of habit, right? A butler, probably Sinhalese, answered the door. The people I'd grown up with hadn't lived there for some time, and in fact the house was now in the hands of foreigners.

"Is Signora Morganti upstairs?"

The Sinhalese butler gazed at me in astonishment, he couldn't understand why I had come in through the back door. He gestured for me to wait and picked up the phone: "Who shall I say?"

There was an internal phone line in the villa. The place was too big to just go and speak to someone in person. Even lunch was announced by the trill of the intercom: "Food's on the table." Taking the time to walk to make the announcement meant letting the pasta get cold.

"I know the way," I replied.

The butler shook his head, he didn't trust me, I'd have to comply with procedure. But before he had a chance to dial the number, I'd already bolted.

I ran quickly, the way I had as a child, when I was afraid of ghosts. And as I climbed the stairs and strode down the hallways, I was thinking of Manon's last words: "If you make my granddaughter suffer any longer, I'll come and *dig* every night in your garden."

OLIVIA WAS IN THE BOSCHERECCIA, a room named after the garden frescoed on its walls, a beautiful trompe l'oeil by Martinelli. She was sitting at her grandmother's desk and leafing through a photo album.

She looked up in surprise: "Valerio, what are you doing here?"

"You made me come all the way from Rome and then you sent your lawyer instead of coming yourself," I replied, standing motionless in the doorway.

She closed the album, taking care to mark the page. "I'm sorry, I admit that I realized a little late. But I understood that it would be a fatal error to sell this house to you, of all people."

She smiled at me, but without using all the muscles in her face, it was just a hint of a smile, the smile of someone who can only roll with the punches. She narrowed her eyes slightly, she didn't seem to have the strength to close them any more than that. Deep down, it was a smile that seemed to spring from kind intentions, but still somehow scanty in its delivery.

But I was very stiff and proud: "You could have come and confessed it to me personally, this *fatal error* of yours. You've confessed so many other mistakes, what difference would one more or one less have made... It would have been a gesture of respect."

I stepped toward her, and she raised her body ever so slightly to let herself be kissed. She wore her grandmother's pearls around her neck, they were knotted at the bottom and dragged on the desk as she extended her face in my direction. I pressed my lips against her cheek, but only for a moment. I tried not to smell or feel: her scent, her flesh, my desires. I preferred to kiss her in a sort of anesthesia.

"You're right," she said. "I made a mistake. Maybe I was afraid."

Olivia had a blank gaze, as if life had smeared onto her cornea, layer upon layer, a courteous veil of distance. The substance of that courtesy rang very similar to a farewell— thank you all so very much, but I'm a little weary—a benevolent and even understanding adieu to the world of deep emotions, something she no longer desired.

Meanwhile Ella Fitzgerald's voice was circulating in the room. *Come on and cry me a river.* It seemed to be coming from the ceiling: *'cause I cried a river over you.* I turned my head up, looking at that labyrinth of loudspeakers, concealed in cavities more secret even than the tunnels bored by woodworms: I wanted to rip them all out. I didn't want to listen to that song, I just didn't want to. *Cry me a river, 'cause I cried a river over you.*

I sat down in the armchair facing her and unbuttoned my overcoat.

"Do your father and your uncle know?" I was unwrapping the scarf from around my neck with too much emphasis, my hands were shaking.

"That I ruined the deal?" She laughed in that undertone of hers, which I wasn't used to. "No. They don't know yet."

"They're not going to be very happy about it."

"I don't care," she replied, twisting Manon's pearls around her fingers.

"You said you couldn't afford to be a sentimentalist."

"That's right. But these are sentiments, not sentimentalism." Then she looked at me, cocking an eyebrow. "But did you come here to talk me into selling you the place, or to say hello to me?"

She was trying to confuse me, so I smiled at her. "Guess."

"To say hello." Her smile broadened.

Then she stood up, she wanted to offer me an aperitif. She said that in her grandparents' cellar there were magnificent wines, wines that hadn't been kept properly, but if you looked carefully, you could still find a perfectly good bottle. She picked up the phone to call the Sinhalese butler, who appeared a short while later with a silver tray and two crystal chalices. The wine, which was poured directly out of a dust-laden bottle, ought perhaps to have been properly decanted. But we were in a hurry to drink a toast to something, anything, there wasn't time to let it breathe.

"Well? Have you returned to Bologna?"

Olivia shrugged. "I had to. I certainly couldn't stay in Milan. I had my ex-husband underfoot every other day, he was capable of waiting hours outside my front door to catch me. A stalker, in other words."

"Is he still waging war on you?"

"We had a hearing just yesterday. You can't imagine the boredom. I was hoping we would at least have a few more things to say about who was to blame for what. But such was not to be. By now, the only subject is money. It's almost more emotionally engaging to go see the accountant."

"Does he want alimony? The apartment?"

"Even my lawyer can't figure out what he wants. He's just kicking up a ruckus, for the pleasure of refusing to grant me my divorce, I think. Does he hope to possess me through bureaucratic channels? What the hell kind of desire is that even?"

"Maybe he's still in love."

Olivia shook her head: "No, he's just completely lost his mind."

"You're the problem, you're too magnetic. Even when you don't want to be."

I told her that we human beings aren't made for such vertiginous, high-flying unions, on the whole we like to live at a lower rate of expense. A nice healthy orgasm, which is also good for warding off prostate cancer, and we're done.

"But that isn't possible with you. You always wind up sticking your fingers into people's dark side. And then you complain about the madness that surrounds you."

"So you're saying that's my fault?"

"You might not be doing it intentionally." I found her touching, now, the way she hung on my every word. "Believe me, people can tolerate only up to certain altitudes, any higher and they need special equipment. It's a matter of survival. In technical terms, the phenomenon is known as hypoxia."

I explained to her that when you go any higher than thirteen thousand feet, or four thousand meters, barometric pressure drops, and with it the quantity of oxygen in the air.

Whereupon our human organism begins to struggle. How imprecise metaphors can be. In our imagination climbing a mountain corresponds to a triumph of freedom: you immediately think of a vast vision, which evokes a great sweep, a deep breath of air. Here I am, I've struggled all the way to the top of a summit, now I am the master of all I survey, and I can finally fill my lungs with this satisfaction. But such is not the case. The exact opposite happens. Elevation is a disturbance.

"Migraines, nausea and vomiting, a feeling of exhaustion, an acceleration of your heartbeat, insomnia, difficulty urinating," I was saying. "Don't look at me like that. I'm not kidding around. You run the risk of pulmonary or cerebral edema."

Olivia burst out laughing, hard. Look at that, I had launched into a ridiculous riff on altitude merely because, to me, she was a fucking mountain to be climbed. A goddamned sheer rock wall, my Everest. Maybe I was making myself ridiculous. But her laughter was stronger than any of my fears: it drew me in and it swept me away. Now I recognize her, I thought to myself. And I happily accepted the avalanche and started laughing with her.

THEN WE POURED ourselves another glass, and now the wine smacked less of tannin. Perhaps we'd conquered the harsher overtones, now the red went down easy and lay sweet on the palate. Olivia asked me how my children were doing.

"Oh, just fine. Filippo has started his adolescent phase at age nine. If he's this argumentative in fourth grade, I can't begin to guess what he'll be like when he gets to high school. Constantly fighting with me, criticizing everything about me. Papa, you're fat. The hamburger you cooked me is disgusting. What on earth are you wearing? And so on and so forth."

Olivia laughed.

"There's not that much to laugh at. I actually wonder if he has Asperger's, he's always glued to his computer: if he wants to tell me something, at this point he just sends me an email. And if I tell him to call his mother, because dinner's ready, he picks up his cell phone and posts a message on Facebook. Benedetta says it's normal, all the kids act this way."

When I mentioned my wife, Olivia's face tightened and she started blinking her eyes rapidly, upset.

"What about Sara?" I asked, to change the subject.

"I'm a little worried." Meanwhile she was biting her nails, she still hadn't shaken that bad habit. "Lately she's been having frequent nightmares, and she wakes up all sweaty, shouting. She walks in her sleep. I hear that this happens to lots of children, that it's not serious, that she'll get over it. I don't know about that. Yesterday I found her in the dog's bed, she'd taken her pillow with her."

In the meantime, Olivia had been forced to give Sara some explanations. Her daughter had the right to know that the man she was divorcing wasn't her father. And when the little girl had asked her where her real Papa was now, Olivia had told her that he was "in heaven," without offering her much of any dangerous description of what heaven looks like, since it's a very controversial matter.

"But you know where Mehdi is now, really? In prison."

"Him, too? Then you must have a weakness for criminals."

"He's not a criminal, you don't know what you're talking about. There hasn't been much coverage of the case in the press, nothing like the uproar about Panahi, even though there have been calls for his release from the film industry. Ahmadinejad doesn't like hearing dissident voices: Mehdi was accused of propaganda against the regime because he shot a full-length documentary about the 2009 elections. He was sentenced to four years, with a ten-year prohibition against leaving Iran, giving interviews, and directing films. He can't write. I was right to tell his daughter that he's dead." Meanwhile she bit her lip. "This is certainly going to kill him."

But she immediately pulled back the sleeve of her blouse and looked at her watch: "Hey, it's already eight o'clock."

"Do you have to go? Do you have plans for dinner?"

Actually, I had plans, somewhere I needed to be. I had train reservations to head home, to rejoin my wife. But I had no desire to board that train.

We exchanged a glance, it only took a moment. We made love, right there, in Manon's house, surrounded by an eighteenth-century trompe l'oeil and, perhaps, some other, larger illusions. When I collapsed, with my nose in her hair, she said: "Well, so there's been a *closing* after all."

2

AN ACT OF COURAGE?

THERE ARE TIMES in anyone's life that are destined to remain unforgettable. That exact year, those particular months, those precise places: you know that you'll carry them with you for all time and you know it even as you're experiencing them, so much so that you gaze on the present with an especially tender eye, in some sense, similar to the way you look at memories. And for me, 2011 was that year.

I loved Olivia with a new love. It was a strange thing: there was a thrilling today and a tomorrow to dream about, but all it took was a snowfall to summon up all of the past. I remember one evening in Bologna, the streetlamps lit up the large falling snowflakes, which looked like backlit gold. We both stood gazing upward, hypnotized. Maybe it was a sign. We thought back to when we lay on our sled and hurtled down the hill—at full speed, hugging each other tight and shouting—and my mother said that sooner or later we'd both split our heads wide open. But we didn't care, as long as we were together we were willing to slam into anything.

The snow had silenced the city all at once, there was nobody else out and about. Our voices echoed in the portico, resonating eerily. And in that somewhat magical, slightly surreal silence, our ghosts couldn't fail to reach us. But we were happy to walk along in their company.

We were strolling along slowly under the Pavaglione portico, arms locked, and we thought we saw Manon. As if she were coming straight toward us, fresh from the hairdresser, wearing one of her fur coats, absolutely indifferent to animal rights except when it came to her poodle. And her crocodile-skin purse and her leather gloves, but how *beautiful* she made all that slaughter look, my God, perhaps because she carried it with an utter gracefulness that made you forget its bloody origins.

We saw Gianni dressed to go skiing, because he was always off to the slopes at the first dusting of white. He was heading for his element: the sky—the mountains were the next closest thing to the sky. A pale-blue windbreaker, sunglasses to withstand the glare of the winter sunlight, or perhaps the overwhelming glow of it all, and ski boots studded with hooks and clasps. He didn't belong to the earth in which they'd found and then buried him, no. His wife had been right about that.

And we saw my father, who, instead, walked out into the snow without a jacket, shovel in hand, to clear the lane for the Morgantis. It was no joke for him. He was expected to put the chains on the tires of all the cars, scatter salt on the linden-lined lane, and knock the icicles off the ledges and cornices with a hoe. And yet he accepted all these chores and responsibilities without objection, and he only got mad at the snow when it broke the branches of his trees.

My papa died shortly after Manon, leaving me, however, with a stunning surprise: Gianni Morganti's watch. My jaw dropped. He'd even put it in his will, to be certain I wouldn't overlook it. The notary read aloud the list of bequests without suspecting the story that lay behind them: "I leave to my son Valerio my mother's necklace—my mother, whom he sadly never met—and Gianni Morganti's watch, in commemoration of a man who was like a grandfather to him."

I wore that watch constantly now, I never took it off, not even when I fell asleep. Only when I took a shower.

Olivia slid the soles of her shoes over the wet marble and touched my wrist.

"Sure, I was convinced that my folks were in the wrong, too, you know. The very idea. Guido seemed incapable of stealing anything."

"We'd always underestimated him."

She looked at my watch with a smile of amusement: "Do you know that I still remember my grandfather wearing it? Because it has a chronometer. Gianni would use it to calculate how long I could stay underwater, holding my breath."

With the same natural ease we showed in summoning up things that had been lost, a short while later we were able to enjoy the present, in all its heartbreaking fleetingness. We needed only enter our favorite restaurant, La Drogheria della Rosa, on Via Cartoleria, brushing off the heavy wet snow, and ask for a table downstairs. The joy of being alive had a very concrete flavor, perhaps that of the mortadella we handed each other. Or the full-bodied taste of a fine Sangiovese, which we chose carefully, attentively studying the wine list, like the good traveling companions we had become—companions in life, or in history, who could really say?

The Olivia sitting across from me, mouth open as she awaited her slice of pleasure or salami, possibly directly from my fingers, was the most moving of all the Olivias I had known. There was such a lust for life in her—*a life together*—a lust for eating and drinking and making love, such a deep desire to enjoy—*together*—that I felt my chest being crushed by happiness. Every now and then I had to take a deep breath, to ease, if only slightly, the pressure I felt in my lungs.

"You know," she was telling me, "it's so important to *understand happiness*. It sounds easy, but it's not. Because it's so simple. And simple things are the hardest to grasp. I've finally realized it only now, it took me almost forty years."

THIS TIME, I really was having trouble moving from one world to another, from one time to another. I had two houses, two cities, two women. There were times when I'd wake up, feeling panicky and disoriented, because I could no longer remember who was sleeping beside me. Then I'd reach out an arm to touch the nearby body and understand where I was.

I would come up with all kinds of excuses to stay far away from Rome, but Benedetta only pretended not to notice that I was spending much more time away than expected. Possessive though she was, she suddenly started overlooking all my absences. As if governed by a deeper intuition, she stopped asking questions or demanding answers ("So you have another meeting in Bologna? Well, bundle up, because it's cold there," and she'd send me off with the gift of a scarf). It's just that I was increasingly weary, emotionally weary, and I knew I couldn't go on like this for much longer.

I realized it one evening on the train, while I was heading back to Rome. In front of me lay a stack of newspapers that I couldn't even bring myself to leaf through. I was only capable of gazing out the window, perhaps because it was dark and it was raining and you couldn't see a thing.

I lost myself in the study of the raindrops, trembling, clinging to the glass, seduced by the spectacle of their struggle to maintain their grip. So I played a game: if this raindrop, battling to keep from being sucked away into the void and the rushing air, manages to hold on to this window all the way to Florence, then I'll make it as well.

Deep down, I'd already made my choice. But I was afraid. Not of my wife. I knew that what awaited me there was a catastrophe, in the etymological sense of the word: namely, a great change. Exhausting, like all great changes—when you suddenly see all your most secure points of reference stripped away—but those have to do with a shift of *things*. My fear was a deeper one, and I was having trouble focusing on it clearly.

I was afraid of what Olivia was capable of unleashing inside me, I think. I'd known her all my life and I felt as disarmed as if I'd only just met her. Perhaps what I needed to do was take matters in hand, rationally. So I said to myself: Olivia is my passion and passion is, notoriously, a mystery. But she's also a woman about whom, after all, I know everything. She has always told me every single thing about her, even when I would rather she hadn't. I can't seriously say that I'm dealing with an enigma here.

Meanwhile I was keeping my eye on my raindrop: good, it's still clinging to the glass. I was very proud of it, it was glued on like a suction cup. Then I felt a pang in my stomach. Ouch: my belly was warning me that things weren't going to be so easy, in this operation.

At that very moment, my cell phone lit up. It was a text from my wife, asking: "When are you going to be home?" The question was unsettling, because I'd never been able to think of that place as *my home*.

Olivia maintained that I often mistook *concrete objects*, which I dealt with all day long, for *true things*. And maybe she was right. One *concrete object* was the villa on the Via Appia Antica that I'd purchased for my wife and my children. And one *true thing* was the depth of the physical relationship that I had with Olivia.

For that matter, ours was an intimacy that had been cultivated over time. The language of the body had grown along with us as *we* grew, it had been modified over the years, but that slightly animalistic foundation, like siblings or puppies sniffing at each other, had persisted unchanged. My skin *knew* her skin in considerable depth. I knew what Olivia had smelled like as a little girl, for instance. Hers was a skin that I'd seen tauten and tense with muscles around age twenty and then slacken and relax at certain points at age thirty. A skin with which I had an ancient and almost terrifying familiarity. When we were children we'd compared warts ("mine is bigger"), we'd smeared ointments onto fungal infections ("What if you catch it?" "I don't mind, it's something of yours") and pried each other's scabs off with our fingernails ("Hold still, I've almost got it off"). It was that kind of an intimacy, a dirty thing, based on peeing in the bathtub when they put us together to soak, laughing heedlessly behind the nanny's back, at all the time she wasted washing us.

As if by a short circuit, I whipped around to look at the window: my raindrop was gone. I'd lost it. Oh my God. Seized with panic, I grabbed my phone and wrote back to my wife, speed-tapping the letters of the text: "I get in at nine. Wait for me and we can eat dinner together." I hit Send. For a moment, I felt calm. Everything's all right. I'm *returning home,* I'll say good night to my children who are surely already in their pajamas, I'll put them to bed, maybe I'll read them a book that they'll both enjoy, and then I'll turn out the light and sit down to dine with Benedetta. But what will I say to her? My anxiety surged upward again.

I picked up my cell phone again: "I'm sorry, sweetheart, I'd forgotten that I promised my sister I'd eat at her place tonight. I haven't seen her in such a long time. Do you mind very much?" I hoped that Benedetta would tell me that it wasn't a problem, because she was tired and didn't feel like eating anything and just wanted to get to sleep early. I waited with my cell phone in hand, eyes glued to the screen. When is she going to text me back? Why isn't she answering me? Is she angry? I was too impatient to wait any longer, so I called her. Bebè had been in the shower, poor thing, that was all. She understood completely, but she'd wait up for me because at the performance Flavia had forgotten her lines and we needed to talk about it. Oh, fuck, the nursery school show! I'd completely forgotten. I hadn't even asked how it had gone, how shameful. She hadn't said her lines? A wave of guilt washed over me. There you go, it's all my fault. My daughter couldn't open her mouth because I wasn't there in the audience, to reassure her. I started mumbling out words. "Well, of course, I can go see my sister some other time," I said. Benedetta insisted there was no reason to overdramatize, these are things that happen. In any case, she'd be delighted to have me home for dinner. Then she apologized, said she had to go and finish drying her hair, otherwise she'd catch a chill. The call ending with this little everyday vignette of her with wet hair left me a wreck.

WHEN I ARRIVED at Termini station, I rushed for a taxi. People were still calling me from the office, but I had neither the interest nor the strength to deal with more problems.

"It's easy to play the queer with other people's assholes!" I replied, ending the phone conversation.

I had discovered that cheap vulgarity really works with certain people, it rings as elegant as a learned quotation, it was a good idea to give others no more nor less than they expected of me.

Meanwhile I was thinking that divorcing Benedetta would also mean finding a new line of work. I certainly couldn't leave her and continue as director of the Bernasconi Group, whose majority shareholders were her and her brother. But I didn't especially mind that. In fact, it seemed like a form of liberation.

I was sick of that world, and especially of its *language*. It really was a matter of words, words that I no longer wanted to use. Words like "requalification," a term we used to describe the act of plowing under and paving with cement. I no longer wanted to describe a landscape as an "area" and discuss "decay" in the face of a path of unspoiled nature when all I plan to do is request authorization to "restore it," or put more bluntly, build over it.

I'd never again have to utter the term "urbanistically integrated" or "local collective," I'd never again speak about "economic revival, tourism, employment, and development," when all I was doing was camouflaging far more concrete technical terms, such as "modification of zoning for use" or "securitization." Never again would I have to write "all-purpose materials" instead of "dirt and sand," in order to up the profit margin on public funding from the regional government. I no longer wanted to contrive things that sounded like "project for a territorial presidio serving a fire-prevention function" just so I could build houses on hillsides in contravention of master zoning plans. No longer would I shamelessly tout "culture, art, and sports, along with long-term, broad-based sustainable projects" as cover for transforming an insane asylum into a luxury residential housing facility with eighty basement garages, or turning a forest into a shopping mall with a multiplex movie theater, or a bay into a port structure, reaching a record density of one boat slip for every forty residents. Nevermore would I feel the need to talk about a "bike path" to justify the construction of a parking lot. I'd finally be able to stop tapping the European Union for contributions to projects involving "agritourism, riding stables, and organic farming, with a view to spreading the understanding of proper environmental culture, and the longer-term objective of sustainable development," only to transform woodsheds into row houses with peak ocean views and the field across the street into a swimming pool. God, what a relief.

I really didn't feel like returning home, especially not while I was thinking about these things. So I wrote to Benedetta again and told her that the train was running late after all because Gypsy vandals had stolen copper from the railway lines, and all rail traffic was blocked. Gypsies always worked as an effective scarecrow with her. I was willing to spend an hour in the train station café as long as it meant I wouldn't have to eat dinner with her. And that, too, should have made me think, perhaps.

THE NEXT MORNING, I woke up and walked into the kitchen in my boxer shorts for a cup of coffee. I was greeted by the sight of a dozen or so housekeepers busy polishing silverware. My wife was fighting with someone on the phone ("No, I requested three crates of Sauterne, not Sauvignon. Are you serious? Now, you're going to send the right wine over immediately, the wine I *asked* for, or I won't be paying you a cent. I want it here within the hour, and I can't care about traffic. I want it here *now*").

I went over to Filippo, who hadn't even said hello to me because he was too absorbed in playing tennis on the television set with his Wii.

"Wait, who are all these people? Do we have a party planned?"

My son replied with a shout of disappointment. I'd made him lose the match. He tossed the controller onto the couch, and now he was mad at me.

"Darn, I've told you a thousand times not to bother me when I'm playing tennis. You messed up my backhand."

I slapped him on the back of his neck. "First: you are not to talk to me like that. Second: you are to say, Good morning, Papa. Third: you are not to play with the Wii for a month because you're a rude little brat."

His sister appeared at the door to the hallway and started shouting: "You hit him! You hit him! I saw you! Mama doesn't want you to hit us. Now I'm going to report you to the police! I'm going to report you!"

I whipped around and in order to put an end to all the laughing and crying, I slapped her, too. In tears, Flavia ran to the kitchen shouting.

"Mamaaa. *Put him in prison*, Mama!"

Filippo, arms crossed and feet on the sofa—with his shoes on—was laughing. I was furious.

My wife walked into the living room, hands on her hips and her daughter clutching her robe, pretending to hide behind her skirts and be afraid of me for the fun of making things worse.

"Well? What's come over you? I've told you a thousand times never to raise a hand to my children!"

"It was just a slap. Symbolic and one hundred percent deserved."

"If you do it again, I swear I'll divorce you. I'll take them away from you, and you'll never see them again."

My eyes danced with delight at the thought. If only.

"All right," I replied.

Luckily, the phone rang. It was a girlfriend of Bebè's, who extended her regrets but unfortunately she wouldn't be able to come to the party, she had the flu and blah blah blah. My wife chirped how sorry she was and dispensed advice about the best medicines to take. Benedetta adored medicines, she guzzled down all sorts of pharmaceuticals, homeopathic and otherwise. From the conversation it was easy to deduce that the party at my house was going to be a fairly sizable one. I racked my brains trying to remember if there was some occasion that I'd forgotten about. Considering the tension in the air, I'd be better off avoiding missteps. I didn't have the nerve to ask questions, though. Who could say how many times we'd talked about it. But I was very preoccupied and, after all, certain topics of conversation bored me so profoundly that I just wouldn't listen. Benedetta would make fun of me because I'd answer "Yes, please" without paying the slightest attention to her questions. Sometimes she'd ambush me to see whether or not I'd been listening ("Darling, it's all right *if I let fifteen men screw me all at once*, isn't it?" And I'd reply "Yes, please" without looking up from my newspaper). But things didn't always end in laughter. More often, in fact, they'd end up in a quarrelsome diatribe. "You never listen to me. You don't care what I say. You're always thinking about other things."

So it seemed wiser to investigate without making it clear to her that I'd completely forgotten about the celebration in question.

"Well? How many guests this evening?"

Benedetta heaved an annoyed sigh: "Fifty people. How many times do I have to tell you? Now, actually, forty-eight, because Beppe and Lucia are sick. That is, she's sick. He's just taking advantage of the opportunity to lie on the sofa and watch the game. She ought to dump him—he has a case of chronic depression and he's just a ball and chain."

I nodded my head, but only to avoid annoying her. What the hell did I care? In fact, I understood him perfectly, I didn't like parties either. Lucky him.

Meanwhile I was desperately trying to come up with something that would get me out of the house immediately. It was Saturday, and something to do with work wouldn't stand up. I could round up the children and take them somewhere. The idea didn't thrill me, I would probably slap them silly at some point. But I really had no alternative.

"Come on, kids. Stop pouting. Get dressed, we're going to the zoo." Filippo pretended he was about to throw up and Flavia, just to make me feel bad right down to the last second, buried her face in her mother's belly, as if I was suggesting feeding her to the lions. I can't lose my temper, I thought to myself, sinking my teeth into my lips, *I can't.*

"A stroll at Villa Borghese and then we could go to the movies? Is there a new animated flick you both want to see?"

That went even worse. My son whined, saying that he was tired. He just wanted to play with his computer, that hadn't been hard to guess. Flavia continued to act offended, in the hope that I would offer to take her for a spin through a toy store, just to win her forgiveness. She wants a present, I know my chickens. It was a technique she'd learned from her mother: make someone feel guilty enough to give you a present. In this specific case, a Glamour & Fashion Barbie. Even now, I could still get away with spending just twenty euros, but the principle was humiliating. I wasn't about to stand for it.

I was sick and tired by now: "Fine, then, I'll go out on my own. I need to take a walk and clear my head."

Benedetta glared daggers at me: "And you're not going to help me?"

I pointed out to her that there were no fewer than ten caterers hard at work in our kitchen, plus our own two Filipino housekeepers, man and wife. But she dug her heels in. She was willing to press-gang me into polishing the silverware, as long as it forced me to stay there. I realized that things weren't going well when she started reeling off a list of my demerits stretching all the way back to the previous Christmas and all the way up to Flavia's nursery school play just the day before ("You weren't there!"). Months and months of recriminations ("You're always traveling!"). Unless I complied, she'd keep swimming upstream like a salmon, all the way back to the summer of 2001, piling up the debt and, obviously, the accrued interest as well.

"What do you want me to do?"

"Let's choose the tablecloths."

"All right."

AT EIGHT O'CLOCK that evening I still hadn't been able to figure out what we were celebrating. I'd been able to grasp only one concept: that this dinner could prove fatal to me unless I figured it out fast. I'm not much at socializing, I don't know what I can do about it. I was usually dragged back and forth by Benedetta, against my will. My wife always said that

I'd better stop whining about it because *it was useful to me*, the only way you can make a career in Italy is through the people you know.

I wandered solitary through the parlors of my house, already drunk. Every now and then Benedetta would cross paths with me, taking the glass out of my hand and threatening me in a low voice: "You're the master of the house, Valerio. Don't make me look like a fucking fool, I'm begging you."

Everyone was congratulating me and giving me their best wishes, but I still hadn't figured out what for. I just thanked them and moved on. Then I discovered that the occasion was our wedding anniversary. Motherfucker, I hadn't bought her so much as a bouquet of flowers. "She'll never let me forget this as long as I live." I poured myself another glass, discreetly, and tried to come up with a plan. I couldn't even call a florist to put together a surprise bouquet, because it was nine in the evening. The only person who could get me out of this mess was my sister. I locked myself in the bathroom and called her.

"Fuck off, Pisè. I've got a tableful of twenty people. Plus, excuse me, what consequences are you afraid of? You're about to leave her. Soon she'll have a lot more to blame you for, not just forgetting an anniversary."

"I'm begging you."

"I don't know where to find flowers at this time of night. If you want, I can cut the geraniums I have in my window box. How about some coke? Come on, nobody doesn't like cocaine."

"Don't be stupid."

"Are the bathrooms already backed up at your house?"

"I need to make a quick recovery here, I need to make an impressive gesture. Try to understand me."

"Well, use tonight to tell her that you're in love with Olivia Morganti! That would be an impressive gesture, and then some."

"Cut it out."

Silence, she was finally giving the matter some thought. She told me that she had a friend, on the Via Tuscolana, that maybe he could do something. Marta had his cell phone number, she could reach out to him and ask if he could come up with something in a hurry, something resembling a wedding cake.

"Something ironic, you know what I mean. Certainly nothing that weighs 350 pounds, and there wouldn't be any genuine pearls studding the frosting. But a gesture to show that you'd been thinking of her," she said, "and on top of it I'll have him put a newlywed couple, in plastic. It'll be good for a laugh."

"Tell him that I'll pay him a thousand euros if he can get it here before midnight."

"You're not giving anyone a thousand euros for a cake. A cake costs thirty euros, when it's expensive. You know how mad that kind of thing makes me. Just let me take care of it."

"Thank you."

"Do you want balloons? I've got a bunch right here— yesterday we celebrated Er Vetraro's daughter's birthday."

"Stop making fun of me."

"Listen, balloons really liven up the show."

"Do whatever you think best."

"Valerio?"

"Yes?"

"This is the last time I'm going to help you. After this, you're going to act like a man."

I walked out of the bathroom and found myself face to face with Domitilla, and she too was very drunk. A renowned architect, the wife of an accountant who was our friend—all the holidays and dinners and Sundays we four had spent together, with and without the children—and a woman I fucked every now and then. I'd never been in love with her, not even for a fleeting second. But our relationship had lasted for years, under the noses of our respective spouses. All the women I'd bedded in my life had only served to cover up an absence. I threw myself into the arms of female friends and acquaintances, in an almost compulsive manner, in the hope of forgetting Olivia. Something that was never going to happen.

"Happy anniversary, sweetheart," she said, as she gave me a peck on each cheek.

"Maybe the last one," I replied.

Her eyes got big: "Wait, what's going on?"

"I want a divorce. Benedetta doesn't know yet, please, don't say anything to anybody. Not even your husband, do me this favor."

Domitilla wasn't taking me seriously. She burst out laughing, long and hard. She pushed me against the wall, looked around furtively, and slid her tongue into my mouth.

"That wasn't our understanding, Valerio."

What on earth was she thinking? That I was talking about leaving my wife for her? What madness was this? Now I was the one who burst out laughing.

"What did you think I was talking about? Certainly not *us*."

She took a step back, put her hands on her hips, and looked at me: "Olivia Morganti again?"

I really did need to speak about it with a friend, and maybe she was the friend—who could say? Who was more intimate than us two? But Domitilla took me down a peg with a highly moralistic little sermon. She of all people, who was regularly fucking all her husband's friends, without the hint of a scruple. Now she was trotting out the Sense of Responsibility and all that sort of thing. Lying is perfectly okay, apparently, and so is cheating, but leaving your wife? Never! She was worse than the average Italian male, even though she considered herself a feminist, put on airs as an intellectual, and posed as a left-wing progressive.

"If you leave Benedetta, you're going to have to leave the Bernasconi Group, too. Have you lost your mind?"

"Wait, but aren't you happy for me? You've always told me that I was a piece-of-shit *palazzinaro*," I chuckled. There, maybe that was the truth. It excited her to be a powerful man's lover, is that it? All the time I've wasted, I thought to myself. All the pointless relationships I've had. I felt like calling Olivia and telling her that I wanted to live with her. Move in with her now. Immediately. And forever.

I thought to myself that quitting my job, losing my wealth, and abandoning my social position didn't bother me at all. When you thought about it, I'd spent my life moving through different worlds, often completely incompatible with each other, and this had allowed me to avoid any sense of belonging. I felt like an outsider wherever I went, in the end, whether in the *borgata* or in high society, in spite of all my compromises and efforts to adapt. Thanks to this permanent outsider status, I was a free man. Capable of giving it all up from today to tomorrow, for instance.

"Are you drunk?"

"Never been more sober in my life."

But we were interrupted by Benedetta, who came striding straight toward me like a general.

"Someone brought a cake. Did you order it?"

"Well, the real present is the new car. But they just weren't able to get it here in time for our anniversary," I invented on two feet, and my playacting brought a flush of shame to my cheeks.

"The Mini?" She hugged me, that kind of thing made her happy and I knew it. "Oh, sweetheart! Thank you, thank you. You picked the one with the leather upholstery, didn't you?"

"Of course."

3

LAST ACT

ONE AFTERNOON, Costantino called me on the phone. He asked if we could have dinner together, just the two of us. Up until that moment, he'd kept a certain distance, avoiding any interference. He'd told me he was sorry to hear about the breakup, but that was all. So I agreed.

"Why of course, happy to see you."

Perhaps he wanted to resolve a few practical matters with me, before involving any lawyers. I knew that Bebè wasn't capable of endorsing a check, so I was hardly surprised. And after all, I had nothing to fear from meeting him: I'd resigned as managing director and CEO of the Bernasconi Group the very same day I moved out of our home.

I was already casting around for another job. Offers were raining down, and I was taking my time to consider things. Changing sector appealed to me and I was about to take an offer from an industrialist who manufactured shoes. I was done with cement, thanks. I preferred less controversial commodities.

We'd arranged to meet on the terrace of the Hotel Minerva, behind the Pantheon. A chic little place, the kind that politicians and journalists like so well. I was feeling chipper and happy to treat him to dinner.

Deep down, I loved my friend Costantino, in spite of our differences. And I was grateful to him. Gratitude is an all-too-seldom experienced emotion, I know that, but I always thought about it: if he hadn't sat down next to me in the class-room on that morning in 1989, my life wouldn't have been what it became. But then, Costantino ought to be grateful to me, too, and not only because he'd made it through high school without flunking and he'd even managed to get a university degree, thanks to the thesis I wrote for him, but also because at the youthful age of twenty-seven I'd taken the Bernasconi Group in hand, just at the most challenging moment, and thanks to me, the company had taken off. I had transformed a family company into a vast empire.

I knotted my tie with some satisfaction. I could boast an impeccable record when it came to my brother-in-law. Admittedly, I was making his sister suffer to some extent, but these things happen. From a professional point of view, I hadn't a thing to apologize for.

When I got there, right on time, he was already sitting at the table.

"Come here, sit down, Valerio, good to see you. While I was waiting, I ordered some champagne."

Fine, the atmosphere seemed untroubled. Costantino was smiling. The terrace was practically deserted. Nearby there was nobody but a Japanese couple dining on *trenette al pesto* in silence, while looking out over the roofs of Rome. Of course, he's not satisfied with the toughest lawyers he can deploy, he wants to negotiate the division of assets in person, that's all. Don't worry, I'll give up anything you want, what do I care? If she thinks for one minute that I feel like fighting over a house at the beach, she's wrong. Bebè can even take my Porsche, I'll just buy myself another car.

"So, have you bought yourself a new boat?" I asked, as if I cared.

"Yes, I got a larger one. A 108-foot Ferretti: a Navetta."

We talked for a while about the boat builder and the specific model. By now I had become more worldly. His world, anyway. I could even converse intelligently about yachts.

"So you had the interiors redone."

"Well, of course, I had to. I don't like American walnut, it feels like you're in an alpine hut. And I wanted the jacuzzi on the flying bridge a little bigger."

"Right you are. And how fast does she go?"

"Eighteen knots, with a cruising speed of sixteen knots."

"Nice."

"I even managed to get them to give me a discount, I'm getting her brand-new at 10.4 million euros instead of 10.8 million."

From there we moved on to our children. For a little while, just to warm up the atmosphere, we talked about how Filippo had won the school cross-country event.

"What an athlete," we agreed.

Actually, after watching that mountain footrace, I'd come away somewhat chilled. It was snowing, the track was covered with ice, the children were slipping and falling one after another like tenpins, flat on their bellies, curve after curve, and Filippo, impassive, simply leaped over them like so many little corpses. Without ever stopping for so much as a second to see if they were hurt—hop—the only thing he cared about was winning.

"He's a fast runner, and he's got outstanding stamina."

"Of course he does."

Now the subject changed to Flavia. She deserved a few compliments, too, before we got to the meat of the matter. I was immediately reminded of a sweet little anecdote.

"Here's a good one, let me tell you this. One evening your niece said something clever, I can't remember what, prompting the admiration of the grown-ups in the room. And one of our friends paid her a compliment: 'You're smart as a whip, sweetheart, when you grow up you can be the prime minister of Italy.' She turned to me, looking worried, with a frown: 'Papa, I don't want to have to go to prison!'"

Luckily, my brother-in-law laughed heartily at that one. Then I started leafing cheerfully through the menu.

"So what should we try? Linguine with shrimp and asparagus?"

Costantino put his hand on his belly, saying he felt pretty full, he'd rather stay light: "I'll just have a *carne cruda all'albese* with a dusting of parmesan cheese and a little salad on the side." He immediately took advantage of the opportunity to give me a lewd wink: "You know, I don't want my lovers to complain. This fatso, they think. And then they don't want me in bed," wink wink.

His gross sexism had always embarrassed me, I couldn't share his bid for solidarity. For starters, Olivia wasn't one of the Brazilian or Russian girls he squired around. But I was even willing to let him drag me onto that territory if it made him happy and willing to solve all the practical issues quickly and without friction.

"Certainly, and a harem doesn't come cheap," I winked, leering right back at him.

"If you'll allow me to offer a piece of advice, the same as I'd give my brother," Costantino said, pouring me more champagne, "if by any chance you're interested in benefiting from my opinion and my experience…"

Whores: his experience extended strictly to whores. Right now, he had a Ukrainian girlfriend who certainly couldn't afford to complain if every so often he chose to try out women from other developing countries (and on this matter he shared the opinion of Zio Vittorio, who always liked to say, in heavy *romanesco* dialect, "*Spòsate una che je devi comprà pure 'e mu-tanne, se voi stà sereno*"—"Marry a girl who needs you to buy her everything, down to her panties, if you want a peaceful life"). So I gave him an icy glare. Oh, no. I didn't want to be rude to him, but I did want him to grasp the concept: his long career with whores was not in any way a pertinent topic.

"Believe me, you have all my understanding. I'm just say-ing from the male point of view," he insisted.

"Man to man, you're telling me?" But Costantino utterly overlooked my irony.

"Exactly. The desire to run away is normal. I mean, it's *forgivable*. Wives just bust your balls and my sister is even more of a ball-buster than the others, believe me, I know, I know," and he laughed again, with salad in his teeth.

I wasn't hungry anymore. One glance at his mouth and I no longer had the slightest appetite.

"I've tried to talk to Bebè a little, you know? She needs to grow up, she still thinks she's fifteen years old. But you don't throw marriages away like this, you need to learn to turn a blind eye."

"Your sister has turned a hundred blind eyes. But it wasn't enough, because I wasn't just asking her to *tolerate*. I want to live with Olivia, and that's another matter."

"Ah, Olivia Morganti," he smiled at me, "she's always been an obsession of yours, ever since we were kids. But now there are *more important things*."

I looked up. What did he mean by that? I'd never been good at deciphering certain languages. Sidelong insinuations were only clear to me in literature: to my mind, the one realm of oblique discourse was literature, even sneakier and more treacherous than the Mafia. That was a shortcoming of mine, though, and I knew it. In my line of work, I often needed to decipher coded messages and so, during certain delicate meetings, I found it best to have Costantino present, to provide his first-rate skills as an interpreter.

"Look, there are some problems. My sister's really taken this badly and she's not listening to reason. So we need to figure out how to stop her."

"You'd better explain more clearly."

"She knows a lot of things, and now she's threatening to spill the beans."

"But she'd ruin the family along with me."

"Yeah, I know. But she doesn't care. She doesn't seem to grasp that side of things. She says: 'Let Dido die with all the Philistines.'"

"Samson."

"Who?"

"Forget it. Just go on."

"Nothing, that's all. There's no way to make her listen to reason."

"But this is absurd."

"She doesn't care about the consequences, let me assure you. Rather than letting Olivia have you, she's willing to send you to jail. And even if that means her own brother has to go behind bars with you, she doesn't care. She's lost her mind."

"Why don't you get her some psychiatric treatment?"

"What do you think, that I haven't tried? But Benedetta, who isn't as much of a fool as you might think, has hired a lawyer. A real bastard, who won't even let me get near her without an appointment."

"Have you explained to her that they're going to freeze all her assets, too? That she won't be able to go into her beautiful apartment in Cortina, for instance, the one she just renovated with the help of her little interior designer girlfriend, because that apartment is in my name?"

"Of course. It was the only way of making it clear to her that her little vendetta was an idiotic piece of bullshit, I thought of it first thing. But she says that her offshore bank accounts are more than enough. Accounts that I set up for her, by the way. Asshole that I am."

"What about your mother? Can't she do anything?"

"Not a thing. My lawyer went to see her yesterday. I wanted him to clarify the situation for her. But once he explained that the charges could range from tax fraud to criminal conspiracy, Mama upbraided and insulted him and threw him out of her home. And immediately afterward she picked up the phone and called me to say that I always seem to surround myself with the wrong sort of people." He lit a cigar. "I even tried to reach out to certain friends, and you know who I mean. But they just shrugged. When you're dealing with a madwoman, what do you want to do about it? If she manages to talk to the magistrates, then how are you going to stop them?"

"Shit."

Costantino braced his head against his hands, one hand on each temple. Then he looked up: "Please, Valerio, go back to her. Just pretend you want to give things another try, I'm begging you. Apologize to her, say anything. Then, in a while, once she's calmed down, you can do what you want. I'm sure that Olivia Morganti will understand."

"It's an unacceptable extortion."

"Trust me, my sister isn't kidding around. She's capable of carrying through on her threat."

"No can do. You're asking too much of me this time."

A WEEK LATER, Costantino's lawyer called me up. He asked if I would drop by his law office, "just to say hello." I told him that I was extremely busy. But he wouldn't give up, he wanted to have a chance to invite me to lunch, *at least*. The risk of wiretaps made that conversation even more equivocal than it already was. It sounded like a gay courtship.

"All right. Let's make it Wednesday."

He'd selected a traditional Roman trattoria, over in Trastevere, full of tourists. He said that it was probably better to avoid places that might be too elegant or full of indiscreet neighbors.

"The people at the next table are Germans, we can speak freely," I sighed as I read through the laminated menu. The photographs of the dishes weren't especially inviting.

"Costantino sent me to see you to let you know that he's left the country. He says that his sister is out of control and that the best thing he can do now is take a nice long trip to countries with no extradition agreement."

"So he's in Brazil?"

"You guessed it. That's why I insisted on seeing you, you know. I couldn't exactly explain things over the phone." He was tucking his cloth napkin into his collar to keep from spattering his shirt with tomato sauce. "There's a new administration in power, we've been left without connections. Costantino told me to tell you that he's really sincerely sorry. That son of a bitch only loves himself, but believe me, he has a soft spot for you. So I felt it was my duty to report these things to you, even though he left the country without paying my fee. Though as far as that goes, over the years, I've paid for a house on the beach, in Sabaudia, by solving his problems for him. I owed him a slight discount on volume."

Was he extorting me, too? Did he mean to tell me that he knew plenty of things about me and that I'd better choose him as a lawyer, before someone else had a chance to hire him?

"I've never much liked Sabaudia," I replied.

The lawyer laughed, wiping his mouth. "My wife did it all. When I signed the deed, at the closing, I hadn't even seen the apartment. *You know how women are . . .*"

He had a few more arrows in his quiver, and I was going to have to be patient and wait for him to take them out and fire them.

"Yes, I've learned," and I smiled, as if I'd taken the bait.

"You know, Costantino and I have done our best to make her understand the consequences. We've explained to Benedetta that if the investigation spreads, and every time there's an investigation like this one, it spreads, it'll happen that someone gets worried. And it's always best never to worry anyone."

"And did Bebè follow your meaning?" If this guy was speaking to my wife in those mysterious allusions, we really were risking a rollicking *commedia all'italiana*.

"Well, of course. For the past several weeks, she has allowed us to see her, strictly in her lawyer's presence."

"And what did she say?"

"She told us that she's willing to be mown down on the riverfront Lungotevere by a hit-and-run driver. After all, she's already deposited all her documents with a notary."

"I don't even recognize her."

"She feels like Joan of Arc. Only she hasn't lost her mind over some ideal, she just wants to destroy you, nothing else."

"And that's fine. But how the fuck has she managed to make such precise moves in a world she knows nothing about? Who told her to collect those documents, and exactly which ones, too, and to deposit them all with a legal notary? Until a month ago, Benedetta didn't even know what a securities account was. Who's maneuvering her?"

"That's exactly the point. Do you remember the old CEO who was there before you? The one that Costantino didn't want to get rid of when you arrived, because he knew about too many things?"

"Certainly. He appointed him honorary president, he paid him a terrifying salary, even though we never saw him. He also bought a villa on Lake Como from him, paying twenty million euros for it, even though it was worth less than ten."

"Exactly. Now his son, the eldest, has just become a lawyer. And he felt the need to give him a hand. He introduced him to little Bebè, who needed a lawyer's counsel."

"Now it's perfectly clear, yes, crystal clear."

Very politely, while sipping an espresso that tasted of dish soap, I announced that I'd soon be coming to visit him in his law offices.

"I'm always very happy to see you, Valerio, you know that. Drop by whenever you please," and he picked up the check, which was ridiculously low, because it was a prix-fixe lunch special.

"Thanks," I said.

THAT SAME EVENING I hurried over to see my sister. The osteria was full because there was a table of diners celebrating a victory by A.S. Roma. They were all shouting, and we needed to huddle close together to be able to talk.

"Oh my God, Pisè, promise me you won't wind up like Max. Think it over carefully, please."

I was a little hurt by the fact that Marta had listened to the string of potential criminal charges without blinking an eye. She hadn't evinced any signs of agitation even when I mentioned Article 416 of the penal code: criminal conspiracy of a Mafia nature. She didn't dream of asking me whether I was innocent or guilty, for instance. Stung, I pointed it out.

"Why should I be shocked? I don't understand why you're being all sensitive."

"So you were fine with having a brother like this?"

"I was fine with having a brother like you, which is quite another matter. I've always loved you for who you are, with all your defects." She stood up, now she was offended.

Defects, she called them. I felt like retorting that technically speaking, they're called crimes, not defects. But I spared her.

"Please, stay here with me. I'm sorry, I'm just a bit confused."

Marta brought two pitchers full of red wine to the table of the Roma fans, then came back to my table. In their honor she had prepared a red-and-yellow chicken, the team colors, with potatoes and red peppers. They certainly couldn't complain.

"Have you talked to Mama?"

"She's the last person on earth I'd want to talk to."

"You're not wrong there. But listen to me, though."

"That's why I'm here."

"Try to calm her down, at least. Your brother-in-law has a point. And try to get between her and that lawyer, who's much more dangerous than she is."

"You say that like it's an easy thing."

"Just give her a couple of straightforward lines, something she can believe in, she can't wait to buy into the idea, trust me."

"I can't do that, for fuck's sake. I just can't."

"Do you think that Olivia won't understand? She's seen more than her share. Even the father of her daughter, that Iranian, wound up behind bars."

"He was opposing a regime, that's quite another matter. The comparison isn't pertinent, if you don't mind my saying so."

"Okay, you've got to go all subtle on me. All I meant to say was that if you ask me, Olivia isn't all that interested."

"Interested in what?"

"Interested in this kind of trouble. She's had plenty of it already in her lifetime. Of this particular kind. I'm sure that she'd be the first to recommend that you take a step back."

"The problem is *me*, Marta. I'm the one who can't take a step back. How am I supposed to sleep at night next to a woman who, in twenty-nine years, has only been able to think about serious matters once, and that was to send me to prison? I'd rather cook my own pasta on a camp stove for the rest of my life."

"If they put you in the same cell as Er Faccia, you'd even be able to enjoy yourself."

"Is he back in prison?"

"He's in and out continuously. You, at least, have lived a very nice life, you have to admit it."

"He came to see me, a few months back. I loaned him twenty thousand euros, and that was the last I saw of him."

"I'll bet it was."

"He confessed that when he nicknamed me Er Principe he never expected that I would become 'a prince to this extent.'"

Marta wiped away a tear, this detail had touched her. Crimes left her indifferent, but nicknames from the *borgata* were quite another matter.

A WEEK LATER I was back on the terrace of the Hotel Minerva, this time with Olivia. It was eleven o'clock at night and she was completely drunk, almost as soused as her mother had been at her eighteenth birthday party.

"Shall we ask for the check?"

I would have preferred to continue our conversation at her hotel, because all through the dinner Olivia had either wept or laughed loudly. Everyone was staring at us.

"So early? Hold on a minute, I have a present for you."

She bent over, rummaged through the purse that she'd dropped on the floor, and extended something under the table.

All right, I was willing to play along. I stuck my hand through the drapery of the tablecloth, smiling. But then the color drained from my face.

"Are you insane?"

"Do you recognize it?"

"Put it away."

"You always wanted to *touch it*. And here it is."

"You don't even have a permit to carry. Are you trying to wind up behind bars, too?" I looked around anxiously. "If someone sees this, sweet Jesus. This place is packed with journalists, they'll write in tomorrow's papers that I'm walking around with a Beretta in my pocket, which is the last thing that we need."

"Go on, take it. It's a souvenir, a piece of memorabilia. My final farewell."

"Are you inviting me to shoot myself?" Meanwhile I'd finally taken it fully in hand, because leaving her with a pistol was probably not a very good idea.

"Or you could always kill me. That way, I'd send *you* to prison," she said, throwing her head back and laughing loudly. "Bribery? Illicit party financing? Criminal conspiracy? I have an even better offer! First-degree murder, with a mandatory life sentence!"

"You're completely drunk. Now let me get the check and then we can get out of here."

I was already on my feet

"But it's a gift. Don't you like gifts?" As she stood up, she knocked over two chairs.

"Did you bring it with you on the train?"

"Yes, of course. In my suitcase."

"You really are out of your mind. It's just a good thing that it isn't loaded."

"Who told you it isn't loaded?"

I froze to the spot. Just then, the waiter came back to hand me my credit card. I quickly signed and dragged her away. Olivia laughed and laughed.

"Did you think I was going to hand you a pair of panties?"

I pushed her into a taxi. She was all over me, acting the fool, trying to slip her hand under my jacket. I had to stop her before she could reach the pistol.

"But I wouldn't recommend you take it home," she said, continuing to laugh. "Your wife might find it. Then she'd figure out I saw you tonight, and she'd shoot you dead."

"With all the noise you made in the restaurant, we certainly didn't go unobserved."

"*Boom!* Aaahhh. The Bernasconis will try to pass it off as suicide, I can already see it. But if they find you floating facedown in a pool tomorrow, I'll go to the police and say it can't be, because the night before you were with me and *you were having the time of your life.*"

"Hold still! Keep it up and you really will wind up killing me."

As soon as we pulled up in front of her hotel, I quickly paid the taxi driver and grabbed her by the arm.

"Now I'm going to put you to bed and then I'll go and hide this little toy in my office. I'll arrange for it to be returned to your father. Let's try to make sure that this idiotic move doesn't have any unpleasant consequences, huh?"

"It was such a thoughtful gift. My grandfather's Beretta. Such a sentimental thing."

"Come on, get moving."

"You break up with me, and instead of causing a scene, I bring you a present. Something you've wanted ever since you were a boy. Where are you going to find another girl like me?"

"Get in the elevator, go on."

She couldn't manage to get the lights to turn on because she had inserted the magnetic key the wrong way. The room door shut behind us and we were standing in the dark. Olivia burst into tears.

"Oh, now, don't start crying."

"But it's not fair."

"Ah, fairness really has nothing to do with it, I know." Silence. I heard a strange little noise, almost like a hamster. *Click, click, click.*

"Olivia, are you biting your nails?"

"No, I swear to you, I'm not."

"Listen, I can tell if you're lying, even in the dark."

"Okay, I'll stop."

"Give me the key so we can turn on the light."

"I'd prefer not to see you anymore."

"As you like."

I could feel her breath, so close. I took a step forward and embraced her. She hugged me tight.

"Take it easy, you're crushing the Beretta into my belly."

"Then a shot really will go off." She sniffed. She started laughing again. "That would be a nice finale, wouldn't it? But the safety's on. This pistol never goes off."

4

THE REDISCOVERED HISTORY

THE ONLY THING I really care about, out of everything I've ever stolen, is an album of photographs with a velvet cover and these numbers, gold and broad, written on the spine with a felt-tip pen: 1975–1984, the numbers running vertically, one below the other.

I managed to slip it into my suitcase just before Manon died, when I went to tour her house, with a view to buying it. Giulio had left me alone in the library for ten minutes or so while he talked to his mother's nurse. He'd asked me to wait for him, he'd just be a moment, because he wanted to give me a ride back to my hotel. Impossible to resist. No one would ever notice that minor theft. I spotted the album, it was on the table. I quickly opened my suitcase and tucked it inside, wedged in with my shirts.

I still have that album, in a drawer that I keep under lock and key, in my office desk (together with Gianni's Beretta, which I have not yet returned to the Morgantis). Manon, who wrote no letters and never kept a diary, had a habit of gluing little strips of light-blue paper down next to the pictures, with captions. The captions had nothing to do with the pictures they flanked: that was the great thing about them. On those little rectangles of paper, cut out with scissors, I found my whole personal history.

When I go to see them, Olivia and Valerio tell me: "Take off your shoes." That way they can be sure I won't leave, because I'm barefoot.

The picture had nothing to do with the caption: it was us, held in our parents' arms, while we stuck our fingers into the icing on the cake that featured three candles shaped like cats. Birthday, 1978, date and occasion noted below. Perhaps Manon meant to convey the idea that we knew only a few words, but we already understood language, with all its innuendos and their consequences. *Take off your shoes.*

I invited Giuliana over. After dinner, the children pretend to smoke, holding breadsticks between their fingers. Then Giuliana asks Olivia, "Why do you smoke so much?" And she replies, "To be happy."

Next to it, the most unremarkable picture imaginable: the two of us in the snow, awkward in our snowsuits, trying to figure out what a sled is. We were much more familiar with bad habits, apparently. And we were already following twisted paths in our pursuit of happiness. Immortalized next to a large plush donkey, we seemed much more innocuous. Manon photographed us like that, the way we were *supposed to be*, but on those little scraps of paper she revealed a much more complex view of things. She was the only one who fully perceived our efforts to probe reality.

Today the children asked me what work I do. I replied: "I take care of the house and the family." They exchanged a glance, they weren't satisfied with that answer. Then they went to my husband and asked him the same question. Gianni smiled: "I build houses." Olivia and Valerio exchanged a second glance, then they came back to me and said: "All right, then, we'll ask him for money for rides at the carnival."

My granddaughter will gulp down anything, alas, she's even developed a taste for truffles on tagliatelle. I wish I'd never let her taste that delicacy, what was I thinking? But when it comes to meat, nothing doing, even if I spoon-feed her: she just spits it out on the plate. To help her get over that, I told her the story of Henry VIII, who used to eat chicken with his hands, because forks hadn't been invented yet. She was captivated by the nonexistence of forks (a detail I'm not even sure of—I should check to see if they had such a thing in Greek and Roman times). On Sunday, my sons came over for lunch and I had the cook roast a chicken with potatoes. Olivia picked up a chicken leg with her fingers and asked: "Can I eat like Henry VIII?" Giulio started laughing: "Why, what are you talking about?" Olivia replied: "He was a king who ate with his hands. He liked women but when he was tired of a wife, he'd just chop off her head." And she ate every last bit of the chicken leg. Stories work, we identify with them.

Corresponding photo: Olivia in a pair of red overalls trying to insert a 45 rpm record into a tape recorder while I pedal a toy car, dripping with sweat. Ordinary children, born in the seventies.

Today, at lunch, I told the story of Polyphemus to Olivia and Valerio. Valerio missed his mouth with his spoon and spilled his mush on a newly reupholstered chair. Olivia was very worried about the damage, as if she'd done it, so she leaned over and said to him, very quietly: "So now what are we going to say to my grandmother?" And he replied, in an undertone: "That No Man did it."

Photo: I'm next to Manon, wearing a bathing cap covered with plastic flowers, as she teaches me to swim without water wings, while Olivia, naked, wanders around the swimming pool in confusion.

Valerio has given Olivia a little necklace of colored beads, which he made himself, and Olivia has put it on to go out to dinner. At the restaurant, a woman asks her: "Where on earth did you buy this lovely piece of jewelry?" Olivia: "From Bulgari."

A scrawled drawing by Olivia, glued to the page, with a scribble of my own on the back. Dated 1980. The house that she'd drawn was all crooked, but underneath, in pencil, there was an explanation ("It's a neglected, invisible house, which every so often reappears, saying alley-oop"). Yes, it was a very neglected house. But someone was paying extremely close attention and noting down all our doubts about the world.

We were watching the Grand Prix. At a certain point I noticed that Valerio had vanished and I went to look for him. He was all alone in the green parlor, sitting on the sofa, looking at the Miró. I asked him what he was doing and he said: "I'm trying to figure out why that monster has a yellow eye."

Olivia is praying, kneeling on the bed. I step closer to hear what she's saying. "Jesus, protect Gianni, so that he can protect us."

I went down into the yard and I found the children lying on my German shepherd, their heads resting on his belly. Valerio was asking Olivia: "Do you think that Wist knows he's a dog?"

A single photo reveals the passion that was devouring me. It's a birthday party and Olivia is trying to free herself from the grip of a playmate who is determined to hold her in his arms, whatever the cost. I'm sitting next to them and watching. I'm also pushing a slice of cake into my mouth to keep from revealing that I'm dying of jealousy. We're six years old, we're in first grade.

I went to pick up Olivia and Valerio at school because my husband is in Rome. In the car, Olivia said to me: "You know, Nonna, there's a boy in my class who always hugs me and tells me that he loves me. But I push him away and try to be as rude to him as I can so that he understands that I wasn't born to be his woman." So I asked: "Wouldn't it be simpler to let him know that he wasn't born to be your man?" And she replied: "That's the one thing he would never admit."

First report cards, slipped in between the pages, mine and hers, stapled together. I check: my grades are higher. I smile. I was already a winner, my mother really couldn't complain.

The teacher had to step away from the classroom for a few minutes, so she left Valerio in charge in her absence, sitting at her desk, with instructions to dictate a problem for the other students and maintain discipline. Olivia couldn't stand it ("I can't take being told what to do by him"). Valerio commented: "I've finally realized what it feels like to have power."

Anyway, I met her again, a few months ago. The year was 2013, but for the first time I felt myself excluded from the gallop: I realized that time had stopped running for me.

I was in London, where I was looking for an apartment because I want to establish my residence there. Like God, I don't want to pay taxes. I was with my wife, because we had to choose the apartment in question, and there are some things that she decides.

I took her to lunch at Nobu, Bebè only likes that kind of place, universally considered chic. A hellish meal. My daughter was playing at dressing up Barbie on the iPad. The Barbies in plastic, with their tangible charge of eroticism, are things of the past. She continued to show us the screen, relentlessly.

"What about this feathered vest, do you like it? Or do you prefer the one with flowers?"

It was exasperating, but at least it covered up our silence. Bebè and I seriously didn't know what to say to each other. Every now and then I'd look over at Filippo, who wouldn't even glance up from his tablet, engaged as he was in exter-minating thousands on a warfare app.

"How do you think she looks more *glam*, with red hair or purple hair?"

Now and then, my wife tried to get a word in edgewise.

"I saw the apartment in Chelsea. I like the neighbor-hood, but the place is too small.

"Ah," I answered. That was my only answer to every-thing: "Ah." By now, I was a man who could only say "Ah."

"This afternoon I'm going to Mayfair. They're selling a three-story detached villa, it might suit us better."

"Ah."

This gripping conversation was interrupted by a text from her brother. Costantino had just become a member of Italy's parliament, thanks to Silvio Berlusconi's locked elec-toral lists.

"What does he say?"

"Nothing, just that he'll be bored in parliament."

"Of course he will."

Then I looked at the time, on the beautiful watch I'd in-herited from my father, and got to my feet. "I'm sorry, I have to go, I have a meeting. Ciao, see you tonight."

My children, very much caught up in the battle or the virtual garbing of Barbie, didn't even look up.

Far too early for the meeting, I left the restaurant for the City. No one could deny me the pleasure of a walk. In the open air, all I wanted was to breathe fresh air.

I caught the tube and got out around the Tate Modern. I wanted to walk along the Thames. It was a beautiful day, a light breeze was tossing the leaves of the plane trees.

Olivia appeared to me there. It was just a fleeting instant, but I'm positive it was her: she went by me on a bicycle. Her daughter trailed after her, a few yards behind. She turned around, but only for a second, as if she'd sensed my presence. We exchanged a glance, I believe. Even though I can't say for certain. It was the briefest interval of time in our lives, and yet in that fraction of a second there was concentrated almost forty years of love. And all of my personal history, rolling away from me like that, with a brief, extemporaneous turn of the pedals.

I didn't stop her, I didn't call after her. But I watched her go for a long time, as she dwindled into the distance, slightly hunched over the handlebars ("Sit up straight, honey").

ACKNOWLEDGMENTS

If I hadn't walked into an osteria one day and if, from that day forward, I hadn't come back to it every single day, I would never have become friends with Valentina. And this novel could never have been written. A special thank-you to her, then to her husband Walter, and to all my friends from Tarallucci e Vino.

A thought of great love goes to my grandmother Dory, who always corrected the proofs of my books. She was unable to read this one, but I know what she would have told me ("Take out a few curse words, honey").